PRAISE FOR THE
ARISTOTLE DETECTIVE SERIES

"Doody weaves the tapestry of the background beautifully and unobtrusively. And she knows how to sustain suspense."

—*Book World*

"The best detective to come along since we said good-bye to Nero Wolfe and Hercule Poirot." —*Lewiston Journal*

"[Margaret Doody] not only makes Greece live but turns Aristotle into a passionate, quirky seeker of truth." —*Detroit News*

"This clever and original detective story set in ancient Athens should suit classicists to a T and enchant all sleuthwatchers... Doody brings the Athens of 322 B.C. to life with skill and verve..."
—*Publishers Weekly*

"...well-paced and memorable not only for its marvelous evocation of what it must have been like to sail the Aegean 2,300 years ago but for a lurking sense of menace beneath the surface detail of daily courtesies, comical misadventures, and breathtakingly beautiful descriptions." —Roderick Beaton

"The Aristotle Detective series by Margaret Doody is historically correct without being pedantic, learned but not tedious, equally ironic and attentive to details."

—Mariarosa Mancuso, *Corriere della Sera*

"This work offers satisfactory detection, a well-proportioned story, nostalgia for lovers of Greece, and special fun for classicists. It is a bonus that it is so well written." —Barbara Levick, *TLS*

"Why did no one think of this before?" —*The Times*

THE *ARISTOTLE DETECTIVE* SERIES

ARISTOTLE

DETECTIVE

Margaret Doody

THE UNIVERSITY OF
CHICAGO PRESS

AN
ARISTOTLE
DETECTIVE
NOVEL

To my sister

MARY ELIZABETH HOWELL-JONES

this book is affectionately dedicated
with the hope that it may please a real classicist

The University of Chicago Press, Chicago 60637
© 1978 by Margaret Doody
All rights reserved
Originally published in 1978
University of Chicago Press edition 2014
Printed in the United States of America

18 17 16 15 14   1 2 3 4 5

ISBN-13: 978-0-226-13170-2 (paper)
ISBN-13: 978-0-226-13184-9 (e-book)
DOI: 10.728/chicago/9780226131849.001.0001

LIBRARY OF CONGRESS CATALOGING-IN-PUBLICATION DATA

Doody, Margaret Anne, author.
    Aristotle detective : an Aristotle detective novel / Margaret Doody.
    pages ; cm
    ISBN 978-0-226-13170-2 (pbk. : alk. paper) -- ISBN 978-0-226-13184-9
(e-book) 1. Aristotle--Fiction. 2. Greece--History--Macedonian Expansion,
359-323 B.C.--Fiction. 3. Athens (Greece)--Fiction. 4. Murder--Investiga-
tion--Fiction. I. Title.
    PR9199.3.D556A89 2014
    823'.914--dc23

                                                        2013042064

CONTENTS

LIST OF CHARACTERS

» Aristotle, son of Nikomakhos: philosopher and head of the Lykeion in Athens, age 53

» Stephanos, son of Nikiarkhos: young man, age 23, now head of his family, former student of Aristotle

» Philemon, son of Lykias: Stephanos' cousin, age 23, sent into exile at age 19 for manslaughter

» Eudoxia: Stephanos' aunt, mother of Philemon

» Stephanos' mother: widowed and given to weeping but not weak

» Theodoros: Stephanos' younger brother, age 7

» Pythias: Aristotle's wife

» Boutades: wealthy man of the aristocratic tribe of the Etioboutadai, age 50, a trierarkh and gentleman of consequence

» Polygnotos: nephew of Boutades, wealthy, producer of a play for the Dionysia

» "The Sinopean": young slave of Polygnotos

» Eutikleides: stout citizen, neighbor and kin to Boutades

» Telemon: wispy and talkative citizen with a limp

» Kleiophoros: jolly citizen who likes telling the news

» Theosophoros: serious citizen, given to dry remarks

» Arkhimenos: noble citizen of distinguished appearance, another trierarkh and associate of Boutades

» Melissa: beautiful young woman, formerly lived in Thebes

» Nousia: old nurse, attendant on Melissa

» Phokon: Aristotle's senior male slave

» Autilos: another of Aristotle's slaves

» Lykias: a toddler

» Mikon: young citizen, one of Stephanos' former schoolfellows

» Dametas: steward of Stephanos' farm, family estate

» Tamia: Dametas' wife, housekeeper at the farm

» Peleios: sailor, once encountered Philemon in Asia Minor

» Sosibios: former soldier in Alexander's army, becomes an active witness for the prosecution

» "Pheidippides": pseudonym adopted by a questionable boatman who also goes by the name of "Philander" when it is necessary to appear in a law court

» Simonides: potter in the agora with usefully disreputable connections

» Kleophon: fish-seller of Peiraeus, a reluctant witness for the prosecution

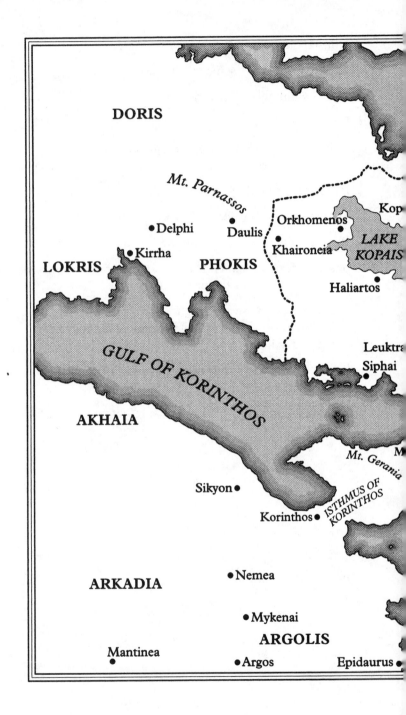

DORIS

Mt. Parnassos

•Delphi   Daulis   Orkhomenos•   Kop

•Kirrha   Khaironeia   *LAKE*
                                KOPAIS
LOKRIS   PHOKIS

                              Haliartos•

                                        Leuktra
GULF OF KORINTHOS   Siphai

AKHAIA

                                        Mt. Gerania   M

Sikyon•   *ISTHMUS OF*
                                        KORINTHOS
            Korinthos•

                    •Nemea
ARKADIA

                    •Mykenai
                    ARGOLIS
Mantinea
•   •Argos   Epidaurus•

Hear me, O Kleio, thou Muse, and support me in the labor
of this history. The word I speak is a true word.

I, Stephanos, son of Nikiarkhos, citizen of Athens, do
hereby relate the strange and untoward adventures which
befell me in the year of the 112th Olympiad. It shall be
known how a man of my house was calumniated, how he
was delivered, how an evil man was brought to justice
through the workings of the mighty gods. Further I shall
celebrate the wisdom of my counselor Aristotle, whom I
call, in the face of all detractors, one of the best of men and
one of the greatest philosophers of the age.

I

I, Stephanos

It was in the month of Boedromion in the waning of the
third full moon after the summer solstice that the terrible
deed was done that was to have so long and arduous a consequence. The day before it happened I had troubles enough
—not that one would say such a thing lest the gods hear and
laugh. But so it was. My father, Nikiarkhos, had died the
spring before and I, a young man of twenty-two years, was
left the head of a family with a mother and a very young
brother to care for, as well as a household of servants and
slaves. My mother had no brothers, and my father's brother
had died, so I was the governor of the home. With a heart still
sore for the loss of a beloved father I had to listen to stewards'
tales of sheep and butter and olives. Instead of studies at the
Lykeion and the converse of philosophers, I had accounts to

read in the midst of women's babbling in the courtyard. The house seemed to be supporting all sorts of hangers-on: feeble old ladies in shawls always taking gruel, and their stout slaves always taking cakes and olives. My mother is a soft-hearted soul, and hospitable. Too much sucking in of olives and wine and cakes and gruel by those who blow nothing back is not forever to be encouraged, as Telemakhos found in Ithaka. At the same time, I had no wish to be hard to kinsmen who were in any true need of my assistance. I was always willing that we should receive my father's brother's widow, poor Aunt Eudoxia. She was always spoken of so, as "poor Eudoxia," not on account of poverty, but because she was always ailing, and because of her great trouble. She was really ill (not grumbling as women do, muttering something is wrong with their insides), yet she could not be persuaded to make her home with us, but insisted on returning to her little house on the outskirts of Athens. It had occurred to me that she feared if she left her residence I might seize the property for my own use. An unjust fear, as the laws of gods and men forbid such wickedness, and I knew as well as she that the property belonged to her only son, Philemon.

This brings me to what Mother called "poor Eudoxia's great sorrow." My mother seldom mentioned the name of Eudoxia's son, feeling he had brought disgrace upon the family. I could not feel that way about him; I had known Philemon well in youth, almost as a brother, and my affection could not vanish even after Philemon's trouble. At the age of nineteen he was involved in a tavern brawl (not his first fight of the sort—Philemon always preferred physical to intellectual discourse). One of Philemon's blows killed a man, and my cousin, without waiting to take leave of us, jumped on the first ship leaving Peiraeus and disappeared into the world. The case was brought to court, but the magistrates were lenient; Philemon was sentenced to exile, on pain of death should he appear again in Athens, but his inheritance was not confiscated. So we could hope an amnesty would someday let him return to his home and his citizenship. We did not know where he was, but heard some confused rumors that he had gone south with the ship, and that after wandering about the southern islands he had become a soldier. This didn't seem unlikely, and certainly at that time soldiers were wanted, as Alexander of Makedonia was pushing his way into Asia Minor. There would be stirring battles which I knew Philemon would enjoy. I hoped he wouldn't get killed. I thought of him quite often in the summer after my father's death, imagining him wandering about the world while I stayed like a stick-in-the-mud at home. I wished he had been around to talk to, but he was not. It was no good saying such things in the hearing of the women, as Aunt Eudoxia would go off into sobs and cry, "My poor boy! I shall never see him again. Ai! Ai!" Then my mother would weep, and the serving woman and the slave girl would start bawling as best they could for company's sake.

These things were not all that sapped my heart. My father had been easy with money, and we had less than I had supposed. It had been arranged that I should marry Kharmia, the daughter of respected citizen Kallimakhos, but since Father's death the respected citizen had drawn back a little on the arrangement. He wanted our family to settle handsome presents on myself and Kharmia at the wedding time, and by midsummer I realized that I would have to sell a vineyard in order to raise the money. It was the smallest and scrattiest of vineyards; I didn't think we could afford a larger bite into the estate. Near the beginning of Boedromion I thought I had made a sale, but after consideration the buyer decided against it, much to my vexation.

I really wanted to get married, despite having so much of women at home. Mother cannot manage a household well; also, she gets entangled in conversation and weeps easily. My brother was too young for serious talk. Besides, I had become used to the idea of Kallimakhos' daughter as my wife. I had heard, and not only from her father—the seller who cannot praise his goods is a simpleton—that she was sensible and industrious, and, from the usual women's gossip, that she was fair to look at, and likely to bear comely children. Not that young people should be over-curious in these matters, but no

3

one wishes to marry a shrewish hunchback, and from a barren woman Aphrodite preserve us. Wife and children of his own—these establish a man and make a citadel about him. My desire for marriage was not merely the longing that can be easily satisfied by a night of sport with an accommodating female in one of the little houses.

On reading what I have set down, I find I have strayed from the subject, which is not the manner of a good rhetorician nor of a trained legal mind. Perhaps I put off the moment that is to come, as I must soon recapture the experience of my first sight of what was vile and fearsome and impious. At least you can now judge why on the night before the memorable third day of the second week of that month I was not able to sleep. I found myself lying awake wondering when, if and how I should marry, and worrying about the wretched vineyard. Eventually I got up and, without bothering to wake a slave, lit a lamp and tried to read. But both head and heart were too dull, so I thought I would take a walk. It was a little before dawn, and soon the city would be stirring.

II

Murder in Athens

I walked through the silent streets, letting the rhythm of my steps ease my thoughts. It was chilly in the wind that springs up just before dawn, and I was glad of my woolen himation over my bare arms and scanty khiton. The birds began to call, and I thought I could hear the gulls' cry. I thought of Philemon ducking aboard the ship, and as I passed a small shrine of Poseidon I said a prayer for my cousin and promised a sacrifice. There was no knowing where he was— he might be at sea.

The breeze blew more freshly; there was a damp scent of

gardens, not quite the smell of summer nor yet of full autumn. Then the east grew gray and the shape of Lykabettos hill became clearly visible. The dawn was coming, a thin saffron spreading slowly along the sky. I could see the street before me and the small shrine of the founder of the Eupatridai in that deme where so many wealthy and noble citizens dwell. The blank street-walls of the great houses were no longer sad-colored, but pale gray. I was still thinking of the sunrise, and trying to recall the most appropriate lines from Homer, when I was startled by a great shriek and cry from the mansion just beyond me.

Before I could get there, the cries had increased in volume, and two men left the house opposite and hastened toward the source of the noise.

The courtyard door was wide open when I came to it, and the two men were hurrying across the yard to the door of the house. A slave was standing in the courtyard, hopping from one foot to another and bellowing, "Master's killed! Master's killed!" his face contorted into a great omega spilling the sound. I passed him, nor did he stop to inquire my name, but continued imbecilically with what he evidently considered his major duty to the house at present and kept on yelling. I followed the other two men, a portly citizen and his house-slave, to the inner door, and I could hear others entering behind me. I didn't know why I felt I must go in; some unthinking curiosity drove me on. Sokrates, as recorded somewhere by Plato, tells a story of a man who knew there were a number of decapitated bodies, recently executed and piled in a heap, behind a wall. The man endeavored to make himself go past the wall without running behind and peering at what was dreadful, but he could not resist. He looked, crying in disgust to his eyes, "There! Feast yourselves on that delicious sight!" Certainly there is some lust, not of the eyes but of the baser mind, to look at terrible things, and so it must have been in my case—though, unlike the man in Sokrates' story, I did not know exactly where I was going, or what I was to see.

I knew soon enough. I followed the other two through the

inner house door and then through another door into a room. My first impression was that it was a fairly large room, dimly lit, with five persons in it besides myself—three Athenian citizens and two slaves. No. There were six other persons in the room, five living and one dead. There in the middle of the floor was the owner of the house, in a poor condition for receiving guests. Respected citizen Boutades, of the clan of the Etioboutadai. Boutades, former khoregos, trierarkh, wealthy patrician, was lying supine on the floor, his body twisted below the waist so that both knees were turned sideways. Trierarkh Boutades was fully dressed in a white linen khiton—or, rather, a khiton that had been white but was now streaked in crimson blood as with some atrocious dye. His glazed eyes gazed steadily up at the ceiling, and an arrow was sticking in his throat.

I do not know 'how long I looked at this sight like one entranced. I felt slightly sick, but not inclined to go away. I might have stayed rooted to the spot, but others coming through the door were shoving me along the wall. I moved cautiously down the wall toward the window. I was aware that there was a table behind me, with an amphora upon it, and even then I was automatically careful of it. More newcomers crowded along the wall by the door. Everyone gave the middle area of the chamber a wide berth.

When I had first looked at Boutades I had felt as if I did so in a long silence, but this could not have been so, for as soon as I started to move I noticed that there was a continuous high-pitched screaming of women from the inner house, and the yell of the slave in the courtyard had not ceased. I realized also that one of the original persons in the room, a dark-haired broad-shouldered man standing at the other side of the body, was speaking passionately.

"Who has done this deed? Who has killed my father's brother? May the vengeance of the gods be upon him!"

It was of course Polygnotos, Boutades' nephew. This man, four years older than I, was already himself something of a public figure in Athens. In his youth he was known as a good gymnast and a fine student. He was now wealthy in his own right, having inherited his father's estate, and latterly it was rumored that he was hoping for and might expect political office. He had recently distinguished himself by offering to be khoregos for the next Celebration of Dionysos. The sponsor of one of these elaborate productions is famous for a lifetime, should the show be a success, and he will also have proved that he is one of the men of greatest substance in Athens, as the cost of presenting the Great Dionysia is measured not in drakhmai but in talents. As a boy I had admired Polygnotos for his stamina in games and for his fluency in debates. I ought to have known him right away, but the room was dim and Persephone had darkened my eyes for a moment. And strong Polygnotos, disheveled in a khiton hastily drawn on so that one shoulder was unfastened, like a slave's garment, Polygnotos pale in the dawn light and trembling slightly with grief and rage, did. not look quite like the bronzed boy I remembered.

"O Zeus," cried Polygnotos, with a rising choking cry, so that the words stifled in his throat, "look upon this offense and bring vengeance on those who work harm to me and my house and tribe! Curses on the assassin!"

"Do you know who did this thing?" asked Eutikleides—the stout citizen from the house across the way. I recalled that he was of some distant tribal kin to Boutades. Eutikleides' flabby cheeks looked sickly in the pale light, but his voice was firm.

"How can I know?" exclaimed Polygnotos. "A villain! A worker in darkness!"

"Be calm, Polygnotos," said old Telemon. "We will have vengeance yet." Telemon, who was standing by Polygnotos' side, had evidently been one of the first comers. Suitable enough, for he was a fellow who loved the news. He was always called "old Telemon" though he was only about the age of Boutades, but he was a thin man with wispy hair and a general air of senility. He had a limp too; the children called him "old Stumpfoot." Polygnotos paid no heed to his words, but stood muttering broken curses and tearing his hair with one hand.

"Yes, Polygnotos, be calm," said Eutikleides. "This is no time for women's work. Tears will have their season, but now tell us what has happened—what you know, that is—so that we may lay the case before the Basileus and see that the arkhon is informed."

"I myself know," said Telemon eagerly. "I was here first, just after poor Boutades drew his final breath. I heard all from the lips of Polygnotos and I saw—"

"I would rather hear all first from the lips of Polygnotos himself," said Eutikleides. "Boy!" addressing the slave, "go to the kitchen and ask for bread and wine to—to be prepared for your master. Soon he will leave this place of horror and have some food."

I think Eutikleides had been on the point of ordering wine to be brought to us, a natural enough gesture in ordinary circumstances, and the result of kindly thought for a man suffering like Polygnotos, but a glance at the floor had checked him and changed his speech. It would have been profane to eat or drink in the presence of such a violent death.

Now Eutikleides reached out an arm and touched Polygnotos comfortingly on the shoulder. His words about the wine and this gesture were the first everyday human acts in this room of death, but Polygnotos hitched his shoulder away as a frightened horse may shudder away from a new master. Eutikleides, rebuffed, let his arm fall back. The slave left quickly, opening the door to the next room and admitting a flood of newborn light from the east and the loud cries of the women. Then the door closed, leaving us to relative silence and the slower western beams.

"Sirs," said Polygnotos in a more tranquil tone, "you shall hear what happened, as well as my confused thoughts and trembling tongue can utter it. All that I know, which is little enough, I shall tell you. This morning early, just as dawn began to break, I was awakened by a noise. I was not perturbed, for my uncle often works—alas! he worked, I must say—in this room late at night or early in the morning. I sat up and reached for my khiton, when I heard a sound louder than the first—a great crash. I jumped up and ran along the gallery and downstairs, dressing myself hastily as I went. I came into this room and—in the near-darkness by the light of the lamp that is yet guttering on that table—I saw what you see. Boutades lay then exactly as he lies now.

"Anguished though I was by his death, and by the unnatural manner of it, I saw at once what must have happened. My poor uncle had been working at that table, facing the window, and in the pale darkness someone had crept near the window and shot him. My uncle had evidently been warned before the fatal shot—perhaps he heard a noise outside, or saw a face. Clearly, he stood up, and the sound that awakened me was doubtless some exclamation, combined with the noise of the stool being pushed back. The murderer must then have shot him instantly, striking him through the throat, and he fell down, there as he lies. His falling was the crash that I heard."

We looked again at Boutades, lying so heavily on the floor, with the large table beyond his feet, between his body and the window. Corpse, table and window were all in a straight line, and the table would have offered no obstacle to an assailant who intended to kill him as he sat there. The stool, pushed away from the table, was still upright. On the table a lamp was flickering in its last drops of oil, and all the paraphernalia of stylus and tablets lay undisturbed.

"What did you do then?" inquired Eutikleides.

"First, of course, I went to my uncle to see if there was life in him, but his spirit had certainly fled before I came through the door."

"What a pity he did not have time to name the murderer," said one of the citizens beside me.

"It's little he could have uttered in such a death as that," said Eutikleides shortly. "What then, Polygnotos?"

"As I looked upon my dear uncle's body, hardly believing what I saw, I thought I heard something move outside the window. I rushed to it and could see a dark shape in the little courtyard outside—the small orchard. It was then that I shrieked to raise the household, and as my cry was still upon the air Telemon here entered with the Sinopean doorkeeper. I shouted that my uncle was murdered, and that the murderer was outside. We all ran from the room and rushed through the courtyard into the enclosed garden. Just as we came through the gate we saw the assassin leap over the wall. I sent the slave to run after him, and Telemon and I returned to my uncle—to this room, I mean. The house was in great uproar, but I shut the women out and stood crying and cursing and wondering what to do. And at this point you, Eutikleides, and all the rest came in to look upon the scene."

"That is the way it was," said Telemon. He had held his peace for a surprising length of time, but now his excited voice came quickly out again. "I was coming to pay a call upon Boutades, and the slave had let me in and escorted me along the court. Just as we came to the house door I heard Polygnotos' cry, and hurried in. I saw—what we all see now —and Polygnotos at the window shouting, "Stop! Stop! Murder! Boutades is slain!" I too hurried to the window—taking care to avoid Boutades, you may be sure. I looked out with Polygnotos and saw a dark figure moving among the trees."

"You should have run to the orchard to take him, instead of wasting time staring out," said Eutikleides.

"So I did," said Telemon. "We all went at once, I and Polygnotos and the slave. Indeed, I was first at the outset, but Polygnotos overtook me at the gate. He runs faster than I can now—my lameness you know. Our Polygnotos is still young and trains his body, though in my youth I was—"

"Yes. Quite so," said Eutikleides dryly. No younger man would have felt it polite to interrupt Telemon, who, after all, was well-born, but Eutikleides was his contemporary. I think the others felt as I did, that the old hobblefoot should have stood aside. He must have been in Polygnotos' way in his childish attempt to get to the orchard first. And what could he have done with a stout and desperate murderer had he reached him—Telemon with his little weedy frame? Of all of us present, Telemon seemed least affected by the horror of the occasion, and most like his usual self.

"But," said Telemon, without waiting for more prompting, "I did see the villain—jumping over the wall. He was going along the top of it, as a cat or dog will sometimes do, and then leaped off and we could hear him running."

"What did he look like?" I asked.

"Well—it was hard to see in that light, gentlemen, and my eyes are not as good as they were. A dark huddled shape—not very tall, I'd say, and yet not small. Not fat, certainly—but I shouldn't like to say thin. Well built. Agile. Probably dark-haired."

"What was he wearing?"

"A long cloak, I think."

"Difficult wear for climbing walls," I said.

"Well, it might have been a short cloak," said Telemon. "Perhaps with a woolen wrap muffling his face. He wasn't naked." Telemon tittered and stopped abruptly.

"Well enough," said Eutikleides. "We have heard all we can and must return to the present." We looked away from each other, and back again at the floor. Oddly enough, as we listened to Polygnotos and Telemon, we had been, I cannot say diverted, but somehow eased. Seeing the previous events in the mind's eye only had taken us away for a time from the corpse, so starkly a corpse, so very dead, to which we now all returned.

The light was quite clear by this time and every detail could be seen—the blood on the floor rapidly drying, the stiff clothes and hair, the glimmer of eye like frozen water. The arrow stood erect from Boutades' throat and cast a shadow on the far door, like a feather. The shadow of the amorphous body with its one feather looked as if Boutades were trying to become a monstrous bird.

As you must see, what made it all so terrible was the arrow. Boutades had been shot by an arrow from a bow—that was undeniable and unbelievable. Had he been killed by a dagger there might have been as much blood, and Boutades would have been just as dead, but it would all have been much more normal, more comprehensible. Any Athenian

11

citizen might have had sword or dagger—but a bow!

The bow is not a common Athenian weapon. In the hands of Artemis and Apollo it is, like everything about them, divine, unsearchable, perhaps symbolic; in the hands of barbarians it is rude, grotesque, dirty and disgusting. Skythian policemen carry the bow—as slaves of the state with a bad job to do—but otherwise it does not belong to the middle world of common life. One might almost as well expect to meet the Minotaur in Athens as a man shot by an arrow. If all the crimes within the walls for the past hundred years were to be laid before our eyes, there would be murders in plenty, no doubt, by various means—but hardly one killing by bowshot.

So it was no wonder that Polygnotos looked pale and trembled, that Eutikleides was ashen-faced, and that I felt the sweat run down the backs of my knees. The bravest man may still be moved to see a violent death, how much more a death as strange as this one. As I gazed, the wonder of the thing grew more impressive than the ugliness of bloody death. I noticed for the first time that the wall opposite me, beyond Polygnotos and Eutikleides and behind a little ornamental table, was painted with a fresco. The scene was harmlessly sensual—a rather languorous Apollo chasing Daphne through a grove—but it occurred to me to wonder if Apollo himself, at first shining of the sun's beams this morning, had not shot Boutades dead with a divine arrow which remained below in the shape of an earthly shaft, to puzzle men and cast mysterious infamy upon the city. I shuddered then, for if this house were under the malediction of a powerful god, it would be madness to oppose the judgment, and folly to sympathize over-much. I clung to Polygnotos' and Telemon's account of the man in the orchard, a human killer.

Eutikleides was stronger than I, who wasted my soul in dreaming. "Come, Polygnotos," he said. "We must do some offices for our kinsman before he can be washed and prepared. Vengeance will be done on the killer, and Boutades' outraged spirit may find peace. First let me do what must be done."

Eutikleides knelt by the body and with one brave gesture sternly pulled the arrow out from the adhesive flesh where it was embedded almost to the full depth of Boutades' neck. The head, with its blood-crusted hair like nasty strands of tarred string, shook and nodded. I could see that Eutikleides flinched slightly at inflicting new injury on the insentient flesh in order to remove the obscene indignity. Polygnotos, seeing his friend with the horrible implement in his hands, started to shake.

"Ai! Ai!" he cried. "This house is accursed!"

"Come, Polygnotos," said Eutikleides. "Let us close his eyes."

Polygnotos knelt stiffly by the corpse and closed Boutades' right eye as Eutikleides closed the left. I could hear Eutikleides breathing heavily, and Polygnotos' hand and arm moved stiffly like a piece of wood. Then slaves were called to bear away the corpse. I had seen one of the slaves in the courtyard; he was quite composed now and silent like a man in the fourth stage of drunkenness. They took Boutades up, their bare feet making queer marks and patterns in the blood on the floor, as if they were walking in paint. I had a vivid glimpse of Boutades' own feet; as he was lifted up, they were nearly level with my eyes. He had been wearing slippers in the house as old men sometimes do to protect their feet from cold floors, and these slippers were of the softest sand-hued leather—but now his feet were all bloody and the leather was discolored as with bright rust, soaked through to the very soles. I thought idly, "A pity that such good slippers should be spoiled,"—as if Boutades should have met his death in more economical wear.

The slaves moved slowly to the door, bearing their vivid burden. I watched them passing the huge wine amphora by the door—one of the enormous ornamental kind with a long neck and great belly, painted with an extravagant Bacchanal scene—and thought, "Poor Boutades, no more wine." It seemed pathetic to leave such wealth just to be dead.

Polygnotos looked dazed. Eutikleides was still very dignified. "Gentlemen," he said, "you have all seen and heard

enough to act as witnesses if called. I must see that the arkhon is informed, and the leaders of tribe and phratry and
deme. First, however, I shall await the return of the slave
who was sent in pursuit. I know, gentlemen, I may call upon
you for assistance. You may depart from this house of sorrow."

We looked for the last time upon the room still painted
freshly with the morning's deed. The sunlight illuminated it
all now—the bright colors of the fresco behind the little
carved table, the desk with its tablets and stylus, the table
and vase behind me, the pompous jar near the carved door-
post. The sunlit room said, "Rejoice in the delights of day"
while the dark stain on the floor said, "Life departs quickly."

We went out silently into the courtyard, but once there we
became more talkative. We all needed to find water for
proper ritual washing to rid ourselves of the contact with
death. Most of us were still fasting. Yet we seemed unwilling
to disperse.

"I can show you the closed garden," said Telemon, "and
the exact spot on the wall where the killer jumped." There
was a murmur of interest, and most of us followed him. The
closed garden was not much to look at—a city garden, with
a few fruit trees and some pot herbs. One section had been
walled off for the women and slaves to do the washing.

"There," said Telemon. "Now, I stood over there, and then
I came here and Polygnotos was just beside me—and just at
that place in the wall we saw him. Only for a brief space, as
long as it takes for the water-clock to let fall one drop. Now,"
he said, turning from the wall and facing the house, "there's
where the murderer must have stood, just back a little from
the window." We walked over, and examined the ground
before the window. It struck me that none of us knew how
far back the killer would have had to stand in order to shoot
effectively. I looked about in the dust to see if I could find
some track of a murderer's feet—if the killer were god or
demon, he would leave no footprints. But the dry dust and
tussocks of coarse grass were soon trampled over by our

party, so I had no means of assuring myself that the killer was human.

I did see something as I peered at the ground—a small object, brown but shiny. I picked it up. It was a piece of horn with a broken bit of wood fixed in its wider end.

"A sheep's horn," said Telemon without much interest. "How came a sheep to cast its horn here?"

"Don't touch it!" said one of the citizens anxiously. "It may be some heathenish thing belonging to one of the foreign slaves, a charm with power to work us ill."

There were quick footsteps in the courtyard, and a young slave entered the small orchard, a slender red-haired boy of about fourteen years. The lad looked about him, evidently expecting to find his new master among us. His breast was heaving like a bellows.

"I ran," he said hoarsely to Telemon. "I ran as hard as I could—for a great way—but I couldn't catch him." His voice trembled, and sweat poured down his pale face, making dusty streaks. Even the barbaric-hued hair was damp with sweat.

"Oh, dear," said Telemon. "There's one hope crushed."

"Wretched fool!" said one of the citizens.

"I did try," said the slave, still addressing Telemon. "Please tell my—my new master—that I tried as hard as I could."

"Be off, you lousy dog, and tell him yourself," said one of the citizens. "Your master's not here. Into the house with you and make yourself useful."

"Here," I interjected as the slave was slowly making off, "better give your master this and tell him we found it under the window."

He took the object in his palm without looking at it and plodded slowly away, his shoulders bent.

"That seems a frightened slave," I said to the man who had examined the thing of horn.

"No wonder," he said. "The dog may count himself lucky to get off with a good flogging. Letting his master's murderer escape! There's gratitude!"

15

"Quite so," said another citizen. "They're all lazy. I doubt if he ran at all as soon as he was out of sight."

"True—all eye-service," "Give them a crumb and they take the cheese": the familiar remarks on this subject arose from all sides.

"Worse than that," said one. "He may have been in the plot from the beginning, so that the chase was false by prearrangement."

There was emphatic agreement.

"He might have shot his master himself. He's a dirty Sinopean—listen to his accent. Barbarian!"

"But he could not have done the murder," I objected. "He was keeping the main gate when Telemon arrived just at the time of the killing."

"So you say," said the man who had first made the suggestion, throwing me a look full of offense. "But if he's such a fast runner—"

"Well said," responded another citizen. "I shall see the phratry is informed, and I expect the slave to be produced at the first hearing."

This dignitary left the orchard, and the rest followed, most of them apparently well satisfied at the notion of the slave's guilt. I lingered, letting them go without my company, as I felt I had made myself unpopular. My senses were returning to me, including the social sense. I looked again at the ground where I had found the heathenish bit of horn, wondering if there were another. There was not, but I saw a thin glitter; I bent and picked up a very small narrow shard of pottery. Just a piece of broken pot, not very interesting. There were no fragments of figures on it. Scratched on one side, however, there was a tiny sign that ran into the broken irregular edges, a small cross, perhaps a potter's mark. I left the orchard and walked out of the courtyard after the others, still holding the fragment and playing with it absent-mindedly, as men sometimes toy with beads or pebbles. It was a hot sunny morning. I felt tired, as if I had already lived and labored through a whole long day.

III

Threnodies and Accusations

When I got home, I purified myself with water. I said nothing to the family of what I had seen. One does not tell everything to women and children. Besides, I did not particularly wish to relive that horrid scene in my memory. And my mother in her present unhappy state would certainly be disturbed, and would weep. I went out as usual. It was the time of full agora. After the dark and violent beginning of that day it was reassuring to find the usual crowds of shoppers and sellers in the porticoes, to see the customary articles—leather, fish, figs—as abundant as always and to hear the potter at his wheel and the sooty smith at his bright work. The sounds were pleasant to my ears, and the cries: "Pots, cooking pots, very cheap!" "Honey, sweet Hymettos honey!" All these were mixed with the buzz of a hundred conversations and various animated disputes. "Two obols for a pair of lousy slippers? Do you take me for an imbecile, son of a pig?" cries a country slave, while nearby a wealthy citizen is warmly objecting to his companion, "Five hundred drakhmai for a shanty and that patch of weeds. Be reasonable!" In an agora the business and pleasure of living seem of permanent importance. Wisdom is not to be sought in the market place—yet, if wisdom is not there, activity is, and variety, and some cessation of care.

Even in this place of life, however, Boutades made his deathly presence felt. When I left the porticoes and went upon the paved space of the agora itself, I found the citizens in their clean white khitons strolling about as usual and conversing, but, instead of the usual variety of topics, each group as I came to it seemed to be discussing Boutades. News travels rapidly in a city. Telemon was much in evidence, perpetually recounting his tale until he got dry, when he would be hustled over to the stalls in the porticoes and well moistened with wine.

There was a tightness in the air, as when a lyre string is stretched too much, and many a man glanced toward the Akropolis where Athena holds her reign over the city. We could see puffs of dark vapor, the smoke of sacrifices, but this did not release our hearts from fear. There was fear in our hearts, fear of an unknown killer who might walk our streets to strike again, and a bigger dread with less shape. A homicide pollutes all—the killer most, then his family, tribe and phratry, and ultimately the whole city until the murder is avenged. As we made the usual sacrifices and prayers and libations, we might be unclean and our prayers a scorn. Athena herself, the clear goddess of wisdom and craft, might abandon the whole city as an offense until we were cleansed.

No, the morning conversation was not so cheerful as usual. I came upon one group which seemed to be discussing drama, and stayed to listen, but the talk soon returned to the inevitable subject.

"I wonder," said one, "if Polygnotos will be khoregos now. With his poor uncle fresh in his grave."

"There are yet seven months before the Dionysia," another answered. "Time enough—if the slayer is caught and executed before then, that is." It was quite obvious that it would not be seemly for Polygnotos to put on a play with an unavenged murder in the family.

"Certainly no one else will be eager for the honor—to pay out all that money. There would be a show of long faces and short purses then, wouldn't there?"

"Besides," said a beardless fair-haired youth (presumably somebody's playfellow), "Polygnotos has already selected the poet—Keramias. The play is nearly finished, and he hoped soon to apply for a khoros. The mask-makers and theater dressers expect to be busy. Everyone thinks Polygnotos will produce something very big—songs and dances and machinery."

"What's the play about?" asked one of the middle-aged citizens.

"I've heard," said another. "Polygnotos told one who told one who told me, in fact—that it is to be about education."

"Humph," said the other. "A moral tale. I hope there's some fun in it. I like the old-fashioned comedies with some good raw jokes and a piss-pot and the sausage-seller and a chorus of pots and pans. Anyway, I didn't ask what the *theme* was—I wanted to know what is it *about?*"

"I know," said the fair youth. "I know one who knows Keramias. It's about Kheiron and Herakles."

"Ugh. An ill omen. Remember the death of Kheiron."

The conversation chilled and the group separated. I left the agora and went back to the porticoes, to the laughing groups about the wine-sellers. Even here, I discovered, the muse of poetry pointed at Boutades. As I walked slowly in the crowded shade, I came upon a ballad-monger, one of the vulgar ragged beggars who collect a few coins by singing the day's news in jerry-built lines of the poorest poetry—mere doggerel stuff, in the rhythm of farm women bringing cabbages to market. This fellow was plying his trade with a hoarse but lusty voice:

"O come, Athenian people, and gather round about me.
I have some awful news to tell, 'tis true so do not doubt me.
Good Boutades of Athens, on this day he was found
Shot by an arrow, and lying on the ground.

Boutades is slain, but 'twas not by spear or knife.
The ground it was all bloody where the arrow took his life.
The wicked murderer was seen, leaping over the bricks—
May the gods curse and kill him, and send him to the Styx!

Boutades met an awful death, while sitting in his room,
A-doing no one any harm, he's sent unto his tomb.
He died a much respected man, fifty years after he was born.
This dreadful murder happened just at the break of morn.

19

Boutades was a trierarkh, a man of an Athens deme.
He did his duty by us all, as it does plainly seem.
His spirit cannot be at ease, for Vengeance cries his friend!
May the killer be caught and tortured and meet a dreadful
end."

It was poor jumbled stuff enough, but, though I was often entertained by the lumpy lines of these traders in bad verse, I could find no amusement in this. I left the agora before noon.

Two days later I went, like everyone else, to Boutades' lying-in-state. The courtyard through which I had hastened on the murder morning was now a scene of formality; a dignified crowd of men was gathered to pay respects. The rise and fall of women's wailing could be heard from the house, as well as the lamenting flutes. There was a large band of musicians, handsomely turned out. Polygnotos in his mourning garment looked heavy-eyed and melancholy, but he bore himself with sad composure. He was surrounded by men of the family and members of the phratry, Eutikleides among them. Polygnotos paid me no heed, though I had been among the first at the scene of death and had beheld him close his uncle's eyes.

Boutades paid none of us any heed. He lay at ease on a fine carved couch, his feet toward the gate. He looked a good deal better than when I saw him last. The women had well performed their grisly task of washing the corpse, and Boutades, though pale, looked as proper and pleased as if he had died in his bed. His white grave-cloth was immaculate—how unlike the khiton he wore when he had last received us—and the women had carefully wound the woolen fillets all the way up the throat, so that no wound was visible. This unusually extensive swaddling had pushed his chin up and gave it an arrogant jut. Lying there with the obol in his mouth, he looked almost smug. The women had crowned him with the customary vine leaves, which added a touch of the bacchanal oddly sorting with the manner of his going. Poor Boutades! I remembered the huge amphora which would never again offer him a drink. As I bent over him to take my last farewell I could smell oregano, and warm honey from the honey-cake in his hand which was melting in the sun. There was also the slight but unmistakable smell of death. Some flies buzzed about the sticky white fingers which would never brush them away.

The hired mourners struck up a fine threnody. They sang heartily, probably encouraged by generous refreshment from the kitchen as well as handsome payments. No one could say that Polygnotos had sent his uncle meanly off. Everything was most correct. The imbecilic slave I had seen, now apparently in his right mind, was decorously in attendance at the gate with the water for purification.

The prothesis had been so normal and so well conducted that I felt somewhat cheered after saying my farewell, as if life might return to its ordinary ways. This feeling was indeed foolish.

I don't know which was worse, the day of the murder or that of the funeral. Although I could not realize it at the time, the day of Boutades' lying-in-state (which was, of course, the day before the funeral) only provided for me a brief respite between two blows.

That is a burial I shall remember until I myself depart from life. As every other citizen did, I got up early in the morning to watch it. The morning—night, rather—was cool: although the stars were still bright in the sky there was a feeling of rain in the air, as if clouds were building up over the sea.

Boutades' body on its bier was drawn on a cart. Probably his friends had not felt quite like carrying on their shoulders a corpse so slaughtered, a body whose irate spirit would be hovering above their heads. The family and phratry all came, however, with Polygnotos at their head, carrying a spear. We had known he would carry it, yet an extra tremor of excitement, almost exhilaration, ran through the crowd at seeing him with it. He looked very stern, as if he were going to war. The procession moved through the streets of Athens. Boutades on his bier was clearly visible, a center of brightness in the light of the torches carried by the slaves; then came the dark group of the women of the family, black-veiled, following the bier to catch Boutades' soul should it drift behind the body. The dark silence of the night streets was cut into shreds by torchlight and lamenting cries. The funeral party with all of us following went through Athens to the Kerameikos. There the procession stopped in a part of the burial ground already well settled by the wealthy and noble. The light flickered on large monuments, tall grave stelai and carved marble as the body of Boutades was deposited in the freshly dug grave. Amidst ululation, kin and friends threw the customary objects into the grave: pots and terracotta figures and even a gold ring shone in the brief glow of torchlight as they fell in a heavy shower. The gravedigger shoveled steadily and there was a dull sound of falling earth. There was no moon, and the stars had hidden their fires. Night waged a battle against the coming dawn, and seemed to grow stronger instead of waning. Just as the grave was filled, a fine rain began to fall.

Polygnotos advanced to the graveside. The slaves held the torches up so that Polygnotos was the only thing clearly illuminated. Carrying his spear, looking large and wavering in the glow cast by the hissing lights outlined against the darkness, he was like some god or hero on the stage. A shudder of anticipation—and of chill from the cold rain—went through the crowd. This was the moment which made this burial different from others. Polygnotos would now make a proclamation against the unknown "doer and killer," a challenge and a threat to the anonymous assassin, charging him (or them) to keep away from all legal and holy things. This utterance, made directly to the unknown assailant whether among us or far away, was a holy utterance made in company with the shade of the murdered man. It was a beginning of vengeance in sight of the gods and of men, and the faceless man-slayer, wherever he might be, would be touched now by an invisible finger. We were all expecting Polygnotos' challenge to be against the intangible and unknown "doer and killer." But Polygnotos surprised us.

He raised his spear on high and began to speak. His voice was clear and deep and well modulated; it carried extremely well. "At the grave of my uncle, Boutades, son of Boutades, of the Etioboutadai, and in presence of his shade, Boutades foully murdered, I, Polygnotos, proclaim to you, Philemon, son of Lykias of Athens, that you are the known murderer, and I charge you to keep from all legal and holy things, from holy water, from wine and libations, from the agora, from the courts, from the temples, and from all sacred places!"

I almost fell against the slave who held my torch. I could hardly believe at first that those were the words I had heard. My cousin Philemon! It was impossible. As life and thought came back to me again, and with them anger, I almost shouted, "You lie!" almost rushed up to Polygnotos himself. I wanted to snatch the spear from his hand and bid him fiercely take back those false words. But I had sense enough to realize this would be foolish; it would be judged unseemly, even impious. The funeral party began to move away, and the crowd was dispersing as I still stood there, the men trying to cover their heads with their himations against the insistent rain.

I could hear excited exclamations around me. No one came to me to offer commiseration or what would have been more welcome, sympathetic anger. Those near me who knew who I was—the man next of kin to a proclaimed murderer in the most heinous crime Athens could remember—moved hastily from my presence.

Even then I could not but think that this was all a mistake, a nightmarish confusion. But this feeling was considerably abated by an ominous fact. Polygnotos with Eutikleides and others of his kin passed not far from me, and as they did so, Eutikleides, with a meaningful look in my direction, said to a questioning citizen, "We go to make a formal charge to the Basileus, and you may hear the proclamation to Philemon made in the agora before this day has ended."

IV

Aristotle at Home

I stumbled home, drenched and shivering. I said nothing to the women of what had passed. During the rest of the morning I had time to think over the events of that alarming funeral, and raised my heart a little by a hope that the Basileus would reject this absurd charge. This hope died almost at once. The Basileus appeared in the agora with Polygnotos and his kin, and the proclamation was made against Philemon before noon.

Everyone knew now, and the legal charge meant that Philemon would surely be tried. It was in vain to try to keep such a thing from the women—news travels fast by back doors, and they had heard of the public proclamation as soon as I did. Aunt Eudoxia had to be faced. She came to me, trembling and tear-stained, throwing herself at my feet as a suppliant.

"Oh, Stephanos, you must save him! You are the man of the family now—you can do something to put it right."

I raised her and sat her on a stool, trying not to hurt the side where her disease pained her. She might not have noticed, her whole body and mind were in such pain.

"Yes, yes," I said soothingly, patting her hand. "This is some horrible mistake that will soon be set right. It is all absurd! Philemon is an exile—he's been away for two years. It is not reasonable even to suspect a man who is not here! They must all see that. We know it would not be reasonable to suspect him in any case. He would not do it, and we know he didn't, and can show it was impossible for him to do it. Even if we have to wait until the first hearing, the Basileus will throw the case out then. It will not even come to a trial."

I was speaking to myself nearly as much as to her, and my words seemed to hearten us both. Eudoxia dried her face and composed herself to speak. She caught eagerly at my words.

"'Not reasonable to suspect a man who is not here.' You tell them that, Stephanos. Make the Basileus see it is foolishness—to suspect a poor exile, so far away. Oh, my poor boy, when shall I see you again?" She started to weep afresh. "Why was his sweet name even tainted with such a foul crime?" She lowered her voice and bent toward me. "I know all about the murder, you know, and so does your mother, though you tried to keep it from us. The slaves were full of the news on that very morning. We didn't talk of it before you because we saw you were out of sorts. We heard you had been there in the house, and wanted to ask you of it, but we felt you did not wish to mention it beside the sacred hearth of Zeus. But I must ask you now—you were there, weren't you?"

"Yes," I said, wondering at the women's unforeseen ability to keep things from me.

"And was anything said then about Philemon? Is that why you were downcast? Were they, even then, saying or hinting, that he had done it?"

"No, Aunt Eudoxia, I assure you by the gods, nothing like that. I didn't feel more concerned than anyone else, except that I was one of the ones who saw Boutades. That was a— by no means a beautiful sight."

I hesitated, but she was looking at me as if she expected me to continue. So I told her of that morning and of what had been said. She listened attentively, not crying. Indeed, her response surprised me. She gave a great countrywoman's snort, honking like a goose through her nose, which she then blew.

"Is that all? If it is, they have nothing—they have pulled out a name from a pot. I'm sure that Boutades' kin are ashamed of such an ugly death in the family, and think if they can tie the murder quickly to someone or other then vengeance will have been done and the city will be easy and forget. They have chosen the name of my poor Philemon because of the old man-slaying charge—but that was in a *fight*, Stephanos, and nothing like this, nothing."

The tears crept to her eyes again. "We all depend on you, Stephanos—poor boy, so young. But make them see reason. We will have justice even if that great family are against us. They think they can do as they like with the name of our house because there are so few men among us—and my Philemon sent away. But you are a man, Stephanos, and a good man—the gods will hear you and punish the Etioboutadai for their falsehood."

She got up, mopping her eyes, and moved her bulky painful body to the door. Before she went, she looked back at me and said almost triumphantly, "They're silly too, Stephanos —silly—aren't they? How can a man who is not there do a murder?"

I seemed to have comforted her. I myself was not so easy, although I kept repeating to myself what we had said: "How can a man who is not there do a murder?" Eudoxia was right about there being so few men in the family. My father and uncle were dead, I had no adult brothers, no cousin—except poor Philemon. There was of course my phratry, but none of the important men in it were close connections. Everything depended on me alone—and I didn't know what to do.

After a sleepless night, I rose and tried to go through the ritual of an ordinary day. I went to the baths, and friends greeted me briefly. I went to the gymnasium, and everyone was too much occupied to join me in any sport. I went to the agora, and citizens were suddenly deep in conversation as I came by. I heard exclamations from the vulgar crowd in the market, and even caught one or two small gestures I was not meant to see, the motions made by country folk and slaves to avert evil emanations from an ominous passer-by. I went home and tried to read, but no book held my attention. My mind was all soreness, like the hot irritation that comes upon a deep cut in the flesh.

In the evening I could bear it no longer. I would go and talk to the man in Athens I most admired and the one who, oddly enough, for all his eminence, was the man least likely to turn me away with cold civility. I needed to clear my mind, I needed intelligent conversation and advice. I would go and talk to Aristotle.

Aristotle was living at that time in a small house near the Lykeion. It was not his house. Aristotle was a foreigner in Athens, a metoikos, and, though the public decree three years ago had conferred honorary citizenship upon him, he was not well thought of by some because of his Makedonian connections. He was not a property-owner; hence Plato could not have bequeathed the old Akademeia to him. Besides, before Plato died, Aristotle had had to leave Athens hastily because the conflict with Makedonia meant increased hostility to the man from Stageira whose family was patronized by Philip. Aristotle was away for thirteen years. There could really be no question of Plato's leaving him the Akademeia. I set this down to contradict base rumors which circulate nowadays saying that Plato and Aristotle were at enmity—a vile slander upon the names of two great men.

When I was a young child the white-haired man who was Plato had been pointed out to me, but I can hardly remember him. I had attended the Akademeia in the latter days of Speusippos' dull reign. When Aristotle had returned to Athens and established his school I joined it and for a short while enjoyed the greatest intellectual pleasure it is possible to know. Coming there from the Akademeia was like watching the weather change from cloudiness to the full light of day. I kept my lecture notes and even after my enforced retirement from the Lykeion at the death of my father, I would return to them occasionally when I wished to keep my mind alive.

Yes, I certainly admired Aristotle sufficiently—but would he take any interest in me? I had not been an outstanding student. Probably he would not recollect who I was. As I drew nearer the house my heart sank at my own temerity.

The house-slave received me courteously and went at once to announce my presence. He brought back word that the master was at dinner but would see me immediately afterward, and conducted me to the front room to wait.

Voices in the next room, audible in this small house, suggested that Aristotle was dining with his wife. Some thought it odd that Aristotle, for so long the recluse of the Akademeia, stealing away from conversation to read by himself, and delighting apparently only in the world of books and philosophical discourse, should have come back after his years of absence and mysterious foreign embassies a married man. Not only married, but to a wife not of the pattern one would design for a philosopher. He had married, while still in foreign parts, an outlandish woman, Pythias, daughter of Hermias of Atarneos. Some unkind folks said Pythias had been Hermias' concubine, not his daughter, but I shall never believe it. The usual women's gossip reported that she was pretty, rather dark-skinned, dressed her hair in a foreign fashion, was neat in her housekeeping and kept herself to herself. She had borne her husband only a daughter.

As I waited in the cheerful small room with its extraordinary quantity of books (Aristotle had books of his own, not just two or three but a number, which he kept at home) I began to feel downhearted again. The slave was deferential enough; he probably took me for one of the young gentlemen of the Lykeion come to take up some intricate discussion unfinished in the day's work—one of Aristotle's most promising pupils whom he would naturally receive at home. I recollected that Aristotle himself had early been recognized by Plato as his best pupil. It was said that Plato called Aristotle "the Mind" and refused to begin a lecture until he was present, saying, "The Mind is not yet with us." We students thought this comical, and sometimes referred to Aristotle (behind his back) as "the Mind." It was not an epithet anyone would use of myself, unless in plainest mockery. And here, instead of being a cultivated young gentleman come to discourse of noble subjects, I was an uninvited visitor, not even now a pupil, a young man in a wretchedly emotional and unphilosophical condition, hoping to lay my sordid personal problem at the feet of the master.

The door opened and Aristotle came in. His smile in greeting me suggested none of the lofty rebuke I had persuaded myself to fear. I sat at his bidding while he settled his bony frame, first arranging a careful cushion at his back.

"I hope, sir," I said hesitantly, "that by the gods' favor I see you in good health."

"Very well," he said briskly. "All except the sciatica. An Attic complaint. But you, Stephanos—" he turned those deep-set blue eyes of his upon me and gazed shrewdly at my face— "you have the look of one who has not slept. You are full of Attic complaints. I think I know why you have come to me."

"Ah," I said sadly, "I scarcely know that myself, save that I must speak to someone clear-minded to arrange my own thoughts. But this is no philosophical matter. Perhaps you too would not wish to converse with me—"

"I know very well what has happened," said Aristotle calmly. "I do not live so much in the groves and lecture rooms that I do not hear what happens in Athens. I know that Boutades has been murdered, and that your cousin is accused. Obviously you will act as his defender. So what is more natural than that you should come to me, your old tutor in Rhetoric as well as in other branches of philosophy? Most sensible. And I," he laughed, "I am not at such a peak of respectability in Athens that I mind being seen talking to you, if that's what you mean."

He shook his head; his large bald spot glowed in the lamplight which also sparkled in the reddish fringe of his remaining hair. He looked rather as one would imagine a fire-spirit, and certainly not especially respectable. I thought to myself, "This is probably my best friend in all Athens."

"I understand," he continued in a deeper tone, "the distress this causes you. But you are wrong to think that yours is not a problem for a philosopher. Fear and pain and anger—these are natural to animals, to men, even, we are told, to the gods. But the human animal exerts itself through the work of the mind—this is the best and most effective remedy against evil that mortals are given. Let your mind now enter the game. But first some wine, to ease your heart a little. We shall drink as we talk.

"Now," he said after the wine was brought and we had made libation, "talk to me and tell me in order all that you know. Set the matter out before us as if you were setting out a problem in geometry."

I told him what had happened, rather as I had told Eudoxia, but more clearly. I told him of my presence in Boutades' house and my view of the body, of what Telemon and Polygnotos had said (as well as I could remember), and of our going into the courtyard and my finding the piece of horn. He listened intently, and insisted on my describing this object.

"Ah," he said, "I know what that is. It is the tip of a Kretan bow—they're rather crude affairs but serviceable enough, it seems. Philemon has been in Krete?"

"Yes," I answered sadly, "when he first left Athens he went on board a grain ship bound for Krete. It's common knowledge."

"Indeed," said Aristotle. "Then that is a point which will obviously be used by the prosecution. Don't look so downcast, Stephanos—we must look at all the facts, and it is a poor rhetorician who goes to argue a case at law without anticipating his opponents. We must know all the facts as far as possible. It is ill policy to wait to be surprised. Whatever is so, is so. Truly, Stephanos, I will not betray you, nor discuss what you say to me with anyone else, but I must ask you—or if you will not answer me, answer yourself: Has Philemon been back? Was he in Athens? Forgive me, but only the truth can help us now."

"No," I said indignantly. "I *know* he has not returned—not ever in these last two years. If he had been here, he would have let me know—or if not myself, then certainly Aunt Eudoxia. He would have seen her—his mother and ill—and I know he has not."

I told Aristotle about my conversation with Aunt Eudoxia. "And she thinks," I said in conclusion, "that Boutades' family want only to avenge themselves as quickly as possible, and that they have picked on Philemon's name because he is of a small family, and not wealthy, and has the old charge of manslaughter sticking to his name."

"She is a wise woman," Aristotle answered. "I feel a great respect for your Aunt Eudoxia."

"And above all," I went on, "Aunt Eudoxia and I both know Philemon. We *know* he would not do such a vile thing, not to be ruler of Athens or to save himself from death."

Aristotle shook his head. "Of little use in a court of law—save perhaps in the courts of Hades, but there, one presumes, truth needs no proof and rhetoric is at an end. I have not asked this question to discourage you," he continued, "but we are thinking at this moment as rhetoricians and men of law. You have this poor consolation, as far as your cousin himself is concerned—Philemon is an exile and still absent from Athens, so, no matter what the outcome of the trial, they cannot make him suffer the utmost penalty. His life is safe—as long as he stays away from Athens. How are you going to get word to him?"

"I can't send to him. I wish I could. If only I knew where he is! Perhaps he may hear about this slander, wherever he is—though I hate to think of the bitter news coming to him alone and far away."

Aristotle sipped his wine and looked at the fire.

"Well," he said briskly, "we wish to take this as our hypothesis: Philemon did not do it. This is the basis of your defense. The argument proceeds, you think, along the lines suggested by your good aunt. He was not there and so he could not do it.

"But there is a corollary to your first hypothesis which leads to a more interesting argument. After all, Eudoxia's proof is only a support of your hypothesis, not a demonstration of it. It is absolute as it goes, but if this prop were knocked out your hypothesis could still be true. If we take it as true, the corollary might be demonstrated. If Philemon did not do it, someone of the class not-Philemon did it. Someone did kill Boutades. Looked at objectively, that is the more interesting point. Find out who did kill Boutades and prove that this person did it, and your theorem stands proved. It is open to you, before the trial, to investigate who did kill Boutades, as well as to find witnesses to prove Philemon's absence."

"To me?" I said, choking over my wine. "That is a task for Herakles. To find some fleet killer who moves like the night wind? Whoever did it may have gone anywhere in the world, and his act may be known only to himself and the gods. What chance have I of finding him in these few weeks?"

"I did not say it could certainly be done," Aristotle said. "But it *might* be done. And you have some time, Stephanos. So—look." He held up four fingers. "The first prodikasia," he said, touching his little finger. "You will be meeting the Basileus and those who are bringing the action for the first hearing in a few weeks' time. That is a short time, certainly—the end of this month. But then," he touched the next finger, "there is a month between that and the second prodikasia. Another month," moving on to the middle finger, "before the third prodikasia. And then another month before the trial itself." He shook the forefinger at me. "There are nearly four months, Stephanos. The sun is still bright now, and the days hot. It will be after midwinter when the trial is held. Much can be done, and much learned, in four months, or even three."

"What should I try to learn? What should I do?" I asked. I felt like an idiot, like the kind of student who is always asking, "What should I read? What should I be thinking about? How do I begin? How do I go on?"

Aristotle only beamed encouragingly and gave me some more wine. "First we must stop wandering away from the point. We should return to the major fact—the murder itself. Your story of that morning is most interesting, Stephanos— and well told too. It is an advantage to our defense that we know—not what really happened, but more than if you had not been there. There is also a distinct disadvantage to your having been there, which I ought to point out. If Polygnotos and his tribe wish, they could assert that you were in league with Philemon and discount you as his defender. I don't think they will do this," he added. "Someone must conduct the defense, and it would be the greater credit to them, as they see it, to overcome a relative of the accused, a true defender. In any case, as to the events of the morning from the time of your arrival there will presumably be little dispute. You know that Philemon's name was not mentioned at that time, and presumably can call witnesses on that point."

Aristotle thought a moment, then shook his head as if in mild vexation. His bright hair, his silver-streaked beard, glimmered in the light as if he were made out of sparks. "Dear me," he said. "I wish I had been in the room myself."

"Do you doubt me?" I asked, rather hurt.

"No—no. But people notice different things, and much talking confuses the eyes. Always remember you weren't present at events of which you were told. Some of those who entered the room with you will now be saying foolish things like 'I was there when Boutades was murdered'—which is a loose and common way of talking. No one was there at that time save the murderer. None of you save Polygnotos was there at the first discovery of the body. Even wiser men may say they were 'as good as there'—but they know only what they remember someone else saying. What did you really see? Describe the room and the objects in it."

I did so.

"How was Boutades lying when you saw him? Where had the arrow gone in?"

I told him that too, pointing at the spot in my own throat —not without a slight shudder.

"Ah! The great vein of the throat, the jugular," said Aristotle cheerfully. "Neatly shot, indeed. And a great deal of blood, you say? Poor Boutades, his unfinished accounts lying there on the table and covered with blood—"

"No," I protested. "There wasn't any blood on the table, I'm quite sure. But there was blood on the floor, a great deal. It had even soaked through Boutades' slippers. And his hair was discolored with it."

"What a good memory! You are observant—I was carelessly assuming that there was blood on the table. I shall make a note of that."

Here he did indeed make a note, jotting something down with his stylus on a wax tablet. He noticed my inquiring glance.

"I shall not put down anything that could convey information to anyone else," he said reassuringly. "I make notes on everything. It is, I imagine, a nervous habit, but better than chewing one's fingernails. And it makes one look wise. It is pleasant to be thought wise; that bestows such inexpensive power over others. But continue with your interesting account. Where were Boutades' slippers most stained?"

"All over—the heels especially."

" 'He did not come dry-shod to the bank of Styx,' " said Aristotle, quoting an elegy. "Very perceptive. Tell me, was the body still bleeding when you saw it? Or was the blood clotted and rust-colored?"

"He was still bleeding when I came in," I said, remembering. "I watched a drop oozing slowly down his throat. But before we left, the blood was still, and most had started to dry, even the puddle on the floor."

All this sort of talk gave me a qualm at the stomach, but Aristotle seemed to take a bright dry interest, as if we had been talking of the proportions of a triangle instead of the body of a man. I remembered that Aristotle's father was a physician, and that the philosopher himself, a descendant of Asklepios, was skilled in medicine. I suppose physicians always have this cool attitude to the body and its doings—an attitude which most others do not share.

"I should like to have seen that body," Aristotle remarked wistfully. "Yes, Boutades' death is very interesting. Why was he dead? Men injure others from four main causes: chance, compulsion, habit and desire. Chance it cannot have been—unless the killer intended to kill someone other than Boutades and made a mistake. Possible but improbable. Habit—certainly not. A habit of killing citizens with arrow shots at dawn would become too noticeable an eccentricity. Compulsion—yes, the killer may have been compelled by the real designer of the murder. Which brings us to the fourth reason, for whoever plotted the murder, whether his was the hand that struck or not, wanted Boutades to die."

"It might have been a madman," I interjected.

"Yes—an irrational craving for the man's death is a possibility. Irrational motives are harder to unravel, although often they come to look like rational ones inside out. The irrational man, say, acting a part in his own mind, sees in his victim an enemy of the state, or the killer of his father, or a person plotting against himself. The insane man usually gives himself away by inappropriate talk. For all we know, the prosecution may allege that Philemon killed Boutades in an act of madness."

"Then all we could do," I said, "would be to introduce instances that show he is sane. But that wouldn't apply, as we have only to show that Philemon was not there."

"Aunt Eudoxia's Proof. Yes." Aristotle frowned. "Proving a negative, always proving a negative! Philemon wasn't there, Philemon wasn't insane, Philemon had no rational motive . . . It is always hard to prove negatives. Let's return to Boutades and why he is dead. The desire for his death is more likely to have been rational. Roughly speaking, there are three types of rational desire involved in such a case: desire for revenge, for self-protection, for gain. Wrath, Fear, Covetousness. Three powerful passions. Boutades is interesting as that bloody corpse. Was he as interesting in life? He must have been, for someone most probably hated him enough to kill him. I think we can say that to prefer a man's goods to his life ranks as hatred. Boutades has distinguished himself. You and I began our talk tonight as if Philemon were the hero of our tale—but if you are right he is not a central personage at all. It is much better to treat Boutades as our central character. As such, he merits attention. You remember in school exercises in rhetoric, how you would be asked to make a speech on the qualities, actions and character of a literary figure? At this moment, I imagine, you could deliver a speech of shrewd remarks on Odysseus the wise, or the lascivious and brutal Aigisthos. Yet Boutades is more to you now than these—and what can you say of his character? Of his actions and qualities?"

I found myself answering:

" 'Boutades was a trierarkh, a man of an Athens deme.
He did his duty by us all, as it does plainly seem.' "

"What is that?"

Rather stupidly I repeated the whole of that inane ballad to Aristotle. It had engraved itself on my mind without my wishing it. Aristotle seemed quite entertained.

"Very fine. Succinct and inaccurate—as poetry and history usually are. *Was* a killer seen leaping over the bricks? "He died a much respected man"—but *did* everyone respect him? *Did* he do his duty by us all? What did he do? Or not do? We might proceed on the assumption that something in his life led to his death."

"I don't know how I'd find out about him," I said. "It would certainly not be possible for me to question his household."

"True. But a household is a sieve, not a stoppered jar. A man's life leaks out, a grain here, a grain there. Someone as big as Boutades doesn't live without trace. The best thing for you is to keep your eyes and ears open, see what you can learn about Boutades—the real man, not a character in a ballad."

"But I want to start somewhere definite," I protested.

"Take one aspect of his life and start investigating that."

"Like his being a trierarkh?"

"Very good."

"That might be possible," I mused, "and certainly, if what we hear is true, there has been a lot of trouble among the trierarkhy, until . . ."

"Excellent, Stephanos. You are thinking for yourself. You were going to add, before your customary tact intervened, 'until your great enemy Demosthenes set everything right with admirably just arrangements about the shipping.' I would not deny Demosthenes' ability, and applaud the justice of his reforms. But that was during the war. Now Demosthenes is powerless, the city is calm, there are fair chances for men to prosper. Old disorders have had a chance to creep in. Oligarkhs are hard to discourage—they have such strong habits. There *might* be something worth finding out in Boutades' relationship with the trierarkhy. The investigation would broaden your mind."

"I shall try to find out what I can," I murmured. I felt I had the beginnings, at least, of a definite task. "Boutades—trierarkhy." It was like having a theme for one's first disquisition in school.

"But above all, Stephanos, be discreet. Over-busyness is irritating—like flies. Boutades' family will not wish to hear the sound of buzzing. Go serenely about your ordinary affairs. And at the first prodikasia be modest and unassuming —as becomes a young man. That will dispose the Basileus favorably to you, and give your opponents no cause for annoyance. A seemly demeanor is an effective rhetorical gesture. What are you planning to say at the first hearing?"

"Aunt Eudoxia's Defense. He wasn't there."

"Yes. Well enough at the start. Your second piece of work —the first in importance, if you will—is to look for witnesses who can testify to Philemon's being elsewhere."

He sighed. "Proving negatives—a tedious course in logic. The scent on the trail of the positive is so much hotter and more exciting—though the trail may be longer. It will be long in any case, I fear. Don't be downcast if you have no witnesses for Philemon by the first prodikasia. A mere formality, after all. Modest demeanor—Philemon wasn't there. That should do for now. At the same time, begin your secret inspection of Boutades' life. Let me know whatever you find out, even slight things not apparently related to the murder."

"So I may come again?"

"Whenever you will," he answered cheerfully. "I look forward to adding to my notes."

I glanced at his wax tablet. It had a very few words on it, disposed thus:

Krete
table
blood slippers
Wrath Fear Avarice

"It's not very much," I said, disappointed. "I've given whole lectures with no more notes than that. Ariadne's thread. A rhetorician, after all, is a true son of Athens' father. He moves through a labyrinth, guiding us until we come face to face with the truth."

We rose and tossed the last of the wine into the fire. The few seconds of prayer were very calming.

"I do wish," said Aristotle, breaking into my silent thoughts, "that I had taken the walk you did that morning. I should like to have seen that room. But perhaps it is just as well I did not. I might have been accused of complicity in the murder myself! What a chance to get rid of the friend of Makedonia!"

I hastily contradicted this preposterous notion, which seemed foolish conceit in him. "No indeed," I said. "Why, Boutades' family are ardent supporters of Makedonia. On every occasion they speak well of Alexander."

"Well said, Stephanos. You know more of public life than I had thought. You know perhaps more than you think. This evening has given me a very good impression of you. You are loyal and clear-minded. Do not let one quality stand in the way of the other. Now farewell, and take some sleep."

His praise and concern were heartening. That night I slept, and in the morning felt better than I had done for several days, although on thinking about our conversation I realized that not much had really been accomplished. Aristotle was not going to be of any direct help—he had not offered to assist me in my investigations. But at least I had clearer ideas, and some thoughts about what I should do in the next while. Aristotle had given me the reassuring impression that my judgment was not despicable. I did, however, feel annoyed about his harking back to the room and wishing he had been there. What would he have seen that I had not? Nothing, quite certainly.

V

Hearing and Overhearing

In the next few days I accustomed myself to cold looks and snubs, and went about Athens looking serene and controlled. My applied serenity was not without some effect in allaying others' hostility toward me; the coldness became a shade less icy, the snubs less evident. Within, I felt constantly anxious. The serenity became heavy on my face like the mask of an actor. I was not really doing anything yet for Philemon's cause, except in so far as my remaining publicly acceptable would ease my position as his defender. Time was going by.

Then, a week after my meeting with Aristotle, something happened. Not much, but something. I picked up my first grain of information. I was idling about the market place, after forcing myself through the daily appearance at the agora, and stopped by a leatherworker's stall. While I was inhaling the bracing odor of leather, thinking lazily of buying some new sandals, I heard chattering voices. A hide thrown over a rope shut off part of the stall's interior, and beyond this partition some women were gossiping—slaves or country-women who would appear in public. I supposed they were waiting for the leatherworker's boy to come and cut out sandals for them. The women spoke with the accents of the town, not the country, and it occurred to me they must be slaves belonging to good families if they were getting shoes for themselves. This is the kind of logical deduction one makes every day without setting all out in syllogisms, and the conclusion was of no interest whatever.

I was about to pass on when I heard a name that kept me fixed where I stood. One woman, lowering her voice, asked the other, "How are you all managing at Boutades' house now?"

"Oh, Zeus!" the other responded emphatically. "We live between the pig-sty and the parlor, as you might say. The young master keeps all in order, and he isn't mean either—but who likes living in a house covered in blood? May I never have another task like cleaning that room, Athena hear me! Then we get in a great fright when we think of the trial. Some say that all the slaves will be called as witnesses, and others that only that poor young lad will be called—and that means torture for a slave. That's the law. Athena be praised, I was at the country estate at the time, and can't be called to the question. But that poor boy—he's getting thinner by the day."

"It's a wicked thing, the law," her friend remarked with indignant sympathy.

There was a short pause, and a third female voice, dryer and older, asked, "What of Boutades' wife? Does she bear her sorrow well?"

"You may say so." The slavewoman of Boutades' household seemed happy to expand on the topic. "Oh, she shows great patience in her affliction. Why, the third day after the funeral she asked me on the sly to get her a young sucking pig, roasted—the master that was used to forbid her to have any. She gorged herself on pig roasted in honey, dripping fat all round her chops—a fine picture of a lady in mourning. But I kept it quiet, and, indeed, I didn't begrudge her. He kept us on short commons enough. Why should she lament for him? He abused her beyond any woman's patience, calling her barren bitch, and beating her. Worse off than the slaves, she was. Never a pair of new sandals, or a new dress for ages —he was mean past belief in his latter days. She didn't produce an heir, and that was the end of her in his eyes."

"Ah, well," said the second woman. "Many a man feels that, especially one with so much to leave as Boutades, and not even a girl child to pass the box to. Neither your old master nor his lady were colts, however—they must have become used to the state of things by that time."

"Ah—that's not what you'd say if you'd heard some of what I've heard. They were by no means in their youth, that's true —him with his fat belly and bad bowels, and her always colicky (she paid dear for her meal on the pig)—but they quarreled as well as if they had just begun. These last few months were the worst of all. She had spirit enough to retort, I'll give her that. There was a big scene between them in the summer. I heard her picking his nits for him in a fine style: 'Ah, *you*' (here the slavewoman shrilly mimicked a lady's voice), 'making a fool of yourself at your age! Do you want to disgrace yourself and the whole family? A fine time to think of a child!—and not your own. Better, instead of wasting your whole estate, to spend a few coins on some good harlot who'll be glad to take your money for what you can't do!'

"Well, I laughed to hear the master so taunted, but he shouted back, 'I'll do what I want!' and called her filthy names I wouldn't repeat. Then he gave her a couple of blows that might make her come to grief indeed, and I stopped laughing. A woman pays dearly for going a journey with her tongue. He was always surly within doors. Ah well, as the slaves' proverb goes, 'A master's manners are no lesson.' "

"Poor thing," said her friend. "She'll be easy now. Many a good thing can be said of widowhood."

"I think it's disgraceful," said the third personage. "A wife ought to behave decently. She seems a bad woman, by your account."

"No," said Boutades' slavewoman judiciously, "I wouldn't say so, and I have to serve her. Easy enough to please, most days, and she can be quite generous. But now she's like a woman in a wind, turning this way and that, crying and laughing by turns, now deep in woe, then bright as tin. Strangely cheerful in a stiff manner, as if she were made of new linen. Do you know she laughed when they told her her husband was dead and how he died—*laughed?* The slaves had to start crying and wailing to cover the sound. I partly think she's not right in the head. She has even quarreled with

Polygnotos—and he's so even-tempered. He was distressed about his uncle's death, but he did his best to speak kindly to her, always. And such a beautiful funeral he got up, under the circumstances—might have done any woman's heart good."

"What did she quarrel with him for?"

"I didn't catch it all. Something about his not having the right to do what he liked with the furniture, that's how it began. Nonsense, of course—and this was only the day after the funeral, and he had given her new clothes and all. But she was shouting at him, and I heard her saying, 'Why don't you give the child something and show you care for your uncle's wishes? Zeus is the father of orphans. None in this house can afford to go against the wishes of the gods, can they? And I know about the boy, remember that.' She went on repeating herself about Zeus and a boy."

Her friend laughed knowingly. "Perhaps this was a love-friend of Polygnotos'."

"Well, perhaps. But *I* think it may have been some bastard child of Polygnotos' that she had heard of. If Boutades had ever had a child, he would have adopted it at once, you may be sure—but he had long lost the power of making any woman bear. At any rate, Polygnotos was displeased, and told her to be quiet. But you see how strangely foolish she is, to quarrel with her nephew who provides her with the very bread she eats."

"Fine affairs indeed," said the older slave. "Life in Athens is not as it used to be, even in the old families. I'm glad I live in the country most of the time now. Food's cheaper too. Have you noticed what a price they charge for cabbage in the market?"

Their talk drifted along to matters of food and marketing. All women have five subjects only—food, clothes, sex, children and scandal. I was, however, grateful for this gossip. Walking slowly away, hoping I hadn't lingered noticeably by the leather-stall, I thought over what they had said. Aristotle was right: a man's household is a sieve.

Here was an insight into Boutades, the good citizen, who was given, it seemed, to sordid quarrels and brutish behavior, whose impotence was domestic knowledge and a familiar shame. I thought about his wife's words, "Do you want to disgrace yourself? A fine time to think of a child." Had he been trying to beget children on some neighbor's wife? That would be a motive for revenge, certainly. The behavior of Boutades' wife seemed not only repulsive, but strange— though I, unmarried, had to admit I knew little of what might be expected in married life. This woman laughed at her husband's death and called secretly for feasts of roast meat. Could a woman draw a bow? I had a sudden picture of her in my mind, the black-veiled woman I had seen at the funeral, bending the bow back with the arrow in its place and sending the arrow into Boutades' throat. Revenge might be sweet, and women have been capable of horrible deeds— consider Medeia. I had something to think about.

The overheard conversation had its effect on my private life. I became more careful in my conduct before our slaves. No one should say of me, "Master's manners are no lesson."

Otherwise, the talk I had heard could be of no immediate use; yet I was heartened. Boutades no longer seemed invincibly respectable and powerful, and this in some odd way made it easier to think coolly about his murder and his outraged kinsmen. It was easier to maintain my calm demeanor, and I took more interest in listening to others. Two days later, when, in the agora, I heard the word "News!" loudly uttered, I joined the group which clustered about the news-bearer almost without fearing hard looks. In fact, nobody paid me much attention; everyone was too interested in the tidings of war.

The citizen who had made the announcement so emphatically was Kleiophoros—a jolly man with light blue eyes set in little pouches, and two chins. He was known as a man both rich and hospitable who had large concerns with trade. He had just bustled into the agora, and his countenance was beaming with the pleasure of having something to impart.

"What do you think?" (He is the sort of man who says "Guess what's for dinner" before feeding you and "What do you think?" before informing you.) "News—news from Tyre!

My ship from Rhodos has just arrived, and the captain brought with him a man from Rhodos who fought in the battle. The siege is ended—last month. Alexander has been again victorious!"

"Ah, indeed," said grave citizen Theosophoros, rather dryly. "Alexander is destined to be victorious, it seems. The star-blessed fate of the commander can hardly count as news now. Who enters in the annals that the sun shone this summer?"

Other hearers were more ready to be informed and impressed.

"What happened? How did the battle go?"

"What a master the young Makedonian is," said Kleiophoros, warming to his subject and evidently bent on doing that subject justice by employing his own kind of rhetoric. "A master of ships and men, both at sea and on land. He moored his ships by the city wall—Tyrians sent divers down to cut the cables. He anchors them again—ropes cut again. But what does Alexander do then? Why, sirs, he uses for cables *chain*, not rope. Divers go down—shock—can't cut them. So the ships stay where they are, right against the city wall, and engines on the ships hammering away. Tchock! Bang!" Kleiophoros gestured with his fists, feeling that the occasion called upon him to mime the action of rams and catapults.

"Ships lying alongside the hole in the wall. Gangways thrown down, resting on broken stone, some of it small as chips—all that's left of that part of the wall. The troops swarm over in their hundreds. Admetos leads the way, waving valiantly—'After me, men!' Then Admetos is hit—spear thrust —whumph!" (Here Kleiophoros smote his own chest.) "The second wave of attackers is led by Alexander himself. Tyrians left the walls and went into the shrine—but fell in the attack like grass under a scythe. Hack! Swish! Uh-h! Argh!" Kleiophoros swung and thrust imaginary spears and swords, imitating in turn the cries of the attackers and the groans of the dying. He seemed to be a war all in himself.

"No one knows how many they lost," he continued, mopping his forehead. "Some say five thousand, some say ten—

and only four hundred of Alexander's army killed in the whole action. Alexander has sacrificed to Herakles in the shrine of Tyre."

"So he is King of Tyre now," said Theosophoros. "Had they allowed him to sacrifice in that shrine at the outset, they would have spared themselves a seven months' siege and increased their chance of dying free and in bed."

"Is it better to yield? Or to fight and die to be free men?" asked young Mikon, one of my former schoolfellows.

"Their god was against them," said Arkhimenos, a noble citizen and a well-known supporter of Makedonia. Gray-haired Arkhimenos was of distinguished appearance, with a broad brow and fine nose—the sort of man who makes a good impression on visiting embassies. His forehead was little lined, save for two deep vertical grooves above his nose, probably created by a habit he had of scowling slightly before he spoke.

"And it must be remembered," Arkhimenos added, "that Alexander gave the cities of Aiolia and Ionia true democracy and restored their own laws. Is it not well done to fight against the tyranny of Persia, which otherwise might threaten ruin to us all, as in the old time? Athens has sent Alexander the golden wreath: this was in acknowledgment not only of his victories but also of his virtues."

"The gods preserve us from trusting to the Athenians' golden crowns," said Theosophoros. "My memory is not so short that I cannot remember Demosthenes being given this honor by a grateful people—and now we hear he is to be tried for it. The wreath of gold is a poor protection. A wise man would sooner pray for a hat against the rain."

"Well," said Kleiophoros, evidently feeling he had been out of the conversation long enough, "Tyre is reduced, and thousands are marching into Egypt. Keep your eye on Alexander! He'll soon be skipping over the old Pyramids. The cities on the coast have started to surrender, although there's a rumor that Gaza wants to hold out and fight. Alexander will be needing more ships soon, surely. Perhaps our fleet may be called into action."

45

"My father thinks so," said Mikon. "He says Alexander cannot leave the fleet he sent back last year in idleness forever. Now Athens has proved its loyalty there will be no sense in leaving the ships with nothing to do. My father says the Athenian fleet will be called out in the spring."

"I've thought as much myself," said Kleiophoros, "and the sailors of the fighting ships think they will be in action next year. But here's one who knows more about naval matters. What do you think, Arkhimenos?"

"It is not possible to know with certainty," Arkhimenos said in his precise tones. "Alexander keeps his own counsel. There is, of course, much speculation. I may, in such a company, go so far as to say that certain possibilities have been discussed. It has been suggested that we may be called upon to make ships of the new kind, with the five-man bank, as they already have in Syracuse. Alexander may be letting the fleet lie at present because he wishes to remodel it."

Kleiophoros nodded sagely. "Peiraeus would be an excellent place in which to build a new fleet, to be sure. I should like to see one of the new ships. What stirring times we live in, indeed, a time of new things."

"We must not seize conclusions," said Arkhimenos. "On the one hand, it may be so. On the other hand, it may not."

"But if true," said Theosophoros, "how satisfactory! There would be such opportunity for the trierarkhy to show what it could do. New timber—and whatever the salt-water things are—all provided at once by our patriotic organization. How well it speaks for Athens that here it is not only a duty but a privilege for a rich and noble man to undertake the care and fitting of one ship of war. 'As a nurse to one babe, so the trierarkh to one ship,' as the saying is. Stirring times these are, too, as my friend Kleiophoros says. But it may be a weary while before Alexander requests a fleet from Athens. He may be tediously cautious where we are concerned."

"Why so?" asked Mikon.

"How soon time flies! We can barely remember now that a few short years ago there was a little fuss made about

Alexander in this city. And recently there was that little matter of King Agis of Sparta trying to get ships and money to fight against the Makedonian. Alexander, being a sensitive man, may fear that an Athenian fleet might be a little of Agis' mind."

"Sparta!" the young man said. "The old enemy! They are on the Persian side, so we are right to support Makedonia. Our old enemies allied against us—what greater sign do we want? Agis is no friend of ours. He went into Krete with Agesilaos and took the cities and made them swear allegiance to the Persians. But we are not Kretan bandits, nor would we fight in Kretan ships."

"Have you seen any of the new ships?" I asked Arkhimenos, really for the sake of something to say. The mention of Krete made me feel embarrassed, and I was foolishly eager to divert the conversation. Some of the others looked at me as if they had just noticed my presence and did not care for it. But Arkhimenos replied politely, saying that he had only heard of the quinquereme from one who had seen such a great vessel. I thought Arkhimenos himself was not happy with the political temper of the discussion. The group began to disperse, but I remained with Arkhimenos. Kleiophoros' remarks had reminded me that this man was a trierarkh. This seemed the opportunity which I needed to begin my investigation of Boutades' relationship with the trierarkhy. Arkhimenos answered me civilly as I pumped him with deferential questions, asking about the importance of Tyre, the effect on trade. With what I hoped would seem youthful enthusiasm I said that I wished I had been in the battle myself. I lied in my throat in saying so, for I thought of Philemon all the while. He might have fought in the siege, for aught I knew. (Had he been injured? Killed? I kept seeing maimed bodies falling off walls.) I piled one untruth upon another; I said I thought of going as a volunteer if our fleet were called out, for I saw this sort of ardent talk was not displeasing to the man. I admired the industry of the trierarkhs, praised an enlightened nobility which had made Athens great, and then

—having swum through this froth to my object as a dog paddles out to fetch a stick—said that I supposed he must lament the loss of Boutades as a trierarkh.

"Yes indeed," he responded. "Very shocking. And Boutades was a most estimable man, most estimable."

This didn't seem, from my point of view, very encouraging. I tried again.

"I had heard," I said vaguely, "that there was some trouble among the trierarkhy, something involving Boutades—that he had not supplied his full amount, or something."

Arkhimenos gave me a severe look. "You must not listen to vulgar rumor. The departed Boutades—peace to his shade—was a most public-spirited man. No trierarkh could less have been spared. Always paid what he owed, gave what he could and devoted his mind to the city's welfare."

This precise speech was decidedly a contrast to the language of the slavewoman—they might have been talking of different men. Arkhimenos spoke as if he were engraving a monument to the departed. As he spoke, his forehead went to and fro in repeated scowls, drawing the vertical lines deeper. My impertinence seemed to have aroused his displeasure. I felt impertinent—and endangered. I could not talk of Boutades easily, and anyone might look at me with detestation, hearing me utter words to the discredit of my cousin's supposed victim. I added hastily that Boutades' benevolence to the city was well known, that the poor would miss a liberal giver of food, and ended, I hoped gracefully, with a compliment to Arkhimenos' own benefactions. I left him, however, still scowling spasmodically, as if his face had little restless currents running just underneath the surface.

I felt freshly discouraged. I had done nothing, except possibly to mark myself as hostile to Boutades—no good thing. All I had learned was what I might have expected—that Boutades was a conscientious public man and had been a pillar of the trierarkhy. Aristotle seemed to be wrong. There could be nothing more of interest to find out about Boutades' life and works. The idea of finding something discreditable about his relationship to the trierarkhy had been spun of my own wishes.

And I had reason to be heavy at heart. The first prodikasia was almost upon me, and I had nothing to offer but Aunt Eudoxia's Defense.

VI

Prytaneion to Peiraeus

The day of the first prodikasia came. Dressed in my best khiton I made my way to the Prytaneion, walking up the narrow streets at the north side of the Akropolis, passing through the crowds of poorer citizens and slaves going about their business. Eye-beams seemed to pierce my shoulders. I felt extremely solitary when I arrived at the Prytaneion, that cold official hall. Usually the male relatives come in a body to support their main speaker and add statements of their own. (My young brother could not assist me—one doesn't take a seven years' child to such affairs.) Polygnotos was there with a good crowd of his friends and kin, dressed in their best and looking prosperous. I was alone.

The Basileus was formally polite to us all. After the preliminary libations he placed the party of the accuser on his right, and myself upon his left, and we began. He recited the bare details of the case, to establish what facts could be agreed upon by both parties. The main points of Boutades' death were brought forward. Polygnotos and his kinsfolk made their statements, to which I assented, keeping an ear open to see if they slipped in anything unexpected or untrue, but for a while all was plain. This examination of the facts acted on me like a medicine; my heart beat less unpleasantly and my hands dried. This was as well, for soon things became less straightforward. After we had agreed that on a certain day

49

in a certain manner Boutades had been slain by a killer who made an escape over the wall, the Basileus asked, "Whom do you accuse of this deed? And wherefore?"

Polygnotos replied, "I accuse Philemon, son of Lykias of Athens, an outlaw of this city already condemned for man-slaying."

"Do you, Philemon's kinsman, assent or deny?"

"I deny it," I said.

"Why do you accuse Philemon, and in what manner is his guilt known to you?"

Eutikleides answered, "He is a known killer, a desperate man. He is known to have taken ship for Krete two years ago. This outlandish murder has been done with an arrow evidently shot from a Kretan bow. Such a man, impoverished and careless of blood, had need for money. Boutades had in his house much money and some jewels. It may be that he intended to rob the place after this murder and was interrupted. Or it may be that he hated the worthy man. But," Eutikleides gave me a triumphant scowl, "he was seen making his escape."

"Who saw him?"

"Telemon, citizen of Athens."

Telemon came forward, looking pleased with himself, nicely dressed and polished for the occasion.

"I, Telemon, heard Polygnotos' cries just as I was coming into the house. I turned to the window and saw a dark figure among the trees. We ran outside—for although lame, sir, I am quite spry when the need arises—and I saw the wicked one jumping over the wall. He had cloth swathed over his head and about his face, but, just as he started to jump, the wrap slid off his head, and I saw he was Philemon. Only for the space of a heartbeat I saw him—but that I did see him, no question."

"I *do* question," I said. "Was it not still dark, particularly at that side of the garden? How could Telemon see so clearly?"

"It was not bright, certainly—not a blazing noonday, ha, ha!" answered Telemon with pert merriment. "But it was just at dawn, gentlemen—light enough to see an ugly face in a puddle if you look, as the saying goes."

"I question that," I said. "Telemon is advanced in honorable age, and his sight is not of the strongest." I suddenly had an idea. "Do you, O Basileus, fetch any well-known citizen of our class and use him to examine Telemon's judgment. The Prytaneion is not bright within; let the windows be shuttered, and then lead the citizen in to the corner of this hall by the door, in the shadow—then see if Telemon can recognize him at that little distance, here."

Telemon looked distinctly offended. "That is not the kind of thing one does at prodikasiai, my lad."

"No," said the Basileus, "such disproofs belong more properly to the trial. But you of Boutades' family are now informed of a defense."

"It does not matter," said Eutikleides, "for we have, and shall have, other proofs. It was Philemon."

I looked directly at Polygnotos. "Did you, who ran with Telemon—did you see him too?"

He sighed, and looked at me kindly. "Alas, what can I say? I am determined not to swear to that. Truly, while we ran, my heart was heavy and my head confused. I saw the wretch leap upon and over the wall—I must have seen what Telemon saw, but face and figure meant nothing to me then. But when Telemon told me it was Philemon, I remembered, and knew he must be right. But I shall not—indeed, I cannot —swear myself to identify him, because I did not recognize him straight away, at the time."

"That is just—nay, magnanimous," said the Basileus.

All I could do was bow to Polygnotos and turn to Telemon again. I felt really puzzled by now.

"But I myself was there at the finding of the body. I came almost as Eutikleides did. And heard Telemon and Polygnotos describing what they had seen. No mention was made of the killer's name—nor even of the possibility that they could identify him. Indeed, I distinctly recall Telemon's saying he could not see the killer. I remember what he said. A dark shape, not tall nor small, not fat nor very thin, not naked. I was there and heard him. Is this not true?" I turned to Eutikleides.

He nodded. "It is true."

"Why did Telemon deny his knowledge then?"

"Well," said Telemon, scuffling his foot. He looked at me with a small venomous frown; I could see he was still annoyed at the slight upon the powers of his eyes. "Because it *is* as you say, sir."

"Exactly," said Eutikleides. "You were there."

There was a short silence.

"It seems odd, does it not," Eutikleides continued, "that the killer's only kinsman should be at the scene of the crime? Almost at once?"

This was nightmarishly near the danger of which Aristotle had warned me. My mouth dried. I turned to the Basileus, my knees trembling slightly.

"Sir, before the most high gods and to you and these gentlemen I protest I am ignorant of this foul crime, nor have I any concern therein other than defending my cousin. I am a young man, ignorant of law and not gifted in speech. I throw myself upon your wisdom and authority, for I do not understand what is being said. Does anyone accuse me?"

"O Stephanos," said the Basileus, "no man takes from you your rights as an Athenian, and there are, as you say, wiser heads to guide you in the law."

He turned to the other party. "It is most irregular, gentlemen, to accuse the defending speaker of complicity after the case has started, unless there are unshakable reasons for it. Does anyone accuse the defender?"

"No," said Polygnotos with dignity. "We consent to take his word that he is no party to the crime, nor have we ever said otherwise. Indeed, on that fatal morning half of Athens flocked to our wretched house—we make nothing strange of his presence. We say merely this: that, as the kinsman of the murderer was among us, Telemon discreetly thought it better to say nothing before him at that moment of what was seen." He looked at me, speaking in natural informal tones. "Don't you see, Stephanos, that it might have made unpleasantness for you too?" He turned to the Basileus again. "We may have done amiss not to have uttered the horrible secret then—but remember we were men amazed. We kept our accusation—a serious matter—not for the vain tumult but for the proper occasion."

"We understand," said the Basileus. "Do you hear this?"

"I hear and answer that the words of honest men must be accepted. Perhaps they saw one who did look something like Philemon—a half-light can lead to strange errors. But it could not have been Philemon. He was not there. You must know he is banned from this city on pain of death. He has not been in Athens for two years. None of us has seen him, not even his invalid mother. He had no cause to hate Boutades, nor would he have attempted theft. In any case, this looks not like a theft, with nothing taken. But Philemon could not have done it. He was not here. That is the one reason we have ever had to be thankful he is an exile."

"You intend to show and prove that this Philemon was absent and could not be the guilty one?"

"I shall bring proofs of that fact."

"You hear the defense, gentlemen of Boutades' clan. The accused was absent."

"We hear and answer that we shall bring proofs that Philemon was present at the time of the deed. We shall bring them by the time of the trial, if not before."

"Has either party more to say at this point? No? You must both come before me next month for the second prodikasia, when statements shall be taken again and any further proofs produced. The prodikasia is over."

Never was a small boy more glad to hear the signal to depart from school. Greatly desponding, I walked down the hill. Every step brought me nearer to the moment when I should have to tell Aunt Eudoxia about the proceedings.

Three days after this first prodikasia the city had fresh melancholy tidings to talk about. Boutades' wife had committed suicide. Her favorite slave had found her (so gossip ran) dead in the morning, decently on her bed, fully dressed, with a cup containing the dregs of a poison (hellebore was the common suggestion) beside her. The sad event showed that sorrow still haunted the walls of this house of Etioboutadai. Yet not altogether mournful—it was a tribute to Boutades that his wife could not survive him, and many approved, saying it showed that proper female sentiment could still be found among the better families. Polygnotos admitted that the woman had been tearful and wandering in her wits since the death of her husband, and he gave her a very decent funeral—as women's funerals go. Her self-slaughter was of a very feminine kind, by the cowardice of poison rather than by the courage of the dagger, but it is women's nature to love pleasure and shun pain.

Rumor fed on this event rather happily than otherwise— it was shocking enough to interest, without having the hideous flavor that had embittered any talk about the earlier death. I pondered over the event gloomily. It seemed as if another thread that might have led me to the real Boutades had broken—even in the vanishing of a woman I did not and could not know.

"I feel surprised by her suicide, as I would not be had I not overheard the slaves in the leather-stall," I explained to Aristotle. I had come to him again, to tell him of the dreary proceedings before the Basileus—and then I found myself telling him all my own disconnected thoughts over the past weeks. "The tall woman in black, throwing a gold ring into the grave of her husband—yes, she was an image of sorrow, she might have committed suicide. But what of the wife who quarreled with Boutades and taunted him with impotence? The woman who laughed and ordered sucking pig in a house of weeping? Why should she, with the grease of a feast, as it were, upon her lips, have drunk a toast to Boutades' shade and gone to seek him in the Underworld?"

"Why indeed?" said Aristotle. "But human nature is not a simple affair—it is difficult for those outside a marriage to fathom it. The woman might have been crushed by the dullness of life without her partner in quarrels. Our habits are stronger than we think. And she might really have loved her husband—a few domestic battles signify little to the contrary.

54

You are young in the ways of men and women, Stephanos, whereas here I am, an old married man, full of wise saws on the subject."

He chuckled, for of course he was himself, if old, not so old in the ways of marriage.

"But the sucking pig," I protested. "Banqueting for joy?"

"That does not quite prove a joy. A sort of hysteria; a childlike reaction to the absence of law. She might have said to herself scores of times, "I would eat sucking pig if my husband didn't forbid it, saying it always gives me indigestion." So when her husband can no longer forbid it, she feels compelled to try this pleasure. But you evidently have your own thoughts on the matter."

I glanced at the closed door and lowered my voice, even though Aristotle's wife and servants were in another part of the house.

"Yes," I said. "I have thought a dreadful thing—even before, it had come to me, and this deed seems to—to fit it, like another side of a triangle. For what other reasons do people commit suicide? From grief born of guilt, or from deadly fear. I had thought that *she*—his wife—might have been the slayer—and now I see it is possible. And she rejoiced at first, but grew heavy with murder and slew herself still without confessing. But she feared she would betray herself if she lived longer."

"It is possible," said Aristotle, not as perturbed as I had expected. "Every human action is possible. But really, Stephanos, a wife has so many good opportunities of murdering her husband—a mess of mushrooms, aconite in the soup, a muffling piece of cloth on the bed—why should she create a great bloodshed and a startling slaughter? Most women hate wounds and blood in any case."

"Klytaimnestra didn't."

"No. But Klytaimnestra had Aigisthos to do the butcher's work for her. I fancy no Aigisthos entered the scene here. And what woman would be such a good shot? One might invite all the women in Athens to shoot arrows at their spouses and little harm would be done."

"She might have done it," I insisted gloomily. "It would not be a long shot. Perhaps she was carrying out a blood feud, or some vow of vengeance. Perhaps he *had* to die in blood. And then she had to die because it was too terrible."

" 'Perhaps he *had* to die in blood,' " Aristotle repeated. "That is quite good, Stephanos. But come—we do not wish Boutades' wife to be guilty, do we? There our chances of clearing Philemon wither almost entirely. There are far too many perhapses in what you say. It still seems to me that this sort of killing is a man's work. At least, one good thing about the prodikasia is that the question of your complicity has been raised and got out of the way."

"But all is worse than before," I objected. "Eutikleides seems truly hostile to me. And now they say they saw Philemon. It is monstrous. I know Telemon could not have seen his face at such an hour and distance."

"That I do heartily believe, myself, and at the trial something can be done to throw doubt upon that evidence. Your proposal of a test of vision was a good one—a pity you used it so soon. We are still left with two things to pursue: (a) Philemon's absence at the time and (b) information about Boutades. If there *were* a blood-feud, it is to Boutades we must turn to find out why."

"There is nowhere," I said, "to look for any of these things."

Aristotle poured me a drink of wine.

"One place I have thought of," he said, "where one might fish for truth. Peiraeus. There are returned sailors who know other travelers—one might have seen or heard of Philemon. There are ships, and the men who work among them, and among these there will be information of Boutades and the trierarkhy. I have an idea that these seamen might help, at least in working out a case for Philemon."

"Yes," I said dubiously. "I could go and ask questions—"

"If you go about asking questions, Stephanos, you will get nothing. A man of good birth and education, proclaiming himself, asking questions. No. Oh, they'd take your money and treat you politely enough, and they would tell you whatever pleases the official ear. Some of them would recognize you at once as the defender in this case. With suspicion and fear and images of torture in the front of their minds, they would take great care to be of no use. You must chatter with people on their normal occasions—at least at first. Don't be yourself, be somebody else. Go in disguise, like Odysseus to the swineherd."

"Disguise? Like a player? Aristotle, such things happen in famous stories, but in real life—"

"In real life it happens as well. How do you think Alexander gets his spies through enemy territory? That reminds me—I must tell you sometime of my travels in Asia. I'm not asking you to attempt a wonderful metamorphosis. Just wander down to Peiraeus in a countryman's garb, with some earth in your fingernails. Look ordinary. Speak in a homely fashion—and not too much. You're a man from the country beyond Athens, come to see a distant relative in Peiraeus. Go into a tavern, drink quietly, look like a tired boor resting his feet. I'm afraid you can do this only two or three times—you don't want to become a noticeable figure. Of course," said Aristotle, warming to his notion, "if you wished to maintain a disguise, you might go regularly as a vegetable-seller—"

"Aristotle, I will *not* sell vegetables in Peiraeus—"

"As you wish. You might not do it too well, in any case. The trouble with you, Stephanos, is that you are so very respectable. Now, I," he said complacently, looking around his elegant room, "am learned, well born, even rich after a fashion —but I am not an Athenian, and not quite respectable. I could act as a vegetable-seller if I had to. Remember, your sacred honor, as an Athenian, as a kinsman, as a man, is pledged to defend Philemon. Nothing not evil in itself can injure your true honor. Was Odysseus a dishonored man? But go to Peiraeus. Tell no one. It is better that your accuser know nothing of it—therefore, not your own kin, not your own household. But try it once or twice."

We stood up, and I was ready to depart.

"Keep the things you see and hear in separate baskets in your mind—like a physician collecting simples. Don't mingle them too soon. And smile occasionally. It is a game of a kind. I will look forward to hearing what you have to tell."

I muttered something about not wanting to take up his time. This was not altogether out of politeness; I was offended at having gone to see the master only to be sent away with instructions to be a peasant—or a vegetable-seller.

"Oh, I always have time to listen to things," said Aristotle blandly.

A country lad in rough homespun and broken shoes stumped toward Peiraeus just before dawn. It was I. It had taken me nearly a week to decide to do as Aristotle had suggested. Then I had to obtain my disguise, and to do this secretly, without confiding in any, not even the slaves, had taken me several days. Now as I set out I felt like a fool, like some country bumpkin in a village play. The broken shoes, not made for me, hurt my feet, so I had to walk slowly. I had left the house very early, so as not to be seen, but I did not wish to arrive in Peiraeus until folk were stirring and one could pass unnoticed through crowded streets. After I had left Athens and come to some waste land, I went to the side of the road and grubbed in the earth, pulling up the coarse grass and slubbering my hands with the roots. I broke a fingernail or two, and clawed the dirt, afterward rubbing my face with my hands. It had been raining and the earth was freshly moist—it felt disgusting under my nails. Once it had begun to get light I peered into a little puddle to look at the result. In the early dawn, reflected in this dirty mirror, I looked foul enough. I gave my face a more artistic rub, to make sure I was all earthen-hued, and went my way again, feeling I would enjoy nothing now so much as a bath.

When I got to fish-smelling Peiraeus, I blundered along to the docks. It was then the beginning of the winter season, the time when ships seek safety from the great gales and lie in port to be repaired and laid by until they set sail again in the spring. Boats were drawn up everywhere along the beach, fishing boats and merchant vessels, many turned upside down or lying on their sides, looking like discarded shells.

The sheds to protect the larger and more valuable ships lay at the far end, and a few of the smaller craft bobbed up and down beside the mole. There were a good many sailors about, and the place was quite noisy with hammers and saws.

I plodded along, mouth ajar and gazing like a yokel—I was really not incurious, as I had never been to the Great Harbor before. At last I came to an empty space by the wall, in the sun, so I took it, like a seat in the theater, and sat back inertly like a peasant on holiday. The sunshine was not excessive; the morning as it advanced was cloudy, and there was a light haze over the sea. The dawn colors had departed from the water, and it was a flat gray expanse; through the haze I could make out a couple of fishing boats close to shore. Far off to my left I could just see the bluff of Sounion, with the great temple on its top, a white smudge. I drew my gaze back to the nearer view; at the spot I had chosen I could watch the repairing of a merchant vessel and listen to the men working on it. The smell of the sea was mixed with the smell of wood, and of tar in little pots bubbling over the fire.

The workers were two men and a lad; they nodded to me when I arrived, but paid me little heed. Their conversation was not, at first, very interesting—instructions from the senior man, insults, jokes, references to other sailors on other ships. Then the younger man said, "Think this pretty cruiser will be out with Aleck come spring?"

"And why not?" answered the other. "Fast runner and all. His Northern Majesty'll want fast runners for them big wars —and Athens' is best, by a long measure. Aye—" he patted the ship's side—"you'll be hearing the sound of shot before long, my girl. You dunderhead!" (to the boy) "Bring some more pitch, you skulker, and look sharp about it, or I'll boil you in it and sell you for sausage!"

"So long since I've been in a battle," said the second man, "that I've forgotten the way of it. Me, I've been doing the grain-ship run this year—Krete and back. There'll be a good deal of that trade, for Athens' cupboard is pretty bare. The merchant run's a steady thing, and no bloody foreigners trying to pound holes in your hull."

"Arkh!" The elder spat on the shingle. "Kitchen work. Me, I wouldn't mind having a bout with them Persians myself. Many's the stout Athenian who joins Aleck's service. Isn't that so, clodhead?" addressing himself to me, evidently—he threw a chip to win my attention. "You'd like to leave your dusty furrows, eh, my friend? Jump on a boat and see the world?"

I gazed at him, opening my mouth silently like one slowly considering a new idea.

"A brisk lad like yourself, my fine earthen vessel, with good muscled arms for rowing and stout legs to run into battle, or run out again—think of the service? See the world—see the coast of Troy, maybe—where Aleck ran about like Akhilleus on the fret."

"Heard of Troy, my friend?" said the other, with condescending wit. "There was a few fights there once, over a whore and a horse."

"Then," said the other, "on to the cities of the coast—head for Egypt—carry a shield, and march like a turtle through the landscape, out to Persia and sack the golden city."

"Ah," said his mate, bursting into lewd song,

> "Darius will be weeping
> And rending of his curls
> When the Greeks are plundering Persian gold
> And pricking Persian girls. . . ."

"That's so," I said with stupid animation. "It's a life for a man, that is. But Athens is good enough for me. And," I added after a pause, "not many Athenians go with Alexander. Not really our war, is it? Makedonians mostly, I reckon."

"That's all *you* know," said the older one. He and his mate whistled as they replaced an old plank with a clean. The boy stirred the tar pot. "There's a good number. Some fighting the Persians for glory and the chance of loot, some for variety's sake—*and* the chance of loot, of course. Say there's a brisk boy who's had a bit of trouble at home—for thieving or fighting it might be, or for reaving sheep—he goes to foreign places and finishes by joining up."

"Not many from Athens," I said obstinately. "I don't know none of that sort."

"Maybe not *your* daring neighbors yet, friend, but there's others. Last summer Asia was crawling with them. When we touched at Ephesos I came upon five or six. A one-eyed fellow called Demokles, I remember. He came from a farm just outside Athens—left a wife and four children." He thumped with his mallet emphatically. "And a skinny lad from the tannery who'd robbed his master's money jar and was in a hurry to join the army. And a tall fellow called Philemon. Nicely spoken, free and easy. He'd come from the city. Treated me to a drink in one of the dockside taverns. Said he'd fought in the big battle and figured to join up again. Wanted to hear the Athens news."

It seemed too good to be true. My heart bounded, but I kept my face steady.

"And what mischief had this one been up to?" I asked.

"Fight in a tavern—so he said. Sent a man to Hades by accident, as you might say, while his blood was up. Sort of thing might happen to anyone—but he had to run for it. Just the sort to make a soldier—big and well muscled. Not quite the build for a sailor, but he'd worked his passage from Krete by taking the oar, however."

"I likes things peaceful," I said. "I'm no thief nor brawler. Fine men to meet on a dark road—your little tanner fellow to pick your pocket and this great roisterer, this Philemon, to knock you over the head."

"Oh," said the second man sarcastically, "if you want to sit under a tree waiting for the olives to drop into your mouth, the services won't do."

"This Philemon was a good fellow," insisted the other. "Now, just between ourselves, *I* think he must be the one there's all the fuss about, yonder." He nodded toward Athens. "Puzzles me how he could have got back again, though, for I'd seen him not two months before, going east-ward. He let on in his drink that he had an old mother in Athens that he'd not see again—but he'd not have risked his

61

outlawed hide for an old woman. And why should he be killing old men at home when there was wars to go to? Sure, he went east where the fighting was, and not here. It's a riddle, but none of my business, says I."

"That's right," said the other. "Keep clear of the law, and of the doings of rich men inside the walls—'tisn't for us."

My heart sang. I said nothing more about Philemon, but I was glued to the place as if I had sat on the pitch. I kept by the two, listening to their tales, admiring their boat. Growing a bit more talkative, I explained how I had come to see a friend who wasn't at home, and that I worked on my father's small land-holding north of Athens. Eventually I persuaded them to take drinks from me at the nearest tavern in Peiraeus—dreadful thin wine it had too, and nearly choked me, combined with the smell of sweat and tar and drying fish in a close room. But I found out the two men's names, without asking, and found too where each had sailed during the summer, and with what captain—so I could identify them clearly, later. It was the older one I wanted to keep track of, of course —the one who'd seen Philemon. Pelieus the sailor, son of a sailor; he had served on a ship bearing a cargo of arms and supplies to the new-taken coastal cities during the summer.

After I drifted away from them, it was a puzzle to know how to spend the rest of daylight. I did not want to go back to Athens until twilight at least. I moved through Peiraeus, pricing fish occasionally and trying not to look noticeable, and then dozed on a lonely part of the gravelly beach. I thought of going to one of the little houses of Aphrodite, with which Peiraeus is well supplied, but I couldn't imagine getting a girl who didn't smell like fried squid. Eventually I left Peiraeus in the early autumn evening, whistling and plodding home on my sore feet, holding two fish on a stick like a rustic who's been to market.

Next day, when I thought about my excursion, I did not feel much elated. Certainly I had learned something; I even had a potential witness of sorts, and I could hope that this sailor would not leave our shore during the winter. But, at best, my possibly reluctant witness could establish only that

Philemon had been on the Asian coast not long before the murder. The accusers could retort that nonetheless he would still have had sufficient time to return to Athens if he wished to do so. I myself felt convinced that Philemon had gone eastward, as the sailor thought he intended. No—the sailor provided a valuable chance to cast doubt on the accusation, as his evidence would strengthen the contention that Philemon was not in Athens at the fatal time, but it was not enough to make my case firm. It would be hoping too much to expect to come by chance upon further information as to Philemon's whereabouts. Yet I was not without hope even for this, for the gods seemed, for the first time, to favor me.

VII

Taverns and Broken Vessels

In the next few days this new hopefulness wavered like an image in water. I realized that the accusers could still put an ill color upon everything. If all that was known was that Philemon was in Asia, it might be said not only that he could have made his way home in time, but also that he was in Asia as a volunteer in the Persian force, assisting the uneasy cities of the coast in their revolt against Alexander. We had no *proof* that he was a soldier of any kind, much less that he was fighting for Alexander, and to suggest this might lead the others to suggest the opposite. I had better not mention the matter at this juncture; to produce my uncertain certainties at the second prodikasia would be to invite trouble.

Despite my earlier dislike of Aristotle's suggestion, I now wished to try my low mumming again. I needed to know more, and I was drawn to Peiraeus. A week later I went again by the Long Wall. This time I purposely avoided the place where I had been first; it seemed unwise to meet my sailor again too soon. I wandered along the dirty streets and by a different area of the docks. I tried another tavern. I learned nothing—except some lively obscenities that were new to me.

Yet I went again, a few days after that. I was like a man who complains of the sour taste of new wine and cannot stop drinking it. This time I wandered by the Kantharos, looking at the great ships of the fleet. I noticed that some were in a most pitiful condition. One, a great war trireme, lay on its side like a wounded cow. Its hull timbers were beginning to warp and rot, and the poop had been smashed. I idly supposed that someone with new timbers and pitch buckets would eventually come and do something to it.

At noon I was sitting in a dark tavern, drinking thin wine and trying to eat sprats cooked in rancid oil. It was a sailors' tavern, and I felt out of place, but I tried to look stolid and blank. The best way of doing this is to be blank and stolid inside: I cleared my mind of thought and gazed idly on the chips and straw and spit on the earthen floor, drearily seeing in them strange patterns, like a mosaic. In a kind of dream I first noticed a party of sailors holding a celebration near to me. I heard them, not because their voices were loud—they were speaking low, in serious conversation—but because one of them in mid-utterance had spoken a name which had power to charm my soul's attention.

"—Boutades. May his soul rot. The planks were cheap unseasoned pine. Rot away, twist like eels, after only two runs. The tar was never made that would keep that parcel of faggots together. Captain knows what I mean. Might as well try to glue a dog's jaws together with spruce gum."

"What did you do then?"

"Ah—we fothered it with an old sail and made a run for it. Neptune be praised. I tramped out to Sounion and made a votive offering, special. But if we'd 'a gone down with all hands, 'twouldn't have been the sea's fault, so to speak. Never seen a vessel more minded to ship water."

"It's an ill thing altogether," said a middle-aged swarthy man with an authoritative manner, whom I took for the captain. "No good comes of speaking against one of the nobles—so keep a still tongue, lads, and don't throw names about. Sacred be the name of the dead, too, and all that—but to send out a ship that will gape like an old man by the fireside as soon as it touches a wave or two! It's not to be borne. I don't mind telling you, seeing we're among friends, like—" and here he leaned across to the others, dropping his voice to an emphatic hushed tone—"I went to see him myself. Right up to the city. I went to tell him my mind."

The others seemed amused and admiring.

"I'll wager he asked you to dinner."

"Did you invite him for a free ride on the good ship *Leaky Pisspot?*"

"Oh, all polite he was—fat as a seal, and bald. 'Yew are under a mis-ap-pre-hension,' says he, speaking rich as a fig, like all those gentry who polish their gums with butter. 'It is citizen Arkhimenos what you must see about this little matter. The *Aphrodite's* his responsibility at the moment. I am sure he will fit out this ship for you.' "

"Did you see Arkhimenos then?"

"For a long while I thought I wasn't going to. Sat about in his courtyard half a day or more—his slaves running out, feeding me, trying to make me drunk or send me away or both. 'Dear! Dear! The trierarkh has just gone out!' 'I'll wait,' says I, 'till he comes back in.' 'The master's very busy now!' *'I'm* in no hurry,' says I, 'for I can't go to sea at the moment, so I'll just sit here in your yard and collect a few of your fleas, thank you.'

"I did see him at last, as the day cooled. He had the advantage of me, sitting there in his fine room (not as fine as Boutades', though) while I was standing in my dust. 'Well, my good man, I'm so busy, what is it?' 'It's like this,' I said, and reeled off my list of things missing and things wrong, starting small and finishing up big.

" 'Twenty ells of rope are missing from the *Aphrodite,'* I says, 'and what we have got is as frayed as my cloak.'

"He smiled on half of his face. 'Dear, dear, what a pity, but hardly a great matter. It is, I'm afraid, good captain, just another case of a thieving slave. The de-teri-oration in manners is *de*-plorable,' says he, 'but let us not worry ourselves about trifles.'

" 'Not such a trifle, neither,' I said, 'but there's the rest as well.' And then I went along brisk with the rest. When I got to the missing blocks and the cracked oars, Arkhimenos blinked. When I mentioned the old sail as was supposed to be new, he turned pale. And when I came booming along to the uncalkable planks and the rest, he turned cheese color, like a girl. Then he stood up, shaking, and cried high like a woman, 'The gods preserve me and keep me from madness, for I think they've a mind to ruin me! I am the dupe of this man and have no redress, Athena aid me!' He tore his hair —what he had—and his face folded like a child's. The thing was a bit like a play, but all wrong with a naked face. Then he remembered to get rid of me before he burst into tears.

" 'Be off with you!' he shouts. 'Do you think I am made of wood and pitch and sailcloth?'

" 'I'm to take it, then,' I says, 'that I am dismissed from service on the *Aphrodite* and must seek employment elsewhere?'

" 'Yes—get out! Get out!' he screams. So that was that, and that was the poor *Aphrodite.* "

"But what happened?" asked the youngest man. "I thought Boutades was trierarkh in charge of the *Aphrodite.* "

"Well, we'll never know the exact rights of it, surely. But what it looks like is that trierarkh Arkhimenos took part or whole of the fitting of the *Aphrodite* off trierarkh Boutades in exchange for a debt. Private-like and between friends— very civil. But what he didn't know was that his friend's ship was in rotten case. It could happen, too, that, say, a man who wanted to make a profit—quite a sizable one—in this barter would ill-fit his own ship ahead of time, pretending to do the job but putting in shoddy goods for new."

"The saving would be pretty considerable. Shipfitters do it if we don't keep an eye on 'em," said one of the men, laughing, "but it's rather a joke for a trierarkh to do it to himself."

"I don't see that," said the young man angrily. "Lives are lost that way—it's a crime—"

"But 'tis rather a joke, all the same," said his good-humored friend, still chuckling. "See a trierarkh sell himself bad rope."

"Grand things, some of these trierarkhs," said the captain. " 'The slave stole it!' I'd like to see it!"

"But can't something be done? A complaint to Antip—"

"Don't be a young fool. And don't spread foolish tales of what I've been saying. Remember, it's best to mention no names. Speak of Citizen One and Citizen Two, if you must, but best to keep quiet except among our own. There's ten kinds of trouble in the city, and who wants to bandy about the name of a man who is horribly dead? As for the rest, we don't know where the wind sits—King Agis and all taking an oar—everyone rowing in different directions, so to speak. Leave politics alone, and get some work for the winter."

"The fleet will be sure to be out in the spring," said the youth with conviction.

"Does seem likely," the captain admitted. "I hope so. But don't take a berth on one of Arkhimenos' ships," he added, winking.

Then one of the men cried, "Hi, Paulos, we must drink again to your baby son—" and there was a filling of cups; the rest was the tedious converse of boisterous friends.

At the beginning of the next week I went to see Aristotle to tell him about my shabby visits to Peiraeus. I was full of thoughts, especially about Arkhimenos. This eminent man had recently praised Boutades to me as "most estimable . . . a very patriotic man . . . very generous"; yet the man who spoke of his friend thus, like an epitaph, had earlier that summer complained that his old acquaintance had ruined him. Perhaps it was not myself only who adopted disguise.

Aristotle was in a cheerful mood that evening, showing me a gift of a large two-handled cup he had received from one of his students. He seemed little disposed to ask me about my doings. I was a bit annoyed—the last time I had seen him he was entirely taken up with the notion that I should sell vegetables in Peiraeus, and now all he wanted to talk about, it appeared, was pottery.

"This comes all the way from Poseidonia," he said. "That's what makes it curious. It isn't often that one sees colonists' ware. The painting is a trifle clumsy—but it is lively." He showed me the squat kotyle. It had an odd recurrent design of very flat palmettoes like bunches of fingers. One side had a picture of Dionysos (in high style); the other, a scene of revelers (in comic style). At the end of that group there was the squat figure of an old man with sparkling eyes and absurdly heavy features, dancing a jig with a bowl on his head.

"A comic piece, isn't it?" said Aristotle. "A bit vulgar, but amusing. The old man dances—all is well. I think the old fellow must have reminded Eubolos of me—a resemblance in the nose and brows, don't you think—and something of my figure? At least it's not a love gift—in the old days cups with figures of Zeus and Ganymede were presented to me by ox-eyed students. There," he added. "I'll set it here, I think." He put it on a table where it caught the firelight. The old man winked and danced. "Next to this flat flask made to look like a duck. That comes from overseas too, from Velathri; they're fond of making things that look like ducks and hens, for some reason. Rather ugly, isn't it? This kotyle is much better made. Do you know that the clay is different from ours? Lighter color—brownish—like Etrurian. Have you seen Etruscan ware? Did you know that it is never the true red ware, the figures are painted in with red paint?"

"No," I said shortly. Then, gathering up my manners, I observed, "You have some fine pieces."

"So I do. That pelike, now, is a beauty." He nodded at the vase, which showed a young man leading a white horse in the midst of a throng of men and gods. "Ornate but graceful. That's fairly old—my father had it. Attic ware. And I have a wine krater in the pure red ware—rather old-fashioned, but it's the only good wine bowl in the house. That one there—" he nodded to a small krater—"with the hunting scene on it is a cheap one, really. It looks like Attic work, but it's Korinthian. Did you know that Korinthian clay is yellow? Not red like ours—so Korinthian potters can't make proper red figures. They look the same, once everything is painted over a wash, but they're not."

"No" I said again, "I didn't. I really haven't thought about pottery much. And we haven't got anything very fine at home."

"Oh, but you should notice things, Stephanos. And pots are very entertaining, whether you own them or not. Some scenes are instructive, some amusing. And everything, including practical craft, is interesting in some way . . . one can speculate. What makes Attic clay so superior in the fashioning, for instance? Let us take our wine from the best krater —it will improve the taste."

"Boutades had a lovely amphora," I remembered. "I saw it in his house."

"Well, Boutades would have some very fine things, wouldn't he? Nothing but the best. And he would have inherited some grand pieces—commemorative vases in honor of a khoregos, family gifts and presents from clients. We Makedonians have had few such heirlooms. But Alexander now—he could fill a house with the lovely pots he has been given in the last few years by admiring Athenians—and Antipater too."

"All with scenes of Akhilleus or of Herakles," I suggested, warming a bit over the wine.

"A good many indeed. Polygnotos will certainly be looked on favorably when as khoregos he produces his play of Herakles. I hear that is coming along very well. The poet has written in some new lines in honor of Alexander's most recent victories."

I thought of the remarks I had once heard about Herakles and the fate of Kheiron, but said nothing.

"Incidentally," said Aristotle more gravely, "I think I must tell you that it has been suggested to Antipater that the murder might be a Persian plot to throw Athens into alarm —and to get rid of one of the city's most influential citizens among those who favor Makedonia."

"Oh," I said glumly. "That's all I need. Philemon as a traitor and Persian plotter."

Aristotle had startled me, for I had recently been thinking that the other side might try to suggest that Philemon had been fighting for the Persians. I felt I ought to be wary in front of Aristotle. As the gloom deepened in my soul, I wondered that I should trust him as my friend—this friend of Antipater, this fussy little man who got expensive presents from students and friends and could sit enjoying himself with his wine and his pots and his books. He was a world away from me, and I wondered why I was there.

"Stop scowling, Stephanos—I am *not* Alexander, and I *don't* run away to Antipater to repeat every conversation I hear." He seemed to read my mind, and he looked at me shrewdly and rather crossly, like a teacher at a troublesome pupil.

"Sorry," I said, looking awkwardly at my feet—like the rustic I had pretended to be. There was a pause.

"I feel such an idiot," I said, stupidly irritable, jerking my cup. "It must be acting this boorish part that's made me so clumsy. It shows that Plato was right about acting. If you act a part in a drama—still more in real life—of a bad or stupid person, it taints the soul and you become like it—him—you know what I mean."

"Ah, so you've been on your hunt." Aristotle was interested. "Do tell me about your boorish part, Stephanos. Your soul seems to be quite untainted—I'm sure nothing's wrong with it."

"I may not have tainted my soul," I answered, "but I certainly tainted my clothes and skin. I went three times, and each time I came back smelling like a fish shop. I even bought fish and took them home. Now the mere thought of sprats, for instance, or squid—especially fried in rancid oil—makes me quite sick."

Aristotle laughed. "Good. If you can't sell vegetables, buy fish. A good disguise, like a cotter from the market, your fruits of the sea dangling from wet twigs."

"I couldn't think how else to get away effectively," I protested.

"As Arion said about the dolphin," finished Aristotle. He

was much amused at his own jest. "Where did you go? I suppose you didn't find out anything? Tell me all about it."

I did so, despite the fact that a few minutes earlier I had thought I would never tell him anything of importance again. Aristotle pulled information gently from you, as a woman draws wool into a thread. Although he seemed so ingenuous, I sometimes thought I knew why he had been an ambassador—and a spy—in Asia in the old days.

I told him about my three visits, and faithfully narrated all the conversation I could remember.

"So," I concluded, "there are three things I have learned. Not really extremely helpful things, but not quite useless. Most important, I now have some information about Philemon."

"Hmm. Yes. And now you have been thrice to Peiraeus. Better not go again, Stephanos. The pitcher can go too often to the well. Yet, Truth lives in a well, after all."

"Now," I added, "I know more about Boutades, but I can't see how that can help. And how can I *know* the captain was telling the truth? No, the information isn't useful to me—I don't see how it could be made to be. But—it is puzzling. Have you noticed, Aristotle, that anything I've heard by chance about Boutades has been unfavorable? And yet he had such a good reputation. I wonder if he wasn't a—a very *hatable* man, so that a lot of people wished he were dead."

"Quite," said Aristotle. "I though we had almost established that earlier—although you were then enthusiastically ready to see his wife as the killer. What's the third thing you have learned?"

"The third? Arkhimenos, of course. This is a man who must really have hated Boutades, although he spoke so beautifully about him after he was dead. What was going on about those ships?"

"I think your bluff friend the captain was probably right in his deductions. The aristocrats are like ducks moving across a pond—serene and beautiful above, but paddling furiously underneath, and kicking up invisible currents beneath the surface."

He paused a moment, then added, "One thing that strikes me is that there's a good deal of money involved. And we have heard some things about money. Boutades' wife had had no new shoes. The man was niggardly in his housekeeping. Was Boutades not as rich as we all supposed? Had he any sudden need for money? Or had he really been quite poor for a long time, so that he needed to save—even to cheat—in order to maintain his position?"

"But," I objected, "Polygnotos, his heir, isn't poor. He has supported the expenses of two good funerals, and he's putting money into the production of the play. And he hasn't sold any of Boutades' lands, or anything of his own."

"True. Of course, Polygnotos inherited a good deal from his father. But, as you say, he seems just as wealthy as one would expect. It is puzzling. Was Boutades just acting upon a personal grudge against Arkhimenos? And why? Or was Boutades feeling so poor that he felt he had to do a shameful thing to an old acquaintance?"

"And a criminal thing," I added stoutly. "Think of the poor sailors."

"I doubt if Boutades' imagination extended so far as to picture flesh-and-blood men in a leaky ship at sea—nor the fate of a bad vessel in a sea fight. His moral sense would, however, presumably have extended so far as to make him realize that cheating another trierarkh to such an extent was not at all the thing."

"And there, too," I said, leaning forward, like the captain in the tavern. "Do you see? Think of how Arkhimenos must have felt—how he did feel! 'I am the dupe of this man and have no redress!' He was beside himself with grief and rage, if we can believe the captain's story—he even forgot that a stranger of low birth was in the room with him. Yet, as far as we know, he said nothing to men of his own kind about his injury—perhaps because it would make him appear foolish. His family, though noble, is now somewhat friendless—you remember, his father and uncle were suspected of being hostile to Philip. So he was without redress. He is such a straight stiff man, too. His passion, if it got the better of him, would be very great, the more so for being concealed. Do you think, Aristotle, that Arkhimenos might—"

In my nervous excitement, as I leaned forward, I somehow jarred my knee against the foot of my wine-cup. The cup sprang from my loose grasp, and shattered. Wine stains spattered the floor, among shards of pottery. I could feel myself blushing heavily.

"Oh, Aristotle! I am so sorry!" I babbled, trying to pick up the useless pieces. "Please let me buy you another—"

"No harm," said Aristotle, smiling. "It was a very cheap cup, truly—although that does not sound too polite, does it, to serve my guests out of cheap cups? I'm sorry it wasn't a better one, which would have made a more satisfactory crash. Don't worry about such a trifle. Pythias and I break cups ourselves. When we begin to feel dull, we throw crockery at each other to keep ourselves in good spirits."

"The floor—" I murmured wretchedly.

"Don't think about it, I beg. The house-slave will have to clean the floor tomorrow in any case."

The wine stains reminded me of those other stains on Boutades' floor. Those also had been cleaned up by efficient house-slaves.

"Look," said Aristotle, gently taking one of the fragments from my hand and holding it out to the firelight. "Remember what I told you about the clays? Well, there you are—red right through. A thick piece, not very elegantly potted—an indifferent design—but it betrays its Attic origin. From the cheapest to the finest, the essential material is the same. There ought to be a moral in that somewhere. If it had been from Etruria, now, it would have been pale brown, with a coarser texture." He threw the fragment into the fire.

He loved detail of this sort. Small peculiar things delighted him—odd in a philosopher who would, one imagines, always prefer to think about the great true things like Beauty and Justice. As far as I was concerned, one piece of fired clay might as well be another. Still, I knew he was chatting to console me for my clumsiness and cover my embarrassment. As I stared at the broken pieces in my hand, I was suddenly reminded of something.

"I found a fragment," I said. "A funny thing. I'd forgotten. That day it was, at Boutades' house. Or, rather, outside, near the window, just lying on the ground. A little piece of pottery from some household object. I thought at the time that a slave must have broken a pot recently and taken the pieces outside and dropped one. That's all."

"Recently? You thought it was recently broken? Why?"

"Well—I don't know. Just my impression. I suppose because the edge was still rather sharp, and because it wasn't pressed into the ground, or caked in dirt."

"Did you show it to anybody?"

"No—the others were leaving. It was only a bit of rubbish. I picked it up and I played with it in my hand for something to do."

"And then dropped it again?"

"I suppose so. No—I didn't. I think I must have taken it away with me. How silly. I remember occupying myself with trying to make out what the sign or letter could be."

"What sign or letter?"

"Something like a small cross. Like this." I sketched it on the floor. "A potter's mark, most likely."

"Was it near the broken edges?"

"Yes—it ran into them, at the top and at the side. The fragment is all broken edge."

"It might be part of an inscription—if it were a good pot. Was the piece thick or thin?"

"Thin—thinner than these," I said clumsily, blushing again.

"Do you know, if you could find this fragment, I should like to have a look at it. I enjoy puzzles. It would be something to make out an inscription from two strokes only. It might be almost as interesting as looking at a whole pot from Poseidonia."

"It's sure to have been thrown away long ago," I said doubtfully. "But I will look."

After making a proper farewell, I left—glad to get away from the scene of my embarrassment. Neither was I unhappy to get away from the wine stains on the floor. They were, in the firelight, too much like something else.

Also, I felt a sense of dread. It had come so pat to the moment, that breaking of the cup and spilling of wine—by me, who never broke things as a rule. It seemed like an omen. It was as if, the moment that Arkhimenos' name was hinted at, the gods, or some dark force from the Underworld, had assented. And Aristotle had never replied to my unfinished question, as if some power had sealed his lips. Instead of being encouraged, I felt frightened. If the gods had told me who the murderer was, I still didn't know what to do. This was not evidence that could be produced at the trial. If I were meant to prove my conclusion, I did not know any more than before how to go about finding proofs.

VIII

Blood and Insults

For want of anything better to do, I began next day to look for the piece of potsherd found on Boutades' grounds. My search was at first half-hearted, for I knew the trivial object must have been swept away long ago. But as I went on looking for the fragment I became more interested; anyone who seeks wishes to find. I turned over my clothes in the press, and looked into jars and under furniture—into well-swept and barren corners, in the stupid manner of all persons looking for a lost object. At last I went quietly into the women's quarters.

In my mother's room I looked into the clothes in her chest, and then began to examine the boxes and jars on the table. I went through her new pnyx of best inlaid boxwood, which my father had given her shortly before his death, and examined her jewels and trinkets; of course, the box was innocent of broken pottery. Then I noticed the old pnyx behind it, a

round one somewhat battered, and opened it. There was a
magpie hoard such as a woman will keep—a broken fibula,
a child's milk-tooth, a lock of hair—and there in the midst of
this detritus was the lost fragment!

I had just picked it up and put it in my sleeve when my
mother appeared in the doorway.

"Dear me, Stephanos, what are you doing here? Why are
you examining my jewel case?"

I thought of an excuse, and smiled weakly, like a child
caught with his hand on the sweetmeats. "To tell the truth,
Mother, I was wondering what you might need as a gift the
next feast day."

She blushed and looked pleased, but said, "Stephanos, my
son, don't spend your money on me. I don't need anything!"
She put her hand on my forehead and looked at me anxiously. "Are you feeling quite well, my child? Your uncle's
wife's uncle—on her mother's side—had his mind turned by
worry. I forget whether it was when he lost all that money,
or whether it was because his rheumatism pained him so
much, but he went very quiet at first, and then he acted very
strange—he would throw things around the house, and then
sing at the top of his voice—sometimes nearly all day, and
very loudly, and nobody could stop him."

"I'm quite well," I assured her. "My mind isn't turned, and
I shall certainly not sing."

"Well, then, my dear," she replied, apparently reassured,
"don't go about the women's quarters. Suppose the serving-
women should notice—it makes such a bad impression. I
hope you're not becoming fidgety at your age, like some men
who poke into all the household affairs. You will get just as
bad as Boutades if you're not careful."

"Boutades?"

"Oh, yes," she answered, sitting comfortably on the bed.
"I do not like to listen to slaves' gossip, of course—but do you
know, Stephanos, in his latter days Boutades became quite
strange in such matters. He took to counting things."

"Counting? What sort of things?"

"Well, he'd pry through his wife's boxes and chests, counting jewels and ornaments. And he made lists of all the furniture—one day he insisted on them bringing up all the pots and dishes in the house, and made a list. Of course, many a man likes to see where his money is going, and what he has, but this was peculiar, wasn't it? Then he went out and bought some more things—like two small amphorai, and ten cups of the best quality—and he added them to his list. The women were quite tired of Boutades' spying and snooping—silly old fool that he was!"

"Perhaps he just wanted something to do," I suggested.

"Is that the case with you, Stephanos? Do you want something to do? Oh, be off to the baths or the agora, and don't become a male housekeeper—it isn't becoming."

"I don't think there's any danger of that," I said.

She smoothed my hair with her hand. "There, Stephanos, you look so tired. Dear, dear, I shouldn't have mentioned that awful man." It was evident to me that since Boutades had been so inconsiderate as to allow his murder to implicate us, she regarded him as a personal enemy of the family. I kissed her.

"In any case," she added, "I don't suppose you would ever be as mean as Boutades. When he gave his wife some fine jewels last spring, he told her she need not expect to take them into the grave with her as a death-offering—they were far too valuable for that. Imagine! I'd rather have a garland of flowers from my good son than the richest ornaments given with such a heart as that."

I looked at her anxiously, thinking I had neglected her in the past few weeks. This was a hard time for her, newly widowed, and probably she and my aunt were shunned by other women now we were under such a cloud.

She noticed my look, though she did not know its source, and patted my hand.

"Don't worry, Stephanos—go off and enjoy yourself. I'll make you a lettuce drink to take tonight before you go to bed. And I think I'll make some of those little honey-cakes Eudoxia is so fond of."

She bustled out, being careful, however, to see that I

preceded her and left the women's quarters in good order. I took the little fragment to my room and put it in a safe place. It was a piece of trash—but still, I had looked for it and found it. I suppose I owed the luck, good or ill, to the fact that my mother is one of those who hate to throw anything away. She must have found the fragment on the floor and then absent-mindedly put it in her box of rubbish. I have never, then or later, bothered to inquire about this—questions would lead only to confusion, and I know that she would never remember how she came upon it.

I went to the agora in a fairly cheerful frame of mind and at noon wandered over to the market stalls to buy something to eat. The day was chilly, and I felt hungry; I stopped by a stall selling cooked meat. As I was idly wondering what to buy, two men came up. They were Theosophoros, with his long chin and usual air of looking for something to criticize, and the good citizen Arkhimenos, thinner and perhaps balder than ever, with the two serious lines on his forehead etched like marks in stone. I fancied these two respectable ones had not recognized that it was I who was standing there; they had seen me from the back only. Since the first prodikasia I had been even less sought after than before.

With reckless affability I greeted these citizens. Arkhimenos merely nodded, but Theosophoros said, "Ah, Stephanos, the young man at law. What a pity your father departed this life when he did—what a pity," shaking his head. "We are all so sorry for your poor masterless household. I wonder that your mother doesn't take better care of you than to let you come out on such a cold and windy day."

"Yes," said Arkhimenos stiffly, "the doctors speak much of colds and fevers at this time of year, and the malefic influence of the stars."

Just as I do not know what possessed my mother to keep something better thrown away, so I do not know what possessed me then to utter words better left unspoken. I had, of course, been brooding upon Arkhimenos—now I had him at hand, I did not wish to let him go. Their insults—implying that I was not a man, not lord of my household—were of the sort to arouse one to action. I assumed joviality, and, throwing a coin to the owner of the meat-stall, I seized a sausage and began to eat with apparent appetite.

"It is, as you say, a chilly day, gentlemen," I said heartily. "Some philosophers think now that the winds drive away the evil humors. Most things work a little good and a little ill. Such a wind is good for the sea and bad for the sailors, as they say." I looked straight at Arkhimenos and continued, "Yes, I think if I were a sailor I would stay ashore—indeed, so I would in all seasons unless I were sure of my boat. Of course, good sail and strong planks can weather rough gales—is it not so, trierarkh?"

I fancied I saw Arkhimenos blink. He scowled at me over his nose.

"No good setting out to sea," I explained, "if the slaves have been allowed to steal the rope and substitute bad planks for good. I suppose Odysseus' raft was of sound planks. But perhaps not. It foundered, you remember? And he had to swim for it. But one could scarce accuse Kalypso of supplying bad materials."

I don't know what brought the *Odyssey* so much into my head; perhaps the previous insults had reminded me of the suitors' treatment of Telemakhos. At any rate, I'll swear that Arkhimenos turned pale at my saucy remarks, while Theosophoros, to whom what I was uttering seemed mere froth, said testily, "What nonsense you talk, Stephanos—of course sailors don't go out in the autumn gales."

"But I was thinking of Odysseus," I said earnestly. "He must have been in the autumn storms—that's why he was wrecked or nearly wrecked so often. I've been reading the poem again lately."

I turned to the meat-seller. "I'll just have some more of that sausage, my good man—if you don't mind, I'd prefer to cut it myself."

The tradesman handed me the knife—and then, driven by the gods know what inner daemon, I did a most strange thing. As I cut through the sausage, holding it awkwardly, I deliberately cut myself with the knife. It was only a small gash, but it produced a great deal of blood, as such little cuts will. The blood spilled over the counter, and the piece of sausage, and my drops of blood with it, fell off and rolled on the stones.

"Oh, dear, now see what I've done," I said in rueful tones, sucking my thumb. " 'And the good food was scattered on the floor,' " I added, quoting from that part of the *Odyssey* where the hero begins shooting the suitors in the banquet hall. There was no doubt about it now—Arkhimenos was turning very pale.

"No need to throw good food to the ground," said the shopman. "And look what you've done to my counter. Keep your blood to yourself."

" 'The floor was slippery with blood,' " I quoted, and then added:

> "Begin—you and the women—to carry the bodies
>   away.
> Then with porous sponges wash the beautiful
>   chairs and the tables.

You have a porous sponge, I hope?" I said to the shopkeeper. "Even if you haven't any beautiful chairs and tables. Clear the gore away. This will help!" I tossed him a drakhma with a lordly air, and he subsided.

I turned from him just in time to see Arkhimenos droop. His face was pale green, as if he were seasick; he grasped the side of the stall to keep from swaying. "Hate the sight of blood," he said hoarsely.

"Tush! I'm not hurt," I said cheerfully. "It's only a scratch. Why, if there were a pretty girl here, I should bow and say gallantly, 'A small sacrifice to *Aphrodite!*' " I emphasized the last word, waving my bloody hand in the air.

Then he did faint, or nearly, slumping to the ground. I moved toward him, but Theosophoros, supporting his friend, turned on me angrily. "Keep away," he said. "Go home and get sober. Didn't your tutor teach you any manners?"

"As you will," I said cheerfully. "Put his head between his

knees." This in fact was what Theosophoros was about to do. "Goodbye," I added. "Who would have thought a man would faint off like a girl, though—like a young girl? I don't know a woman who would do so, for such a nothing." I said all this loudly, hoping Arkhimenos might be conscious.

If only I had not said those foolish words and done that foolish thing—like a small boy showing off. If I had remained decently respectful, I might have spared myself much trouble and some danger. But as I left the market place I felt nothing but pleasure, as if I had struck a blow for Philemon. I was still without logical proofs of anything, but I felt my conviction about the omen was supported. The affair of the ill-fated ships galled Arkhimenos, undoubtedly. What sounded to his friend like my drunken maunderings had evidently made sense to the trierarkh. His loss and worry over the *Aphrodite* were close to his secret heart. But there was more—the sight of blood, the references to the *Odyssey* —had these not overset him so much because they brought to mind his revenge on the man who had cheated him? Why else should he faint? Truly, men do not swoon at sight of a scratch. But hearing the reference to a bloody vengeance by bow and arrow, combined with the sight of real blood, might well be too much for the murderer. Yes, Arkhimenos must be fearful. How stupid it was of me that day to think of Arkhimenos' fear, and not of my own!

On the day of the second prodikasia I was sober-minded enough. The opposing company were there, dressed in new winter clothes of fine fulled wool and looking even more impressive. Grave Eutikleides in his winter bulkiness appeared more than ever a bulwark of civic decency. Even Telemon looked well dressed, serious and not too stupid. Polygnotos, a trifle thinner, looked handsome still, but more like a responsible middle-aged man of affairs—he seemed a great deal older than me now. I noticed that his attendant was the rusty-haired Sinopean, the slave whom I had seen just after the murder when he returned breathless from pursuing the assassin. I recalled the remarks that had then been made about him. Certainly, no one now seemed at all disposed to attribute the murder to a slave or slaves. Nor did it seem likely that the whip had been applied to this fellow for letting the murderer escape. He wore a new tunic and looked stout and sleek, waiting cheerfully outside the door. I could not help sighing. If only the murder had been the iniquity of slaves, how much happier it had been with me and mine.

The proceedings went on at first much as I expected; we merely covered old ground. I repeated my defense, that Philemon could not have been in Athens at the time. I was still not certain whether, when we came to new matter, I ought to mention that I hoped to produce a sailor who could help in establishing the fact that Philemon had been elsewhere. However, I was forestalled. For when the Basileus turned to the other side to ask if they had any new material to produce, Eutikleides said loudly, "Yes, indeed, my lord." I was of course all attention.

"We have," said Eutikleides, clearing his throat, "new evidence as to the activities of the accused, and as to where he was—hem!—evidence which contradicts the assertions made by the defense." He looked sharply at me. "There is, my lord, a certain soldier, one of Alexander's troops, recently returned wounded from the wars. He is a poor man, but he is one of our phratry. He has told us that the accused, Philemon, also fought in the great battle by the town of Issos. But —gentlemen—Philemon fought *on the Persian side.*"

He paused to let that sink in. My knee-strings nearly gave way. This was one of the most horrible things that could be said about a man. "Mede-lover" is a most vicious taunt; in the past, families have been exiled for "Mede-loving." To fight for the Persians is treachery. Alexander had shown what he thought of it after the battle at the Granikos, when he ordered that all the Greeks who had fought for Darius be slain out of hand. Philemon and his estate could expect no mercy from the civic powers if this could be proven against him— even, perhaps, if it merely became common belief. As those whose political sentiments were against Alexander had to keep their views hidden, old popular feeling could find expression unchecked. All men, gentle and simple, could exe-crate Philemon as they pleased. I felt as if I were being sewn into a sack, so that I could not move nor breathe.

"After the rout of the Persians," continued Eutikleides, "when the misbegotten mercenaries fell out of love with the coward Darius, this man, like some other renegades, made his way westward by way of the disaffected cities."

He must have guessed that I was frantically trying to re-member dates and calculate times, for he added, "The battle by Issos took place over a year ago now—he had many months in which to return. This soldier got news of him at Sidon—Philemon had already returned to Greece by ship. He had a scar over his eye from a wound in battle, so men remembered him readily."

There was a short silence. I found my voice.

"Where is this witness—this soldier? Produce him!"

"My lord," said Eutikleides, "we thought it wisest not to produce the man at this time. He is wounded and ill—the cold weather is bad for his health. He will be produced be-fore you at a later season. Meanwhile, we have taken note of his evidence, which we will offer to you in writing, if you will accept it."

"His name?" asked the Basileus.

"Pardon me, my lord." Eutikleides looked at me. "It is, I know, irregular to conceal a name—but really . . . so many dangers. A weak man, injured, not well able to defend him-self. He has no need of enemies," with a significant glance at me as if I were a sturdy rascal who would as soon knock a man about the head with a billet of wood as look at him. "His name shall be produced at the proper time, when we set forth the man to speak for himself."

"Yes," said Polygnotos. "Take this, if you will, as a state-ment of intent merely. But it did not seem right to withhold this forthcoming evidence, considering the proper function of the prodikasia."

"Very well," said the Basileus. "What say you, Stephanos?"

"This is a monstrous accusation," I said as forcefully as I could. "And from a nameless man, too! My lord, who can refute a shadow? And if this man is to be found, who can prove that it was Philemon that he saw? At such a time as this, we may say of any man absent from the city, if we wish to slander his name, 'Oh, he went to fight for the Persians.' All that we know of Philemon is that he went away and remained away—but he was not a man to fight against the Greeks." There was a titter from someone (Telemon, probably). I had phrased my last remark badly. Was it not for fighting against one particular Greek that Philemon had first been sentenced?

I went on hastily: "I cannot allow that this is proper evidence, lacking the witness or a document signed by him. It can be accepted only as a statement of intent—if my lord please. I certainly cannot defend my cousin against a man who does not yet exist before this court."

I could think of nothing more to say. It would be the height of stupidity to suggest that even if Philemon had fought for Darius that didn't prove he was a murderer of Boutades. Logically that was still true, but rhetorically such an argument would have been the same as admitting in advance that Philemon was a traitor—and that I must deny and deny. It would have been foolhardy to refer to my bit of supposititious evidence, that a sailor had seen Philemon far away a while before the murder. That could too easily be twisted to fit in with their tale. I would have to think, to decide if in future I could use the sailor's story at all. At that moment my mind was paralyzed. The idea that Philemon had fought for the Persians, once accepted, was sufficient without the guilt of murder to deprive him of property and to keep him in miserable exile forever—exile with perhaps a reward for any Greek or Makedonian who might take his life.

The Basileus asked if we had more to say, but nothing was added and we were soon allowed to depart. That was just as well, certainly—I could not have stood for another half-hour. I was trembling almost visibly, and I felt an urgent need to relieve myself.

We filed out decorously, through the little crowd outside the door—the crowd of aimless fellows ever to be found where anything might be happening. Polygnotos went off, attended by the sleek Sinopean lad, and Eutikleides went bustling along the hill of Hephaistos with some important clients who had awaited him. I darted off to a convenient grove where I could relieve my bursting bladder and bowels in private. When I started down the path again, I nearly stumbled into Telemon, doddering along as usual.

"You do not look well," he commented. "Distressing for you, very distressing."

I cursed in my soul, and gritted my teeth. How odious is pity from those whom we dislike or distrust.

"I'm quite well, I thank you," I said, and set off walking as briskly as I could. But the limping old fool seemed determined to keep up with me, and chattered merrily at my side, as if we were coming away from a party.

"There's Eutikleides, gone on ahead. Very busy man, Eutikleides. He knows how to conduct business, too, don't you think? That's why we got out in such reasonable time. Another sort of man would spin everything out. And Polygnotos too. Such a head on him, although he's so young. Do you know he's planting new olive trees? That estate will certainly flourish. And I said to him, 'What about extending the house, Polygnotos—building materials will not get any cheaper these days.' And he said that was precisely what he would do, once his duties as khoregos were out of the way."

"I hope the play is going well," I said coolly.

"Yes indeed. Such costumes! No expense spared. Alexander will be pleased. I suppose he won't be here, but he's bound to appreciate the compliment in the story of Herakles. Do you know, I think Polygnotos is just the sort of man—the new young Athenian nobleman—that Alexander will like. Alexander is sure to want Athens put on a firm footing—a firm footing. Antipater has invited Polygnotos to his house. Polygnotos is to go as soon as he returns from Korinthos."

"So he's going to Korinthos, is he?"

"Yes, on business. To collect a debt owed to his uncle. He sets off today. So conscientious. And such a fine respect for his uncle's memory—if you'll excuse me mentioning it. Polygnotos has had the most beautiful tombstone made—the best Karian marble and lovely carving. Figures in relief." His hands sketched them in the air. "Boutades with his wife, don't you know, and a description of his services. Tekhnophilos, the best worker in stone, has it in his shop now—it's nearly completed. People go there just to see it—you should too. It's a real work of art. It took him a while to get the marble."

I agreed that it sounded very handsome.

"Well, as I was saying—Antipater's invitation looks as if Polygnotos were respected in political matters, doesn't it? He has such a knowledge of affairs. I told him, 'Polygnotos, the stars look favorable now.' Even if this nasty business has happened to his house, the stars look well. Antipater needs intelligent and sensible men about him—like the teacher Aristotle he's so friendly with. I can imagine Polygnotos working well with Aristotle—quite the Guardian and the Philosopher. Polygnotos knew him in the Lykeion, of course —and you too, didn't you? But there, I was forgetting you didn't have much time for your studies. What a pity."

My head ached. I could not tell exactly what this garrulous Telemon was trying to do to me, but I could not believe our conversation—his conversation, rather—was an accident. Perhaps Eutikleides had told him to speak to me; perhaps he had thought of it for himself. He might have a more cleverly malicious mind than I had given him credit for—or all this might be simple nature. No matter. I saw in my mind the picture that other Athenians must see: on the one hand, the poor Stephanos, with nothing but a family of women and a reprobate cousin—on the other, the splendid Polygnotos, with all his clan to assist him and rejoice in his success. I had hinted that their witness didn't exist—but I knew he had sufficient existence. Somewhere in the phratry there was an old soldier. Someone in the phratry would supply what was wanted. It would do me no good to assert that the witness was suborned—he might have needed no direct buying in his desire to please. Perhaps it was all true, too—horrible thought! I could not say in my heart that I was sure Philemon would never fight for the Persians—he might perhaps join any fight that was going. It was all doubt, and life tasted bitter.

"You are very quiet, Stephanos," said Telemon solicitously.

"Yes," I said. "I was thinking about what you were saying."

That was true enough. Everything Telemon said carried one message. Leave us alone, don't bother trying too hard to defend your kinsman. It is hopeless. They had said it through the shocking "evidence" and now Telemon was saying it again, telling me of the glory of their tribe. We are strong; you are weak. And they *were* strong, sure to be pleasing in the sight of all earthly powers. Heavenly powers and earthly are not quite in accord always about these things, but the stories that tell us so are not very comforting. I thought of Oidipous at his grave at Kolonos, leaving Kreon and his sons and Thebes to ruin things their own way.

Even my friendship with Aristotle seemed dubious and shadowy. Perhaps Telemon intended to remind me how tenuous was my acquaintance with this man from Makedonia. There was little likelihood that the friend of Alexander would wish to interest himself in a soldier of Darius! Nothing that had been mine seemed mine at that gray hour. I was to be more anxious, more frightened—nay, terrified—later, but there was nothing to come so horrible as that time when my world seemed to slip from my numb grasp while I watched colorlessly, like a shade. Who would have thought a fool like Telemon could kill a man with words?

At the bottom of the hill I saw two men whom I knew; they had been talking to the others who had come from the court. Theosophoros and Arkhimenos remained, watching us with cold eyes. As we came by, the stately Arkhimenos amazed me by crying out: "Mede-lover! Mede-kisser! Arse-licker to Darius!"

At least these words jolted me out of my lethargy, for which I thank him. Not only were the insults themselves a shock, but one expects such rude language from oafs on the street, not from a somber citizen. He could not be accused of veiled sarcasm.

Theosophoros was more like his old self. As I came closer, he merely said, "Do let us see your Persian stuffs and carpets, cousin of Philemon—you have kept them to yourself for too long."

Telemon shrugged, left me and went on his way. I answered, "These insults are unworthy of you, Theosophoros. You know that I have no more Persian stuffs than yourself— and no more reason to have, either!"

Arkhimenos moved forward and grimaced at me, showing all his teeth. He looked like a grinning skull with two vertical lines drawn in charcoal on its forehead. "Ah-rh-ha!" he said, deep in his throat. "See the impudent whelp of a Mede-loving tribe. Persian-king-lovers!" (The word he used this time was not as polite as "lover.")

"Citizen Arkhimenos—this is not bec—"

"So? What are you going to do? Tell that to Alexander! Darius' darling!" He made an obscene gesture with his fingers. "Why not go and fight for the Egyptians? They do their fighting lying down. 'O soldier, going off to war, with a little prick-lance wobbling all before!' " (This was a snatch of street-urchins' ditty.) "Ha! Ha! Get a sword in your belly, sword in your belly!"

He was hopping up and down with excitement, and his face had become flushed. I turned away from them both, muttering, "It is stupid to try to speak reasonably to you—"

"Ha! Eutikleides'll give you reasons—more reasons than grapes this autumn!"

Theosophoros tried to restrain him, but his brutal delight kept finding vent in little showers of laughter. That was the emotion I was watching—not hate so much as delight. Joy. Relief perhaps, too. I could not tell.

"Get a sword in your belly," he repeated as I went on down the street. Theosophoros drew him away in the opposite direction, but Arkhimenos could still not resist cackling, with little shrieks, "Get a sword in your belly!"

I suddenly knew that he was mad.

Well, at least the insane sometimes enjoy themselves. I was sane (probably, on the whole) and all joy seemed gone. I crawled back home and went to my bed. There, where no one could see or hear, I wept, silently, but for a long time.

IX

Family Matters

I cannot say what moved me to go to Peiraeus a few days later. I had no definite plan or hopes. Perhaps I looked on Peiraeus as a place of good fortune for me. If that were so, I was most grievously deceived.

The year was moving swiftly into winter. The sea wind was cold, although there was some sunshine between swift-flying clouds. Muffled in a worn cloak of unbleached wool, I mingled with the shabbier folk of the port and wandered about the Peiraeus market. Not that there was much to see there —a squalid place it is, with a footing of mud, dung and fishbones, and the stalls offer little but the cheap food and rough pots that the poor can buy.

I remember I was standing by a little heap of inferior vegetables smelling of decay. A streak of sun lighting the green-and-yellow leaves must have cast its light upon my face as well. Suddenly, I felt a tug at my sleeve.

"My lord! My lord!" Turning, I saw at my side a toothless old woman, her face wrinkled like cobbler's wax. Her deep-veined hand with the brown spots of age upon it clawed my arm. It was not a particularly clean or attractive hand.

"Woman, be off—"

"My lord! My mistress bids you come to her!" The crone lowered her voice and hissed, "Your kinswoman has need of you."

"I know of no—"

"Hush!" she implored, laying a chapped finger on her mouth. "I saw you in Peiraeus before, and have waited for your coming again. I know your name, and will tell you all, but not here. Come."

I felt some apprehension. It crossed my mind, after Ar-khimenos' behavior, that this might be some snare, that I might be decoyed away to my destruction if I followed this hag. On the other hand, she looked like one of the Fates, standing there, and all men are obedient to Fate. Had I not come to Peiraeus searching for the unknown? I certainly had imagined nothing in this guise, and wished ardently that she would not breathe the streams of garlic and rotting tooth-stumps into my face. I shook her hand off, but answered, "I will come."

"Follow me, then. Not openly. Be discreet."

She shifted off through the moving throngs, and I followed her at a distance. It was not that easy a task, for she looked from the back like all poor old women, a shapeless bundle of dark rags. When we left the crowded place, she threaded her way (quickly for her age) through streets and then noisome lanes, by waste land and hovels, and I followed, like Theseus threading the labyrinth. Not once did she cast a backward glance. Had she been Orpheus, Euridyke had been free—but I felt she was leading me deeper into an Underworld, not out of it. At last she stopped by a small house—though that seems too dignified a word for this poor dwelling. The walls were unwashed, and showed deep cracks. Outside, in the lane by the door, there were little heaps of refuse.

"Come in," said my ragged Sibyl, and I entered. I came into a small room with smoky walls. In a little brazier burned a very few olive stones. The insistent odor of a nearby privy was making its presence felt. However, there were some signs of housekeeping. On a table, some dishes, exquisitely clean, were arranged in order. There were two wooden stools, and a leather chair which had seen better days—one leg was slightly cracked—but had received the attention of some polish. The doorway into the next room was covered by a curtain of good tapestry showing Penelope at her loom; it was the worse for age, but had been neatly mended in several places. A small high window, half covered with dingy parchment, let in some air and the dull daylight. It was not a beautiful residence, but neither did it seem very sinister. I was not frightened that it was a trap, but I was puzzled.

"Sit down," said my guide, showing me the leather chair. "Will the gentleman not take something to eat or drink?"

"No, I thank you," said I hastily.

"Oh, but Stephanos, the son of Nikiarkhos, must take food in our house. I will heat some water, and you must drink our camomile before you go."

She put the pan of water upon the brazier and then turned to face me.

"The son of Nikiarkhos is wondering why he is here. I have heard you described. Saw you in Peiraeus a while back—recognized the nobleman under the old clothes. I thought, 'He must be helping Philemon in some way—so why not approach him when he comes again?' You love your kinsman well, and aid Philemon, son of Lykias, in his trouble—is it not so?"

"Yes, that is so," I agreed.

"We believe there is nothing not impious you would not do to aid him and his—is it so?"

"There is nothing," I said earnestly, "nothing the gods allow that I would not do for Philemon, my cousin." It flashed through my mind that she or those known to her had some evidence that would help my cause, and my heart leaped.

"Kinship is a sacred tie, my lord. Ah, sir, I speak for your kin; I, the old servingwoman Nousia, come to you in their name as a suppliant." She suddenly threw herself dramatically on her knees and embraced mine as I sat in the cracked leather chair.

I felt embarrassed rather than majestic. I said, raising her, "All is well between us—but how on earth can I know what you are talking about?"

She was enjoying her part. I felt she had rehearsed this scene many times in her head. "First, my lord, swear that even if you will not do what I ask—I and another defenseless woman—you will do us no harm."

I considered. I had no mind to do harm to old women, and it did not appear likely that it would be profitable to do so, so it seemed safe enough to promise. I thought I saw the Penelope curtain move.

"I swear," I said.

"Praise be to Zeus! Now hear me."

"Sit down," I said in a kind tone; it disturbed me to have the old woman standing so close by me, waving her arms, with elf-locks sliding down from under her head-covering. She sat, a comfortably hunched bundle, like any poor old gossip by the fire.

"Thus it is, sir. You know your cousin Philemon—or perhaps I should say, knew him?"

"Yes, of course."

"Well, he was a young rogue, but good-hearted, and you may not have known all about him. In fact, you didn't. I have a surprise for you. What would you say if I were to tell you that your cousin Philemon was married?"

"Philemon? *Married?* But he wasn't—"

She cackled with laughter. Gone was the figure from a drama, and the homely language regained sovereignty, deposing the noble forms of speech that had ruled her tongue before.

"Oh-oh. But he was, now. A bit of a lad with the women was your Philemon, as you'll say. But this ain't one of those affairs. He was a real gentleman; he knew what was due to gentry. He was married, right and tight, before he left Athens. To a most respectable young lady, too—Athenian descent, and all done proper."

"I can hardly believe *that.* Why, a marriage is something a whole family knows about. It can't be a hole-and-corner affair—it isn't legal!"

She frowned. "Legal enough, don't you worry. Nor don't you cast any slurs on my nice young lady as I've nursed from childhood—and her mother before her. Melissa, daughter of Arkhias, she is. She went to her wedding as much a virgin, pure as silver, as any noble bride in Athens. We can show you the wedding sheet with the spot on it, if you've a mind to see it. Her kin all knew—there was a proper betrothal beforehand, there were witnesses. But there were reasons why

Philemon couldn't tell his family. It isn't as pretty as it might be, I'll admit, but it was right enough. And there's no good making trouble in families now the thing's done, and well done, is there?"

She was enjoying herself, like all old women given a chance to gossip on about marriage and women's matters. She absent-mindedly picked up a withered olive from a plate and popped it into her mouth to refresh herself for her discourse.

"There might have been disagreements about the dowry. Melissa has a good dowry, you see, but we can't exactly lay hands on it at the moment. Philemon expected everything would turn out well—and as for marrying young, why, with his father dead, it was his *duty* to marry and produce an heir. Well, only a few weeks after the wedding Philemon got into that nasty business and had to be off. He moved us out here, under a false name. And here we've been. And—" she looked at me brightly, chewing on the olive stone— "there's a son of the marriage by now. Your nephew. A fine sturdy boy."

"Where is this person?" I asked. My head was spinning.

"Over there." She nodded at the curtain, which slid hastily back into place. "She's a respectable married woman. Of course, you can't see her until you acknowledge her a kinswoman. Wouldn't be decent at all."

Here was a quandary. I couldn't clap eyes on this Melissa —couldn't decide for myself if she were whore, mistress or wife—until I had acknowledged her as a wife. Women have a way of manipulating the proprieties to their own advantage. The encounter had led to a kind of trap, after all.

"You are a kind and just man, sir," she said coaxingly. "You could not want your relatives to starve. You've done your best for young Philemon in the law case—we've heard—but things are taking nastier turns now, and what's to become of us? What's to become of the dear baby boy, I'd like to know?" She suddenly began to keen, rocking back and forth on her stool and lamenting, "Oh, oh, we'll starve, or be persecuted out of the place. Friendless and homeless! Oh, deary me! Old bones and young bones, dying on the cold stones! Oh Athena,

93

aid us! Oh, deary me!" She made my head buzz.

"Very well," I said. "I'll see her."

"See who?" said the old crone sharply, in the middle of her keening.

"The wife of Philemon," I said resignedly. As I thought of it, I realized that my *vow* bound me only to working these women no harm —and I didn't see that I would want to do that, no matter what the woman was. As for saying I would see her as a kinswoman—well, there were no male witnesses, or even gentlewomen, in the place, and I could always deny it later.

The old woman stopped her lament as if she cut it off with a knife, and went over to the aperture, calling in soft tones, "Ah, my lady, my Melissa! Your kinsman will see you, wife of Philemon."

The curtain moved slowly aside. A woman entered.

"Good day to you, wife of Philemon," I said, the words sticking in my throat.

She was young and slender and very beautiful. Her hair was golden, as I could see from the few curls that escaped her head-covering. To my disappointment, she looked not at all like an hetaira; she was dressed modestly, like the wife of any citizen, and not at all splendidly. This was surely no courtesan. She stood at the threshold, looking at me with deep blue eyes, very gravely—then she came gracefully across the floor and knelt at my feet, touching my knees.

"Kinswoman and suppliant, too, I come, Stephanos, son of Nikiarkhos, cousin of my husband, Philemon," she said in a low voice.

I raised her and said, "Welcome is the sight of my cousin's spouse"—although few sights could have been less welcome, despite her beauty. I gestured that she should sit, and she perched demurely upon a stool, with the old woman behind her beaming and nodding. The room felt stuffy, and looked even grubbier than before. The girl seemed like a lily growing on a refuse heap. Despite myself, I was moved to pity; even if she were only Philemon's mistress, I would still see that she was given some money.

"Tell me, wife of my cousin, where do you come from? And, I must ask, how comes it to be that you were married without anyone's knowing?"

She looked at me reproachfully. "Not without *anyone's* knowing. It was a true marriage. But we are ill-starred. Let me explain." She drew a quivering breath, and began her narrative.

"My father's name was Arkhias. He was a man of Athens. Although we were Athenians, we were in Thebes at the time of the—the trouble a few years ago. That was an awful time —soldiers killing and looting. I know nothing of political matters" (I thought perhaps she did not wish to utter any anti-Makedonian sentiments) "but I know we had to flee for our lives—our house was damaged, and my mother was killed before we left Thebes. Like many others, we came back to Athens, our rightful home. Father and I met Philemon when we first came into Athens with others who sought refuge here. I was a child and he was a child. But he gave us a drink of water—we always remembered. My father was not very well. We took shelter in a cousin's home—a little farm off the Sounion road. We met Philemon again about three years later. A thief attacked Father and me on the road from Athens to Sounion and snatched our bundles—Philemon was near, and caught the man and gave our things back to us. After that, he came to see my father sometimes. Everything was very correct. I lived in the women's quarters, with my cousin's wife, and Nousia, and did the spinning."

"Did your father have no son?"

"That's one of our troubles, you see. I had a brother, but I don't know where he is. In Sparta somewhere, I'm afraid" (in hushed tones). "And our money and things were all in Thebes. My father always promised a good dowry for me, and there is a *lot* of money somewhere. Some of it my father gave to a friend, a Theban in good standing with Makedonia, so I understand, just before the storm broke—so all we have to do is go back and collect it when things are peaceful. Some fine amphorai and some silver things, I remember, and good stuffs, as well as money."

"Hm," said I. "Are there any documents?"

"I think there are—somewhere. I know nothing about business. My father and Philemon used to talk about it—I suppose Philemon knows. Anyway, this Theban is an *honest* man, else my father would not have trusted him with the money and things."

"Hm-m," I said again. Whether she were telling me the truth or not, it seemed to me as likely that Philemon would get a dowry as that he would get honey from a wasp's nest.

"My poor father was very worried when he knew he was dying. You see, sir, how unfortunate it is—with my brother perhaps serving King Agis, what was to become of me and the money? So Father offered me in marriage to Philemon, and his will made Philemon his heir if his son died. Philemon was quite pleased at the idea of marrying me, after he had considered the matter," she added primly.

Poor Philemon! Everyone knows that no sensible man marries for beauty. Indeed, in a well-conducted family where such matters are properly arranged, bride and bridegroom do not see each other before the wedding. But Philemon was not sensible—the glimpse of blue eyes and a pathetic story might have been too much for him.

"It was *not* imprudent," she said, a bit defiantly, as if reading my thoughts. "I know the marriage might seem a bit— well, not quite nice, you know. I was very sorry to have such a small wedding. And I know his relatives should have been there. But my father and Philemon knew that his kindred might make difficulties about the dowry, and about my brother and our misfortunes. If his father had been alive, it would have been quite different, of course."

"How was the wedding managed, then?"

"There was a proper betrothal ceremony, and my father made over the dowry—I mean the promise of it—to Philemon. My cousin was a witness and one of his friends. Then we married and lived in my cousin's house."

"You should have lived in Philemon's house! That makes a marriage," I said severely.

"But he didn't want to bother his mother with it all—she's

ill, I hear, and old. But he did tell her about it later, I think. He said he would, anyway. It would be much easier to arrange the public side of things once he had the money. We didn't want people to say he was marrying *beneath* him."

"When were you going to do something about it?"

"As soon as things got peaceful. You see, some money and family treasure—gold and things that wouldn't rot or get broken—were buried in the garden of our old house in Thebes. Philemon thought it would be fun to go and dig it up."

Philemon thought it would be fun to go and dig it up! Yes, there truly I could recognize my cousin.

"I had some wedding gifts. I've had to sell some now, of course—Nousia does all that for me; I try not to stir out of the house. But look at that cup and bowl—they are Philemon's."

I looked at them. They were indeed Philemon's from his own home—I had seen them in earlier days.

"I shan't part with *those*," she said. "Everything went against us—my cousin died, and his wife went back to her brother. And poor Philemon got involved in that *trouble*. Just before he got away, he brought me here and put me in this little house. We live here under another name, of course. I go as the wife of Ephoros. I didn't know it, but I was pregnant when he left—the baby is nearly a year and a half old now. Of course, as a woman alone—especially under a false name—I couldn't present him to the phratries and demesmen, could I? He's a lovely boy. See—I'll show him to you."

She got up and went into the next room, returning quickly with a small child. It looked sleepy, but tottered obediently along on its plump legs.

"Here's your nephew," she said proudly, while the old woman made cooing noises. She pushed the child toward me —it clutched at her skirts and said dismally, "Mamma!," looking at me with displeasure.

Another dilemma. If I touched the child, I would be acknowledging it as a legitimate member of the family. She solved the problem, rather unfairly, by popping it into my lap. I peered at its face—the boy was well kept and healthy, at any rate, and in a surprisingly good state as to cleanliness. He gave promise of a sturdier sort of good looks than his mother's. Women and old men can claim to see family resemblances of the most detailed kind in infant faces. I have no skill in this sort of reading. The child had tight-curling hair, and its eyes were brown. There was nothing to indicate that it was not Philemon's. Indeed, as the boy struck me with a strong little fist I rather thought he must be of Philemon's getting. But no child bears marks of legitimacy or illegitimacy in face or behavior. I awkwardly handed it back to its mother.

"His name is Lykias," she said proudly.

I repressed a retort. Here was boldness—to call an illegitimate child after his paternal grandfather! And even if he were legitimate, he did not, strictly speaking, have a name; he had been presented to no one in authority, accepted into no tribe or deme. My faith wavered. Anyway, I thought bitterly, it would be I who had to pay to keep the child from starving, legitimate offspring or not.

"Pa-pa!" said the child, standing with one hand on my knee. "Where Pa-pa?"

I could not suppose the baby itself had been coached, but it was a most effective performance.

The old woman beamed. "There, you remind him of his father—you see, he sees the likeness."

"That is touching indeed," I said dryly, "seeing he has never seen his father."

There was a short pause.

"Pa-pa!" said the child again, confidently.

"Well, he *has* seen his father," said the lady of the house defiantly. "Many times. How do you suppose we've kept going all this time? What do you think we would have had to live on?"

"Do you mean that Philemon has been back? Here to Peiraeus? In Athens?"

"Hush! Yes, he's been back. I'm *pregnant* again, cannot you tell?" (Alas for inexperience! I could, now that she mentioned it.) "His second child. But he hasn't come in a long time—and he mustn't come now, things are much too bad with the things people are saying—about fighting for Persians, and all that. We've all got to hide even deeper." She suddenly started to weep. Crystal tears flooded out of those large blue eyes. "I've nothing to live on!" she said. "We must have something to live on—else how can I feed my children?"

The old hag began to snivel too, for company.

I stood up. I had to get away from this stuffy room and weeping women.

"Oh," said Nousia, "you haven't had your camomile."

"Never mind that," I said. I looked at the young woman. "Don't cry. Look. You will be safe. Here is some money for now—" and I shook what coins I had with me upon the table. "And within a few days I shall bring some more—and perhaps other things too," I added, glancing around the room.

"Oh, thank you, sir," both women said at once; the older one added practically, "When?"

"Meet me in the market place just after dawn, three days from now," I said, recklessly committing myself. "But before I go, tell me one thing—" I addressed Philemon's woman of the golden hair. "Tell me, for I must know—when was Philemon last here?"

She had stopped weeping, and looked at me piteously. Then she said slowly, "I haven't seen him for about two months, sir. Not since the month of Boedromion."

I stumbled out of the place and hastened away through the back lanes of Peiraeus. These last words beat upon my brain like a silversmith's hammer on soft metal. "The month of Boedromion"—the time when Boutades was killed. My whole case—the one of which I had been certain in my heart —fell into ruins. I had thought I had known that Aunt Eudoxia's Defense was true, even if terribly difficult to prove. "Philemon was not there." But now—either what these women had said was a tissue of lies, got up by who knew what infernal enemy, or for their own purposes; or it was true (or true except as to the connection being a true marriage). If Philemon had been in Athens at the appropriate time, then I had no defense—except in my soul the still firm belief that he had nothing to do with the murder.

The need to know tortured me. There was one person who might confirm or deny the truth of what I had just heard. I walked home swiftly, as if my feet were winged, and marched in upon my mother and Aunt Eudoxia, who were eating honey-cakes happily together. I seized my astonished aunt by the arm and drew her roughly to the chamber—the best chamber, where in happier times I had received guests. I shut the door.

I suppose I must have looked like a madman—never before had I been rough with Aunt Eudoxia. I saw that she was terrified, pale and shaking, and that I had jolted her side where she was carrying her pain, but at that moment I had little mercy. I let go of her arm and confronted her, throwing my questions at her in a stern whisper.

"Aunt Eudoxia, I know all about it. Philemon has been back in Athens—hasn't he? Hasn't he? He was here during Boedromion—wasn't he? Answer me! And spare me lies or evasions. By Zeus! I want the truth!"

I hoped that she would burst into indignant and puzzled denials. But her face fell like a wall caving in, letting me see behind the usual pained patient expression the anxiety of a long-harbored guilty knowledge, now struggling into the open.

"Oh—yes," she whispered. "I don't know how you know, Stephanos, but—he *has* been back in Athens. He came in secret, several times. To see his old mother. I thought we kept it so cleverly! But now—oh, Athena!—and I thought torture would not wring it from me!"

She was crying, and dropped into a chair. I was glad she was not going to kneel to me—I'd had enough of that for one day.

"It doesn't matter," I said. "Whether you told me or not, I've found out. I know that Philemon was here at the time of—at that time. I've been talking with someone else who has reason to know."

"Who is that?"

"Only Philemon's wife," I said.

Then Aunt Eudoxia fainted.

X

Puzzles in Writing

When Aristotle, to my surprise, summoned me to see him, I went without much heart. He had of course heard about the second prodikasia, and said he wished to tell me that "not everybody" believed that Philemon had been fighting for the Persians. I took this to mean that the higher powers were reserving their judgment.

"And," he added cheerfully, "this evidence is late and incomplete. The whole still seems to be rather an hypothesis than a proof."

"Oh," I said bitterly. "That's last week's trouble. As the poet says,

'What threatened us before and looked so bleak,
Though still to come, seems idle memory
Now this black cloud shoots lightning o'er our heads.' "

"Expressive," he said, "but not very good poetry, do you think? What is this black cloud? Has something new arisen?"

"Yes," I said flatly. "But it is—private—in the family—and I ought not to tell you. You have been kind—and you are wise —but this is a thing personal and most puzzling, with perhaps the gravest consequences."

"You are becoming quite an orator, Stephanos. You arouse my keenest attention; already I am trying to guess. And how judiciously you flatter me. The wise are always ambitious—to be thought wise. As for the kindness—well, we are especially friendly to anyone who praises us for the good qualities we are not sure we do possess. So now you have swayed me entirely; perhaps you should tell me this grave and puzzling matter. You have my promise of silence even if I cannot assist you."

Feeling guilty at betraying a family secret and shame, I was moved to pour out to him everything about the women in Peiraeus.

"I don't know what to think," I said in conclusion. "Sometimes I think it's all true; sometimes I think only some is true—that she was Philemon's mistress, not his wife. Who knows who is father of the child she bears? But what does it matter if we free Philemon of a sordid entanglement? The important thing is that she says he was here in Boedromion. It could be some vicious plot to extort money from us—I've thought of that."

"It could," he agreed. "But it would be rather a risk for them to associate themselves with such a family. Pardon me, but you are all under a cloud (dear me, poetry again) and not rich. A girl so beautiful would be better off with some wealthy protector. But, of course, she could be a prostitute, pregnant and cast off, who is looking desperately for support while she is unable to engage in her usual occupation. She might be willing to say anything—for pay. But a prostitute's evidence could be rejected. Athenian juries are not very fond of prostitutes—in public." He laughed, as one who knows his world. I found him very irritating at that moment.

"Oh, Athena help us!" I said desperately. He still hadn't understood. "It matters to me. You haven't seen—Aunt Eudoxia's Defense was always a lie! She has admitted now that she knew Philemon was here. He had been to see her—several times, and at *that* time. So to that extent—on the worst point of all—the girl's story is true. And if no one else were to know it, I know it now. The one *fact* I myself depended on has gone."

There was a dead silence for perhaps a minute.

"Now you see it," I said unhappily. "You will believe he must be guilty now. All I can ask you is to say nothing—not to interfere."

"Do *you* now believe Philemon is guilty?" he asked me directly.

"No," I said. "This will seem mad. But I believe it less than ever, if that were possible."

"Why?"

"Because I've been more and more reminded of Philemon. The real Philemon—reckless, impulsive and good-natured. All this with the woman—it's a mess, but it seems natural and, in a curious way, ordinary. And the child did look like the child he'd have. Oh, it's so difficult to explain. But there's no more motive for Philemon to do away with Boutades than there was before. In my mind I've been turning it about and about—but in my *heart* I think—feel—that Melissa believes she is married to Philemon. I find it hard to think of her as an enemy—more like an extra burden."

"Aside from her catastrophic admission, what does Aunt Eudoxia have to say?"

"Well—she says Philemon once started to say something about a girl, and he cut him off—she said she didn't want to hear about his doings with women. When I talked to her, she was at first quite clear that we didn't have to acknowledge this female. Even if there were some sort of ceremony, this wasn't a real marriage, the girl was probably a scheming slut, and anyway a foreigner. But when she thought about the child she began to weaken. Says she wants to see a grandchild before she dies. All this wench would have to do would be to show the baby to Aunt Eudoxia and cry, and she'd be accepted in the course of an afternoon."

"No," said Aristotle firmly. "Don't let that happen. Keep the girl away from your family's houses, and keep your family —especially Aunt Eudoxia—away from her. There must not be any visible links. Not now. Make your womenfolk hold their tongues."

"What can I do? I can scarcely go about looking for traces of kin in Sounion, finding out if there were a marriage, and digging up Thebes. All that would take months at the best of times. It's impossible to find out about the legitimacy of the marriage at this point."

"Hum." Aristotle fitted the points of his fingers together judiciously. "You feel that she is, or thinks she is, Philemon's wife. At this point, you had better proceed as if dealing with his wife and child. If she is an impostor, trying merely to extort money for support, she may thus be satisfied. If she is Philemon's wife—or even a deluded concubine who thinks she's a wife—your family would owe her and her children some support. It is a risk, of course. She may be acting under someone else's direction. She may have been bought by the other side. It's a risk you have to take. Put nothing in writing, and have no witnesses to your transactions. If things go awry, she can be discredited, and she will have no proofs that you have acknowledged her as *one of the family*. You could always say that she merely told you she had an illegitimate child by Philemon and you gave trivial succor out of pity before you knew of her bad character. Foisting spurious children upon citizens isn't well seen, so a jury would probably side with you if the accusers used such a dung-spattered weapon."

"I see," I answered. "But I feel that her story is basically true. So it would be wrong not to help them. At least it's one thing I *can* do for Philemon."

"True. But secretly, *secretly*, Stephanos. Don't go to the house again. Meet the old servant and get as much as you can out of her. Be watchful for any slip that shows their story is false. But remember this." He leaned forward earnestly. "If these are Philemon's wife and child, they are *in danger*. So you owe it to them and to Philemon to take the utmost care."

"In danger?" I repeated, stupefied.

"Yes. Indeed, yes. It is becoming clear to me that the best way you can assist them is to remove them to some foreign place as speedily as possible. That would also supply a test— for the truer Melissa's story, the more willing she would be to go. If she is set to entrap you with a false tale, she would do her best not to leave. There I think I can help you. She can go to Makedonia until it is safe to return. I can say a word to the right people, and secure a cart and some guides. If you can pay the cart hire and supply money for provisions, the rest is simple. Leave it to me. Shall we say the fifth day of the next decade? That's the middle of the month. I think it will take that long, but we shouldn't leave it any longer." His mind seemed to move like a water-beetle on the surface of a stream. I could not follow him.

"In danger?" I said again. "How in danger?"

"I have been partly swayed by your faith in the woman. Either she is a danger to you, of the sort we have mentioned —and by sending her away we get rid of that too—or she is, as you think in your heart, Philemon's wife, and, in that case, in peril. Someone hates Philemon. *Hates* him. And everything belonging to him. And hates you too, now. I wonder why."

"Hates us! But that's ridiculous. Philemon killed a man in a fight, it's true—but the family received compensation. They are lowly people, and have never mentioned revenge. And as for me—I have harmed none, nor did my father ever do injury to any man. Someone might be angry with me for some thoughtless word, I suppose—"

"No, not angry. I sense the presence of hatred—something more deadly than anger, and more sure. Anger can be cured by time, but hatred cannot. Haven't you noticed the differences? The angry man aims at giving pain to his object—he wants him to feel, to suffer. The man who hates is secure, detached—he doesn't care whether his victim feels pain or not, as long as he can annihilate him. An angry man may eventually pity those who offended, but the hater will never pity. Real hatred stops being personal. After earthquakes and lightning and so on, it's the most deadly thing in the world. I fear that your antagonist—Philemon's and yours—is a hater, not just an angry man."

"But who," I said, rather overcome by all this, "who could hate us? Hate me?"

"Not you, perhaps," he said thoughtfully. "Not as yourself. Something you represent. As people can hate others involved in a political cause which they abhor."

"Oh, yes," I said slowly. A little light wavered into the darkness. "I was forgetting. Somebody hated me just the other day." I told him of Arkhimenos' insults—and of Theosophoros too, and his sarcasms, but chiefly of Arkhimenos' obscene outcry. When Aristotle pressed me for more, I related the whole of the incident at the meat-stall.

Aristotle sighed.

"What are we to do with you? The young are very rash. That was most unwise. Don't, I beg you, make enemies—or, having made them, don't inflame them any more."

"You have frightened me now," I said seriously, "with your talk of hatred."

"A little fear is medicinal—too much robs us of our wits. As for my discourse on hatred—quite in the lecturer's style, was it not? I must make use of it sometime if I haven't already. I might be wrong about it in this case—but I think not. Hatred exists, I am sure—but why? Strange how things come about," he went on in a more jovial tone, looking at me benignly. "I wanted to talk to you about pots again, and instead I lectured on hatred. How could these two things be combined? A scene of hatred on a vase? Or just a hateful pot? I don't suppose you remembered to bring me that fragment, by the way?"

I had remembered to bring it with me, wrapped in a small piece of cloth, though I'd nearly forgotten it. It seemed most trivial now, but I meekly produced it. Aristotle was as delighted as if I'd given him a whole pot of intricate design. He turned it over and over in his long fingers, and brought it to his eyes, then held it away from him.

"Feel the edges," he said. "This was broken shortly before it was found. Good Athenian ware it is. Look at the red clay, and the fine glaze."

To my eyes, there was still nothing very pretty about a small piece of broken dish.

"If you like that kind of thing," I said, slightly sarcastic (I must have been feeling better), "there's a very nice kitchen-heap behind our house where you could find pieces of all the cups we have broken in the last ten years. I'll make you a present of the whole collection."

"Come, Stephanos, don't make fun of your old teacher. I don't think," he added more seriously, "that this is a potter's mark. It looks like part of a proper inscription. I think this is a bit of a letter. Stephanos—doesn't that look like a letter to you?"

I looked over his shoulder, idly. At first I saw nothing I had not seen before. And then—I saw a letter in the mark. It looked like part of a written word, with its fine sure strokes, and not a mere sign meant to stay by itself. And the letter I saw was the obvious one. Phi, Φ, which is often made in the form of a cross, thus ✛ or thus ✛. Phi, which is the beginning of Philemon.

"It looks like a—" I began, out of the habit which makes one answer a teacher's question. Then I stopped. "I can't be sure," I ended lamely.

"I will keep this, if you don't mind," Aristotle said. I did mind, and wished to take it back, but of course I said nothing. Better to treat it as a matter of no importance. For the first time it struck me that the Kretan bow-tip had been meant to be found in order to make my cousin seem the criminal. Perhaps this fragment was another piece of false evidence, deliberately placed. I sought confusedly for explanations— but I would keep my mouth shut.

"When is a pot not a pot?" Aristotle asked cheerfully. "When it's broken. Thinking about pots and wine-jars and so on reminds me. I'm going to dine soon with the rich citizen Kleiophoros. There's an estimable man. Full of chatter and untroubled by ideas. I must go into good society more often. It polishes the manners. And there is much to be said for dining with rich men—their wine is very good. Don't forget about the departure next week. Money for hire of wagon— I shall take care of the rest."

I met the old woman again in Peiraeus, at the spot which she had indicated near the market place. Her beauty was no brighter on second viewing, and I disliked the thought of requesting a private conversation, but she forestalled me by saying, "I think, sir, you and I should have a little quiet talk, out of harm's way. Follow me to the seashore." I followed her winding trail—it seemed to be becoming a habit. We went again through back lanes and poverty, but this time we came eventually to a solitary stretch of beach, away from the shipping and fishermen.

It was not a good day for strolling by the seaside. The air was chill, and the water itself looked gray and mean, as if it too were poverty-stricken. The coarse sand and gravel crunched harshly under our feet.

"Here," I said, glad to give away the bundle I'd been trying to conceal. "There are some child's clothes and a blanket, and some figs and cheese and a jar of honey. And here's some money," dropping it into her claw. She examined it, and bit the coins, unembarrassed. "It isn't much, but it should be enough for your mistress and the child for a while." I hadn't been able to give much, naturally, for a good deal would have to be spent on the hire of a cart—how to find it all had given me a sleepless night.

To my relief, she chuckled with pleasure at the taste of the coins, seeming to consider the gift quite handsome.

"Sir, many thanks to you. Oh, the blessing of not having to worry about the price of tomorrow's dinner. And of course my mistress must be well cared for now—her carrying a child, and winter coming on. Of course, my lord, it ain't scarcely good manners for you to come to my lady's house while the master's away. The neighbors would talk, and take it wrong, not knowing the facts. A woman's reputation is a fragile thing, especially in a dirty place like Peiraeus—where my lady really shouldn't be."

"Look," I said hastily. "Your mistress, her child and you must get away from here—from Peiraeus and from Athens —to somewhere safe. As you say yourself, this isn't a fit place for her. And it's no good now waiting for Philemon—he certainly can't come at this time. The trial will come soon and the wife of an accused murderer is in a difficult position. Will you trust me? I have a plan."

"I'm not that fond of Peiraeus," she said with a loud and juicy sniff, "not so that it'd break my heart to leave it—nor my mistress's neither, not now. And I can see your mind better than she—you don't want anyone to know that Philemon has been here, and it's easier to conduct the case with us out of the way. Fair enough. But look—you wouldn't be thinking of any nasty business, would you? Spiriting away the inconvenient wife that the family don't want, and strangling her and her child and her servant, and throwing the bodies into a ditch? I've heard of such tales."

"Great Zeus, no!" I said indignantly. "I swear by Zeus, the protector of the suppliant, the stranger, the widow and the fatherless, that such an idea is abhorrent to my mind, and I would not do it for any advantage in this world. I promise your mistress can trust to my honor."

"It had better be," she said cryptically, and muttered a stream of oaths. I gathered an undignified and painful vengeance would be mine at the hands of several gods if I did any harm to Melissa. Then she brightened.

"I do trust you, deary—my lord, I mean. It's in the face—you can always tell. I agree with you really—'tis better for us to be away from here at such a bad time. It *is* a bad time, isn't it?" Her eyes, between the dozens of wrinkles, searched my face. "You think it's going badly for my master, don't you?"

"Yes." There seemed no reason not to be blunt.

"Well, now," she said thoughtfully, "I've always thought you'd a right to know everything. I mean, I've thought so since we decided to turn to you. I'm not easy in my mind."

"What is it?" I said patiently. I feared more revelations. Either it would be something insinuatingly mendicant, but trivial, like the number of holes in the child's garments, or it would be some new blow. Good heavens . . . *more* children, perhaps?

"I want to tell you. Melissa don't. So I'm breaking a bond, in a way, though I never did swear real solemn—and she just sort of took it for granted. But now everything's such a puzzle, and nothing don't make much sense, but you can't help wondering if there isn't sense somewhere. Melissa don't think about things, but I do. Sometimes you take a bundle of wool on the spindle and you tease it and pull it but nary a proper thread will come—then, on a sudden, it comes, regular, and keeps going. That's like life, that is."

"Quite so," I said dryly. "I admire your philosophy." (But one should never use irony on inferiors and women.) "What do you want to say?"

"If I tell you, sir, you won't tell the mistress I've told you?"

"No," I said curtly. "I'm used to keeping secrets by now." I said this with a very manly air—and then blushed. Hadn't I told all my secrets to Aristotle?

"True," she said cheerfully. "A gentleman knows how to manage things. But, sir, you must listen now and let me tell my tale my own way."

"Certainly," I said. The wind seemed colder, and the water grayer; some seabirds made derisive noises. I felt no inclination to listen to a long tale. If Homer, revived, had risen before me on that desolate strand and had said brightly, "I've got a new epic!" I should have said, "Can't we go indoors to hear it?" and would then have added, "Won't tomorrow do?" But I had to remain, marching along the beach, listening to this croaking bundle, who punctuated her utterances by hawking and spitting. There were some good reasons for listening to her in the open air.

She blew her nose into the wind, and began.

"You don't know—the gods willing, you never will know, —what the siege of Thebes was like. I wonder to be still alive, I do. Eight years ago it was, but I remember it like last week —wish I didn't. I can remember," she added, "the omens that came before, when everyone was struck with dread— we were like people living in a dream. There was a spider's web appeared in the temple of Demeter—a great big thing, the size of a cloak, shining like a rainbow, all beautiful and unnatural. Everyone went to see it—and then the augurs said that it was a sign that the gods had departed from the city. And at Dirke a strange ripple kept running along the surface of the water—a wave the color of blood. They said it signified slaughter. Well, the slaughter came soon enough, once Alexander's men breached the walls. It was all yelling, and confusion, and some of ours killing their own by mistake. We ran out of the city as soon as we could, and just kept going—Melissa's parents and the child and I—but what a run! Twisting and turning and stumbling, and our mouths full of the taste of terror. What sights! Heaps of corpses at the street corners and in the lanes outside the city. Melissa's mother lagged behind, after a time, and she was taken. I saw her killed, sir. I kept the child's face covered. Melissa never knew how her mother died, nor that I saw it. That's one secret that I *have* kept. But I think Melissa always sensed that her poor little mother's death was very terrible. Oh ye gods, to be women!—and not to have revenge!" She cleared her throat and spat hard onto the sand.

"Melissa saw enough sights on that journey to turn her blood cold forever. The gods be thanked that she got out alive and free—children smaller than her were killed, or were herded away and sold as slaves, some crying for their mothers, and some for their mother's milk. Melissa wasn't twelve then. She kept her life, and her freedom, and her health and her virginity—oh, it's true we were blessed!—but even keeping these things doesn't mean you stay as you were before. The reason I'm telling you all this is that it's made her very fearful. Almost until her marriage she kept having nightmares. She's Athenian by rights, but she's not the same as a nice Athenian young lady would be who hadn't known all that. She frightens easier than some would do. Her husband makes her feel braver, and she feels easier when I'm around. She needs me—we mustn't be separated, at least not until she can live with her husband at ease and proper—and I pray I'll be allowed to stay with her till I die. Pray, sir, that you never see the fall of a city the gods have forsaken!"

"So I do," I said, not unsympathetically.

"Melissa, as I said, was nigh twelve then, and nearly as lovely as she is now. She got her growth early, too. You know about her first meeting with Philemon—but there was someone else she met during that flight. His name—" she looked at me— "was Boutades."

"Oh?"

"Yes. He was one of the citizens who were supposed to look into the affairs of those from Thebes who sought refuge in Athens. He saw Melissa, unveiled with her hair down, on her first entry into the city. I remember him, too—his big face, so well fed. I thought, 'You've never seen any danger, that's clear!' He was greatly taken with her, poor child, and asked her to be his mistress—in rather coarse terms. Such things may happen to the most virtuous in time of war, when good women are homeless. The poor girl cried and veiled herself, and her father was there and soon told him no. Her father was clever enough to mislead Boutades about the place they were going to live in, so he couldn't find her. Then she stayed at her cousin's, and all came about as we told you before. *But* —this man Boutades—what is really extraordinary—never forgot her, or so he said when he found her again. He did find her again, years later, after the marriage, when Philemon was in exile and the child had been born. He seemed besotted. Funny, he was rich enough to buy love at any house of Aphrodite or to keep half a dozen women if that was his fancy. Sometimes I've wondered if he were quite right in his head. However, men getting on in years sometimes turn quite childish, insisting on one toy and nothing else will do. The oddest thing of all is that he took to the boy child as much as to Melissa herself—though commonly men don't like babies, and if you want to trap a man's love you'd best keep anything in swaddling clothes out of sight. He offered her— that position—again. *And* he said he'd adopt the child, properly and legally. He hung over the boy like an old grandmother, or a new father. Nay, when she put him off and explained about her marriage, he said he'd adopt Philemon as well, and give father and baby son a place in his will. He said all this in secret, you understand. We had to meet in a little deserted hut, and when he talked business he made me go outside, but I listened through the door. There wasn't anything improper went on—and he was old and fat, so Melissa could have run away, easy, if there'd been trouble. Nothing wrong happened, I do assure you," looking into my frowning face, "only he made the offer like I say. Made it twice, in fact."

"Oh, indeed? And was Melissa pleased?"

"Don't take it so, sir. Of course she said no. But the second time she said it more timidly. That was in the middle of last summer, and she was very hard pressed and low in her spirits. Philemon hadn't been back for a while, and, what was worst of all, we heard a rumor that Philemon was dead. Do not be harsh with her in your mind. Remember she is but a woman, and her duty and desire told her to bring up her child in good health and good circumstances."

"I'm glad to hear Melissa is a good mother," I interjected ironically.

"Consider, sir," reproachfully, "consider her distress, her hardship. A young wife—perhaps a young widow, with a child, and no one to turn to. She could not go to your family, as she was unacknowledged and if you too thought Philemon was dead you could easy turn her away. Poor my lady! She begins to weep and have those fearful dreams again, many nights. Remember, I have said she feels fear more than most. Thebes gone—mother killed—father dead—husband banished and now mayhap dead likewise.

"They—she and Boutades, I mean—met again for a third time, and this time he made a written agreement, on tablets, which he gave to her. He promised he would marry her when his wife died, if Melissa was a widow, and even said she needn't sleep with him as long as she gave herself to no other (save her husband if he returned) and he might adopt her husband *and* the boy and look after her. Not many men would be so generous. She would probably have assented, but then your cousin came—her husband—not dead at all, thank the gods. So she didn't need to take up the offer. And then you know Boutades was killed, so she couldn't take it if she wanted to."

"Great Athena!" I said blankly. "Did she tell anyone of this —this plan?"

"Of course not. It was a very secret idea. And he—Boutades, you know—said *nobody* must know until it was all legally settled. No one. Of course she wouldn't breathe a word to a soul. She told me particularly not to tell you, for you might cast us off."

"Where," I said hoarsely, "are these tablets? And what exactly is on them?"

Her eyes glazed over, like a lizard's.

"Oh, as to that, sir, who could say? She's destroyed them now, most like. I haven't laid eyes on them since the summer. And as for what was on them—I only know what I've told you. You must know, your honor, I can't read."

"Why did you tell me all this?"

"Because I thought you ought to know, sir. And besides ... you're a citizen ... I was sure you'd know if—was anything left in Boutades' cash-box for her and the child? When he died—in his will?"

"No. Certainly not." I couldn't decide if this old woman was a cunning creature or an imbecile.

"Well, but after all that? He meant to adopt the child at least—maybe that was what he mainly wanted. Wouldn't the child have a claim of some kind? Or Philemon? It wouldn't be right for Melissa to claim aught, the wife of another man and all, but what about young Lykias? Could we not press the matter—in years to come, anyway?"

"I doubt it very much indeed," I said angrily. This woman was too absurd. "He left no such record. Even if your tablets could be produced, they'd be thrown out of court and Melissa's whole family would be tainted. Athenians don't care for freaks of that kind with a citizen's property. Had the child been legally adopted, he would have a claim. This hole-and-corner affair gives him nothing. Any sensible man will tell you the same. Keep it dark and try to forget it."

"Well, you know best, sir," she said dubiously. "I can easy promise to say nothing to anybody else about it, if that's what you're worried about. Now—I have kept you a great while, and should return home. My lady will be worried. Our gracious thanks for the gift. When do you want to arrange about our going?"

I hastily made arrangements to meet her again to tell her

114

about the final plan; she calmly agreed to everything. I let her make her way up the beach and slowly followed. As I turned into Peiraeus, thinking so deeply I was scarce aware of what was around me, I was jerked awake by an unpleasant sight. I saw in front of me an Athenian slave whom I knew —a gangling ill-favored fellow with a face like a young bull's. He was one of Arkhimenos' slaves—I had often seen him. This fellow was gazing after the old woman. I thought he saw me and, seeing me, turned away. Had he seen us together? Of course, he could have been in Peiraeus on quite ordinary business, I told myself, and perhaps my unpleasant sensations merely arose from the fact that I disliked any reminder of Arkhimenos' existence.

I had little room for new unpleasant thoughts—I had to accommodate so many recently. Was the woman telling the truth? Or were she and Melissa concocting some gigantic lie for their own purposes? In any case, the old creature was hardly stupid. She must know that she had just given me a horrible gift. I had always known that Philemon could have no motive for murdering Boutades—or, at least, I had thought I'd known. Now—well. The woman Nousia must realize she had just supplied me with a motive for Philemon —one of the oldest motives of all. Murder from jealousy. Revenge for the seduction of his wife.

I determined on one thing. This motive must at all costs be concealed. Boutades' kin must never know of it—that would ensure the triumph of their case. I would fight on, and deceive everybody. If the women wanted to make me their milch cow, let it be so. I would pay them. I would get them away, I swore by Hades, if it were at all possible. And I would conceal—I *must* conceal—all of this from Aristotle, while ruthlessly accepting the assistance he was willing to provide. I *couldn't* tell him this.

There was that damning fragment of pottery with the incriminating letter upon it—perhaps it did come from something belonging to my cousin. Perhaps it was real evidence of a dreadful truth. How I hoped Aristotle would not use it against us. I could hardly hope his sharp eyes had not read

115

the inscribed character as I had. But perhaps he still felt, reasonably, that there was no necessary connection between a pot with the first letter of Philemon's name on it and the murder. I could not tell him the latest news. Once he knew that Philemon had such a strong motive, he might turn against us, offering evidence to the other side. I couldn't let that happen. I could not afford even to let him withdraw from supporting my case—when I needed his help to spirit the women away to Makedonia, and to supply refuge for them there. I would be a liar. I would cheat my best friend. What worth was all that talk in the Akademeia and Lykeion about Justice and Virtue? Just talk. I had one clear duty—to my cousin—and all the philosophers could whistle for my virtue. If in doing what I had to do I became a wicked man, so be it.

XI

Fire and Darkness

With my new iniquity hardening upon me like drying clay, I went to see Aristotle. Swallowing my guilt, I begged that the women and the child should be sent to Makedonia sooner than we had first designed. Aristotle said it might be possible—the military envoys who were going from Athens to Pella, and who had consented to act as escort to the family, might be able to set out on the third day rather than the fifth. Aristotle assured me that two trusty Makedonian servants who were returning to Stageira would take care of the women and child. He had told everyone concerned that the expected travelers were relatives of his sister's husband who needed to return home; the woman's husband had died in the wars. The travelers would be well provided for; the journey ought not to be too dangerous. His cheerful plans did nothing to lessen my guilt.

The party was to set off at dawn on the third day from Aristotle's house. I was to meet Melissa and Nousia at an agreed point in Peiraeus—for instance, some abandoned hut not too far from their dwelling. (I blushed, remembering how recently I had heard of meetings in an abandoned hut.) If I met them after midnight and conducted them to Aristotle's house, they could depart quietly while I returned to rest in my own bed.

Aristotle was pleased with his organization of things. "I always claim," he said complacently, "that the philosopher is not the least, but the most practical of men." He was also extremely conversational about the dinner party at the house of Kleiophoros—he wanted to tell me who was there, what they drank, what they talked about.

"They say the tombstone for Boutades is nearly completed," he said. "It's supposed to be very fine, and certainly large. I must have a look at it. There was a good deal said too about the play for the Dionysia. A great spectacle. The mask-makers are already at work. The music is to be very impressive; I hope it won't deafen us. But the actor Timosthenes has a great cold, and does nothing but swallow honey and camomile and indulge in fears that he may lose his voice and never get it back again."

"It's months before the play," I said absently, thinking to myself: 'But it isn't many weeks before the trial.' I wondered how I could go on like this—so full of anxiety, so full of deception.

"The poet has already been given a present by Polygnotos. Some people are already quoting the play. Parts were recited to me last night—for instance:

> 'Oh, Kheiron, less than man and more than man,
> Thy wisdom makes the downcast mind arise.
> How pleasant education, like the showers,
> Drops richness on the dry and drooping spirit,
> Making that teem and bear like fruitful spring.'

117

I don't think much of this poetry. A centaur isn't a shower of rain—and spring isn't *fruit*ful. What do you think of it?"

"I'm not really a judge," I said with bored modesty.

"Nonsense. But you should read more poetry, Stephanos. It seems to me that you have a drooping heart which needs a fruitful spring."

"I'm quite well," I said politely. "I shall feel happier, of course, when these people are safely on their way."

"Quite so. But you can't make it happen any faster. Life goes on. Do you know there is a good deal of speculation about the commemoration of this great production? They wonder whether Polygnotos will have a special vase made, with pictures of scenes from the play on it, and who could produce such a piece of art now. Kleiophoros reminded me of the beautiful krater that Boutades' father—*the* important Boutades, even more influential than his son—had made in remembrance of *his* achievement as khoregos. Have you ever seen it?"

"No," I said shortly. I wanted to leave Aristotle, but here he was insisting upon chattering about plays and vases—in indelicate connection with a name I hated to hear.

"It is evidently a beautiful object from the play you know. It was the play of Herakles and Laomedon. It shows the poet Demetrios and the lyre-player Kharinos, and in the center Pronomos the flute-player. Around them are the satyr-actors, with the great satyr, wearing leopard skin. They say each figure is lovely—Herakles with the lion's head, and Laomedon and Hesione. I must see this krater—the thought makes my mouth water. I suppose Polygnotos will have to be content with something much simpler. I wish I had been on visiting terms with Boutades. Are you listening, Stephanos? Have you ever seen this vase?"

"No," I said. "I wasn't on visiting terms with Boutades either. Nor am I likely to be so with Polygnotos," I added bitterly.

"Are you sure you haven't seen it?" he pressed me. "Would you remember?"

"Yes, I'm sure," I said impatiently. "Of course I'd remember a painting like that. Theosophoros has something a bit like it, which I did see once—at least, it had six satyrs on it, with furry tails, dancing in a grove."

"Not the same at all," Aristotle said briskly. "I just thought that I should like another opinion on it, if that were possible. Kleiophoros is somewhat undiscriminating in his praise. Still, it is undeniable that he is developing in taste. We all agreed that the new art is much inferior to the old. It is good to have one's judgment confirmed by such an authority on matters of art as the good citizen Kleiophoros, is it not? He has, however, no prejudice against the new furniture—his home is full of it. Very rich. Gives me the backache."

How true it is that we can easily become irritated with those whom we have injured. It is difficult to gossip pleasantly with a man whom you are deceiving heartlessly—at least, when you are new to deception. I withdrew as soon as I could. Next day I met Nousia and gave her the message, leaving her to manage the details of their removal from the house. We were to meet at a certain deserted hut—perhaps a goat-shed—which she pointed out to me. I wondered if that were the place Melissa had met Boutades. After that, there seemed nothing to do but wait.

The eventful night came. I had planned to have some sleep before departing, but I could take no rest. I set off much earlier than I had intended; we were not to meet until the moon had set, but I persuaded myself that it would be better to be on my way.

When I came to Peiraeus the moon was still visible. It was very cold. A few falling leaves sifted through the darkness and brushed against my face. All the houses in the back streets seemed quiet and shut; my own footfalls seemed loud. Once a few drunken revelers disturbed the dark peace. I easily avoided them, and all was silence again.

I should, of course, have gone to the hut, to wait there, as planned. My restlessness, which gripped me like the shivering of fever, made the idea of waiting very painful. I suddenly wanted to see if I could find the dwelling house and hurry the women on—it seemed as if any time not spent in bustle and hurry was wasted. We had agreed that it would be better not to risk our being seen together in Peiraeus, but this scheme of caution now appeared ridiculous. Who would see us in this dark and silent town? In my folly I decided to try to find the house—blessed be the gods that it was so, and blessed too is the rashness that is sometimes not folly, but the work of the gods through us.

Just as I was coming to the house, pleased to find I was at the right place, I heard a noise—a sound of footfalls, of steps not mine. I stopped and then moved forward hastily. At the same time I saw spheres of light wavering confusedly about the house I sought, illuminating it suddenly, as if three or four small red suns had risen about it. The very cracks in the plaster were visible, as clearly as if it were daylight. The strange dancing lights moved again.

There was the rush as of a falling star, and a crackling noise. The roof showed a leap of flame like an oil lamp. Cries arose from within the house. I rushed forward and collided with a bulky object which—it took me a moment to realize—was a man. He struggled viciously. Before I set out on the lonely road I had secretly armed myself with a small dagger; I brought it out, quickly if clumsily, and slashed my opponent on the arm. My unknown enemy darted into the dark.

I rushed into the house. It was full of smoke, and on the floor was one of the balls of fire, crackling. As I came to it, I saw that it was a torch of pine and tow. I grasped the remaining handle and flung it out into the street.

"Oh, sir!" There was Nousia, clutching the table and coughing in the smoke. There too was Melissa, pale as the moon, clutching her little boy in her arms. "Come!" I said. Once I had thrown out the fiery ball, Nousia recovered her senses, and she was busily grabbing things up in a hurry—baskets and bundles. Melissa began to do the same, more weakly, and we were bumping into each other in the smoke. It was not too dark—alas, it was growing brighter overhead where the first torch was burning through the thatch. And the window patching had also caught fire, so the window seemed to be spurting odd sunshine.

"My child!" said Melissa and thrust the squirming infant into my arms. She hadn't seen the dagger still in my hand. "Come on!" I said in a kind of whispered scream. The roof was made only of dry seaweed and poor straw, and burning showers began to fall about us. Another torch came through the window. Melissa, to my surprise more quick-witted and quick-acting than I would have expected, imitated my actions and hurled this missile outside. She was not, however, so fortunate as I—her dress caught fire, and Nousia, coughing and tremulous, beat upon it with a cloth.

"Now!" I cried. We could hardly breathe clearly, despite the open door—and the open window, through which someone unknown was firing at us.

We all three rushed to the door at once, Melissa's garment still smoldering and Nousia beating at it as they ran, her skinny arm like a flail. I felt relieved when we came into the street, where at least there was air to breathe and the roof would not fall upon us. But Melissa abruptly turned and darted back into the house. I was certain that she had gone demented, and recalled a tale my mother once had told me, of a man who, when his house caught fire, insisted on returning to the burning building and hid under his bed, where he was burned to a crisp. I thrust the child upon Nousia, much as Melissa had given him to me, and ran back into the house —to see Melissa struggling toward me triumphantly with the Penelope curtain in her arms. She must have torn it from its moorings in the twinkling of an eye. "Mustn't forget this," she said stupidly. I pushed her out of the door.

Then we were all in the street again, jumping over the cast-off torches and running. Melissa seized her child and carried it away, while Nousia struggled with the bundles. We panted and stumbled, our lungs unsettled by smoke, and our legs weak under us. Nousia was soon fairly recovered, and made good progress; I took the child again from its mother, to assist her, so even I went slowly. I looked at Melissa anxiously; her breath came in gasps, and I feared she was ill. Like people in a bad but comic dream, we continued to pound slowly, ridiculously, toward our destination, through the dark streets. The moon had not yet quite set.

Suddenly there was a mocking laugh beside me, and a torch wavered, casting red light and blotting out the pale moon. I gave the child to Melissa again. "Run!" I cried to the women. Then I turned to face my assailant. I was nearly blinded by the light, and his face was in darkness and waving shadows. Perhaps he had blackened his face with soot to make himself invisible. I knew I myself was horribly visible.

"Oh, Stephanos!" a voice whispered softly.

"Who is that?" I cried, but the voice answered nothing. A dog started to howl from somewhere nearby.

Another dark shape with a torch loomed up on my left side. I felt somehow that this enemy on my left was the one I had already wounded. Maddened by rage, I rushed at him again. I slashed with my dagger, aiming for the darkness below the torch to find the arm that held it—and I was rewarded. The torch fell (singeing my hair a little). I jumped over the fire and attacked again; I knew my dagger struck flesh. The assailant on my right moved no closer, and this gave me courage; if he refused to assist his companion, then he was not very brave. I turned and ran toward that torch, baring my teeth and uttering angry noises—not words, just noises, as dogs do. The torch bobbed away. I ran the more eagerly, and soon the sound of heavy rapid footfalls told me that this foe was on the run. I hastened after him, with my dagger in my hand. The torch-bearer whom I had wounded at least twice started to follow me, but I could soon hear his steps falter and then cease. Some part of my mind took note of what my ears were telling me—that the man who was wounded was running in bare feet, whereas the man in front of me was wearing sandals. Both must have been wearing very dark clothes. I hunted fiercely after the running enemy in sandals—he once the pursuer, now the pursued. He had soon cast aside the torch, and we now ran through dark alleyways without benefit of light. The moon set, and Peiraeus was as dark as the inside of a pot.

Once my enemy tried to trap me by hiding between two houses and waiting for me to pass so he could jump out at me. Fortunately my ears told me this without my thinking about it. I crept round the corner upon him and turned so abruptly that he was almost taken; he was certainly surprised—I heard his high gasp as I nearly touched him. Evidently his hearing was not as good as mine. He was off again—and so was I. Peiraeus is a ridiculous place for a race, especially at night. I slipped once in a patch of dung, and kept bumping into things. So too did he. We must have looked like two children playing a game.

I cursed myself for not being able to catch him. My dagger itched to be at its target. But I was partly undone by having breathed smoke. I was also aware that I ought to go back and look to the safety of the women and the child. Once I was certain that this enemy was now harmless, trying only to get away, I forced myself to drop out of the game, hoping he would not realize for some time that I had gone. I liked to think of him running still, pursued only by empty air.

Once the excitement of the chase was gone, however, my own condition was not enviable. I was breathing very heavily, and my legs felt like old rags. I was also lost.

I must have wasted more than half an hour, rambling and stumbling and losing myself in benighted winding lanes and dead ends, before I came to the hut. I whispered cautiously, "Nousia!" No sound except the sighing wind. I gave a low call again, and went into the hut. It felt completely empty, and no one answered me. It suddenly came to me that Philemon's wife and child (and the old woman too, of course) had been intercepted and killed—while in my care, too. Where were their bodies? They might be anywhere.

Suddenly, a man's voice said "Sir?" in a low tone; someone had come out from behind the hut.

"O Zeus, not again!" I muttered, and weakly grasped my dagger.

123

"Sir? Is this Aristotle's friend? Is that Stephanos, son of Nikiarkhos?"

"Yes. Who are you?"

"Oh, sir, I thought you'd never come. I'm Aristotle's slave. I've been waiting for you for over an hour. My master sent two of us to help you—in case of trouble."

"Well, there's trouble enough," I said. "I'm nearly exhausted—I've fought two men—and, for the sake of Zeus, do you know anything about the women?"

I expected him to say, "What women? Where?" or something equally soothing. I was astonished when he replied calmly, "Oh, yes, they're all right. The other—my fellow, Autilos—has gone on ahead with them."

"Where have they gone?" I said, almost angrily. I felt petulant, like a child, annoyed that they had not waited for me.

"Why, sir, as I told you. To our house. The master said to bring them home."

"O great Athena!" I muttered blankly, partly in thanks and partly in dismay. Here was Aristotle, from whom I was keeping such a secret, helping in my enterprise far beyond expectation—as he certainly would not, if he knew.

"Well," the slave replied, surprised, "they're his own kin, aren't they? Or his wife's or something? And, no matter how anxious they may be to be getting on in their travels, they won't go tonight—or this morning, rather. You should see the girl! Worn out. There's been some sort of fire. You come back with me now and you'll see how things are."

The slave solicitously took me under the elbow, and we made our way back to Athens, with me leaning on him and stumbling along. I had had enough sense to hide away my dagger. Anyone seeing us on the last couple of miles would have thought I was a drunkard being seen home from a revel.

By the time I arrived at the house, there was a promise of dawn in the pallid east.

"I must see Aristotle," I said, as if I'd come on a social call.

"The master has not yet arisen. Have a wash!" said the

slave, with more urgency than politeness. I hoped he hadn't seen any bloodstains. But when he took me in and washed me, I could see nothing worse on my hands than dirt. I washed my hair vigorously to get rid of the smell of burning. My brains began to stir again as the water cooled my head.

I was moderately presentable by the time I saw Aristotle. The slave had even lent me one of his master's clean khitons. The victim of my treachery invited me to breakfast with him; over a stoup of warming wine and some bread we conversed. Aristotle seemed not at all put out by the upheaval in his domestic arrangements.

I told him about the fire, and the fighting with the invisible men, and the pursuit in the dark, while he listened attentively. He told me not to be anxious about the young woman; Pythias had described her condition to him, and he had prescribed for her. Melissa was, it appeared, fatigued rather than greatly hurt.

"The little boy is in good health," he continued. "I have seen him. A splendid infant. My little daughter will entertain him with her toys. And the old woman is surprisingly well, too—and tries to take care of the child and her mistress, but she has been ordered to sleep. They will not, however, be fit to travel today. By the greatest luck, the journey of Antipater's envoys is slightly delayed as well. So, if the gods are willing, the party shall set out in two days' time. I have sent the cart away from the courtyard, so as not to attract undue attention. All is well here. For the sake of all of us, Stephanos, go back to your home and take some sleep."

Aristotle looked at me thoughtfully. "Your courage last night deserves praise. But do not tempt the Fates. Do not visit me while the women and child are still here. Avoid going out after dusk, and keep from obscure lanes and waste ground. I would rather you stayed unharmed."

I departed. Before I reached my house, the momentary wakefulness of dawn had vanished, and my very knees sank from tiredness. I groped my way to my bed, and fell into a sleep as deep and dark as Lethe.

XII

Swords and Stones

Aristotle had warned me to keep away from his home while his "relatives" were there. I fretted very much at this, although I had no desire to see the women—and, besides, it would not have been at all proper for me to see those who were (ostensibly) another man's female relative and her child and slave, guests in the women's quarters of his home. But I constantly wondered what was happening. I sweated lest Aunt Eudoxia could read behind my forehead. If she got wind of the matter, I could picture her rushing to Melissa, claiming her as a daughter-in-law and bringing her grandchild home, thus ratifying the most dubious marriage and bringing dangers on all our heads.

At last on the third day, in response to a cryptic message sent from Aristotle, I met him by daylight in a grove by the Lykeion when the students were gone. He spoke in a low tone, pacing up and down as he loved to do.

"They are gone," he said. "They went off at dawn, in the manner arranged."

"I am sorry," I said truthfully, "that these troubles of mine intruded into your home."

"No trouble," said he. "The child was much admired by everyone. He even called me 'Papa'—he seems to be somewhat lacking in discrimination. My wife and little Pythias enjoyed playing with him." He sighed. "It is sad that we have no sons. I've been given all gifts save that one." He gazed into the distance.

I felt this was a dangerous topic. I might say, "Why don't you adopt a son?" I feared I might stupidly find myself adding, "I know of a case which would surprise you. . . ."

Aristotle roused himself. "From what Pythias told me of the young woman, it seemed quite safe for her to travel. There were no signs of fever, nor yet of miscarrying. Pythias talked with her, and did not think badly of her. She says the young woman is well bred and modest. A woman's opinion of another woman is worth having. My wife also says that the old Nousia watches over her mistress like sixty parents." He chuckled. "I gather Nousia was not greatly beloved by the female slaves. At first they pitied her as a poor creature, but she soon put that right. She scolded in all directions, and treated the modest elegance of our house and its arrangements with the condescension of one who is accustomed to households of the highest nobility!"

"I believe you," I said feelingly. "She is the most dreadful old hag."

"Do you know, I think Pythias quite liked her. She was quite struck by the woman's loyalty to her mistress. And do not forget how well the old woman managed on that dreadful night. She can evidently cease her clacking at the right time."

"That is so," I assented. My own valiant efforts on that occasion had seemed daily less impressive. No Herakles, I had not destroyed my enemy, but had spent my time running about dark streets.

Aristotle continued, without noticing my mood. "Pythias says they were both very proud. We dressed them in Makedonian style. Melissa would accept clothes and the loan of a fur rug only on the plea that they were necessary for their safety and the baby's well-being. But they wouldn't accept anything fine—Pythias says they were quick to resent any imputation that their own possessions were not perfectly adequate. That speaks well for them—it is not mendicant behavior. So I think that they were not wittingly trying to extort anything from you dishonestly. Anyway, Pythias says she took the opportunity while Melissa slept and Nousia watched her mistress to go through their possessions and to add a few things which they will want upon the road. My wife also employed herself in sewing and mending—which she much enjoys. She sews and weaves like the princess she is. A real Penelope! That reminds me—you mentioned a curtain with a pattern of Penelope upon it. Pythias mentioned it too —it had been badly burned in two places and the edges were frayed. She cleaned and mended it—in private, so as not to hurt the women's feelings. It was a good piece of stuff, she said, so they must have been in a house of some quality at one time." He laughed. "You might say we had three Penelopes in the house: the one on the tapestry; the fair-haired woman with her son, waiting for her absent husband—and my dark-haired comely Pythias, sewing and weaving. I am but a poor Odysseus myself—though I have traveled in my time. Your cousin seems more the part. But he had better not return."

I said hastily, "Odysseus had no one to whom he owed a debt of gratitude as I do to you—except Mentor, of course, and there I acknowledge the resemblance. But I shall repay you for the things you have given my cousin's wife, since I must call her so. Philemon will repay me, of course, so all will be proper."

He looked distressed. "My foolish tongue! A few poor things that we do not need and were glad to give. I wished only to bring to your attention the fact that the women's behavior is not beggar-like. There were no whining thanks, no hints, and they did not accept quite half of what they were offered. For things lent I cannot possibly take recompense, and the things given were, I am ashamed to say, old and not of value. But give me two drakhmai if you wish, whenever you will, and we will say no more of it. Do you know that I am to dine with Polygnotos two nights hence?"

At this change of subject I said, "Oh?" without surprise. What Telemon had said was true. Polygnotos was becoming a man of great importance in Athens, and naturally he would wish to be well with the Makedonian philosopher, the friend of Antipater.

"Yes. I am honored. You see, at present I go into society. Hippomenes and Laios have spoken to me most favorably about Polygnotos."

I sighed. Hippomenes and Laios were among the friends

and agents of Antipater, strong supporters of Alexander. Certainly Polygnotos was well seen by the very highest in authority.

"They were saying," Aristotle added, "that they met Polygnotos by chance just outside Korinthos two months ago, and traveled back with him. They thought his views on business matters most sound, and were much impressed by his work as khoregos. They too will be at this dinner—quite a high gathering."

"I hope you enjoy the evening," I said politely. "I shall send the money for the women's clothes soon. And I should be deeply obliged if you would send me any information you may receive about their progress."

That day I said nothing to Aristotle about Philemon's trial. How could I ask for more assistance and advice when I had been taking so much, with both hands and without scruple? I might speak haughtily about repaying him for a few garments—how could I repay the astounding hospitality to dubious strangers? If the women were not dishonest, I certainly was.

I was uneasily conscious that the third prodikasia was coming closer and closer and I had nothing prepared in my mind. I had no idea what I would say, or even what the other side might bring against us. The smoke I had breathed in the house in Peiraeus seemed to have affected my mind—it was thick and cloudy.

Three days after the departure of Melissa and her child I was in the agora, endeavoring to appear like a confident citizen without cares. It was but little pleasure to me; few indeed now were those who deigned to say so much as "Good day." It was a relief to find something to watch or listen to. I harkened attentively to a rhetor making a speech about the grain trade, paused at a forge to watch a smith beating bronze. When the herald who made the proclamations of the day came into the agora, I gladly gave him my attention. I heard the usual trivial things: descriptions of lost animals, an account of two stolen jars of wine. My attention wandered—

and then I was astonished to hear the following announcement:

> "Hear ye all! Men of Athens, hear ye! By authority of Antipater and permission of the Basileus, Aristotle the philosopher proclaims that he wishes to buy or to borrow examples of weapons. Weapons of war, and armor, old and new, Athenian and foreign. For the purpose of studying instruments of war, and thus aiding our armies in the East. Weapons and armor to be taken to Aristotle's home. A sum of money will be offered to those wishing to sell, price depending on the value. Hear ye!"

I thought I had imagined this strange proclamation, but the herald went through it again. A buzz of comment arose from high citizens and the vulgar alike. I caught odd remarks:

"A sword's a sword—what is there to examine in that?"

"Well, I suppose these philosophers have to prove they are good for something."

"Aristotle will now make war in his study."

"He can have my wife for a sum of money—now, she's an offensive weapon!"

As I went from the agora, I was startled to see that long loutish slave of Arkhimenos' standing by a chestnut-seller's stall on the opposite corner. I did not think he was noticing me. His torso and arms were almost completely hidden by his brown homespun tunic, but a gesture caught my eye. It was his *left* hand which shot out to receive the chestnuts. Then I saw that his right hand and wrist were swathed in cloth bound on with leather. The fellow held that arm stiffly. I thought of my dagger.

It was not my little bronze dagger which I brought as an offering to Aristotle's house that afternoon. I disliked the idea of walking abroad without having it (now clean again) secreted about my person, although an Athenian should not go armed in the city. I had decided to take a weapon of some sort to the philosopher's home, for the errand would provide me with an excuse for visiting him without exciting comment. I was also consumed with curiosity about this strange new whim of his. So I took an old sword which had first belonged to my grandfather—not a very good sword, being nicked on the edge.

When I came to the philosopher's house, the courtyard was very crowded, and busy with comers and goers. There were some well-born citizens among them, but for the most part these were common folk. The slave at the gate had just turned out some low fellow, a brawler. This fellow was angrily jumping up against the wall and beating it, crying, "Give me back my pike! May you rot in Hades! Give it back!"

"Not until you're cool, sir," said the slave smoothly, pushing me in. He wiped his hair from his brow. "That's the second fight we've had this afternoon," he remarked to me wearily. "It really doesn't do to invite all these vulgar persons with weapons to the house. Why aren't they in the army?"

I resented his remarks. He was a Makedonian slave and I could see he regarded the lower classes of the Athenians as beneath him. I passed in haughtily, sword girt about my waist, and joined the waiting crew.

We looked like some insane army, raised by a beggared king. No two were dressed or weaponed quite alike. Here was a man with a great antique leather shield and no sword —there was one with an old bent sword and no shield or body armor. A hulking young yellow-haired knave had a dainty dagger, and a dwarfish frail graybeard carried an old Persian sword of the largest size. A thin-headed little fellow wore an old helmet shaped like a pot of metal, which kept slipping down and obscuring his face.

There was some animated talk about the weapons and their history, rather like parodies of passages in the *Iliad*. Some folk I thought were indulging themselves in fiction, bragging of the great battles they or their ancestors had been engaged in, making themselves out to be members of very important families indeed. A few known scapegraces, scourings of the worst part of the city or of Peiraeus—men whose very mothers would have hooted like hoopoes if they had

131

ever claimed so much as a father, let alone a family—boasted of their grandfathers' greatness, or explained in implausible detail that someone too eminent to be named had given them the prize they bore as a reward of valor. Some ill dressed and frankly ill-suited to the price of the weapon they carried, explained when pressed how they had "just happened to find" such a thing.

The door opened and Aristotle emerged in company with Eutikleides. The philosopher was speaking earnestly to this citizen.

"Most honored, O Eutikleides. It is indeed a privilege." Aristotle's glance fell upon the rest of us distantly. "This good citizen," he explained to us all at large, "has offered to me for my examination the arms and armor which his great-great-grandfather bore in the battle of Plataiai. What objects of veneration! It is a most patriotic cause to which you, O Eutikleides, contribute. Yes, sir, I understand that this is a loan— who would part with such honored heirlooms? Many thanks to you and to your family; your spirit sets a civic example, and commends itself to Alexander."

The little crowd listened patiently, as men must when philosophers speak to great citizens. This was a public speech of thanks; even to me it seemed stuffy. Eutikleides' face was relaxed and pleased; he seemed to be washing himself in the public praise. He left, almost beaming, in company with a thin-faced country fellow with a limp, to whom he offered his arm with condescending affability. He seemed a much pleasanter Eutikleides than the one I had come to know at the prodikasiai; I could even see why some men liked him. He was strong, he had wealth, he could be approached in the formal ways which simplify the complexities of social intercourse. He could be generous to those who respected him— like the little man he now had in tow. It struck me, watching him, that, as some bodies need a special diet in order to flourish, so it is with some minds. Eutikleides was one of those who flourish on success, on praise. All men like these things, but some men can be their better selves only while these constantly supply nourishment. I admired Eutikleides more than before, and thought that I would not like to see him when he was offered failure in his dish.

Aristotle took no particular notice of me, beyond asking another citizen and myself if we would mind waiting for a short while. He saw some of the poorer folk first: he saw each man alone, within the house, for a minute or two. I thought it was perhaps to spare their blushes when they were offered the sum of money—but such delicacy seemed unnecessary. The conversation and chaffing went on among those waiting in the courtyard.

"Why don't you join the wars, grandfather?" to the diminutive gray-haired ancient. "You're of age!"

"Hey, Simonides, cast away that bent small sword! Get yourself a big long lance—and then see whether your girl will have you!"

"What's this Makedonian going to do to the things, then?"

"Some say," said a nervous ill-clad man, probably a freedman, "that he's going to kill a slave a day—one with each of the weapons—until he's tried them all and sees which kills best."

"Roasted eggs of Leda! No! He makes each one who brings him a mortal tool—like that there old javelin like of what you're carrying—he makes him kill a man with the weapon he's brought. And if he can't do it fast enough, the philosopher knows how to encourage him. That's called raising troops."

The puny freedman blanched. I saw that the slave who kept the gate was giggling behind his hands.

Eventually the group thinned. The other citizen was seen first, and then I entered with my ancestral sword.

Aristotle's room was a sight. It looked like an armory kept by a drunken housewife. Heaps of lances, pikes and javelins lay about on the floor like unfaggoted branches. There were swords and daggers everywhere. An old helmet stood upside down on a table, like a strange bowl. I nearly sat on a villainous-looking rusty iron sword, and my foot hit a bronze breastplate.

Aristotle himself sat upon the head of a javelin and sprang

up immediately. "I shall have to take the chairs away," he murmured. He walked restlessly about his treasures, touching first one and then another.

"Isn't it wonderful!" he said expansively. "Look at all this! I feel that I, unaided, could make war against a whole city. That's a Thrakian javelin. That's a modern Makedonian shield—a little damaged—as worn by the Foot-Companions. Its strap has gone. That's an old-fashioned Greek shield—see the difference? The Makedonian one is short and round, and strapped to the body—the soldiers fight with both hands."

I gave him my offering.

"Ah," he said, inspecting it. "Greek. About fifty years old. You should never let a leather scabbard get so dry. The blade has become very dull," he added. "Still, it will fill in the history."

"You may *borrow* it, if it's of any use," I said. I certainly didn't want to take an obol or two like most of my recent companions in the yard.

"Who would have thought there was so much in Athens?" Aristotle was enthusiastic. "It is better than one could have hoped. You see, not only do people have their ancestors' weapons from the old wars, but now those who return from Alexander's wars have trophies and weapons—at least, the damaged ones. That's a sarissa—one which has seen better days." He pointed to a very long slender pike with an iron blade at the point; the blade was a foot long at least, and looked dangerous. The thin haft was splintered in the middle, and I could see that hollow branches had been joined over a bronze tube to make this slender pole. The handle end was splintered and chewed-looking.

"It should have a butt-spike—to ram into the ground—but that's gone. Sarissas can be fixed in the earth, raised like a fence against a charge, although their main use is *in* a charge. Both offensive and defensive—an intelligent weapon. Makedonian. Difficult to manage at first, though—such a length."

"Well, don't stumble against the blade." He was excited, like a child with new toys. I could see that he was going to be happily engaged in his new occupation for weeks and months. Would he any longer be interested in my law case?

"The man who brought that sarissa had taken it home with him from the wars. That man with Eutikleides. I rather think he is to be the witness against you—the one who will swear to Philemon's presence on—on the wrong side, you know. Don't be surprised if you see him again soon. He has been in the wars, that's certain."

"Oh," I said gloomily. That afternoon in the courtyard I had forgotten the third prodikasia and how soon it was to come.

Aristotle picked up a pike and dropped it.

"My hands and arms aren't as strong as they should be. I ate and drank too much last night, I fear. Not very philosophic—but the food was very good—and such wine! I told you I was to dine with Polygnotos?"

"Yes."

"A very select gathering; Eutikleides was there. And at last I saw for myself the famous room; happily, we didn't dine there. But we went into it. It is quite clean now, and there are purifying sacrifices regularly. Hippomenes said it looked just as it had in Boutades' time, and Polygnotos said he tried to keep it so in honor of his uncle's memory. Our host said he liked to keep things where they belonged. Then he smiled rather sadly, and quoted Homer—or paraphrased, rather:

'Farewell, Boutades, I greet you even in Hades.
For all that I promised you in time past I accomplish.'

That wasn't exactly cheerful, but then everyone fell to praising the room again, and its furnishings. Some things he had kept locked away during the nasty time of the funerals and so on, but now everything was back in place. Still, I was glad to get out."

The quotation from Homer did not exactly cheer me—for were not the lines from the *Iliad* taken from Akhilleus' threats of vengeance promised to an injured shade? Aristotle absently tried on a Thrakian helmet, and stood brooding in the middle of the room. He looked very odd, with his eyes gleaming on both sides of the sharp strip of bronze—the nose-piece made him look like some sharp-beaked bird.

"I can't remember," he said suddenly in a puzzled voice, "where everything is in this room now—if I look away, I mean. So much has been added since this morning. Does one remember best the things that should be here? Or the things that shouldn't?" He put his hands over the eye-holes of the helmet for some seconds. He looked positively grotesque. Then he took his hands away and blinked.

"There, I knew I'd forgotten one thing. I'd counted twenty-three objects which came this afternoon—including your sword. And now I remembered twenty-two, and my own furniture as well. But I'd forgotten one thing—the helmet on my own silly head. Still, not bad. *You* try, Stephanos. Take a good look about you, then shut your eyes and tell me aloud what is in the room—and, if possible, where."

There seemed nothing to do but to humor him in his game. I shut my eyes and described the objects in the room. I muddled pikes with lances, and forgot the breastplate under my chair, but I did not do badly.

"Good!" said Aristotle. He clapped a bowl-shaped helmet on my head. It was too large, and slipped over my nose. "Memory is the mother of the Muses. This room is a great jumble. I dislike disorder. I must tidy everything away, and make a list sorting like with like, in proper categories."

I smiled. Aristotle's love of lists and categories was a source of fun to his students. Once when he was lecturing to us in the groves and we were trotting after him, a mongrel dog had joined him, and we had interrupted him at the end of a sentence to ask teasingly, "Aristotle, of what category is this?" The master had answered smartly, "Category of student. Mother's habits deplorable, ancestry unknown, manner ingratiating, speaks out of turn and attends lectures without understanding them."

"I dislike disorder," Aristotle repeated. "But life is often untidy. It's a mistake to expect too much order. Now—you of

136

the good memory—tell me what was in Boutades' room when you saw it."

"I told you once," I protested.

"Long ago. Now tell me again."

I felt foolish, but remembering was not as painful an ordeal as it might have been, now we were playing some silly game with helmets on our heads. I remembered very clearly—despite the fact that it was so long ago. How could I forget?

Aristotle blinked again when I had finished, and shook his head once, slowly. He removed his helmet and gazed into it as though looking for bees.

Suddenly, there was a loud knock at the door, which was opened before the knock had finished sounding. A short square man entered, a man in a workman's tunic which frankly revealed dirty muscular legs with great knotted knees, and long brawny arms. The limbs shooting from his short torso looked like oak branches growing out of a bush.

"Sorry, master, but ain't you going to see a man? I been standing about, your worship, *that* long, and must be off. So I just gave that slave of yours the slip, for a forge won't work on its own, please your honor."

"I see," said Aristotle, straightening his ruffled hair—what there was of it. "Do you have something to sell?"

"That's the way of it, sir. Says I to yon slave, 'Your master wouldn't want to miss this. If he hears he's missed it, he'll be in a right fury and likely kick you from disappointment. Not many have brought such,' says I. 'Not with *such* a history'—red hot, you might say, from the war itself."

"Oh? A valuable weapon?"

"Valuable, is it?" The smith, or whatever he was, glanced curiously at me as I sat there, my face obscured, I hoped, by the helmet; he presumably thought that I was a somebody-or-other, perhaps a slave, taking part in one of the philosopher's mysterious experiments with weapons, for he said approvingly, "At work already, I see," and turned back to Aristotle.

"Valuable? You may say so. Sir, the most deadly weapon in this world or in any other, if properly handled. It's as mortal

137

as the lightning bolt, without quite as much noise—and I've brought two of 'em."

"Where?" said Aristotle, for the man had no iron-tipped lance or gleaming bronze implement about him.

"Hush!" he said darkly. "I've brought 'em wrapped up." He pointed to a large leather bag which he had dropped at his feet. "They are *that* valuable. Used at Tyre. These very ones. Will you buy 'em, sir? For Alexander too, whom the gods preserve. I'd like to give 'em for nothing—but that isn't really just (you philosophers say 'just') to a man's family. And I've got a good wife and five little ones to support. So I fear I must be after selling them for money. Though it don't seem right to do so neither. Wasn't it through the doing of one like these that I lost a front tooth and nearly lost my head entirely? So I'm asking six obols—that's only three apiece."

I could see Aristotle's curiosity was aroused. So was mine. What had the fellow got in that leather bag? I wondered uneasily if he were carrying snakes, and tried to recall if I had ever heard that poisonous serpents were used by Alexander's forces against the enemy. I didn't think so. Some similar thought must have come to Aristotle, for he said, "What is it, man? Are they alive? I must see them first."

"No—not alive. Not what you might call alive, *now,*" said the man cautiously. "I don't scarcely like to show 'em—not unless they're sold. Perhaps I shouldn't part with them." He hitched up his bag. "Let me tell you the story of the siege of Tyre, your honor."

"No, thank you, friend," said Aristotle. "*Four* obols—if you can convince me that these weapons are real weapons, and used in the siege of Tyre."

"Convince, is it? You'll be convinced when you see them. By the sacred hearth of Zeus, don't I swear they were used in the siege of Tyre?" He looked happily at the four obols that Aristotle handed him, and stored them in his mouth.

"Now let me see these things," said Aristotle.

The weapon-seller, with an expression full of caution, set the bag on the floor, loosened the neck, put his hands in and drew out—two stones.

Aristotle began to smile. "Yes," he said dryly. "Stones. Most deadly weapons indeed."

"That's right," said the smith. "To be sure they are that, sir." He handed the stones reverently to Aristotle. Each was rounded, and about the size of a man's two fists pressed together. They looked quite stone-like, gray and uninteresting.

"These here stones is two of the very ones that were used in the catapults at Tyre. I picked them up after, from by the holes in the wall. These are but the smaller ones, like—there was some as big as your head, or bigger. You should have heard it—'swish' in the air and then 'thud—crunch' against the wall as the stones was shot over. Them's some of the most deadly weapons in the world. Spears can break, and swords can bend or chip, or go rusty—and a good shield can stop either at times. But there's not much can stop a stone flying through the air once it takes off, and it does pretty powerful damage where it stops, even through a helmet. And they don't break easy, nor rust at all. Much obliged to your worship and all prosperity to you." The creature bowed himself out, but turned at the door to say in coaxing tones, "I might be able—"

"Listen, smith," said Aristotle. "Play ducks-and-drakes if you will, but no other games with stones. They're dangerous objects, as you say. No need to hazard your safety with bringing bigger ones. Do you understand me?"

"Yes, sir," said the man, with a ghost of a wink, and closed the door.

Aristotle burst out laughing. "That's one of the cleverest men in all Athens! He should be given public office—sent on an embassy! I never thought I should see the day when anyone would make me pay good money for stones—not marble, no, nor porphyry, but two stones I might take from the roadside any day. I let myself break the first rule in business—which is always to see what you're buying before you lay your money down."

I looked at the objects curiously. "Were they really used at the siege of Tyre?"

"Impossible to tell, Stephanos. One of them has come heavily against something—but it could have been hurled against any wall in Athens this morning and then kicked along the road. It's not impossible that they've been used at Tyre. But it is equally—no, much more—likely that they've never been far away. A useful lesson, Stephanos. Two lessons. One: Don't buy weapons concealed in a bag. Two: Any common object can be used as a weapon under the right conditions. What the man said is perfectly true. Such missiles did indeed wreak havoc upon Tyre, and other cities before that. It is right I should be reminded that there are many kinds of weapons. Perhaps I spent my four obols rather well, after all."

He sat down—first removing the javelin from his chair—and looked at the round gray objects in his hands, like one in deep thought. I had to ask him twice if he knew anything of the women's progress.

"What? Oh, yes. I heard today. They are traveling steadily, if slowly; Melissa is taking the journey well, and so is the child. They should be in Boiotia by now; they will not be in Pella until the spring."

He put the stones down, looked at the javelin and made stabbing motions with it, frightening me a little.

"With this, the force must come from a man's arm and body. A bow or a catapult supplies force, and hence speed. But at a distance one may be less accurate. Which is the more valuable, Stephanos?"

"It depends, I suppose," I said, "on the conditions under which one fights. Sometimes you might need hand-to-hand encounter—sometimes, as in besieging a town, you'd need to cover a distance."

"Hm. Yes. That's so. Quite." He picked up a dully pointed object of medium size from among the heap of javelins and pikes and put it on the table. "A Skythian arrow, Stephanos. I wonder." He picked it up and tried stabbing the air with the arrow. "Could you use it as a short lance?"

I felt uneasy as he sat there making these meaningless threatening gestures. I didn't wish to hear of arrows any more than was necessary. Aristotle seemed rather dangerous in that room bristling with lethal objects. The slave came to tell his master that a few more people with weapons to sell were at the door, and I got up to leave.

"The third prodikasia is in a few days." I said wistfully. But he didn't seem in the mood for offering extensive advice.

"Oh—yes. Tell them they can't prove Philemon was there. If their soldier appears against you, hint kindly that illness has weakened his mental faculties. But be very respectful of his honorable service, mind. Think of all the young men you know who look like Philemon. Badger them with questions about recognition. That's all you can do at the moment."

I left him still frowning at the arrow and waving it forward in the air. However, he spoke cheerfully to me while performing these grim motions.

"Goodbye, Stephanos—and, by the way, say nothing of that last purchase of mine, or I'll do you a mischief. Think of the lewd jokes it would cause! But if ever I seem overbearing and foolishly proud of my intellect, you may always murmur to me, 'That leather bag contained stones.' "

XIII

The Last Prodikasia

On the day before the third prodikasia I was walking along the great street that runs under the south side of the Akropolis (the street with all the festival monuments in it) when I heard a buzz of voices.

"Is it not huge!"

"What magnificent carving!"

People pressed forward to see something coming down the street, so I did too. Coming towards us was a wheeled cart pulled by two mules and pushed by slaves. In the cart was something white that gleamed in the thin winter sunshine like a hill of snow, something packed tightly round with bundles of straw and held upright by slaves. As this came closer, I could see what it was. A monument. A tombstone. I knew whose it must be, even before I saw it. Fascinated, I moved toward the cart and stood at the edge of the road to watch it as it passed.

The stone was a splendid piece of pure marble, exquisitely cut and shaped. Upon it there were carved the sitting figures of Boutades and his wife, sculpted in high relief. There was Boutades, moving slowly past me. It was a shock to see his face, now so familiar to my waking dreams. The heavy face and figure were somewhat refined by the sculptor's sense of the beautiful; the arrogant nature which looked out at you from those sightless eyes had acquired a dignity more than in life, and not all the lines on his face had been reproduced. Still, it was a good and telling likeness, unmistakable, even to the way the hair grew. Of course, there was no suggestion of the horror of the man's end, or of the grimace which that face had worn just after death that fatal morning. His thin wife sat submissively by her husband's side, every line in her body in its attractively flowing khiton suggesting graceful obedience. They looked a happy and prosperous middle-aged couple.

I began to read the inscription under the figures, telling of Boutades' rank, services and many virtues, and expressing the sorrows of his survivors, especially of his nephew, Polygnotos, who had caused the monument to be made. Nothing was said about the manner of these people's deaths. I was aware of noises of approbation from the small crowd about me. I do not know at what point I became uneasy, hearing the sounds change to murmurs of disapproval, even horror. I looked up—and saw one of those near me nudging his neighbor and drawing back; both then looked at me with expressions of angry fright.

"He is desecrating the monument!" one said.

I realized that my own shadow was falling athwart the pure glistening stone, darkening the very face of Boutades. Now one of the slaves pushing the cart (probably a slave who had once served Boutades himself in life) recognized me too, and frowning, made the sign which averts evil influences. I was grieved and ashamed. It was true—my presence here was a kind of pollution. I should have had the sense to go another way directly I realized what was coming up the street. "Oh, Boutades," I thought, "*I* am no malign influence upon *you*. Rather, your very shade, or your image pictured in stone, has power to do me harm." I turned away quickly, and took a long walk before I dared to present myself in the agora. Still the monument hung upon my mind; I could imagine it, and the seated Boutades with his wife passing through the Dipylon Gate to the grave at the Kerameikos. Those white figures, mocking me, were constantly before my inner eye.

On the day of the prodikasia itself I knew when I awakened in the morning that I had caught a cold. It was beginning in that tedious way colds do, tickling the back of my nose and prickling my throat. My voice sounded strange, twanging like a broken lyre string. Talking was going to be an effort. I wrapped myself up in my warmest clothing.

All my opponents looked quite well. Eutikleides seemed larger than ever, his skin shining sleekly. Polygnotos was, as usual, clear-eyed, with rosy cheeks. I knew my own face was yellowy pale, and my eyes watery. We two could be stood side by side as emblems of Health and Sickness. The very slave of Polygnotos, the Sinopean who as usual had accompanied his master, looked plumper than before, and was beaming, as if he expected to be fed with good things at noon. And Telemon was fidgeting about with enough activity for two men.

The proceedings at first were exactly as on the previous occasions. I went through them dully. My head felt heavy and stupid—not merely from the rheum in it. I knew I would have to lie, and that frightened me. The Basileus unwittingly made it easier for me by saying, "May we take it that your defense is the same as before, Stephanos? That your cousin was absent?"

"Yes," I said. That was true—in a way—I thought. *They* might *assume* that, truly. So I wasn't precisely breaking my oath by the gods. Still, I wondered if the offended gods would punish me—they would know I had meant to lie, and in their name. The gods aren't to be taken in with stale tricks.

The talk went on, and I was almost in a daze. Then suddenly I realized that Eutikleides had just said, "Here is our witness, as spoken of in the last prodikasia," and he pushed forward the little man who had brought the sarissa to Aristotle.

This quondam soldier was introduced as Sosibios, an Athenian from one of the country demes. The history of his service under Alexander was given, and upon Eutikleides' sympathetic questioning the man described how he had been wounded. It was all very honorable. When he was asked further questions by the Basileus, he answered readily. This Sosibios had a thin unpleasant voice; his words came out in little bundles. He seemed a bit in awe of his surroundings: a muscle by his mouth twitched from time to time when he was speaking, as if he had a tic. Although he conducted himself very properly, I found this man in no way agreeable.

He gave a description—which would have interested me much at another time, and from another man—of the battle near Issos town, and the rout of the Persians. He said further that when he and fellow foot-soldiers were trying to follow the cavalry across the river Payas, they were heavily oppressed and constrained, both by the swift river and by the opposing enemy. As ranks drifted apart, soldiers from the enemy side hurled themselves into the river and up the bank and fought with Alexander's men, very fiercely.

"And," he said, "the really terrible thing, gentlemen, was that the Persians facing us on the other bank, and then crossing and cutting us down, were not *Persian* soldiers, no, but Greeks. They called out to us in Greek—horrible insults. I saw Philemon of Athens then—at first across the river, facing me. Then on our side of the ford. Fighting, he was, and yelling, nearby."

"Did you know him?" asked Polygnotos, perhaps with some doubt in his voice. "How could you recognize him?"

"Knew him—seen him before. In Athens in the old days."

"Did you see him again on that day—in the battle?" asked the Basileus.

"Yes. Crossed the banks, we did. Pursuit. Cavalry cut off the Mede-loving Greeks. They began to run. Alexander had all the Persians on the run at dusk." He chuckled. "Darius flew away like a bird in his chariot, hardly touched ground. Certainly I saw this Philemon again. Making off at speed ahead of us. Wounded on one side of his face. But we didn't catch him."

"Did you see him or hear of him later?"

"Didn't see him—no. Heard of him later—at Sidon. He'd been passing through, going home to Athens. People remembered him. I stayed with the army until I got wounded at Tyre."

"So, you see," said Eutikleides, taking up the case. "This man Philemon was recognized fighting among the Persians. He was wounded. It was not safe for him to stay in Asia as Alexander advanced—we know what revenge Alexander has taken on Greek traitors who fought for Persians! So this skulker decided to return home. There was ample time for him to return to Athens before the time in question—the time of the murder."

I had to examine the witness. I didn't know quite what to say. "How did you know it was Philemon? Did he give his name?"

The man hesitated, looking at Eutikleides. "Yes," he said. "I think he did. He certainly did at Sidon—to a few."

"You *think*—but you're not sure. You cannot remember. Is it not true that you merely had an impression that this man in the battle was Philemon? You saw a man who looked somewhat like him."

"No. I knew him."

"Come," I said. My brain was clearing a little. "Describe this man. Describe him as clearly as you can."

"Well, he was tall—"

"How tall? Very, *very* tall?"

"No—not exceedingly tall. But tall, not short. Well built, and well muscled, agile."

"What color was his hair?"

"Brown."

"What sort of brown?"

"Just brown. Not black-brown. Rather curly."

"Did he have a helmet on?" I asked, remembering the last interview with Aristotle.

"Er—no. I don't think so. Or a small one, maybe; I could still see his hair, so it can't have covered his head completely."

"What color were his eyes?"

"Brown."

"Describe his voice."

The man looked nonplussed; voices weren't things to be described.

"Just a voice. A young man's—clear." He looked at Eutikleides again. "With an Athenian accent," he added triumphantly.

"Any marks, moles or blemishes?"

"No, sir. Save for the scar he has now, from the wound he got that day."

"Ah! That scar from the wound you say he received in battle. What sort of wound? A slash? A three-cornered tear? A hole in the face? Was it by the ear—or by the eye—or the chin?"

"Along the cheekbone, and down."

"On which side of his face?"

Sosibios touched his own face on both sides, hesitantly.

"You aren't looking into a pool," I said rather nastily. "What side?"

He hesitated again. "On the right, I think. Might have been the left. No—it was the right." Eutikleides looked at his witness with annoyance.

"Sir," I said to the witness, coldly. "Let us exercise your memory and your powers of description. Describe to me Glaukon, son of Glaukon, and Euphrastion, son of Dekagones, both of whom you have seen."

These were young men of Athens, from respected families, and both lads were celebrated for their athletic feats—anyone would have seen them. They were nearly Philemon's age. The witness looked reluctant to proceed in this task, but the Basileus intervened, and supported me. Sosibios went haltingly through descriptions of both youths.

"There," I said when he had finished. "Glaukon is tall, but not too tall, and well shaped, with brown hair and eyes. So is Euphrastion. That is what your description amounts to. And you say both are muscular, and neither has any blemishes on the body. You might have added that of course both speak with an Athenian accent! Who could recognize either of these men clearly from such a description? Who could pick out one individual and say, 'This account applies to him and to no other!' In one particular, indeed, you are at fault—Euphrastion has slate-gray eyes. How easily you make him resemble Glaukon. All men of a certain age and in good health look much alike to this witness." I turned to the court at large. "His description of the man he calls Philemon, whom he saw in the fury of battle, could be a description of half a dozen young men of Athens at least—probably of many more." I was elated now, and feeling more clear-headed. I turned again to the witness to press my questions.

"When did this battle begin? At what time of year was it? And what time of day?"

"This time of year, about—a little earlier. And the battle began—oh, middle of the afternoon."

"Yes," I agreed. "That's unusually late for the onset of a battle, but Alexander was careful in arranging troops, and took his time. What was the river like?" I asked.

"Cold," he said with feeling.

"It must have been very hard for you," I said sympathetically, "to fight and to have to cross a river at the same time. It can't have been easy, as you say you had to wait until the cavalry crossed over."

"Yes," he said with proud reminiscence, "it wasn't easy. Even for the cavalry it wasn't—let alone for us. The very horses got stuck in the mud, gentlemen, so you can imagine what it was like for us, trying to cross."

"Was it very muddy?" I asked innocently.

"Muddy! More mud than you've ever seen, not if it rained in Athens for a month. You should have seen the horses trying to scramble up—the last horses, after the first had gone. All churned up, and no more foothold than ice."

"So both sides of the ford were churned up. There would be spray from the horses and men in the river, then—muddy spray, too. Did you get any mud on yourself?"

"Course I did. We all did. Fighting's not going to a party—keeping your clothes clean. You couldn't get near the river without—" he paused, trying to think.

"Without getting covered in mud," I finished. "That would be just as true for men on the enemy side, wouldn't it? The foot-soldiers who hurled themselves across at you after your horsemen had crossed—they would have slithered down one muddy bank and up another—getting soaked in a river of dirty water in between."

Sosibios nodded unhappily.

"So, sir," I said to the Basileus. "Here we have a witness whose recollections and powers of description are not very accurate at the best of times. This witness claims to have seen and recognized a particular man—no close acquaintance, just someone he'd seen about Athens. This man he describes very generally, despite the pretense of supplying detail. The witness then says he saw this man on one very confused and busy occasion—full of danger and distraction, when the witness himself would have his attention fully occupied in preserving his life. Moreover, he claims to have seen this particular individual in what must have been the later part of the afternoon on a late autumn day. He claims that he saw this man again, somewhat after that, at a distance, from behind, in the dark—or dusk, at best.

"This man when Sosibios saw him at anything like close quarters *must* have been covered with dirt—having been muddied, then soaked in a dirty river, then covered with mud again. This person could in no way be easily distinguishable from other Greek enemy soldiers. That there were—alas!—Greeks fighting on the Persian side, no one denies. And most of these enemy Greeks would have been young men, tall and hardy, fit for active service, all at that moment yelling, with faces distorted, and all streaked with mud, with wet and muddy hair. The witness Sosibios may in fact have seen a young tall Greek in that condition. There is no identification at all. All else is mere baseless surmise."

"He said he was Philemon," interjected Eutikleides. "He said so when making his way through Sidon."

"Ah—but do we know that this mysterious person who passed through Sidon was the same as the man at the battle? Certainly not. This witness has very shaky impressions. A man in Sidon might have said that he was, for instance, Philomenes of Orynthos—which this soldier misheard. There might have been another Philemon—very probably hundreds of Philemons in Greece—with or without a scar. Or the man whom he saw in battle may have reminded him vaguely of my cousin—as we have seen, men are in his mind much alike—and the only person in Sidon who made mention of a name might have been the witness himself. In the carelessness to which men give tongue when they make remarks over their wine, he may have said when he heard of a man with a scar, 'Oh, yes, Philemon,' meaning 'the Philemon-like man whom I saw in the fight.' Then he could persuade himself that they were one and the same, the man who passed through Sidon and the man at the battle—and my cousin Philemon. We may be talking all the time of three different men. He does not claim that he met the man with the scar in Sidon. I insist there is no identification here worth bothering with, not in logic and reason. It is all—" I tried to smile serenely— "all froth and mud."

The other side shook their heads, but said little. Eutikleides looked angry and stubborn, and said all would be done at the trial. By that time, he said, they hoped to have a witness who could depose, not only as this man had done, that Philemon could have been in Athens, but that he was actually there. "In which case," he added in a mocking tone, "the objections raised rather trivially by the defender to this witness's statement will fall to the ground."

So that was that. I sneezed three times, very violently, and everyone drew back from the shower. The Basileus brought proceedings to a close. My head had cleared remarkably during my examination of the witness, but now it ached. I felt rather proud of my exertions, but I also knew that I could do no more to knock this witness's statement down during the trial than I had just done now. And at the trial he would be prepared by this preliminary bout. So the whole conversation might go quite differently then. And even if it went then just as it had gone this morning, I wondered how the citizenry gathered at the Areopagos would take it. Perhaps they would side emotionally with the soldier, and be willing to take all he said against Philemon, no matter how slight and illogical it was. Throw enough mud, and some will stick. Oh well, I had thrown a little mud myself now. Yet, if Eutikleides made good his threat to produce at the trial a witness who had seen Philemon in Athens, all was nearly as good as lost. A month ago I might have taken this threat lightly. Now I knew that there probably were persons in Athens or at least Peiraeus who had seen Philemon. I wondered that my opponents had not sniffed the scent of the trail that led to Peiraeus. Perhaps they were keeping something back? I sneezed again and went out. My throat felt raw. I remembered the actor who had a bad cold and was so frightened of losing his voice, and was aware of a fellow-feeling. Suppose I lost my voice permanently before the trial—and had to appear and *whisper* before the multitude of Athens!

By the path, his thin gray hair ruffled by the breeze, stood my hateful acquaintance Arkhimenos. He haunted me, it seemed, like figures in dreams which return night after night. I felt weary, for I had been through all this before. Even before he spoke, I felt we were to enact the same play over—and there was Theosophoros, the same audience. Well, I would change this tiresome play if I could. I would enlarge the audience. I determined to remain close to my opponents, not to be isolated, so we departed in a loose-knit group, proceeding down the path. In front of me I could see Eutikleides' broad back and thick neck, and Polygnotos with his devoted slave trotting beside him. I was only three paces or so behind them when Arkhimenos spoke to me. I still hoped that shame of acting madly before such respectable persons would suppress his filthy rudeness. My desire for an encounter with him was by no means large, and I knew that I ought not to give voice to the angry suspicions bubbling in my brain—not here, not now.

Arkhimenos spoke to me in a low hissing tone, full of distilled poison, like a snake's tooth. "O Stephanos! Mede-lover! Cousin of a Mede-lover! Take your little pestle to the wars and pound spices for the Persians!"

I said nothing, very crossly. The man trotted beside me on the path with light steps, almost dancing.

"Leave off battering the girls and try battering some walls! You mede-lover! Yah—you leaky chamber-pot—getting of babies, that's all you're fit for. The warm nest—eh, Mede-lover? Make love to the Persians—ask them to unstone you and set you to guard their women! But make sure Alexander's men don't come and prick you with a great big sword!"

I was embarrassed and enraged. I could see that those in front of me could hear—and, I thought bitterly, they're probably enjoying what they hear.

"Ha! Ha! Get a sword in your belly!" cried Arkhimenos gleefully. Despite my shame and anger, what he said stirred something in my mind which could almost be an idea. My anger was turbulent and I remembered the slave with the bound hand.

"My life is no concern of yours, you dried kernel without a nut," I answered. I managed my voice fairly well, although I croaked a bit—I did not want to descend to mean-spirited whispering. I went on, glaring at my antagonist, noticing the working of the vertical lines on his flushed face. "Some people are very good at running from danger, are they not? Patter-patter—some feet are quick to run away! Those who attack citizens had better go warily. Remember, fool, those who attack at night are seen in the day. There are always marks left behind. The slave who holds the torch may himself be singed. If you rely on a slave, remember, his discretion is not worth two straws. Indecent deeds against the helpless at night—what pride and honor is there! There is law in Athens yet. Think on it. Go home, you cowardly idiot, and mind your behavior, or you will have keepers to lock your hot madness in a cooling room."

"Get a sword in your belly," Arkhimenos whispered. He did not look so happy.

Theosophoros interposed. "Such rudeness! To a respected citizen, and one old enough to be your grandfather. I suppose these are the new Mede-loving manners and we must accustom ourselves to them."

"Mede-lover!" announced Arkhimenos sulkily. "Dirty dog!"

"Yes," said Theosophoros. "It will take us time to become used to such barbarian magnificence. Overpowering, really. Come away, citizen."

He guided Arkhimenos down the path, not to assist tottering steps (for the man was strong in his striding) but to prevent his running back to me. The scene had not been altogether satisfactory, but at least I had altered some of the lines. In a play, I thought dreamily, I and Arkhimenos would be the protagonists, and Theosophoros the leader of the khoros, but the whole troop—Eutikleides, the soldier Sosibios, Polygnotos, Telemon and all—should be in the khoros, and should not have their backs to us. The exchange had not been entirely satisfactory—the insults had degraded me. Yet at least I had warned Arkhimenos that I knew it was he who had set fire to Melissa's house, and I hoped I had scared him. If it were he—how could I be *quite* sure? Had he actually been present? Was it he whom I had chased through the dark lanes of Peiraeus? I thought so now, more than ever —but why?

I went home to try to think, but by the time I arrived all I wished to do was to lie down. I spent the rest of the day over steaming bowls of steeped herbs, trying to clear my head. I awakened late the next morning feeling a little better, but not much. My mother herself brought me my breakfast and sat beside me. In an effort to entertain me, she told me some pieces of household news which interested me not at all. Then she added generously, "And there's a little piece of news in the city which might interest you, Stephanos. I'm sure any misfortune that happens to *that* house is grateful to me. Now you've finished breakfast, I'll tell you."

"Tell me what?"

"Why, one of the slaves who used to belong to Boutades is dead—fell over a cliff in the Parnes, they say. Polygnotos sent him on an errand yesterday at midday. He did not return, and in the morning his body was found by some shepherds. Our slaves heard the news."

"Yes," said Aunt Eudoxia, who had crept into the room to enjoy the pleasure of conversation. "Some say robbers got him, and I'm sure I wish it was so—anyone who took wealth from them would be welcome to it for all of me. He had a few coins on him, and they're gone—but it might have been the shepherds, you know. The tablets he carried were still there. And there were no marks of fighting, no scratches—the shepherds have just brought the body into town, and some in Athens have seen the corpse. There was no sign of a struggle—only a slight bruise on the head. The head-bone was broken."

"Ah, well," said my mother. "He missed his footing in the dusk and fell—probably he had been drinking when he shouldn't. They're so careless, these slaves. He was but a poor silly Sinopean fellow—most likely he had not wits enough to keep to the path."

"They found him under the cliff—all in a sprawl," said my aunt. "There was no bleeding, so for a moment they thought he might be alive, but when they touched him they knew he had been a corpse for a while."

"Polygnotos is very vexed," said my mother brightly. "Oh, very cut up about it he is. That was his pet slave—went with him everywhere—devoted, he said. They say Polygnotos couldn't believe it at first. But it's no great matter," she sighed. "He'll just get a new one. I wish more harm than that to him, Athena knows. I wish the whole family would fall over a cliff—and Eutikleides too!"

153

"Mother!" I protested. "Take care the gods don't hear your wicked wish and punish you."

"They deserve it," she said stoutly. "Making us miserable! I wish at least Polygnotos' every rising would be to hear bad news—and the same for all the family!"

As I have said, my mother took the whole action of the prosecution as a deep personal insult.

"Ah!" said Aunt Eudoxia, laying her hand solemnly on her heart. "It's a judgment of the gods on them, that's what it is."

I hoped very much it wasn't. It had darted into my head while I heard this news that perhaps the Sinopean slave had himself been the murderer of Boutades. I remembered him as I had seen him on the day of the murder, sweating from running, pale, trembling, and I recalled someone saying, "That's a frightened slave." If the fellow had died by the judgment of the gods—then what could I do at the trial? What was the law for if the gods punished the murderer first, not leaving the innocent a way to clear himself? If only I had thought of this earlier—I could at the trial have called this slave as a witness, put him to the torture, exacted a confession. Now he was out of my hands. I felt as vexed as Polygnotos over his loss. What would I do? I had had a good idea too late.

XIV

A Day at the Farm

The next morning I awoke feeling much better. I had previously appointed that day as one on which I would go out to our farm, and I knew the steward and his wife would be expecting me. Our Athenian household wanted more oil and some cheese. So I set off in company with one of our slaves, who carried with him in two bags the dung and refuse from our kitchen midden to spread upon the farm's soil and make it rich; on the way back he would make himself useful by attending the mule cart with a load of cheese and oil. This slave did not smell like a pot of ointment, and I kept a distance between us. That, however, did not discourage him from chattering. He insisted on telling me about the accident that had befallen the Sinopean, and what the corpse looked like—all pale, with the side of the head by the temple quite pashed in "like a broken crust"—so I had to hear about it all over again.

It was just noon when we arrived. The sun shone full and pale in the winter sky; we were nearing the year's shortest day now. The farmhouse, though only a small rough-built place, looked inviting; I was glad to come out of the cold air to sit by a fire of olive stones and branches and take some wine with Dametas and his wife, Tamia.

I had known Dametas and Tamia since my childhood. Tamia cannot have been so old then, not at the time of my birth, for she had given me suck when my mother was ill, but now she seemed a very old woman indeed, her face wrinkled and her cheerful smile almost entirely toothless. These two had worked on the farm for many years. Now Dametas was old and growing blind, and his work-hardened hands with their broken nails had, I noticed, a persistent tremor. I thought with alarm that I would have to find a new steward soon. Dametas was old, might become helpless and bed-ridden—might even die. It was shocking, like thinking of one of the pillars of Herakles toppling. Tamia, too—as she led me about proudly to inspect the weaving, the storerooms and all the women's work—she seemed to move lamely. When she inspected the woven cloth, she held her eyes very close to it. It became evident to me that her hearing was failing, too. When she attempted to answer my remarks, she kept her dull eyes anxiously fixed on my face, trying to guess my meaning and conceal her infirmity. Talking with her was irritating and depressing, dear to me as she was. How long could she possibly do the work as it should be done?

And slaves could be uttering all kinds of insolent remarks
—she wouldn't hear them.

I had hoped to be cheered by my visit to the farm, for I had
always loved it, but I was a man now, with all the worries of
a man. I inspected the pigs, and looked at the fields. The slave
I had brought with me was sent off to spread the dung and
then to cut wood. Dametas and I talked animatedly about
farm matters, and Tamia cooked fresh cakes, and gave them
to me with honey "for your throat." When Dametas and I
inspected the room where the oil was stored, I did feel somewhat cheered at the sight of the rows of jars. The oil which
I tasted was excellent.

"We've saved some of the last olives for you to see," said
Dametas. "The ones from the late-fruiting trees on the side
of the hill. Come and watch. I know how you like seeing the
olives pressed."

Watching this had been one of my favorite amusements as
a child, and I thought wryly that to Dametas and his wife I
was forever a child. Nevertheless, I found I still did enjoy the
sight. The woman worked the grindstone so that it turned in
its circle, slowly, shaking, and there was a scraping noise—
and then the crushed fruit spat itself into the trough. These
crushed olives, now without their stones, were collected with
their juices and put into baskets. I followed to the outhouse
where they were to be pressed, and watched the heavy lid
being put on the basket; Tamia raised her end of a lever
which pressed down hard upon the wet crushed olives. The
oil oozed through the wicker, and fell into the earthenware
basins below. "Drip-drop. Drip-drop." Slow at first, and then
slightly faster, a thin trail of honey-colored fatness, dropping
in little globs more compact and clinging than water drops.
Tamia smiled and beamed and pressed, and I stared, feeling
my worry drain away as the oil oozed and dropped so satisfac-
torily, first from one hole in the wicker basket, then from
another.

A shadow fell across the press. I turned to the doorway.
The shadow was cast by the bulky body of Eutikleides.

"Stephanos, son of Nikiarkhos?" he said, quite politely.

"Yes, O Eutikleides," I replied, and hastened outside, as if to greet him. I didn't want the peaceful olive-shed polluted by his presence.

He seemed in no haste to move. "A good oil crop this year," he said, "but it is late for the pressing." His tone, although still polite, implied that I was a feckless manager. Tamia kept on with her pressing, but she nodded in acknowledgment of the stranger, and grinned her toothless welcome.

Eutikleides and I walked outdoors. It was past mid-afternoon now, the blue shadows were lengthening.

"I was visiting a tenant nearby," he explained, "and decided to see you at once, as I found out you were here, for the business is pressing. It is about that matter of a debt owed by your father to me. I fear I must ask you for payment—and soon."

"My father?" I asked, astonished. "He owed no money to you."

"It is true that Nikiarkhos was not in debt to me. But he was indebted to my guest-friend, Agesander—you do remember that?"

I scraped about through my mind and recalled that month of Boedromion, just before the murder and the accusation had driven almost all else from my mind, when I had been going through the accounts. Then I had been worried also about how to raise enough money so that I might marry the daughter of Kallimakhos—how far back that hope seemed. I could remember having thought that I would have to settle debts first, and Agesander's among them. I had not been able to sell the poor vineyard; Agesander had not pressed me for payment, and in the anxiety of Philemon's case I had forgotten about the matter. It is shameful to forget a debt—yes, but a young man who has to relinquish his own wedding is likely to think that everyone else might also postpone pleasures. I blushed—and saw that Eutikleides was pleased with his advantage.

"It is true," I said. "I do owe money to Agesander."

"Two hundred drakhmai," said Eutikleides with brisk satisfaction.

"It's not as much as that," I retorted. "Agesander lent my father one hundred and twenty drakhmai—"

"Ah, but there's the interest, Stephanos, the interest. A loan for a short time has become a protracted borrowing. You owe a good deal of interest now."

"But it was an arrangement between friends—citizens—"

"It was a matter of business, my dear boy. Of course."

"And why is Agesander not here himself? It is with him that I should discuss it."

"My dear Stephanos." Eutikleides was almost avuncular. He tucked his arm through mine and we paced along; I was humiliated in this firm grip, as if I were being conducted to jail. "Of course," he went on, "it was to Agesander that your father owed the money. But Agesander is a kinsman of mine and also my guest-friend. Consider! He has had losses, so, to assist him, I have purchased all the debts that are owed to him. Hence I am now your creditor."

"You!" I said, outraged.

"Do not be foolish, dear boy. But I fear you are foolish— headstrong and full of whims. But then, you are young. Allowance must be made. And yet—look at this farm," he said contemptuously, waving his free hand about my domain. "Falling to pieces. That old dodderer who let me in—he is aged and incompetent. A person in your circumstances ought to live quietly on the land, working with his own hands to provide for his family."

"My father was of as good name and condition as yourself," I said hotly. "I am of good family."

"Many good families descend in the world. Look at things as they are. Who knows," he added complacently, "even *my* family in centuries to come may be as reduced as you are now. But your temper is easily heated. You won't take advice, I see."

He fixed me with his cold eyes, slate color and hard as stone. The strength of his arm seemed immense in a man of his age.

"Be sensible, or it will be the worse for you. Of course I want the money. Of course you must pay me."

Angry with myself for doing so, I yet started to plead: "But think what a difficult time this is for me—and my father has not long been dead. Can't it wait until—can't it wait?"

"Do you think me a woman, to be moved by pleas—or tears? Your sort are always under special difficulties. I hate whiners and cringers—so like a certain type of dog. Do not think you can evade me, or you will be sorry."

"You will do anything to get money?" I said impertinently. Resentment and despair made me bold. "I thought true Athenians, whose ancestors fought at Marathon, despised usury, too!"

His arm was like the lever that squeezed the poor olives.

"Your silly words cannot vex me—I'm not here to bandy sentiments with you. I have paid Agesander the debt and interest owing. Now of course I will get what is my own. You are not at your nurse's knee now—neither are you dealing with a man of straw. Go home to mother and whimper, or jaunt about your cabbage patch like a child playing farms *if* you like—but, remember, you must pay."

I swallowed, and fought to bring the conversation back to a more reasonable level.

"Look," I said, as quietly as I could. "I can and will pay the debt. Come—I will show you." I led him to the oil storeroom and pointed at the rows of great jars. "There," I said. "I have all that to sell. I can raise much on that alone. The rest will follow shortly, when I've sold some—other things."

The precious oil! To sell it all at once, and immediately to hand over the proceeds to a creditor! There went the cooking oil for our household and for the farm; there too went the money to pay for winter necessaries. I could see Eutikleides recognized what it meant to me, for he smiled with grim pleasure.

"Very well. But the first payment must be soon."

"By the end of this week," I promised.

"And there will not be much time allowed after that for the rest," he continued.

We were interrupted in our conference by wild screams from nearby. "Ai! Ai!" I rushed toward the cries, dragging

Eutikleides with me; he loosened his hold. By the pile of wood not far from the back of the house crouched my slave, in a pitiable condition. He was rocking back and forth, holding in front of him a hand dripping blood. He held it up to his mouth, but couldn't suck it because he wanted to use his mouth for screaming, and every time he looked at the hand his terrified cries became louder. He had evidently chopped off the tip of a finger. It was a ghastly sight. Eutikleides did not seem to find it so. He moved closer and smiled, as if the sight of blood gave him pleasure, and stood watching for some moments. Then he frowned contemptuously at the slave.

"Hush that noise!" he said brutally, and, going over to the poor fellow, he shook him. The astounded sufferer choked in his bawling and looked with fresh fear at this important severe stranger.

"There! That's the way to deal with them," said Eutikleides. "They get hysterical—like women. One needs to bring them to their senses—what little they have. A careless dunderhead." He looked at me, and I could see that he was thinking, "What a poor ill-managed household is this, where the very slaves are stupid enough to chop off their own fingers. Like master, like men."

By this time a crowd had gathered, all the slaves clustering about and Tamia clicking her tongue and making soothing noises. Eutikleides stalked away toward the gate; I followed unwillingly.

"What a bustling place is yours," he said sarcastically. "Never a moment's repose." I had not thought before that Eutikleides could be ironic; he had never seemed witty. "Remember that debt, Stephanos. I hope not to have occasion to remind you of it again."

I watched him going down the road—this large dangerous man. It seemed odd that only so recently I had been thinking that I could see why people liked him—liked *him!* Probably Agesander liked him—a generous guest-friend who gave help and protection. But he was not just the pompous and

160

respectable man that I had thought him. There was a very strong will—perhaps enjoyment of cruelty. These things were at the roots of that strength which made the gratitude of those whom he protected. There was in this man, I reflected, more liveliness (though of a distasteful kind) than I had before given him credit for. Other men might do his will, eagerly even, not just respecting a well-born stout citizen, but responding to a real force. Never had I hated him so much—never had I seen him so clearly as a leader of men.

But why was he so against me? I felt as if our whole family were being ground and crushed, like the olives under the heavy stone that moved slowly, relentlessly, and made them into dripping pulp. The stone is not cruel—it is doing what it must.

I leaned against the gate wearily, and endeavored to think. Suppose—I thought suddenly—suppose Eutikleides had murdered Boutades for some reason. For money, perhaps. Suppose there were some secret cause. Had Eutikleides felt the need for revenge upon Boutades? I remembered that Eutikleides had arrived at Boutades' house when I did, after the murder. So—he would have had time to commit it, to get away and return. But then, he had not been breathless. Would he necessarily have had to be breathless? The physical contact with the man had taught me how strong he was. Certainly the sight of blood—as in my slave's case—did not disturb him in the least. And he disliked sentiment—so perhaps the sight of an old friend (or acquaintance) weltering in his gore would not have upset him unduly. Then—he could squeeze me, the feeble defender, in order to be sure that the murder was placed at the door of a convenient and helpless victim. Who was really conducting the case of the accusers? Eutikleides. Who asked questions, prompted speakers, brought in a witness? Eutikleides. As I looked back, I realized that he had loomed very large throughout the prodikasiai.

In that case, I was to Eutikleides the only frail obstacle in his course. And even if he had done the murder, what could I do about it? I didn't want to think he was the killer. It made things too difficult—like being asked to push down a tower with your bare hands. But I could not help my suspicion—it was an uneasy temptation in my mind, like a sore tooth which one wants to bite on.

I sneezed several times; my cold was coming back. I left the gate and went indoors to get a little warmth from the fire.

The slave's finger had been bound up, and he was being carefully cosseted by Tamia, who was feeding him hot broth. The man looked up in fright when I appeared, but when he saw that I was alone his features relaxed, and he went back to his broth. What was to be done with the fellow? He was certainly not well enough to drive the cart back with the load of oil and cheese; I would have to do it myself, later.

Once I had warmed myself I was too restless to remain within the house. I walked about the outbuildings, strolled through fields, trying to think. I told Dametas, as he blundered carefully among the cows, that tonight I would be taking away things to sell, as well as goods needed at home. He nodded placidly; he didn't realize that I would be trying to sell almost everything, leaving us all—master, family, steward and slaves—if not starving, certainly much pinched for the rest of the winter. I ground my teeth. Two hundred drakhmai is not a large sum. But to someone like myself—to have to pay it all at once! Cursed be he who first invented usury! When I stopped to consider, I realized that I might have contested the size of the debt, but now I had committed myself by agreeing to the sum Eutikleides had named, so that it would not be legal now to make a protest. My creditor would not take kindly to a protest, either—that was certain, and the last thing I needed was more brangle and litigation.

Gloomily I kept stumping about the farm as the shadows lengthened. In the slow-gathering blue dusk I found myself walking about the olive grove, looking at the great life-giving trees almost without seeing them. At the far end of the grove there were two sacred trees, sanctified to Athena, a little apart from the others. It was dark in the shadows of the trees, dark and very shadowy where the trees of the goddess reigned. The only sound was the rustling of leaves. Then I heard another sound through the leafy whisper—a sound as if someone had moved very slightly against the bole of one of the sacred trees. I walked quickly toward the place, then paused: all was silent. I moved, and soon I heard the noise again, as if someone had moved cautiously, quickly, from one tree to another. I could feel eyes looking at me, looking into my back. I turned and tried to go quietly, facing the trees from whence the sound came—where, in the shadows, behind the twisted boles, someone was watching.

My feet turned quietly, but my nose ruined the effect. I sneezed twice, very thoroughly, trumpeting through the grove. A voice whispered, "O Stephanos?" At these familiar words heard so recently on a violent occasion the hair rose on the back of my neck. What a fool I had been to come out into a dark place alone. I should have heeded Aristotle's warning. Even on my own land I was not necessarily safe. Eutikleides, for instance, had had no difficulty in finding his way to me.

"O Stephanos?" the mocking voice—a young man's voice —said. I stood quite still to face my foe in the shadows. There was a stirring behind the curving trunk of a great tree. I strained my eyes through the darkening air; first I saw the white blur of a face, and then I saw the whole shape of a man —a man who came stealing toward me through the dim alley between the trees. The figure grew clearer. And then—I could have fainted. For standing before me in the twilit grove was my cousin. Philemon. I could identify him clearly, despite what I had said about the difficulty Sosibios would have had in recognizing anyone in the half-dark. My cousin Philemon. It was he, and no other.

"Good day, Stephanos. How are you—aside from your cold?"

I ran toward my dear cousin whom I had not seen for over two years and embraced him, and while I embraced him I groaned aloud with sorrow.

"What are you doing here?" I asked in a sort of despairing whisper. "By Zeus, King of Gods and Men—by Athena, goddess of this grove, you should not be here. Don't you know your life is in danger?"

He held me away from him and smiled reassuringly. "It's rather a long story. I'm so glad it was you, Stepho. I didn't know who was coming along at first. *I'm* all right—I've been a soldier. I can take care of myself."

"Why are you here? You're a banished man—and now you're accused of murder—"

"Yes, yes, I know. But—well—you won't believe this, and I'm afraid you won't approve—but the fact is, I've a wife—"

"Yes," I said impatiently. "I know all about that."

He was surprised. "What? You do? Doesn't that beat the world? I thought you'd be thunderstruck. Well, so naturally I came to see that my wife and child were all right. And to get them out of Athens. Things could be rather unpleasant for them, from what I hear."

"They could indeed," I said firmly. "But Melissa and her child are all right. I've packed them safely out of Athens."

"Well, fancy that! So I needn't have come, after all. Aren't you clever, Stephanos?" His admiration was genuine. "How did you come to know? You are so clever—and Melissa, too, for a woman. I dare say you settled it between you. That's a big load off my mind, I can tell you. And there was I, worrying—where are they?"

"On their way to Makedonia—if the gods are kind."

"How did—"

"Oh, hush, do," I said, my nerves tearing. "This is not the time for long stories. It's your safety we have to think about. You're a banished man, and an accused murderer, and an attainted renegade soldier of the Persians, and the gods know what else besides—as far as most of Athens is concerned. Somebody seems to want your property and perhaps your life—and you come sauntering here! I suppose next thing you'll want to drop into one of the barber's shops in the market for a chat! You idiot, we've got to get you away as quickly as possible!"

"Don't talk all in a rush, Stepho. I can't take it all in," he complained good-naturedly. "Yes, I know that it is a dangerous turn—we've come to a slippery corner, but rein in and take it on all wheels."

That was my cousin, I remembered, always talking in the slang of the races or the games.

"Time! We have no time. You must get out. It was mad to come—utterly mad. Why didn't you send a message to me, instead?"

"Oh, I did think of it, but couldn't quite think what to say, or how to put it so as to be safe if the message went wrong. And I wanted to see Melissa and the boy again. Mother, too. When I thought that Melissa and little Lykias might be in danger, of course I had to come—it was my business. I've been here before, you know, and I always got away!"

I remembered something else that I'd forgotten about my cousin Philemon. He was stupid. Daring, yes, but rather stupid.

"You can just give up any idea of seeing Aunt Eudoxia this time," I said severely. "She's well—up and about, you know. But I'm not having you trotting through the streets of Athens. You'd be taken before my very eyes—and executed before a month was out. Publicly shackled to the plank, exposed and then strangled or clubbed to death— that's execution for murder, you know. And that would be your fate—unless a patriotic Persian-hooting mob got to you first."

I threw him all the frightening things I could think of, hoping that he *would* be frightened. It was always very hard to make Philemon feel scared. He looked puzzled rather than dismayed, as if a game of hide-and-seek had gone wrong.

"What about me?" I went on, in the same vein. "I'm hazarding my own life if it is known—suspected even—that I've given you shelter. You're not to go prancing around making a fool of yourself. If you want to die, I don't. I have had to speak for you at the prodikasiai, and I shall have to defend you at your trial. You need to keep us both alive if Aunt

Eudoxia is going to keep her little property—and your wife and baby their subsistence and good name!"

"Oh," he said blankly. "I thought it would be so splendid seeing you, Stephanos. And now you're angry. Don't be angry. I did everything for the best. And I'll do anything you say."

"Good. Let me think—where have you been today?"

"Oh—just hanging about near the farm. I lay in that little forest over there—and I didn't come here until it began to grow dark. I thought maybe I could bed down in an outbuilding. I always liked the farm—and I knew where I was, you know, no trouble finding my way. You see, I came to Peiraeus last night at midnight and tried to look up Melissa—and there she was, gone! And the house burned down. Gave me a shock, I can tell you. I came on up here, keeping outside the city walls, before dawn. Thought I'd lie low for a while and then perhaps come and look for you some night."

"No one has seen you?"

"Not that I know of."

"Let us hope not. We'll have to chance it. What's to do now?"

"Can you give me a place to sleep here? Then tomorrow—"

"Tomorrow—to Hades. We must go now. Tonight."

"But—"

"Oh, do shut up and let me think!"

He waited patiently, while I sneezed and held my head and thought, just as he used to wait in our boyhood for me to think of a new game.

"Have you any money?" I asked.

"Yes—a little—not much—about ten drakhs."

"Not enough. I suppose—could you ride a horse—for a long distance?"

"Yes, I can!" He spoke proudly. "I could ride when I was a child, you know, and I've learned more in the army. I looked after some of the Companions' horses for a while."

"Good." If he knew enough to sit on a horse for a couple of stadia, I could trust to his instinct and endurance to keep him on horseback for a hundred parasangs—as long as he didn't break the animal's legs through carelessness.

"Well," I said. "For the moment I'm going to hide you in the barn. Soon you will be put secretly into a cart and we'll go away. You'll have to keep absolutely quiet—don't even whisper until I say you may. All right?"

"Oh, yes. You'll make enough noise for the two of us, Stepho—you keep sneezing and you're breathing like an old horse."

That was true enough. The phlegm had gathered in my throat. I allowed myself to cough freely. Then, making elaborate signs for quiet, I led him through the grove, down a field and into an outhouse which sheltered the cows and milchgoats, and hid him in the straw. I then went to Dametas and said brusquely: "It is necessary for me to take as much of what is salable with me as I can. The man who was here today—he is pressing me for a debt that must be paid right away."

"Oh, deary," said Tamia. "That big man. I didn't think he looked pleasant at all."

I ignored her sympathy. "I've been thinking about it, and I've decided. I'll have to take the largest cart and two mules. I want the oil jars put on first, packed about with clean straw, and then the cheeses and most of the cloth can be put around the jars. Draw the cart up near the barn. I'll get the mules, and then I'll see to the oil."

Dametas said it was so late I ought to sleep at the farm and go off in the morning.

"No," I said firmly. "I must get off tonight. I think I can make a good sale to a man I know of who lives out near Megara. I'll send a message home."

I spoke to the slave with the chopped finger, telling him to go home and inform my mother that I found it necessary to make a large sale quickly and was going to Megara with the farm cart; I might be away for four or five days, but she was not to worry if I took longer. He was impressed with this message, and repeated it carefully.

"If anyone comes about the debt," I added, "she is to tell them that I'm seeing to it as quickly as I can." I gave the fellow a few obols to soothe his injury; I was grateful that he was able to be sent as a messenger but too injured to be expected to accompany me.

Quickly and coolly I selected jars of oil (almost all we had), bolts of cloth, cheeses. Slaves bustled about and packed the things carefully in the cart. It grew truly dark—we were working by torchlight before we finished. I still sneezed occasionally; if it had been myself instead of Philemon who was hidden in the straw, I wouldn't have had any prospect of escaping detection, even by Tamia. I rearranged the packing carefully to my satisfaction, making sure that there was room to spare for a man to lie in.

When we had finished, I took a quick bite and sup, and accepted Dametas' offer of an old wool cloak that he wore for farm work. It was a heavy thing of greasy wool, and not too clean—it smelled of Dametas and of manure—but it was very warm.

Now came the tricky part. Dametas and Tamia accompanied me to the wagon, as I knew they would. I sent Tamia back into the house for a jar of honey—and asked Dametas to go to the gate. When their backs were turned, I whistled softly. Philemon emerged. I shoved him into the cart, covering him with straw and then with cloth and cheeses. He was almost entirely covered when Tamia returned. I took the honey-jar and rammed it a bit too forcefully behind Philemon's knee—there was a small yelp, but she heard nothing. She gave me my provisions for the journey. Just as Dametas came back, I noticed that Philemon's foot was sticking out— I hastily covered as much of it as I could with a cloth. Slowly we set off, Dametas holding a torch to light my way. It was good and dark—but in the torchlight I could still see Philemon's great toe. My steward made his farewells, with good wishes, by the gate, and I walked away, leading the mules by the head and encouraging them. (I hoped they were very strong.) Out on the road there was just enough moonlight to see by—I could even see the shape of Philemon's foot under the cloth and sticking out. Thank the gods that my steward was almost blind, and that his wife was almost blind and deaf.

XV

Journey to Euboia

We went slowly along the track, myself with the mules and Philemon in the cart. I had told my steward and my mother that I was going eastward beyond Hymettos toward Megara, and hoped inquirers would be satisfied with that while I went in the other direction. When I thought of Eutikleides, my heart sank; he might inquire after me—and what would I be able to pay him at the end of *this* journey?

I was on a desperate venture indeed—Philemon's life was certainly at stake, and probably mine. The best I could hope for if my plan succeeded was financial ruin or something near it—all because my dare-luck cousin had insisted on running back into the net.

After we had covered about eight stadia, I stopped, to let Philemon breathe and stretch his limbs, and also in order to be able to repack him properly.

"It's very cramping," he complained.

"Never mind," I retorted. "There are worse cramps on the tympanon. I'm going to hide you properly this time."

He made no objection, but asked meekly, "Where are we going, Stepho?"

"I'm not going to tell you that yet until I've thought it out carefully myself. I'm thinking—if you know what that means."

"Sneezing, more like it," he retorted.

I merely added, "We must take you a long way out of Athens."

"A long way? Riding like this? Ugh!" He got in again. "Stepho—suppose I need to piss while we're on the road?"

"Don't you dare piss on those cheeses," I said crossly. I

relented, and added, "If you want to signal me to stop, move that jar of honey back and forth thrice. But give me warning well in advance, mind. You're a man and a soldier, and should be able to hold your water."

He chuckled, and subsided beneath straw and cheeses and cloth. I stumped along through the night, sneezing or coughing when I felt like it. The night was clear, but cold; we were well into the month of Poseidon. Yet my head felt better in the clear air, and I was able to concentrate.

At first it had come to me that I might try to take Philemon into and through Boiotia until we had caught up with Melissa and her troop. But I would be away from Athens for too long; Melissa and her escort were a long way ahead of us, and we would have to go slowly. The best thing to do would be to cut off the distance, sending Philemon alone on some route which would lose him from sight more easily. Before morning I had gone through my revised plan several times, and could find no fault in it—save that it was tricky and dangerous. But so was every alternative.

We stopped in misty dawn. I hid Philemon behind a thicket and shared my bread and wine with him. Presently a couple of country fellows passed by; they glanced at me incuriously. I realized that, sitting there wrapped up in Dametas' old dungy cloak, with my red eyes watering, I looked like a country laborer myself, and probably older than my years. This gave me an idea.

I sat there mumbling my piece of bread and muttering to the thicket. "We're going to Euboia," I informed the bushes. "Melissa and all are on their way to Makedonia, with an escort of Antipater's men. They should be in Pella by early spring. In Khalkis I'll buy you a horse and you must ride on alone, making your way through Thessalia toward Makedonia. Your name is Leander, you're a wounded soldier returning from the wars, looking for a wife who thinks you dead. Now—repeat that."

The bush whispered back meekly. It had taken it all in correctly.

"But how did Mel—"

"Hush! I'll explain later—if there's time."

I looked carefully in all directions, and then made him rush quickly into the wagon. But as I covered him up this time, I saw in the dawn light something that gave me pause. On his face, on the left side where the cheek meets the hairline, was a scar—not a new one, but most decidedly a scar, of almost the length of my thumb. I went on, pondering sadly.

There was much uphill work, and much lengthening of the distance in tracks that twisted about the hills. I was frightened of letting Philemon get out to lighten the load. About halfway to Dekeleia I found an empty woodcutter's hut, with the ashes of a fire outside. I took the whitest ashes and rubbed them through my hair, to make myself into a gray-haired man; looking into a pool, I felt satisfied with the effect. I also rubbed Philemon's face and hands with ashes mixed with oil so that he looked sallow and grimy, with a peasant complexion of old dirt. Now, if we sat together by the roadside, he too might pass muster. The change also helped to disguise his scar—which I did not mention.

I wished I had another cloak like Dametas', and I got my wish. Perhaps my luck held because I kept pouring libations to the deities of every grove and stream we passed—it doesn't do to take chances. Anyway, outside Dekeleia I met an old peasant who sold me his tattered cloak for three obols and a small cheese. I laid the cloak I had been wearing on the cart, and put on the "new" one. It did not smell very pretty, but I pretended it was much warmer, and the old man and I parted with mutual satisfaction.

I really was pleased—even though I soon had cause to scratch myself. The fleas had evidently enjoyed this garment for a long while. Philemon was pleased too, when I gave him Dametas' cloak and allowed him to get out and walk. He said he liked Dametas and didn't mind his smell. He also enjoyed the fun of disguising—it was always easy to persuade him to enjoy any novelty.

We went on as far as we could, not resting until the moon set. We slept on cart straw spread on the ground, wrapped in our peasant cloaks.

I awoke very early, and gazed into the heavens above; I could see Orion striding away toward dawn. I remembered how as little boys Philemon and I had slept outdoors during soft summer nights, waking up to chatter about the brave things we had done and were going to do. How far apart our lives had become, it seemed—and yet it was Philemon who was with me.

"You awake, Stepho?"

"Philemon," I said suddenly, "how did you come by that scar?"

"That? Oh—sword-cut. Nothing very serious. I told you I was a soldier."

"Where was the battle?"

"The battle near Issos, by the river Payas—you must have heard of it."

"The—that battle? Oh, Philemon, how could you?"

"What do you mean, how could I? Easy enough. A lot of Greeks joined up. I did almost as soon as I reached Asia, and marched along with the best. It was a great fight, Stepho— I wouldn't have missed it for anything."

"Better than fights in taverns, I suppose."

"Don't be stuffy. You're just jealous. You ought to have seen those Persians run! And Darius hared off first! Pretty poor in a king, isn't it?"

"Oh—then—you didn't fight on the Persian side?"

"What d'ye mean?" His voice came belligerently out of the darkness. "Course not. Did you believe that?"

"I didn't know what to think." I told him the details of the accusation at the last prodikasia, "and then," I added, "I saw you had a scar after all—so I began to fear—"

"Nonsense. Almost everyone gets scars in battle. Sosibios. Don't recall him—but then I wasn't in the very front. Did some pretty Persian-chasing, though. After the battle Alexander sent a lot of the Greek troops away. Pity, when the fun was just starting. Too many Makedonians about—I'd like to join an all-Greek army. Though the commander knows what he's doing. As I was wounded, I was among the first to be disbanded. I did pass through Sidon later, it's true."

I asked him about the conversation in Sidon. He thought he did remember something of the kind, but added that he'd talked to more soldiers and sailors than he could count. He gave me the name of his Makedonian captain and I engraved it in my memory.

Now we were talking, I wanted to go on. I must know the truth. In a sense, the truth could make no difference: I would spend everything, my blood if necessary, for Philemon's safety, were he seven times a murderer. But I wanted to know.

"Philemon—did you realize that he—Boutades—knew Melissa slightly?"

"Yes. But I've been wanting to ask—how comes it that *you* know Melissa?"

I explained quickly about my meetings with Nousia and Melissa; I didn't utter my doubts about the legality of the union.

"That's like Nousia. She's good at thinking of things in a pinch." He was quite pleased. "It's turned out quite well. Yes, I knew Boutades knew Melissa—a bit more than slightly, really, but no harm in it. He wanted to adopt Lykias. Imagine!"

"What did you think—"

"Oh—it just seemed funny when she told me. I could imagine a man's losing his wits about Melissa once he'd seen her —but then, he seemed just as mad over the child. And when Melissa explained about being already married, he wanted to adopt me. Can you imagine—*me*, in fine array, pottering about Boutades' pompous house? What would my poor mother have thought? Of course, Boutades was very polite about it, and rather nice, really—but I didn't care too much for him. Thought there were some rotten nuts in his brain-shell. So I said no as politely as I could."

"What? You mean—you've met Boutades?"

"Yes. We met once, in Aigina, early last summer. Very quietly. The women knew nothing of it. I thought it might be a trick. So we didn't meet on the island—I stayed in a boat. But it wasn't a trick. He spoke very flatteringly, and told me about his possessions, and all the money he had."

"He told you of such things?"

"Yes—in detail. He even had a list with him. He was very proud of it all—kept saying he was prosperous. It quite amazed me, how much he did have. He even told me of some debts that were owed to him." Philemon chuckled, a bit uneasily. "Do you know, he told me a very curious tale. It seems he had a friend, and about two and a half years ago this friend got into trouble—he assaulted some wretched slave-girl from a farm off the Megara road. Beat her so that she was nearly dead and was left a complete cripple. She was a favorite of the family, and they insisted on compensation. This friend had all his money invested in cargoes or something, so Boutades lent him money to pay—he had to pay heavily, because he wanted it quiet and out of the courts. Part of this loan was still to be repaid to Boutades—quite a lot. Boutades told me this as if it were a good investment. What do you think of it?"

"I don't like it."

"Nor me. Pretty nasty, really. Lovely friends Boutades must have had. Still, he had wealth, and was quite a powerful citizen. He spoke of arranging an amnesty for me soon. I can tell you, *that* was a temptation!"

"Why on earth would he want you?"

"I haven't an idea. Don't know why he was so keen on me, except he is—he was—doting on the subject of children. Polygnotos hasn't married, has he? Which is stupid of him. Now, I've done my duty, like a good citizen. Think of it, Stepho—in a way, I'm your elder now, as I'm a husband and father."

"Philemon—I'm going to ask you a question, and you must answer with the truth, swearing a solemn oath to the gods. I in turn shall swear that I will spend my substance and my blood to get you safely away and to clear your name, whatever your answer may be."

"That's all terribly serious, Stepho. You'd be good at law. You have the rhetorician's voice—all solemn and emphatic, with lots of words."

"Swear!" I urged him. We both swore the most solemn oaths, as the dawn crept upon us.

"Here's the question," I said, taking a deep breath. "Philemon—did you kill Boutades?"

"NO!" he exploded in a thunderous voice. In the pale light I could see his grimy face with indignant eyes glaring at me. He stood up. "By Father Zeus and all the gods, no! So—my own cousin thinks I go off to the wars as a Mede-lover and then come back and kill an old man in his chamber! Because the old man wanted to adopt me and I'm allergic to wealthy fathers, I suppose? Fine cousin you are, thinking horrible things of me. By Dionysos, I'd like to hit you for that!"

He stood above me, blazing like fire. I got up, but as soon as I was standing he punched me in the chest, and I collapsed on the ground.

"Come on," he said, waving his fists and dancing about like a boxer.

I grabbed his knees as a suppliant. "Peace! Please, Philemon! I'm truly sorry—but I won't be very useful to you if you knock me into the ground now!"

He glared at me, and then he started to laugh. He helped me to my feet—but by then we were both laughing so much we sat down and laughed together. I hadn't been so happy in months. The worst thing of all had been the growing secret fear that my cousin had been the assassin.

"Now, between friends and no need for oaths," I said when I got my breath back. "Where were you on the night of the murder? Were you in Athens? Could anyone have seen you?"

"Between friends *and* still under oath," he answered, "someone might have seen me in Athens a couple of days before, when I went to see my mother—or in Peiraeus on the day before the murder morning. It's funny, you know—I had been thinking of going to see my mother again, but I suddenly got cautious, so after dusk I made for Hydra."

"*You* were cautious?"

"Yes. It's the effect of being a father," he explained. "I'm lucky in having some friends among some boatmen. Well—not friends exactly, and rather funny boatmen. The law might not care for them too much. They're a bit scaly, like lizards that run into cracks. First you see them, then you don't. I suspect some of them are Spartans, and outlawed Spartans at that. You don't ask questions and they don't ask questions."

"But they might offer proof. Who are they? What are their names?"

"They won't appear in a court of law, my sausage. Too shy for that. Still—two of them go by the names of Pheidias and Pheidippides when they're in town. I wouldn't go so far as to say those lovely names are truly theirs. If you want to get in touch with them, go to Simonides the potter off the market square. You just say, "The red pots mustn't be baked at the wrong time of the moon," and scratch a picture of a tree on a potsherd or a tablet. He'll take it as if it were an order, and ask where the pots should be delivered, and someone will turn up. So I understand—but I've never met Simonides myself, mind—market area too dangerous."

I wished to continue talking to this restored cousin and friend, but the dawn light was clear now, and we had to depart.

I walked along very happily that day, singing from sheer lightness of heart. Aunt Eudoxia's Defense was right!—which was more than she knew. Philemon was not there. Philemon did not do it. I was thankful that the vision in my own mind of an unfamiliar Philemon committing a ghastly crime was gone forever.

It would be too long to tell of our adventures on the road. It was a tedious journey, and uncomfortable, especially for Philemon. As we got farther from Athens, I let him out more often, which was of no little help in going up hills. Yet small things, like stopping to buy provisions, seemed dangerous. We spent our nights—two more of them—in the same way as before. One night it rained, and my cold returned. In the nights we had the chance to talk, and Philemon told me of all his roamings and of various exploits. I told him about all that had happened in Athens concerning him, stressing Aristotle's help in getting Melissa away. He did not know Aristotle, and was not, apparently, too impressed by my account of him. "Sounds a funny old man," he said tolerantly, "but I'll repay him, you can be certain. He has done handsomely by us. He's a great talker, isn't he? Those old philosophers are always sitting down and prosing."

"Not Aristotle—he's a peripa—"

"Well, walking about and prosing, then. Making themselves sound important with syllogisms and what-d'ye-call-'em-emes. Why don't we just call a bronze mirror a bronze mirror, and a turd a turd, and so forth, and let it go at that? You have to be careful of these sophistical fellows—they can argue that black is white so as you believe them if you give 'em a chance."

We drew on through Attica and into the borders of Boiotia, toward the strait of Epeiros, Philemon riding in his inglorious fashion. When we were too near habitation or people for me to talk to him, I chanted occasionally to the cart to keep him entertained and informed.

> "We're in Boiotia now—hmm.
> These Boiotians,
> Some live by the ocean
> And some in the hills—hmm, ho!"

I sang happily to the oil jars.

When we passed through Orynthos, I sang in a low muttering tone to warn him to keep hidden. The honey-jar started to wiggle and bob about—the agreed signal. I went on hastily, singing and humming in my cold-broken voice:

> "I'd like to relieve myself,
> but I can't just yet.
> No . . . no . . . hmm.
> It's very bad manners
> To piss in a market,
> Yes, very bad manners
>
> And rather dangerous.
> I don't want to offend anyone,

177

No, I don't want to offend;
Least said, soonest mended . . . hmm.
But I can't stay here for long."

I was annoyed at Philemon, for his signal meant we had to
pass quickly through Orynthos, and I had planned on buying
some bread and wine there. But, when I stopped the cart, he
was laughing silently—he said he'd done that to see what I'd
do or say.

We went down into Delion and along the coast track, approaching the narrow strait of Epeiros, where the ocean does
such peculiar things, bounding up and down several times a
day at irregular hours. And there before us was the great
bridge to Euboia. I had heard about it often; the building of
it was thought a great feat when it had been made, eighty
years before. This bridge had given the Boiotians and not the
Athenians mastery over Euboia. The island was, however, a
dangerous country for an Athenian criminal, although not
nearly as dangerous as Attika itself. We had commerce with
Euboia, and of course now it too was under the Makedonian
peace. If it were known that an Athenian criminal—an accused homicide—had passed through Euboia and had been
given any kind of assistance, Athens could take any men of
Euboia within its own walls and threaten them with the
penalty; a neighboring city would not be anxious to let one
of our criminals go free. Still—it was safer than Attika, if only
because no one would expect Philemon to be there. But we
would have to be careful.

Just after dawn we crossed the big bridge; it gave me a
funny feeling to look down and see ocean water moving
below me on both sides—I'd never seen anything like it before.

The big city of Euboia, metal-working Khalkis, looked impressive in the early morning light as we approached. Opposite Khalkis, on the Boiotian side of the strait, I could see
another city rising white on a hill top. That must be Aulis,
famous Aulis where Iphigenia was sacrificed. I imagined the
strait crowded with Agamemnon's ships, all waiting for the

wind. How had the women of Khalkis gone across to Aulis to plead for the victim and lament with her? There was no bridge in that day. Into my mind came some lines from Euripides' play: Iphigenia's passionate saying, "Truly the sweetest enjoyment of man is to behold the sun," and Akhilleus' somber plea: "Remember, Death is a fearful thing."

As unobtrusively as possible we passed through Khalkis, a prosperous town glimmering with new stucco houses. As we went by a butcher's shop I picked up a piece of pig's offal, a bloody piece of entrails on the ground. My gorge rose—I hadn't had anything to eat that day—but I kept the slimy thing in my palm.

About an hour's walk beyond Khalkis, in a stretch of countryside with farms visible in the distance, I found a secluded place by some trees and let Philemon out of his straw-tickling prison.

"Fresh air at last! By Dionysos, I'm as crumpled as parsley! Where are we?"

I told him, without wasting time in referring to Euripides. At the best of times Philemon was never much interested in literary conversation. But he was interested in the bridge.

"I wish I'd seen that—and I'd like to see Khalkis too."

"Well, you can't. And you must stay here. Promise me you will sit quietly in the shade of these trees wrapped up in your cloak—and don't move until I come back."

"Shade, is it? Stepho—it's not midsummer, if you haven't noticed. Cold enough to freeze the very seed of you. What would I be sitting in the shade for?"

"I don't want you to be seen," I explained patiently. "Here —wrap the cloak about you. And you can take the bottle of wine. Just sit there—not too visible. I want you to look like a laborer who's been drinking his breakfast and gone into a doze."

"Oh. I don't mind if I can have the wine."

"Now," I said, "I'm going to change my appearance too." I traced a line down my right forearm with a piece of charcoal, and then with the pig's blood from the slimy offal I painted along the line, a long thin wound. The blood dried quickly in the cool air, so that I seemed to have a wound just starting to heal—the sort that leaves a scar forever after. I ate some bread, and gave the rest to Philemon. Giving him last instructions to sit there and wait, I turned the mules about and set off back to Khalkis with my load.

When I came into the city, one of the first places I saw in the road to the market was a barber's shop. I was strongly tempted to have my hair and beard trimmed and to take a wash; I felt really unclean and uncomfortable, and those fleas from the peasant's cloak had been making themselves thoroughly at home. I stepped into the shop—but inside I caught a glimpse of myself in a bronze mirror. The sight was so rough, so ghastly, that it gave me pause—for a second I did not know that it was myself at whom I gazed. My experience was little like that of Narkissos. I hastily left the shop. If I could hardly recognize myself in this rough condition, it would be all the harder for anyone else to know me—and anyone who described this person in Khalkis would not be giving a very good account of Stephanos of Athens. My excursions to Peiraeus had hardened my spirit—I no longer minded looking like a villainously low person. The "scar" should help too. It had struck me, remembering Sosibios, that men more readily remember strange distinguishing marks than realities of an ordinary kind.

Since what I had to do in Khalkis had perforce to be public, it was best to be remembered in Khalkis as the dirty unkempt countryman with a wound on his forearm—impossible to connect with the clean Stephanos whose arms were covered with whole skin. I led my cart to the market place, and was soon busy calling out my wares.

"Oil! Fresh good oil of Attika!"

Business was brisk; soon I was handing out jars, receiving money, making change. My arm constantly revealed its blood-stained stripe to my customers.

"How did you come by that?" one of them wished to know.

"Friend did it—with a knife," I answered briefly.

"What a good fellow! There's Attic friendship indeed!" I

did not waste time defending my own city to these foreigners. It felt odd to be in a strange city; the handsome monuments of the place look different from ours, and some of the very letters in the inscriptions are differently made. I had not done much traveling before, and I wished that I had leisure to wander about and explore the place. I was even tempted when some of the better class of barterers tried offering me objects in Khalkis bronze—beautifully made—but money—money in coins—was my object.

The quality of the oil of Attika is so well known, and our own was so good, that I finished selling it sooner than I had anticipated. The cheeses and woven stuffs were harder to sell: some cheeses had been squashed on the journey, and the cloth looked less attractive when dusty. However, I sold these also, after a while, and was then able to drive out of the city. I allowed myself the luxury of sitting in the empty cart and riding—this one time—and I ate a piece of one of the unsalably crushed cheeses on the way.

It was still fairly early in the afternoon when I got back to Philemon's grove. Lo! there he was, still sitting, with an empty leather bottle by his side.

"You've been a long while," he said.

"Not as long as I feared," I answered. "I've sold the goods and obtained the money. Now—this is the really hard part. We shall have to buy a horse. That's going to take some time and trouble, I fear. Euboia isn't Argos."

"Needn't take all that long, maybe," he answered. "I've been looking about me while you were gone. See that field over there—in that farm with the orchard?" He pointed to a valley about ten bowshots away. "There are horses in that paddock, Stepho. And one of them would be a good riding horse."

I tied the mules, and we walked toward the farm. As we came closer I could see the horses he mentioned more clearly —I didn't have Philemon's perfect sight.

"It's that black one," he explained. "A gelding. About four years old, I imagine. A lot of power, and some speed too."

"It loooks rather rough," I said dubiously. The horse in

question had a patchy shaggy coat, and its mane was in tangles.

"Never mind the coat," said Philemon. "Look at the way he *moves*. I tell you, Stepho, I've looked after horses in the army. Trust my judgment—I know what I'm talking about."

I decided I would have to trust his judgment. I knew little about horses; riding is for rich people going on long journeys, or for old men, invalids and soldiers. I warned Philemon to keep silent, but I took his advice about what price to offer when we approached the farmer. This man seemed surprised to find horse-buyers suddenly on such a winter's day. I explained that we couldn't afford a very good horse, and had picked out what seemed the cheapest in the paddock, but that we needed one, as our own had died and my brother, who was a trifle lame, needed to see his uncle in Thessalia. (Philemon limped most impressively—I hoped he wouldn't exaggerate.) The farmer let us see the beast—my cousin peered into its mouth, and rode it once about the field. "It would *do*," he said laconically.

"Well, Pheidias," I said to this lame brother, "it's up to you. We can look elsewhere if you wish."

The farmer, becoming more interested, interposed to point out all his horse's many merits. After some animated bargaining, we got the horse—at thirty drakhmai less than the sum I expected to pay. Philemon was elated as we left the farm. We returned to the mules and the empty cart, and I drove along the road with Philemon while he rode his new mount. (The farmer had "thrown in" a cheap bridle.)

"It was magnificent of you to buy me this, Stepho. Won't I try a canter once I have a stretch of flat! Pity he's not looking as he should—I'll soon put that right with a bit of docking and grooming."

"Don't do anything of the kind," I said earnestly. "Feed your horse well, and treat him carefully. But as for its appearance—it is much better if you leave the horse looking rough and shaggy. It suits you better."

"Suits me better? Well, of all the—"

"Yes," I said impatiently. "Can't you see? You're a lame

country fellow, not rich. There you are, a bit dirty, wearing a thick serviceable country cloak. The horse as it looks now matches the man you're supposed to be. But if you get that beast looking like a fine charger in Alexander's army, it will sort ill with your appearance—you'll be suspected of horse-stealing, at the least! Don't try any wild tricks either—be careful of its hoofs and knees. All our safety depends on your riding a long distance, unnoticed."

Philemon looked a bit obstinate.

"It seems such a pity—"

"It will be a greater pity if you are caught and jailed—or discovered and sent back to Athens in chains for execution. Nothing must go wrong. Now—at that next bend in the road I shall say farewell to you. I must return to Athens, and you must go on alone."

He was silent and thoughtful. We rode more slowly along to the next bend, where he dismounted. The road was empty, save for ourselves.

"Here," I said, drawing a map in the dust of the road. "This is the direction in which you must go to come to the strait of Artemision. Cross safely—don't try it in a storm. When you get to the other side, you'll be in Thessalia. Keep going north —the road north will bring you to Larissa. You'll have to find out there how best to get across the Olympos mountains. Probably best if you try to keep to the coast. Far beyond, there's a river mouth where the Lydias joins the Axios. Cross the Lydias and between the rivers is the city of Pella. Probably there you will find Melissa, but you must be discreet in searching for her. I will try to send money to you in Pella, but that will not be easy; you probably will not hear from me until spring. Don't gallop all the way to Makedonia. In Makedonia you are Leander the soldier, looking for your wife who thought you were dead and has gone to live with her kindred. There's money for you—all I can spare."

He repeated what I had said, and understood the map; I erased it with my foot. I reached out my arms to embrace him.

"Stephanos—I've been thinking. You've just sold *all* your

oil to get me the horse and to give me this money—haven't you? And you have risked your life in getting me here. Oh, Stepho—I and my children's children will remember you. It's so difficult to find the words—"

"Find no words," I said hastily. "Are you not my cousin? Your best repayment lies in taking care of your safety."

Sorrowfully, we embraced, and tears came into the eyes of both of us.

"Farewell," I said. "I pray for you to Zeus, Father of Gods and Men, Friend of the Wanderer. Go now! Go quickly! And we will, I pray, have leisure in a later time to talk of these things."

With a graceful movement he sprang upon his horse and started to ride away. The horse broke into a slow trot, and soon Philemon was far beyond me, vanishing along that road. He did ride well, my centaur cousin. He looked back once more, in order to wave. I waved too, and watched him until the cloaked rider on his black horse was just a large dark dot in the distance, ever moving farther and farther away. The gods alone knew when I would see him again.

XVI

Return to Athens

Realizing that I could travel more rapidly on foot than with the mules and cart, especially in winter and over a hill country, I reluctantly sold the whole equipage to a householder on the Epeiros side of Khalkis, and walked back to Athens. The weather was less pleasant than it had been during the journey with Philemon; there were heavy clouds and scudding winds and rain; in the hills I was twice caught in light flurries of snow. I went through the Parnes hills as quickly as possible, when I got there, not having much liking for the region. The distance home seemed long and wearisome, although the traveling time was halved on the journey back. In a barber's shop in Dekeleia I had my beard trimmed and was washed. I had scrubbed off the "scar" shortly after crossing the bridge—now I had left behind the unkempt scar-armed peasant who sold oil in the market place of Khalkis.

Even so, my mother was distressed at my appearance, exclaiming how tired I looked, how travel-stained. She inquired, naturally enough, about the selling of the oil. I gulped, and said that I had bad news to report: the cart had overturned, spilling both oil-jars and cheeses, so the hoped-for profits had vanished almost entirely.

She saw my misery, and did not reproach me with my (supposed) carelessness. It went to my heart to see her making a little collection of her finer things "to sell," she told me. "We'll settle the debt with that nasty Eutikleides, of course we will. He always disliked your father, ever since Nikiarkhos outstripped him in a race when they were young."

My mother was also full of suggestions, some wise, some foolish, as to what we could do without. I feared our economies would mean that she and Aunt Eudoxia would live on fennel and go about in rags. To think that Eutikleides could bring us to this! Yet the first important thing I had to do was to begin to pay off this creditor. The day after my return, I walked to his house and stood about in his courtyard, in the manner of a humble tradesman or a suppliant for favors.

"You're a day late," he said coldly when he deigned to see me.

I gave him what I thought I could reasonably give at that time—seventy drakhmai. That was the amount I had allowed myself to keep back from Philemon when added to the sum realized on the sale of the cart.

"That's not much," said Eutikleides disparagingly. "I expected on this day—or rather, yesterday—to receive at least half of the amount due to me."

My heart sank. I had so hoped he would be mollified.

"It's all I have at the moment."

"What—after selling all your oil?"

"Some of the oil-jars got broken while I was going to Megara."

A thin smile, like a knife blade, shaped itself on his lips. He was enjoying my discomfiture.

"That was careless. I did not promise to make allowances for stupidity, son of Nikiarkhos."

"Worse things than that have happened on the Megara road," I said with the rashness of resentment.

His eyes looked angry. "Do not be silly and insolent. Doubtless worse happens, but this is a serious matter—for you. Whether you sell your oil or choose to pour it on the road, I still must be paid."

I swallowed my pride, and hung my head meekly.

"You must," he continued, "bring me at least thirty drakhmai to make up that first hundred. And soon. Let me see— bring them the day after tomorrow, in the evening. I will allow you that much time, although I should not be so generous. You must have other things you can sell. It's easily done."

I pushed some false and cringing words of thanks through my teeth and departed, hating him. Looking on his odious face again, I thought that indeed I might be looking upon the murderer of Boutades. Was he also the man of the Megara road? It was evident certainly that he had no love of myself or my kindred. Probably my mother was right; he was not the sort of man who would like losing a race, nor would he forgive the victor who triumphed over him.

Despite my anxiety about money and my fierce feelings about Eutikleides, I had a kind of joy perpetually with me. My heart sang whenever I thought of two things. Philemon has escaped! Philemon is innocent! I could no longer resist the temptation of calling upon Aristotle, in spite of his warning that I should not visit his house too often. I told my mother that I wished to consult a physician about my health; she worried about my lingering cold, so she accepted this as reasonable. Aristotle was sometimes willing to act as an ordinary physician, and people often tried to consult him, though rare and curious ailments were more to his taste.

I told him of my excuse, and he insisted upon acting his

part properly; he gazed down my throat and prescribed the usual remedies. He then looked at me critically and added: "You have also been very fatigued of late, Stephanos. Don't you think it imprudent to walk long distances in the winter-time with that cold, especially pulling a load?"

"How did you know?"

"Simple—for a medical man. You are thinner, you are burned by sun and wind. Your arms are more muscular than before; your right hand is somewhat callused."

"Ah, well," I said, "you have heard that I took our oil to sell —in the Megara direction."

"I might have heard that," he admitted. "But, do you know, I fancy you went on a longer journey than to Megara? Yes—and on that journey you didn't care, I think, to be recognized. I hope your uncouth garments were not too un-comfortable."

"How did you know that?" I was truly startled.

"By the fact that you have gone unshaven for some days while on this journey. Your face is brown and roughened— but your beard has grown unchecked; you shaved at last, for parts of your face are a purer shade altogether. If you had gone to sell oil in your own person, you would have kept up appearances. There are barber's shops on the way to Megara —and, indeed, elsewhere. So I deduce that you let your beard grow because you wished to alter your appearance— and perhaps you didn't care to enter shops. Not comfortable —and an unwashed beard offers harbor to fleas. The clothes you have been wearing recently have also brought you into close connection with those animals—I can see the marks of the bites. You have gone a distance— in a disguise—and therefore not to Megara, as you tell others."

"Oh," I said. "That's all quite simple."

"Yes. It isn't wonderful when I give you my reasons. Obser-vation and logic. But—do you know—my curiosity tempts me to employ my logic even further. Why would Stephanos have taken such an arduous journey at this time, and in poor health too? Because he had to take this journey—in disguise —suddenly. My speculations, I assure you, are entertaining."

187

I had been debating inwardly whether to tell Aristotle about Philemon and his escape; this decided me. His mischievous logic might lead him too close to the truth anyway. I did wish to tell him everything. But still I hesitated.

"Aristotle," I said earnestly, "I wish to tell you of something strange—joyful but dangerous news. I must beg you to swear to tell no others about the matter—to pretend, even to your very self, that you haven't heard it. For on this the law touches me and mine—though before the gods I could do no other, and my spirit is free of remorse. But your knowledge might make you also accountable to law. I have already said too much."

Aristotle walked briskly about his room, the room which was still crowded with weapons of war, now neatly arranged. He frowned for an instant, and touched a spear—a helmet— a bowl—and then turned to me, smiling.

"Very well," he said, "I shall promise as much. If I cannot help you, I swear not to hinder you. I will take the most solemn oath—will that satisfy you?"

After he had sworn and made libation, he perched on a chair and said eagerly, "Now!" like a boy about to hear a new tale. I wondered whether his curiosity was stronger than his sense of justice. In a manner, he shocked me by being so willing to evade the law, even though his oath was a great relief to me.

"I've seen Philemon," I announced dramatically.

He nodded. "I guessed that—guessed it before I swore. I don't buy many stones in bags. Really, Stephanos, you are too transparent. But what did you do with him?"

I told Aristotle everything—well, almost everything. I was still careful to select my facts as I related them. But I told him about meeting Philemon and the details of the escape and journey to Euboia, the purchase of the horse, and the farewell.

"That is truly wonderful," he said with satisfaction. "You have shown yourself persevering and resourceful—I congratulate you."

I could feel my own pride washing across my face.

"So now your dear cousin—who, I must say, seems to me somewhat foolhardy and thoughtless—is away from Athens and journeying to join his wife and child. The only drawback seems to be that you are greatly impoverished by the expedition—that and a trifling matter of your being vulnerable to conviction for having harbored and assisted a prohibited exile who illegally returned while accused of murder. For your sake, I hope no one has seen you. I do hope no one else notices the anomaly of the red-and-white face. Pay attention to details—they are important. But then, most people are unobservant. Your idea about the scar was clever."

"I thought it was rather good," I admitted.

"The strange thing about you, Stephanos, is that with depleted coffers, fresh anxieties about the law and slight physical debility, you are happy—almost exultant. How to explain that? You are not fevered—physically, at least. You have new confidence when one would think you ought to be at your prayers."

"Yes—yes, truly!" I said. It came out in a thoughtless rush. "Philemon is innocent! I know that now—he is *certainly* not guilty."

"My dear Stephanos!" For the first time Aristotle was surprised. He got up and began to walk about the room again. "I thought that was our fundamental hypothesis. Why this exultation at something I thought we were to take for granted? This is most interesting. Come now—when and why did you begin to suspect that Philemon was guilty?" He fixed me with his bright penetrating eyes.

My pride fell into wretchedness. I had dug a pit for myself. I had thought artfully not to tell him all parts of the tale. True, I had a strong wish also to ease my conscience and now I would have to confess to him—but what would he think of my duplicity?

"Oh, Aristotle," I murmured. "I have done you great wrong. The knowledge of it has burned my spirit for the whole time—but I beg you to listen to me as a suppliant—" I began to kneel.

"Oh, leave the formalities and let's hear it," he said. "In

what way have you abused your poor old teacher?"

"By letting you assist me in aiding the woman and child to escape when I thought Philemon was guilty," I said bluntly.

"Aha! Such deceit! I'm surprised at you, Stephanos—well, not altogether. How did you come to this remarkable conclusion? When? You had always thought him guilty—is that it?"

"No indeed, indeed not. But then I found not only that he had been here in Boedromion but also that he had a motive."

"And what was his motive? Not a general pleasure in sending old men to the grave—habits of war and so on?"

"No. Something you'd never have thought of." I explained about Boutades and the vague adoption plans of which I had heard from Nousia—plans or propositions regarding Melissa which I had thought she must have tried to keep secret from her husband.

"So," I concluded, "I knew—or thought I knew *then*—that Philemon had a motive. Jealousy. He found out—so I thought —that another man was trying to take his wife and child. And he came into Athens and slew the seducer in his own house."

"Hmm. Boutades doesn't seem to have been a very successful seducer. We may take it that he didn't succeed or Melissa would not have been living in such poor circumstances. The tablets that Nousia mentioned . . ." He got up abruptly. "Really, Stephanos—you are a dunderhead! It's so annoying! Because of your own fears and pig-headed deductions you've let that woman walk away—ride away, rather— with the most valuable piece of evidence. The best thing we've had yet—if we had it! Great Athena, grant thy people wisdom! To think that those very tablets were probably under my roof for two days. It's enough to make a man's soul sweat! I wonder if we could recover them—but there's so little time before the trial. Only two decades and two days. No, I don't think we can hope to send for them."

"I would not give you anything that would incriminate Philemon," I protested. "I have given you enough already— that fragment I stupidly offered to you. The fragment found at the place of the murder—and with Philemon's name on it."

"Philemon's name?" He seemed truly perplexed.

"Well—with a Phi—"

"What? You fool—it's not a Phi. Your mind is too full of Philemon. Don't you see, it's—well, never mind. But we do need those writings which Melissa possesses. Now, tell me the rest. Having dismally concluded that Philemon was guilty of murder in a jealous rage—and having caused me to use my influence to spirit away the wife of a homicide (as you supposed), what made you change your mind?"

I told him about Philemon's indignation at the charge of homicide when I asked him the question, and of his response to the accusation of having fought on the Persian side. When he heard of my cousin's behavior, the philosopher laughed. The idea of my being knocked down seemed to please him.

But then he said soberly, "So, on the word of a roisterer, because he knocks you down, you are willing to believe that all is crystalline? There's logic, certainly."

"It's not like that," I protested. "You don't know Philemon. And he swore the great oath—and he knew I'd help him to the last coin, the last drop of my blood even, whether he were innocent or guilty. He may not be a philosopher, but he is an honest person. Once I talked to him, I needed no more proof. But there is more, if you wish to hear it."

I told him about Philemon's meeting with Boutades, and what Philemon said had passed.

"So you see," I said, "Philemon was not vengeful. And if it were money which he wanted (which was not so) he would have done best to let Boutades adopt him. If he had been adopted, an outsider might say that he had come back and killed Boutades to make himself heir to a fortune. But we know he wasn't adopted—he wasn't an heir, and didn't wish to be."

"So your tale goes," he responded. "A pretty story—with no witnesses."

"Well—there perhaps are witnesses of a kind," I replied thoughtfully. "Philemon mentioned some friends who were sailors—of a rather dubious kind, I grant. Like lizards, he said. Anyway, they were the ones he was with on the boat to

Aigina on the fatal night. So, by the way, Aunt Eudoxia's Defense was right after all, even if she didn't know it." I explained fully, including Philemon's cryptic remarks about how one might send a message to these strange sailors.

Aristotle shook his head. "Would you want to bring a case into court with witnesses who are the next thing to pirates? The lizards will probably disappear into the next crack in the wall and become modestly invisible. If they exist."

"I'm sure they exist. Why are you trying to accuse Philemon just as I know he's innocent? To shake me? I shall never be shaken again in my faith in his innocence, no matter how much is uttered against him."

"A good rhetorician looks at the objections to his case," said Aristotle mildly. "Come. You have done very well by your cousin. I shall be the accuser no more. But don't you think you have deserved a little punishment for having deceived me so shamefully? Oh—those writings! If only we could lay hands upon the tablets? Why don't we have them? Why didn't *you* take them, at least? *Where* were they? No—hush. I want to think."

We were silent for several minutes. Aristotle fidgeted with a breastplate, an elaborate metal one with the figure of Akhilleus on it.

"I know where the tablets were hidden," he said suddenly. "You know as well, if you'd stop to consider."

"No," I said. "I don't."

"What does this remind you of?" He held up the breastplate.

"Fighting."

"Yes—but the figure? The picture?"

"Akhilleus. The Trojan War."

"Yes—and?"

"Well—the *Iliad,* I suppose."

"And the *Iliad* reminds you of? What word goes with it?"

"Homer. The *Odyssey.* "

"Right. A foolish exercise. But this figure assisted my deliberations. Now you know where the tablets probably were concealed."

"No, I'm afraid I don't," I said. It was like being at school.

"Yes. What did Melissa value so much that she rushed back into the house to rescue it?"

"Oh! The Penelope curtain!"

"Aye. Indeed. And that same tapestry of Penelope, the piece of cloth used as a door curtain, would have been weighted at the bottom, to stop it waving about too much in the wind. Curtains used in such a manner are often weighed down with pebbles or bits of potsherd in the hem. But in this case—great Athena, goddess of the loom—why did you let that cloth slip from our hands? Wait a moment, though. My wife mended the curtain while Melissa slept. I'll ask Pythias if she noticed anything."

He slipped out. I was left to myself for a while, wondering if Aristotle did believe that Philemon was guilty at the very time, now, when I was so sure—nay, I *knew!*—that he was innocent. It seemed an irony.

Suddenly I heard feet running toward the room. I looked up, startled, but it was my host himself who burst in. He was beaming, sparkling to the very ends of his hair. Both hands were full.

"The gods at last are good to us!" he exclaimed. "Thanks be to most bountiful Athena, who guided my skillful wife. Look!"

He stretched out his hand toward me. He held four small tablets, one whole and three broken. Clay tablets with writing on them.

"The writings are delivered into our hands," he said triumphantly. "When my wife mended the tapestry, she noticed the hem was much dirtied and frayed. She rewove the bottom and sewed it up again, but forgot to replace these. She didn't think them any more valuable than the customary weights, but when she realized they'd been left she kept them in case they were letters. By now Melissa may have noticed her loss." He laid the tablets out on a low table and carefully fitted the pieces together. "Now," he said, "we can read them."

We pored over them for a few minutes, but my anxious

eyes ran ahead of my mind, and I could not at first understand what I read.

"Aha," said Aristotle. "This looks like a draft, and not a full legal document. Philemon would know, too, that an adoption isn't valid without a ceremony and documents of consent signed by two parties. Melissa might not know about legal niceties. You see—it is a statement of a proposal that Boutades should adopt Philemon, son of Lykias, and make him his heir, and Philemon's son Lykias his grandson, with allowance for maintenance and adornments for the wife. I'm not sure we have it all, but it seems likely that it is complete. And there's Boutades' signature at the end." His face grew solemn. "You see what this means?"

"Well," I answered, "it seems to reinforce what Philemon said."

"Yes. It seems so. It is a point—one that would stand up in a court of law—that there is little to be gained by a man if he were to kill a generous adoptive father before the adoption took place. Of course," he added, with his awful readiness to see flaws, "these might be forged. If Melissa wanted to protect Philemon, for instance. But why bother? If there were original tablets of an incriminating nature, why not just destroy them? It's easy to destroy tablets, isn't it?" he said with a sharp look at me. "How would you do it?"

"Burn them," I said promptly, "or grind them to powder. Or—a quicker way—just throw them into a river, or into the sea."

"Yes. No trouble to destroy tablets. Or parchment, for that matter, or papyrus such as the Egyptians use. The only writing that is lasting is that engraved on marble or cut in bronze—though Ares and Khronos can destroy even those. Written words are so fragile. But we will preserve these. I shall keep the tablets—safer that way, if you agree? From what Pythias says about the state of the curtain hem, these objects had been there awhile—had begun to wear the cloth—and the hem had never been re-sewn. That too makes me sure that these are the original and real writings, made not later than last summer. A good hiding place she found—but not a secure place—the tablets are broken."

"Yes, you keep them," I said. "It is safer—though the gods only know if and how I can use them to advantage in the trial. But my house will soon have no places to keep anything at all—we'll all be as poor as Melissa was if Eutikleides has his way," I added. I hadn't meant to whine about my affairs, but excitement had loosened my tongue.

"What has Eutikleides been doing?"

I explained about the grievous debt and Eutikleides' behavior; I also told Aristotle of the suspicion of Eutikleides that had entered my mind on that fateful day at the farm.

"And soon after I started to hate the man, and to think him cruel, Philemon told me an odd story that Boutades told him. A tale of a wealthy man who nearly killed a slave-girl belonging to a good family near Megara—and how this man had to pay, and Boutades lent him money, which hadn't been repaid."

"And you think this man was Eutikleides?"

"He seems cruel enough," and I told Aristotle about Eutikleides' cruel behavior to our poor slave.

"Interesting," said Aristotle. "Going on the hypothesis (for the moment) that both Philemon's and Boutades' stories are true—then it tells us as much about Boutades as about the other man."

"How is that?"

"Why was Boutades so careful to protect his friend? So careful that even in his will he mentions no such debt? I remember the will well enough, and there was nothing to accord with that—nor in the accounts of his estate. Not even, 'Make sure A or B pays the remaining number of drakhmai for a debt which he knows of.' One would think that Boutades himself must have been present at the scene of the assault—if there's anything in this story. Thus he would be careful that nothing would be known about it, lest it reflect upon him." He sighed. "No, I don't see Boutades as a man of violence, really—but if he were drunken, and in company with this drunken Other, he might have encouraged the brutality of someone else. He would seem to have good knowledge of the affair. Lending money to the guilty person would give him power over him, whoever he was. Power is pleasant. And money too—we know that Boutades found that very pleasant, particularly as he got older. Suppose the other man had to pay Boutades constantly—more than the debt itself? Paying him for his power—his power of speech or silence."

"Well, if that had been going on," I said, "the man at Megara wouldn't have been Eutikleides. Eutikleides and Boutades were very good friends."

"Oh, simple heart," he said mockingly. "The leech embraces his host. After all, a man may wrong his enemies because that is pleasant; he may equally wrong his friends because that is easy. It is as a rule a terrible thing to be at another man's mercy; and if we have done anything horrible, those in the secret terrify us with the thought that they may betray us. If Boutades told Philemon this tale, it would seem that he enjoyed his power, wanted to tell someone about it, though perhaps not the whole."

"Do you think," I persisted, "that it could be Eutikleides who could have done such a thing? Murdered—or nearly murdered—the slave-girl?"

"Most men are possible murderers. But each according to his nature. Some would say your cousin Philemon was a murderer before he was exiled."

"But that was manslaughter—in a fair fight."

"Quite so. Your cousin is the sort of doughty champion who is always urging others to use their fists. A young man's view, a young man's crime. I hope if he lives to grow gray hairs that he changes his views. This other crime at Megara seems more like the crime of a young man than an old one. Rash. A crime of lust, of peculiar lust it may be."

"You don't think, then, that Eutikleides—"

"I don't say that. I don't say it has to be a young man—but it would be someone with too much juvenility in his character. As a rule, men do wrong to others whenever they have power to do it, according to anger and appetite. But these differ in different men. Boutades would not have been a fighter. Tavern brawls would not have suited him. He would enjoy exerting pressure, but he would have to think it safe."

"And Eutikleides?"

"Eutikleides likes exerting force—as you have cause to know. Don't worry overmuch about the money, by the way. I think we could find a buyer for your little vineyard."

He waved off my awkward thanks, and proceeded, "Eutikleides is much more of a physical man than Boutades. He is strongly controlled, except where he thinks it safe not to be, but he has strong passions. A passion for authority. Be careful of him, Stephanos. Do not antagonize him. Eutikleides thinks himself a lucky man. Feeling lucky encourages only one virtue—gratitude to the gods. The lucky man (or he who feels himself to be so) will do venturesome things, good or bad, feeling sure he will succeed. On the other hand, there are persistent failures who will argue to themselves that this one time they must succeed in a rash move, by their own self-pleasing interpretation of what they see as chance. The unlucky person might also be more daring out of a sense of despair. In general, the lucky man who has been rational will associate rationality with his own fortune. When engaging in a daring business, he will plan it well, even in audacity— while the unlucky man (I refer all the time to subjective feelings about luck) will be more likely to distrust reason and to act on sudden impulse. The appetites might be the same (love of power, money, sex, revenge) but the manner of acting will be different. The man's age, his position, his feelings about his own luck will determine his actions. Do you see, Stephanos? If we look at a crime long enough and hard enough we can see the personality of the criminal written upon it."

"I suppose so," I said politely. I could not help thinking that Aristotle, with all this lecturing digression, was evading a central issue. He was refusing at present to discuss directly the possibility that Eutikleides might be the murderer— even when it was he who had gone so far as to speculate that perhaps Eutikleides had been drained of money by Boutades. I didn't want to think of Eutikleides either, yet the idea gripped me. I shivered.

He looked at me kindly. "Go home and drink all the possets the good women of your house prepare. As for me—do you know what I intend to do tomorrow? In the afternoon I am giving my lecture, but in the morning—I think I shall pay a visit to someone who won't be at home. At least, I shall make sure he isn't at home at the hour I shall call. That's strange, isn't it? Do you make anything of it?"

"No," I said truthfully, and coughed.

"You have been exerting yourself while feverish. Now, that's a state well known in medicine for its effects on the brain. The mind is dulled and stupefied—or is it stimulated and over-active? I forget which."

He gave me a smile of impish innocence.

XVII

Aristotle Plans a Journey

Next morning, with the thought of the debt hanging over me, I set out to sell some of our more valuable possessions. It went to my heart to take my mother's little store of jewels and fine ointment-jars, and her best painted knee-tray—I was glad my father did not have to endure the sight of his son plundering the beloved wife and mother. In this sordid task I at least accomplished my purpose of raising some of the money for Eutikleides. Thanks be to Hermes—to whom I had been praying recently as devoutly as if I were a merchant or a thief.

In the afternoon I went to one of the special lectures given by Aristotle which the public might hear for a fee. I did this partly in the hope of seeing him privately afterward and hearing an explanation of his mysterious words of the night before. Whom had he called upon? Why had he gone to see one who was not at home? Also, attending the lecture in my best clothes, and paying the fee, I seemed to re-establish myself as an educated gentleman after the humiliating experience of the morning. Athens at large must not know of my poverty, my cares. When I went to the trial at the Areopagos, I must be a citizen in good repute, commanding respect.

I was not able to enjoy the lecture very much, despite my appearance of thoughtful attention. Aristotle seemed very remote: a public man and a philosopher thoroughly absorbed in his subject. He lectured in his usual manner, speaking quickly, his eyes alight with interest, making rapid jests by the way for the attentive to catch. His subject was Comedy; I am sure his remarks were good and witty, his range of references impressive—but I kept losing the thread of his discourse. I tried to make notes, but soon gave up the attempt. (Fortunately this lecture was one of a set of lectures which were later written down and have happily been kept for all posterity.) Comedy was not the subject nearest me on that day.

Afterward I joined the little group near the master—he was still talking to the eager listeners who asked questions, comparing modern comedy with old, discussing the relative merits of Axionikos and Antiphanes in comparison with Aristophanes. Only when the little group of admirers was thinning out did he deign to notice me.

"About that sword, Stephanos, son of Nikiarkhos—I wish to ask you some questions. If you would be so kind—my history, you know," he explained to the remaining scholars. "And you too, Eubolos—about this history of your great-grandfather's armor used in the Spartan wars."

He took both of us into his house, and entered first into a long conversation with Eubolos, without giving me overmuch notice. Not until Eubolos left, flattered by the attention paid to his family and its armor, did I have the chance to speak to the master.

"I saw you in the audience," he said. "What did you think of it?"

"The lecture? Oh—very fine," I said politely.

"Poor Stephanos. No leisure for comedies. No doubt you are more interested in my visit of this morning. I have something to show you—"

"Please, sir," said the slave, sticking his head in at the door, "there's another person who wants to see you. Selling weapons—says he cannot wait."

"Show him in, then," said Aristotle, with an apologetic grimace at me.

A man entered. I recognized him. It was one of the sailors whom I had heard in conversation in the tavern in Peiraeus many months ago—the captain. His eyes passed over me without recognition; he turned to Aristotle.

"Beg pardon, sir, for interrupting, I'm sure. But I have this to sell, hearing you were collecting weapons to make a book of and help the army."

Unlike the obnoxious smith, he had no mysterious objects concealed in a bag. The object he wished to sell was openly displayed.

"Aha," said Aristotle. "A bow."

The man laid it on the table—I hated the sight. Aristotle did not.

"In good condition, too," he said, fingering it. "String still on it, and not slack. How did you come by it?"

"Friend of mine, your honor, who's a sailor—and he got it from a returned soldier. Uncommon, isn't it? And it's yours for two drakhmai."

"I suppose," said Aristotle dryly, "it's because your wife and children are in poor circumstances, otherwise you wouldn't wish to part with such a precious and historic object."

"I wouldn't say that, sir. I'm not in bad circumstances. My wife is dead, bless her, and my children grown up and able to fend for themselves, barring the daughter. I thought you wanted such things and, well—what good is a bow to me? I'm only asking what it's worth."

"You are in the right, friend," said Aristotle. "You seem an honest man. I'm sorry I spoke so testily—having to do with chaffering has made me querulous. I shall pay what you ask. I suppose you haven't more like it?"

"No, sir." The man had his own dignity, and had accepted Aristotle's apology with grace. "What would I be collecting weapons for? Especially as it looks as if our fleet is not to fight until the gods know when. And if I were in an engagement—which may happen before my days run out—I should hope to be armed properly like an Athenian with lance or sword, and not fighting with one of those Persian things."

"Very true," said Aristotle. "Yes, you are right—this is a Persian bow. I haven't many bows in my collection. As they are used by the armies of both sides, I wish I were able to examine more of them."

"Some might come my way, I suppose," said the sailor dubiously. "Some have taken them from the Makedonian archers—old bows and arrows, I mean, as keepsakes—but they'd be broken and of little use. Why don't you get some fresh from Makedonia? I suppose you aren't interested in Kretan bows? They're pretty poor things, considering, rough made, but they've been used in battle."

"Certainly," said Aristotle. "Have you any Kretan bows to sell?"

"I do not, sir, no. You might try the crews of the grain ships. But I suppose you've already been examining the Kretan bow belonging to citizen Arkhimenos, the arkhon."

"Oh—Arkhimenos has a Kretan bow?"

"To be sure, sir. At least he did. One such was given him last spring by a sailor back from Krete. He had no other present to offer, you see. And the citizen is rather fond of warlike things. He kept it in the big room where he did his accounts and saw to his business. I had—ahem!—occasion to visit him once myself. I saw it there."

"Well, well," said Aristotle. "I shall ask citizen Arkhimenos if I can borrow it—I should have a look at it. He probably does not want to sell. Thank you for your help—come again if you have anything else which might be of use to me. Here's your money."

He saw the sailor out, quite ceremoniously. When we were alone again, he turned to me, his eyes alight with intention.

"We must pursue this, Stephanos. At once. I shall not rest until we have a look at it—a Kretan bow!"

"Words of ill omen to me," I said, making a gesture to avert ill luck.

"Let us pour a libation and set out at once," my host insisted. Soon we were on the great road to the city, walking very rapidly.

"I don't want to call on Arkhimenos—I don't want to see him," I protested.

"No. Quite right. You shouldn't come in with me. When we get near his home, you go on ahead, and linger about by the shrines under the Akropolis. I'll look for you after I've finished seeing him. I hope he is in!"

We arrived fairly soon at the house of Arkhimenos. He lived near to the Akropolis, in a fine residence, although it was not quite as wealthy and grand as the homes of Boutades and Eutikleides in the aristocratic deme by the Hill of the Muses. I was glad to pass by, having no desire to encounter the man of insults. While I waited, I made offerings at several shrines.

When Aristotle did appear, he passed me by with barely a nod. I understood that I was meant to follow him, without our speaking in company within this crowded public area of the city. He set a rapid pace, and I followed him to the unfinished temple of Zeus, remnant of the hated rule of Peisistratos. This was not far from my own home. Grass grows about the ruined unused temple; nearby is a grove surrounding the more modest shrine of Zeus where men offer sacrifice. Here Deukalion and Pyrrha stood, the last survivors of mankind, and watched the flood waters recede and vanish through the hole in the rocks, and here they threw the stones that turned into men and women to re-people the beautiful earth. The place feels calm and holy.

It was in the quiet grove that Aristotle stopped and I caught up with him. There was no one else about.

"Have you got the bow?" I demanded.

"No. Indeed not. Stephanos, that is a very strange man. Do you know, he insulted me—*me!* He called me a foreigner to my face!"

"Is that all?" I said, unimpressed. "He has worse than that at his command, believe me."

"I had hardly met Arkhimenos before," said Aristotle, "only a little, in polite formalities, you understand. And then he seemed very grave, correct and stiff. So he was when I first called—but then! That is a man in great distress, I think."

"What happened?"

"I called upon him, and he saw me in the room which the sailor mentioned—the large room. After the ordinary compliments, I mentioned my work—stressing the patriotic value of everything, you may be sure. And he was all smiles and how-can-I-help-you's. Then I said I hoped perhaps he, being of rich and good family, might have some family armor which he could lend me, and he talked on, with much pompousness, about his grandfather. I think, by the way, that his good family made a little political mistake during the rule of the Thirty which their descendants have been anxious to erase. But nevertheless our conversation was extremely ordinary—and then I said I had heard that he possessed as a curiosity an implement in which I was interested—a Kretan bow. Stephanos, the man turned pale before my eyes!"

"Well?"

"For a moment he said nothing. Then he said he didn't think he had such a thing. I said I'd heard about it—I fear I exaggerated, Stephanos, for I gave the impression that several people had told me of it. Then he said, 'Oh, that old thing!' I said, 'True, cheap bows quickly become useless if not well kept. I understand this bow was true Kretan, tipped with horn?'

"He began to mumble to himself, changing color. Then he said, 'You vile metoikoi! Don't know why they allow you in! Always you are above yourselves!'

"I kept my temper, and reminded him of my duty to Alexander, and the value of my services. He came round and smiled a flowery polite smile, saying he wished he could help me, but that the bow was gone. I asked if he had given it away. He said hastily, 'No, it was stolen some time ago.' I expressed sympathy, and he repeated that it was a nearly valueless object—some slave must have taken it. Then I said in a shocked manner, 'That should have been looked to—a slave with a weapon is dangerous. It is an offense to condone such a theft.' Thus pressed, he said, 'I don't know who took it, sometime last summer—it was gone, and I didn't care for it.' 'No,' I said, 'I suppose you don't need one in Athens in the ordinary way of things.'

"He frowned and muttered something about being sorry not to be able to assist me further. I went out, but on the way I heard him talking to himself in a very odd manner. There was a good deal of general obscenity. But one of the things he said in his ravings was, 'That accursed bow! Would I had never set eyes upon the thing!'

"There," Aristotle finished. "I have given you a complete narration. Bring your judgment to bear upon it. What do you think?"

"It seems obvious now," I said. "My suspicions—my earlier suspicions—are right, after all. It must have been Arkhimenos who killed Boutades. He had a motive after being cheated over the ship. He had the weapon—and then destroyed it. But the tip of the bow broke off and was left under Boutades' window."

"He had the weapon indeed, I think—at least, he had it once. My clumsy game of chance has brought success, I believe. At hazard one may win. The die will never turn in your favor if you don't play."

"You are not a gamester," I said, surprised.

"Not with the dice or stones for money—no. But at this game of kottabos, I have flicked the target and gained the prize. Indeed, I have a prize in my sleeve now. It was of this that I meant to speak to you before we were interrupted by that excellent nautical person. Look! What do you think of this?"

He held out his hand and showed me a chip of pottery, a thin sliver no longer than the nail on my little finger.

"Tell me what it is."

I looked dutifully at the object. "It's a chip," I said, "a small fragment—from a pot, I suppose."

"Yes. Well—what else? What does it tell you?"

I turned it over and back again.

"Little chips of pots don't tell you anything," I said with heavy sarcasm. "They're not rhetoricians—they know their place, which is the midden heap. This isn't useful for anything," I went on. "It's not big enough to write a note on. It's just a little chip from a pot—perhaps a large one—painted in red and glazed."

"Come on. Do you notice nothing more? What color is the earthenware?"

"Yellow—rather dull and yellowish. A color like nothing very much, really. But the red paint has sunk in quite deeply."

"So—the clay was yellow?"

"Yes. I suppose so. I thought at first it must be red, as usual. Aristotle, why talk of pottery now—with not even a whole basin or jug?"

"I shall talk of it no more at present." He sighed. "Perhaps you are right. If you knew where I had paid my call uninvited while the master of the house was out—and stopped for a few minutes in his room to write a message— But no. My dear fellow, you are tired—and your own safety must be your major concern."

"Say, rather, the trial," I reminded him bitterly. "That occupies much of my mind at present."

"It is of that too that I was thinking," he said. "Do not let today's suspicions affect your behavior or take hold of your mind. Keep your own counsel until I return."

"Return? You're going away?"

"Yes—did I not mention it? It is suddenly necessary for me

to go away on business. I must go tomorrow at dawn. My investigations of weaponry leave me no peace, as I complain to everyone. Yes—I shall go away. I may have to make part of the journey by boat. In this weather too! Southward I'm bound—down to the isthmus of Korinthos, if not farther. Accursed be he who first invented winter traveling! Sacrifice to Poseidon for me while I'm away."

"I shall indeed," I said politely. "And I hope you have a good journey, and success in your undertaking." Inwardly, I almost wanted to reproach him for deserting me—which was foolish, for I was not his responsibility, and, in any case, what could he do?

"I shall be back before the trial, of course," he said. "If it's any comfort to you, Stephanos, of course I shall help you with your speeches."

"What should I do now? What should I be doing about Arkhimenos?"

"Do nothing, Stephanos. I mean that. Leave Arkhimenos with a great space about him. I beg you to be careful. Accept no gifts. Do not go out alone, if you can help it, especially at night. Avoid lonely places. Remember the case of the Sinopean slave."

"The one whose foot slipped in the Parnes hills?"

"The one whose head came into contact with a hard object in the Parnes hills. Remember the valuable lecture delivered by the cheerful merchant of the stones. Distance isn't safety. In fact, you won't be safe until after the trial."

"So," I said glumly, "I'm to sit at home like a woman and do nothing? My poor cousin!"

"Well," said Aristotle cautiously, "you might take up your cousin's hint and try to send a message to his dubious piratical companions—although I would leave that for a while. If one of them would be willing to swear to Philemon's having been on the way to Aigina at the time of the murder, it might be of some use—if matters are desperate enough. But I hope for better things. Don't you see, Stephanos, we are nearing success at last. Let us make here our prayers to Father Zeus."

We prayed at the little shrine and departed. The unpainted statues and unfinished pillars of the abandoned temple shone white and gaunt as we passed it. That roofless building, so grand in aspiration, so ruinous and incomplete, seemed to me a fitting emblem of my case for the defense at this trial.

XVIII

Peril and Approach of Death

Aristotle was going—indeed, must have gone. That was the thought with which I woke up next morning. I would have to manage preparations for the trial by myself. I decided to seek out this mysterious Simonides, the potter whom Philemon had mentioned, and to try to send a message by him to one of the possibly nefarious but useful navigators. If I could press one of these sailors to be a witness at the trial, swearing to Philemon's absence at the fatal time, that would be something.

From what Philemon had told me, I knew Simonides' shop was off the market on the road that leads to the Akharnian Gate, in an area full of the smaller and less successful businesses. I found it without much trouble; it was easily identified, for on the cracked wooden stall some illiterate had scrawled, in charcoal, a dirty and anatomically dubious picture, and added the remark, "Simonides is fukker." The master of the shop rather belied this lewd description; he was a thin swarthy-faced man with a peevish expression, sweating among his wares. This shop was not one of the great ceramic works, certainly, nor did its appearance inspire much confidence. There were only a couple of boys in evidence to assist the owner. The floor was spattered with old blotches of clay;

evidently the master didn't add to his labors by aspiring to great cleanliness. The pots on view were fairly rough. There were a few decent black kalyxes, but no fine painted work, and the bulk of his ware seemed to be rough-thrown water-jars of the stout kind used by slave-girls when they go to the well to draw water, or large rough basins of the sort men use to vomit in after a party.

"Simonides the potter?" I asked, although I knew it must be he.

"Yes—sir?" he said with a mixture of deference and impatience.

I gulped and said, "The red pots were not very satisfactory," and added carefully, "The red pots mustn't be baked at the wrong time of the moon."

"Oh? Very sorry to hear it. Would you care to give another order, sir?"

"Yes," I said. "Supply me with these, if you please."

I gave him the message, scratched on a piece of broken jug, a potsherd of the kind that is ordinarily used for writing short messages on. One side of it had already been used, some while back, for a shopping list. On the remaining side I had scratched the design (which I hoped looked like what it was supposed to be) of a flat-branched tree, and under it had written "Pheidippides or Pheid." I abbreviated the latter name for the sake of space; I had given preference to "Pheidippides" because the name suggested speed.

Simonides did not suggest speed. He glanced casually at the message and said, "A large order is rather difficult for us at this time. There may be some delay. I really can't promise —maybe in a week or two—but it's not certain."

"Do what you can," I said, rather dejected by these hints. It would seem that Simonides had doubts about the probable appearance of the questionable sailors.

"Some time in the next two weeks," I said firmly. "Sooner rather than later. The . . . the party . . . you understand. We shall need to be well provided. If you can't help me, I shall have to go elsewhere."

"I don't know if any shop elsewhere could help you now

with such a large order at short notice," he said with some insolence in his tone. "But I'll do what I can, sir." He went on in a more whining shopkeeper's manner, "Not my fault, is it? How can I foretell? I'm not a soothsayer. I'll do my best, but such a large order—it comes expensive, your honor."

I sighed and put my money (ten drakhmai) down. "Take this as an earnest," I said, "and to help purchase materials, but there will be no more until something has been delivered, or at least until I've heard from you that the order is being carried out."

"Very good. Your name and address, sir? So we can send a message."

Reluctantly, I muttered my reply. If he or his confederates were to come to me privately, of course he had to know.

"Very well. You might expect to hear from us next week. I understand the need for haste, to be sure—but it's not a good time, your honor, and that's a fact. However—if you are really in *need* of the things—"

He glanced at me very shrewdly. I felt uneasily that he knew all about me, and perhaps about Philemon's last escape as well. Such a curious personage might well have secret sources of information, dirty streams flowing underground to bubble up in his dirty shop.

Simonides tossed my message down carelessly with a heap of other notes scrawled on similar shards—orders for one hydra, two lekythoi and so on—with perhaps some strange messages like mine among them. He nodded, with a lordly air of dismissal; this lordliness was oddly counteracted by his next action, which was to lay his finger beside his nose very wisely. "Very good, sir," he said, screwing up his eyes with the suggestion of a smile—the first sign of a smile I had seen in him—while he tapped his nose two or three times, as if he were delicately taking it into his confidence.

My visit to Eutikleides in the evening overshadowed the rest of the day. There are many worse things than money worries, as I had good cause to know already. (And I was to have much greater cause to know this before that day was over.) But money worries, if ignoble, are pertinacious; having them is like sitting on an anthill, or walking among wasps.

I dressed carefully for my visit (I wished to appear neither too rich nor too poor) and walked across Athens to the wealthy deme by the Hill of the Muses. Eutikleides' grand mansion was just opposite the house which I still thought of as Boutades' residence. I glanced at that ill-starred abode, remembering that early morning when all our troubles had started. I decided I did not much care for this deme, despite its imposing houses and the fine pure air from the hills.

I was let in at the gate of Eutikleides' home readily enough, but the master seemed in no hurry to see me, despite his insistence on punctuality. I was left to enjoy my own company in a cool and draughty anteroom for nearly two hours. My temper was not improved by this experience, but of course I had to control all manifestations of resentment. When Eutikleides did at last deign to see me, I felt he was perfectly aware of both these facts, and enjoyed them. He made no apology, but merely said, "Well, Stephanos, I hope you have brought the money *this* time."

"Yes," I said. "Here it is." I could not resist adding, "Had I known you were to be engaged for such a time, I could have come later."

"But then you would have had to walk here in the dark. I am often engaged in pressing business, as I'm sure you understand; there are many demands on my time."

I was reminded of Simonides and his talk of delays.

"Everyone seems to be very busy these days," I said dryly. "I did not mind waiting," I added with untruthful loftiness. "I can think of philosophy wherever I am, and that occupies me."

"Quite. You should consider the nature of virtue, Stephanos—especially prudence. I recommend it to your attention. That comes into philosophy, I believe. You have just given me thirty drakhmai—only thirty to add to the previous seventy. Half of the debt. I am a busy man, and punctilious in matters of business, and I expect the same from others. You will, I hope, have the remaining one hundred drakhmai for me—when? Shall we say in three days?"

"I cannot say that," I replied flatly. "I shall have to sell a small piece of land—that takes time."

"Oh? Selling land, are we? I hope you are not trying to sell ancestral land, Stephanos. Remember there are laws against that."

Anger rose in my throat. I knew the law as well as he.

"Of course," I said. "It isn't true family land—just a detached vineyard, acquired by my father."

"Nikiarkhos was often imprudent in his purchases. And who wants to buy a vineyard in the winter? Of course, Stephanos, I cannot wait upon your imagined transaction in the future—it's no concern of mine. You must pay me the money, whatever you do with your little pieces of sour land. I will, however, be generous again, although it's against my better judgment. You must pay me the outstanding sum, plus the interest. I will give you twenty days."

I blushed angrily in spite of myself. That meant I should have to pay him on the day before the trial! He must know I had enough on my mind without that. I looked at him and saw that he did know quite well, so I swallowed my words of protest and merely replied, as calmly as I could, "Yes. I will pay you then. And much can happen in twenty days—or in twenty-one."

"Quite. That's understood, then. Now I need keep you no longer. I will see you when you bring the last payment."

His rudeness was beyond belief. He had not even done me the common courtesy of offering me a cup of wine. I might have been a slave come on an errand—and in good houses slaves are offered better hospitality. I left, seething with rage. I might not be able to sell the vineyard—that was true. And what then? Important days before the trial would be wasted in nervous efforts to try to raise one hundred drakhmai, and I would go to the trial disadvantaged by the oppression of mean cares and humiliated by uncomfortable sacrifices. The whole family would have to live very poorly indeed—at least through the rest of the winter.

When I came out of Eutikleides' house, some peculiar instinct made me turn away from the direction in which I had come. I suppose I did not want to pass Boutades' house again, but I was hardly aware of my direction until I found I was approaching the path that runs up to the top of the Hill of the Muses. I did not mind, although it was now night, and very dark. I knew the path quite well. Once at the top, after passing the shrine, I would find the path down on the other side, and there would be streets and houses again. I had a torch with me, which I had kindled by the light held by Eutikleides' gatekeeper, and there was nothing unpleasant in taking a short stroll on the little peak before going home. Indeed, I welcomed the chance to mutter curses to myself in the small wilderness and to take out my rage in an energetic walk. So I went up to the top of the Hill of the Muses. It was not to be for me in any way a place of the Muses at that time. Sweet Thalia, lovely Erato, graceful Terpsikhore—what thought you of the desecration of that night? But painfully now I call upon Mnemosyne to help me remember.

I walked in the vigor of my anger, hardly noticing my surroundings. Then, in the midst of my turbulent reverie, I felt that there was someone walking behind me. I paused. All was silent—there was only the murmur of the winter wind moving through trees. I went on, and soon again thought I heard footsteps. I could see nothing beyond the flickering pool of light cast by my torch. But suddenly my mind presented to me some stored impressions which I had not been at leisure to read at the time and told me uneasily that someone had been following me up the street—had perhaps been following me from Eutikleides' very gate.

Too late I remembered Aristotle's warning about keeping away from lonely places. Why had I not brought someone with me? A slave, even? But my anger and shame at the errand to Eutikleides had made going alone seem natural. What about the Sinopean slave—how had he died? It seemed important and interesting to know. I walked as quickly as I could, almost running, and then I was quite sure I was pursued. At the top of the hill, near the flat place by the shrine, I paused and looked about.

212

Then I could see another torch—too close. My own torch told my pursuer or pursuers where I was. Suppose he— they—wished to hurl something at me—such as stones? I was all too visible. On an impulse I threw down my torch and extinguished it. Now I could see but little, but my pursuers could see less. I moved quickly, not quite know- ing where I was going (it was in fact toward the stone shrine itself). The way was rough, and tree roots impeded me. I thought grimly that my greatest prowess seemed to be in running—not the most heroic activity. Escaping, running, running away—my life seemed made up of these. I ought to fight like a man.

I need not have worried. I was going to have some fighting, whether I wished it or not. For the torch-holder had gained on me, and just as he came close I knew that he was not alone —there were more running footsteps behind him. I turned in desperation, my back to the shrine.

The next thing I knew, someone had caught me a great blow on the shoulder. I could see the body of a man holding his torch—with a bulbous ugly face beneath the light—the face of no man I had ever seen before. The fact that he did not know me evidently did not lessen his animosity. He could see all too well for the purpose of battering me. Remembering my previous fight, I ignored his dangerous right arm and made a leap for the left one, which held the torch. I struck with both my hands, wrenched the torch away and stamped on it. I was struck by the man's feet while I was doing this, but while I stamped on the torch I managed to give him a blow in the stomach with my right fist. We were now in darkness. Something swished through the air—I slewed to the left and heard a heavy thud as the object hit the shrine. A club! That was what it must be! I jumped through the darkness in the direction of the at- tacker and to my surprise caught an arm. I twisted it back, and heard a grunt of hurt and anger. I grabbed at the weapon—which I could guess at only, not seeing it—and screwed the man's wrist back, wrenching the club away from his fingers. He kept trying to kick me, but I was now aware that that was his device, and kept moving my feet and legs out of the way. I think I was quicker-moving than he expected. Triumphantly, I got his club in my own grip. But just as I got the weapon, someone else came about the other side of me and hit me a great blow in the small of the back.

I staggered and screamed with the pain, but wasted no time in directing a violent blow at random at my first attacker, who was now (I hoped) unarmed. I got him in the lower belly and must have hurt him, though my blow was not as strong as it would have been a few seconds before. Then the attacker at my back grasped my shoulder. I kicked out, not hitting him, but throwing him a trifle off balance. I ducked down and shook my shoulder, managing to loosen his grip and, turning as much as I was able, hit a blow at this second assailant's legs with my club. He let me go at once, but I soon found it was only to get both hands free to raise his club above his head and bring it down. Hastily, I moved out of the way as the implement was descending, and whammed him on the side, just as he brought his weapon down on empty air. I hit again, twice, and this second man must have received at least one violent blow on the neck or head, for I heard a groan, and he slumped to the ground and was quiet.

All this happened very quickly. So far I had done reasonably well. I had disarmed one assailant, and seriously (I hoped) wounded another. This beginning of the fight had lasted only a few seconds, nor did I yet know the strength of forces against me. For now yet another man with the usual club (they might all have been trying to impersonate Herakles) sprang at me. And he brought his wooden weapon fiercely whistling down upon my upper right arm. Had he got the elbow, as he nearly did, I don't think I would ever have been able to write this. At the time, I thought that my arm must be broken.

I let out a cry of pain and dropped the club which I was holding, but in the next second had presence of mind enough to kick it aside in the darkness—just as the first man, whose club I had taken, made a clever grab at my ankles. He caught me and sent me sprawling. His companion, the latecomer who had just disarmed me, hit me twice in the belly with his short plank. He was bending over to do this, I knew—just as he knew more or less where all of my body was now. So when the fellow who had grabbed my ankles let go in order to find better places for hitting, I arched my body and kicked as hard as I could toward the belly or groin of the one who was striking me. He staggered, and I leaped up and started to run —or hobble—away from the place of the shrine, going quite blindly in the direction of the slope. My breathing after all this would have told anyone where I was, even had my foot-steps not given me away. They were soon upon me again, and again I was struck in the back. I sank to my knees. But as one of my assailants moved about to the front of me, trying to hit my face, I reached for his leg, found it—and, bobbing my head like a bird or snake, I bit it fiercely, as if I'd been a dog.

His surprise was very great, and his anger not less so. He cried out to his friend, "Curse him! He bites!" His companion growled angrily and found my neck, which he punched with his bare fists, very viciously.

There are some spots in the neck which can be extraordinarily painful when hit. I felt dizzy. He did it again. My gorge rose. I stood up—the one I had bitten got me in the stomach. I vomited, suddenly and to my own surprise. I suppose he was in the way of my offering. Some dirty words were uttered, and the one who had hit me in the neck did it again. I was struck in the face also, repeatedly; I could feel blood trickling out of my nose. Then the club whistled dangerously and crashed into my cheek. That was how I lost two of my big side-teeth. Fist-blows rained down upon my chest, and into my back and belly. I punched out feebly, trying to stand upright. In a way it was surprising that they weren't using the club more, but we were standing together fighting in a dark knot, and I suppose the one with the club was wary of injuring his fellow. I tried weakly to reach for my dagger; it is the mercy of the gods that I didn't find it, for if I had done so they could easily have taken it from me and used it to finish me whenever they pleased.

They kept punching me industriously. They were evidently big men in good condition. I knew that we were fighting very seriously, and that this was in no way a joke. This exercise with the fists was only a prelude. As I weakened, the man with the club began to use it more freely. As the club came down on my back, on my shoulder, I realized it had nails driven into it. I could feel skin and flesh being torn away.

Very clearly in the midst of horrid pain and whirling mist within the eyes, I thought, "They are doing this until I fall down again. Then they are going to kill me. Once I have fallen, there is no need to be cautious about using the club —it will be easy then to batter my head in."

This small clear part of my tormented mind, still trying to do its duty, then asked plaintively, "Why am I standing here letting them kill me?"

This ingenuous question spurred me into action. I dodged (rather slowly it must have been) between the two men and started to run. They were, I think, surprised, as they had ceased to expect any interesting action from me. Of course they came after me. In a few seconds a blow from the nailed club tore into my buttocks and nearly crippled me for good (though if the blow had stopped me from running "for good" would have meant for about one minute longer). Another swipe got me in the shoulder—the same shoulder that had been so cruelly mauled before. I kept on running as stars and lightnings shot behind my eyes, and eternal darkness seemed to be beyond these strange lights. There was a roaring like the sea in my head—great waves in which I would drown in a few minutes. Hardly aware of what was happening, I burst through some bushes at the same moment that I received a glancing blow on the head. I went falling—falling—falling— bouncing and rolling over on bushes and stones, with every jolt a sense-tearing agony. Then I stopped feeling anything at all, and darkness closed both my eyes.

XIX

Thoughts of Death

I woke up at dawn. I say "woke up," but it did not feel like
an ordinary awakening—more as if I were a nearly drowned
man floating to the surface of the sea. My sight was narrow
and dull, as if I were looking at the world through slits. I could
see rough stones, a few blades of grass, appearing mon-
strously large. There was a roaring in my head that wouldn't
let me see clearly; my head ached as if it were coming apart.
I closed my eyes again—opened them after a while and tried
to move. The effort hurt so much that I gave over and slept
again.

I don't know how long I remained thus, sleeping and waking in short fits. Things became a trifle clearer each time I
opened my eyes. I could hear someone groaning and realized
it was myself. Then I became more rational and made a
serious effort to see if my bones were broken. At first I
thought I could not move my left leg, and became extremely
frightened; then I found that I could move it, although it
hurt. As the dawn light increased, I could make out streaks
of blood on my hands and on my tattered dirty khiton. Some
fragments of memory came back to me. I knew that I was
Stephanos and not just a groaning pained animal coming out
of darkness. I recalled something of the last night. Eventually
I gathered strength and heaved myself up until I was nearly
sitting—and looked about me through narrowed eyes which
still saw in a blur. I was near the bottom of a hillside, in a
thicket under an outcrop of rock. I tilted my head—nauseat-
ingly—and could make out above me the slope of the hill. In
scarred earth and bruised vegetation I could trace the path

of my fall. There were some marks of feet a little distance away, but not beside me. I thought hazily that my assailants must have hit me just as I fell over the brow of the hill; coming down after me by a safer route, they had descried my huddled shape and had thought I was dead. Probably I had not moved nor made a sound for a long time.

Then a great faintness came over me and I lay down again in oblivion. But soon I came to the surface once more, feeling that I wished to vomit (my mouth tasted terrible, full of the flavor of old blood and bile), but found this was not possible; the endeavor shook my wounded carcass, and hot irons seemed to tear through my bones. Looking at the bloody stains, I realized that I had been ripped open by the nailed club. The cold of the night air must have caused my wounds to dry quickly, which was good, as I must have retained some blood. Almost every visible piece of my body (and much was visible, for my khiton was fluttering rags) was a large bruise. A light rain had fallen in the night; everything felt damp and clammy. It came to me that it was no good to sit here, musing on my injuries. I needed warmth, clothes, medicine—human help of all kinds—and I must try to get home. Soon I made myself try.

That was a braver decision than my determination to see Philemon safely to Euboia, and cost much more trouble. He who thinks it was a slight matter should try crawling down a hillside with a wounded body and deranged head—with eyes that are swollen from blows and nearly useless, and numb fingers that refuse to grip. I slithered on my belly most of the way down,like a snake but much more slowly. I felt every pebble on the way as distinctly as if it had been a man's fist.

When I got to the bottom of the hill, I raised myself on my hands and knees and crawled like an infant. I groaned from time to time, I know, but did not cry. All the tears I'd ever shed could not have done justice to the pain I was feeling. Every now and then the pain and the roaring and blindness overpowered me and I fell flat and went into darkness again. But when my eyes opened to light, I crawled steadily a little farther . . . and a little farther.

At last I reached a roadway. I wasn't quite sure where it was, but I could see it was some kind of street, with houses further down. I felt an additional terror—the people might come out of their houses and see this bloody abject thing shaming their fine street—this tattered animal squatting like a toad.

Behind me came a clatter of hooves. I could not turn my head to look, but the noise came near, and far above me I saw the legs of a man, and his body in buff woolen, and the legs of a mule, and its belly. Things look very strange from the level of the road, I assure you. I conquered my shame, and cried "Help!"

At least, so I intended, but it was so faint an utterance that the man did not hear me. I groaned, and tried again to cry out. This time he stopped and looked down.

"Athena preserve us!" He didn't approve of me at all, I could see—and his first impulse was to move on again.

"Help," I said more clearly. "Good citizen of Athens—overtaken by thieves—nearly killed."

He scratched his head. "Oh," he said slowly. Then, "How do I know you aren't a robber yourself? I've heard of such, waylaying innocent passers-by. I'm a poor man, I am," he added loudly, "without an obol about me, a poor slave of a poor man, Athena help me!"

"Not a robber," I muttered. "Good citizen. Take me home. Reward. In the name of Zeus!" I went into darkness again, but when I awoke, he was still there.

"You do look a bit poorly," he said. I thought he would never have made a reputation as a physician—this diagnosis seemed most inadequate. "How much?"

"Five drakhmai."

He looked doubtful still. "Ten!" I said. Who cared if I were ever able to repay debts or not?

"Right. What name—what house?"

I told him, and then he said, "Up you get, sir," and grabbed me with ungentle hands. He flung me over the mule's back, as blithely as if I had been a sack of barley. My headache was in no wise improved by my head being upside down, dropping over the mule's flank. We set off. The jolting made me feel violently sick before we had gone four paces, but I still had nothing in me to vomit. The movement of the beast under me was like the torture. Pain seemed an element, like the sea, and I was plunged into it. I shut my eyes, and merciful Nature saw to it that I knew nothing.

When I next awoke, it was to find myself lying flat on something softer than a mule's backbone. And I could see an anxious tear-stained face bending over me. My mother.

"Oh, he's alive!" she cried. "Speak to me, my son! Oh, Stephanos—the man who brought you home said he had a dead man with him who lived here—and I thought you were dead, my child! Thanks be to Zeus!"

I shut my eyes, and opened them. "I'm dying," I said, flatly and authoritatively, and went back to sleep.

The next hours—a day or two days—were mere pain and sleep, but some part of my mind still tried to function. It came to me as I lay there, awake sometimes behind closed lids, that someone unknown had certainly tried to compass my death. "And I wish I were dead!" I thought bitterly—an impious thought. Then, as reason still struggled, I thought, "If I'm still alive, I'm not safe," and it struck me that the only way to safety, apart from dying outright, was to pretend to be dead—or, as this wasn't possible, to pretend to be dying. Whoever sought my life would be very disappointed when he found out I still breathed—but he might be willing to wait if he thought that success was merely postponed for a short time. Yes—I must pretend to be dying.

In the first two or three days I managed this splendidly, of course, with no help from acting. The next few days weren't so difficult either, as far as pretending went. A night of lying wounded on an open hillside in the rain is not good for the health, and the cold which I'd thought I'd vanquished came back in a hideous manifestation, with so much struggling for breath that I feared I must have contracted one of those vicious afflictions of the lungs that soon carry a man to the grave. Perhaps I had something of the sort in a fairly mild form; I learned later that I was much fevered, and one night delirious. I knew for myself that there was a period in which I was much troubled by hideous dreams—in which a swollen Boutades came toward me with a club, which then turned into a jar of oil which he poured down my throat until I nearly drowned.

Yes, I gave a very good impression of a dying man during those first days. At the very outset I had been so completely convincing that the first news Athens heard was that I *was* dead. My enemy thus enjoyed about forty hours of peaceful pleasure before the news went around that I was only very gravely ill and wounded, having been attacked by thieves, and was not expected to live. After six or seven days my role became more difficult. My chest was clearing (bless my mother's devoted attention) and my body began to mend—even those hideous flesh wounds made by the nails, wounds which my mother had carefully poulticed to draw out poisons. In a way, I felt worse as I got better, as I was awake more of the time; instead of submitting meekly to the pain, I wanted to grumble about it. With a great labor of the will, I forced myself not to talk, not to move, and tried to keep refusing the food which once I had not wanted at all and now began to crave.

I had one visitor during those first days, a man who insisted upon being allowed to see me, saying that he was a friend of Aristotle who had important matters to discuss. This was a citizen Diokles, who, when he saw me, told me he had come to buy the vineyard which he'd heard I wanted to sell. He had prepared the writings, and we completed the transaction then and there, with me lying on my bed. The citizen left me two hundred and fifty drakhmai in a leather bag; I kept the money jealously to myself for a long while, not daring to tell even my mother in case the wonderful riches should vanish. I don't know if this sale would have been good in a court of law had there been anyone who wished to contest it, for I was perhaps not quite sane at the time. The buyer of the vineyard had become mingled with the apparitions of my fever dreams, and there were moments afterward when I doubted his existence. The whole business, however, was happily real enough.

My condition improved, and this caused difficulties for someone who wished to appear dying. I had to take my mother into my confidence. To my surprise, she understood me quite readily when I explained that I thought the attack was ordered by my enemies, and that I would not be safe unless it was thought that I was like to die. She even thought of ways of keeping up the deception. The slave-girl who brought my food saw only that she took it away almost untasted; my mother ministered to me secretly. She went about the women's quarters pale and weeping (tears partly from real relief) and kept up keening and lamentation. Other members of the household and even my Aunt Eudoxia saw me only as a pale figure wrapped in bandages, eyes shut, breathing laboriously. As I found out later, the reports of my condition that went about Athens were quite satisfactory. The slave-girl told all her acquaintances at the well that the master was "grinding his breath like a millstone, and as pale as snow"; this and similar descriptions were taken in at all the best houses, and in agora and kitchen regrets for my early demise mingled with discussions of the dreadful outrages committed by thieves. (Though of course some stout souls contended my death would be the gods' punishment of our family.)

Meanwhile on my lonely couch in the darkened room I had leisure to think. I had told my mother that my enemies had ordered the attack on me, and so I thought—but who was my enemy? I went over the evening's visit to Eutikleides. Had he arranged to keep me waiting in order to ensure that I left at some chosen time, in the darkness? Why had I given it out that I had gone to sell my oil on the Megara road—of all unlucky places? What a gift I had given my antagonists that night by foolishly going up the hill! I didn't think I would recognize my attackers again, even the bulbous-faced man whose visage I had glimpsed for a moment. There was no report of a body found at the top of the hill, so the man I had knocked down must not have been much harmed. By now they would be all well away, or well concealed. I wondered if they had been paid yet, or would have to wait for my funeral.

In this irksome period of recovery, about eleven days after the assault, I had another visitor—one whom I certainly did not expect. He forced his way into my room, over the protests of the household, saying that he had a message which he must impart if I still breathed. I looked at the person in feeble surprise. He was a stocky man with a brown weather-beaten complexion; his limbs were sinewy, but his belly bulged like a cooking bowl, in the manner of one who has indulged the taste for drink, and there were circles like cooked eggs under his small eyes. He strutted in importantly on his flat feet and stood beside me, looking as if he expected a welcome.

"Well?" I asked.

"From Simonides," he said, with a significant jerk of his head at the house-slave.

I dismissed this servant, and my visitor shut the door. "Who are you?" I whispered. "What do you want?"

"Ho, me lad," he said in a low tone, nodding. "Thought you'd be glad to see me. 'Tain't what I want—what *you* want, more likely. Name's Pheidippides." He twinkled through his little piggy eyes and scratched his chest with an easy gesture.

"Oh. Yes, I did want to see you. Can you—"

"Steady. Haul in and I'll check cargo." He made a grab for my wrist, to my alarm, and felt it in his plump hairy paw, as if he had been a physician; then he felt my brow. "Not bad," he muttered. "Well calked too," with a glance at the bandages. "Seaworthy. Better than I thought it might be." He sat familiarly on the edge of the bed, and spat out a bit of the bay leaf he'd been chewing. "Well, my son, landed in the broth, haven't we? No good waiting for the pot to be put on the fire again. No, no. Leave it to me."

"Wait," I said. "Perhaps you have the wrong notion. I didn't ask for you to come to look after my health—"

"Ah," he said wisely. "Nothing like sea air for the health. Fresh air and distance—the cure of many ills."

"What did you think I asked to see you for?" I asked, rather puzzled.

He screwed up his eyes knowingly. "Well—you want the goods shipped, don't you? None too soon. Let's talk about the price. Can be done tonight."

"The goods?"

"Aye. Bag of wheat sent over the sea—bundle of hide stowed under the hatch. Bacon removed from the smoking house. Say bye-bye to the old moon. That's the notion, ain't it?"

"Bye-bye to the—"

"Looky," he said impatiently. "It's plain as the nose on your face—and that's no beauty since it's been hammered, is it? You asked for me when you knew trouble was coming. Sorry I couldn't help before the iron was hot—but you don't want to wait for the next blacksmith, do you? You want to get away—I can arrange it. Vanish. Healthier outside than in, as they say."

"Oh," I said illumined. "No, thank you very much. I don't want to vanish." (I must admit that for a second the idea had its attractions, however.) "I want you," I whispered boldly, "to promise to appear as a witness to swear that my cousin Philemon was journeying with you to Aigina on a certain night—if that's the truth."

He stood up hastily. "That's the truth, right enough, my lad, but not for saying aloud. 'Twasn't for none such that I came along here friendly-like and offered you some help. I'm not twisting my cables. No law courts for me. Not healthy."

"I can—er—recompense you well for any trouble," I insisted.

He shook his head, more regretfully. "Nay. I'm not facing no jury. Not for any cargo. I'm a leaky vessel, master, as far as law and the like goes. You can't paint a rotten raft up to look like a trireme, and that's a fact."

"Please, think of it—" I whispered desperately. "Don't say no right away. I could make it worth your while. If I could promise you safety and a good character—could I send a message to you again?"

"Can't promise where I'll be. No good thinking of trying to impress me and put me in as a witness under torture. I'll be getting away and you'll not be able to find me again without my wish."

"No desire to injure you," I croaked hoarsely. "But consider—please. You would not be the poorer—I mean, the loss of business time would be made up, you understand."

He winked, but his face returned to its frown. "I *might* think on it—more likely not." He edged to the door. "Say nothing, mind." He then announced, very loudly, "The pots will receive our attention, sir, soon," and stalked out.

This visit left me little happiness; it would seem I had done little or nothing for Philemon. The next days were melancholy ones; the process of getting better slowly is not pleasant at the best of times. I felt such profound compassion for myself that at times other persons, even my cousin, figured but little in my mind.

Yet I was getting better. And the trial was growing nearer. On the seventeenth day I was able to walk about the chamber for quite a long time (of course, I did this secretly). And I was sitting in my chair in the evening when I heard eager footsteps coming toward the room. I expected that the slave would fend off visitors, but I had just risen to go back to my couch and be dying again when the door opened. And who should come in but—Aristotle himself!

"I come as your physician," he announced cheerfully. "I told them not to let anyone in while I examined you." His bright countenance seemed to bring life into my dull prison. He closed the door. "Let's have a look at you—hm, yes, you do seem in a poor way." He chuckled in an undertone, and added more softly, "But not in such a poor way as some would have it, I do believe. Oh, you foolish Stephanos! Didn't I warn you about lonely places? What really happened?"

Whispering for secrecy's sake, I told him all about my plot of "dying."

"The best thing you could have done," he said. "Under the

225

circumstances. Let me see those wounds." When he had finished examining me, he said that the wounds were healing nicely. "Though you will be a man with a scar right enough from now on," he added. "I was quite vexed when I came back to Athens and found that you had been beset by ruffians and were just waiting to be ferried over the Styx. The trial hasn't been put off, has it?"

"No," I said.

"Excellent! Stephanos, I'm sure we've found a way to win the case—that is, if we can keep you alive for the next four days. Thank Athena, you are nearly well! You see, part of my plan depends on your assistance. I need you to help me do something difficult and dangerous and so intimately connected with your cause that I would hesitate to ask the assistance of any other. And I cannot do it by myself, not being a Herakles."

"I'll do it, whatever it is," I said eagerly.

"Wait, then. But are you well enough to go out into the night—and to help me move a heavy object? It will take strenuous effort."

"I feel well enough to do anything that will win the case," I said. Hope and strength had grown during the time that he was there. He might have been Hermes, a divine messenger come to help me in my need.

"I suppose it's a risk," Aristotle grumbled, perching on a chair. "It would be best to take it, however. With your permission, I will wait here, under pretense of attending to you; I will ask for spice cloths and so on, and seem to treat your illness. Send all your servants to bed. At midnight a litter is to come for me. Then, instead of myself, you will leave secretly in the litter, while I walk humbly behind. When we have come near our destination, you too will get out and walk. In dead of night we will undertake our secret work. Then—I think it would be best if you were to come quietly home with me. Your mother will have to be told of your visit to me, but try to keep it from all others. If it is discovered—well, I am only trying to treat you with remedies known in Makedonia, and with oriental medicines brewed by my wife.

But it's best if it is thought you are still dying comfortably at home."

"But—" I objected. "What is the strange work we are to do? Where are we going?"

"I'll not tell you for a little while yet, I think. It's not precisely pleasant—not a thing to brood upon beforehand."

This was not satisfactory. But there was nothing for it but to trust him. I had my mother summoned, while Aristotle waited in an anteroom, as was decent. I told her of my proposed visit and the need for secrecy, but not about the rest of the plan. Reluctantly, she agreed, and said she would tell the household that Aristotle's medicines must be administered only by herself during the next few days. I gave into her keeping the money which I now had from the sale of the vineyard, and commanded her to have the sum owing to Eutikleides sent to him by a trusty slave, as from me, on the day appointed. Then the spices and cordials were brought as directed; Aristotle made me breathe balsam and take some hot wine.

The time went slowly. "How did your journey go?" I asked, making conversation.

"Very well indeed," he said. "It is because of that that I think we stand a very good chance of winning your case for you."

"Then you mean—you went on business of mine?"

"Yes. Mainly. And I found what I was looking for. I knew it was there, but I wasn't sure I'd find it."

"I'm not a child," I said crossly. "Now—tell me. And tell me also where we are going, and what we are to do."

"They come to the same thing," he answered. "So I shall tell you the answer to the last question first. What I am asking of you—it's not a pretty thing to request of a man even in good health and spirits. And it has its dangers—the law might have something to say." He laughed. "But you're not too squeamish about the law in a good cause, are you, Stephanos? I can repay you now for the trick you played on me."

"Tell me—at once," I ordered. "Where are we going?"

He told me. When he informed me of where we were

going, I shivered. When he told me what we were to do, my hair rose of its own accord. When he told me of what he expected to find—and why he expected to find it there—I could say nothing. I rose at once and followed him into the night.

XX

At Hekate's Crossroads

It was many days since I had been out of doors, and the very air of the world seemed strange. I had not long to complain of the night air, for Aristotle bustled me into the litter, which was close and cramping and smelled powerfully of damp leather and old straw. I could see nothing, but I could feel every motion of the slaves who carried me, and wished I had insisted on going upon my own feet. It seemed dishonorable, too, to go about thus, like an old fat grandmother. I was not unhappy when Aristotle ordered my conveyance to stop.

"You will have to walk now," he said. "You do feel able, do you not?" He looked at me as I crawled out of the litter; all those days of lying bedridden seemed to have weakened my legs. But he said, "Good," and gave me a torch to carry. We trotted off at a brisk pace (at least, it seemed so to me); turning a corner, we left slaves and litter behind us. By a little grove we turned again. "I thought it better not to let even my slaves know our precise destination," Aristotle said.

Soon I knew certainly where I was—on the great Eleusinian Road, where it runs through the Kerameikos. We went along it, Aristotle glancing back from time to time to see if any other passengers were about; it is a much frequented road, but on this cold winter's night we could see no one.

We were walking toward the meeting of the Three Ways; the Crossroads of Hekate, Artemis the Terrible, goddess of death and darkness. Above us shone her planet, Phoibe, the cool sister of the warm sun, naked and slender. We approached the Sanctuary of Hekate, the dark altar polished by the moon. There on that moon-struck death-encircled crossroads, there if ever was a place of prayer to Artemis. I prayed earnestly to the goddess, and my heart sank within me, as I thought she might not approve our errand. This was her world, her hour. Out of that whispering night what divine arrows might not be driven forth?

Even my companion was still murmuring his own prayers as we turned up one of the little paths that wind among the graves. Fitful gusts of wind made me shiver, despite my warm cloak; far above, little clouds were driven across heaven, and sailed past the moon as ships will move by a bright shore-beacon. The undersides of the clouds turned silver as they passed the moon, and in like fashion the dark shapes of the grave-stelai shone white suddenly as our torchlight fell on them. Now one monument would appear to our vision, now another. Abruptly, whole carved scenes would leap to the eye, flickering into an illusion of life—a man's head here, staring at us, then a laughing child embraced by sorrowful parents. This garden of dust and bone seemed full of living eyes, watching us; I felt as if surrounded by a hundred presences.

Oh, if what many deem true is so indeed, and the intellectual spirit, forever divorced from flesh, descends to Hades after death, what a horror must that be, that first vision by the banks of the Styx of so many shades like itself! Surely each spirit, still remembering living flesh and cheerful day, must shrink away in fright, itself a shadow, from all the other shadows.

My thoughts had wandered thus, gloomily, so that for a few minutes I almost forgot why we were where we were. Not so my animated companion. He seemed as serene as if he were in his study at home, and he walked easily, although the piercing air could not have been any pleasure to his rheumatism. He stopped suddenly and waved his torch at a block of stone—which sprang suddenly into vivid whiteness. Boutades. His face glowered disdainfully at me. Yes, Boutades and his wife, as I had seen them once before, on the day the tombstone was drawn through the streets.

"Here," said Aristotle softly. He planted his torch upright in the ground, and motioned me to do the same. The wind blew the flames a little, sufficiently to make the light ripple and shake across the carved figures, so that Boutades seemed to smile—to scowl—or to make a little grimace like a man afflicted with indigestion. I nearly laughed.

"To work," said Aristotle. He threw back his cloak, and there at his sides were two long metal poles. He had been wearing these—as a man will wear a sword—girt round his waist with a piece of rope. My admiration for his strength increased; walking thus encumbered could not have been easy.

"Crowbars," he whispered. "And something to dig with." He handed me a large trowel. "Dig!" he ordered me. Obediently, I worked at the earth around the base of the stone.

"Earth's already quite loose," I said with some surprise.

"Give it to me," said Aristotle, and he seized the trowel and began to dig also, very delicately, feeling the base of the stone with his hands. "Yes, it is certainly looser in the middle. No, we don't want to put the crowbar there. But we'll try here and here, I think."

He dug for a while, moving the earth carefully and depositing it in little mounds. "Now," he said. "Try your crowbar there, to the left, and I'll try mine to the right."

When the metal bars were in position, he whispered, "Now! Heave!"

We both tried at once. The stone stood immobile. We tried again to pry it away from the earth. It budged slightly—a very little. I could feel sweat bursting out on my forehead. "Humph," said Aristotle ruefully. He looked about him and saw nearby a small stele, a column, unkempt, which had fallen on its side. "There," he said. "Let's carry that over. Put it in front of the tomb, just a short distance in front."

The column moved easily away from the ground, but was no little weight to carry—about the weight of a grown child of fourteen years, I should judge. Ordinarily I should not have minded it, but that night the work made me gasp for breath.

"Sit down," said Aristotle, glancing at me. "Now—watch." He put the crowbar under Boutades' monument, as before, but rested part of the metal pole on the column. "This might make things a good deal easier. You try it." I doubted him, although I obeyed. Yet he was right, for when we both worked, the stone began to give way, with far less pressure than we had exerted in our earlier efforts.

Boutades and his wife looked astonished as they began to tilt over backward, and then they vanished from our view; the stone fell slowly with a soft thud upon the ground. In front of us now was only a black patch of grave earth. Aristotle crouched beside it and began to dig with the trowel.

"There," he said, "where the earth felt loose at first— follow the line of that and— Ah!"

He scrabbled in the earth and drew out a piece of something. "Don't use the trowel, dig with your hands."

I began to dig, and in the mold which clung to my fingers I found a hardness and drew up a dirty fragment of broken pot. We set the shards in a neat pile, and continued to dig, like children playing in the sand. The pieces were close together, and it was not long before we had a pile of fragments. Then I stopped finding them, and Aristotle had already begun to clean those we had found, using a piece of rag.

"Look," he said. With his earth-stained fingers he handed a large piece to me.

In the torchlight I could see that it was a fragment of painted pottery with part of a picture on it—a picture of someone in a furry robe.

"Dionysos," said Aristotle knowledgeably. He arranged the pieces rapidly, frowning at them in great concentration, and like magic a picture grew under his hands: the picture of a festival play, Dionysos, and the flute-player, and a khoros of satyrs.

"One more piece," said Aristotle, rushing over to the earthen plot and digging furiously. "There!" He put in the missing piece—and there it all was: the scene from a vase, on the fragments of the vase itself ranged round in a circle. Red clay fragments, glazed and painted, almost dancing in the torchlight with a red and black and white scene of joy, the delicate figures clearly visible, though here and there earth still clung to them. The painted scene was the work of a master artist, and a contrast indeed to the gloomy world about us.

"That's wonderful," I said.

Aristotle took the compliment entirely to himself. "I told you it would be there. I could arrange the pieces so quickly because I have had a chance to study the picture. And the inscription at the base looks as I thought it would."

I turned my eyes away from the brilliant picture and gazed at the dull fragments which formed the base of the bowl. There was the whole inscription. The letters showed faintly in the torchlight, but I could make them out: "I belong to Boutades." One piece was still missing—when I fitted that in, the lower part of the β in the owner's name would be complete. I had carried away with me not a Phi, but part of a Beta.

"Yes," said Aristotle. "We can restore the last piece. All the parts together make a whole—though I fear some of this lovely work has vanished forever in atoms of dust. We have all we can ever have—it is enough. I'll take these, for the moment."

He picked up the fragments carefully, and wrapped them in raw sheep's wool; then he put the woolen parcel in a leather bag which he wore about his neck.

"I see," I said dully. I felt no triumph, for I dimly recognized that this find meant that a fearful task lay ahead of me. And the meaning of murder which the fragments spelled out was horrible—I still could hardly comprehend it.

"At least we can go home now," I said.

"Oh, no, we can't. Not until we have made the premises respectable." Aristotle nodded toward the overturned stone, and began to shovel the little mounds of earth back where they belonged.

It was just as hard getting the stone into place as it had been to remove it—harder, if anything, for we had to be very careful to move it back steadily and fit it exactly into its original position. After Boutades' monument was in place, we had to carry the column back to *its* place too. (This time it was the weight of a stout man in middle age.) Then Aristotle produced a brush and began brushing down the tomb of Boutades where it had touched the earth. After that, he swept the ground around the tomb.

"I'm afraid the signs of our presence will be noticeable," he said. "Thank goodness the ground is quite hard. We really need some rain. Snow would be best—but that's too much to expect."

"You might order a tempest and an earthquake while you're about it," I said with heavy sarcasm.

"Poor Stephanos. You're not feeling very well, are you? My wife will have some food prepared for us—and hot wine and medicines for you. Still—be careful what you say, whatever the excuse—it doesn't do to tempt the gods."

We set off again; Aristotle kindly refused my half-hearted offers of help in carrying the implements. Our torches had burned very low, and went out before we had come to the place where the Eleusinian road leaves the Kerameikos. We went on slowly, in darkness. I'm sure we had not been over an hour in the graveyard, yet I was more tired than I had been after the whole of the journey with Philemon. The darkness I disliked very heartily; I remembered that other night of darkness on the Hill of the Muses, and kept imagining running feet behind me.

When we returned to the slaves, I was even glad to get into the litter. I fell into a sleep almost straight away, but not an easy sleep, for my half-waking dreams were colored red and white and black in broken pictures—the broken festival which we had unearthed by Hekate's Crossroads.

XXI

Aristotle Teaches Rhetoric

The next day I felt rather ill again, and Aristotle's medical knowledge was of some service to me—as he pointed out. I could have retorted that he himself was partly responsible for my relapse; it is not the best cure for invalids, this going about on midwinter nights to raise tombstones and rob graveyards. I was not, however, in the best spirits for repartee. Everything seemed dreary and distant. I saw that Aristotle was worried about me—and Pythias too, so I gathered, for she kept sending me medicinal drinks, some of them Eastern concoctions which I had never tasted before. By evening I grew light-headed, and even jocular; next morning I awoke feeling much better, except for a slight ache between the brows.

It was on that day, three days before the trial, that Aristotle started working with me on the evidence. We sat in his room, which still bore traces of his weapon collection, and went over matters together. My wonder grew as I saw all that I had not recognized before. Aristotle walked about the room, lecturing, while I would interrupt to question or to argue. It was like going through the first lessons in geometry at breakneck speed. The concepts seemed new, the logic irresistible. I went through the material on my own several times, so that I was satisfied we had it in the best order, and complete. We also discussed different orders of presentation, depending on what the accuser might say. Then I sent messages to my witnesses—one had already been summoned by Aristotle—once I was satisfied as to which persons should speak. Aristotle himself sent messages to two of my witnesses, but what they were I knew not. I didn't think he would attempt anything (such as a bribe) which could endanger our case at the Areopagos. I was content in my own mind because I was certain that all I required of the witnesses was that they should speak the truth and nothing else.

This day of hard study was wonderfully soothing to my mind. Repeating the facts, considering them as mental objects like propositions in mathematics, made my work seem an intellectual exercise, comprehensible and even pleasurable. I fitted the facts together in my mind, making patterns, as Aristotle had fitted together the fragments of the pot. Now I know why some men can take pleasure in such work, even making it into a kind of profession, as some philosophers and students of rhetoric spend their time in preparing legal cases for other men.

Aristotle was not, of course, one of those who sell their ingenuity to plaintiffs and defendants. Yet on this occasion, for no hire, he showed how well he could prepare a case, how far he surpassed all those rhetoric-mongers whose famous speeches are held up for admiration. That evening we began to work on the embodiment of the case—on the pure rhetoric itself. Aristotle did not do what would have been so easy for him—write out whole speeches and give them to me. No —he was a teacher, and he set his mind to a harder task—to eliciting from *me* the proper wording for my own speech— just as he always did with students in the Lykeion in disputations. This is true mastery—to give, as it were, voice to the dumb. As he said, speeches written by another man and committed to memory by the pleader have always a false sound in the utterance. And what can be more inharmonious than to hear some rough uncouth fellow speak in elegant silver phrases, or some weakling sounding high terms like Agamemnon rallying his troops?

Aristotle sat opposite me and listened. He did not spare friendly criticism.

"Hmm," he would say, "I don't like that purple phrase." Or, "That statement was lame—your main point was lost." Or he might even laugh gently, saying, "That storm-of-rain style at that juncture sounds ill—too gusty. Suitable for the large jury of citizens at common court, who might be ready to weep. But remember that your jury is entirely composed of ex-arkhons, the most dignified men in Athens. Always remember your audience—that's the first rule in rhetoric."

He once commented, "That turn of phrase sounds *too* conceited and clever. The jury have all sat in other courts—they've heard that kind of thing before. This case is too serious—they won't want to smile at witty effects, and might feel you were trying to cover up a weak point. Use wit, yes—but sparingly. Frankness and the effect of orderly passion—whatever does not suit with the whole effect is better cast aside."

But he would also applaud a good phrase, a keen remark or an expressive tone. He reminded me how to hold my hands in an easy manner when not making gestures (you never know until you have tried speaking in public how awkward the hands can be). He had a sharp eye for gesture, well or ill applied. Once he interrupted me, chuckling, saying, "That looks too much like a man cutting down a sapling with a hatchet."

"Well," I said, sitting down, "you show me. I'm tired." Then Aristotle arose and commenced an impromptu speech in an imaginary law court—a rustic pleading for the restitution of a bronze bowl—with such inane earnestness, such fine phrases patched onto fustian and such a multitude of jerky gestures that I was rendered helpless with laughter. Aristotle then adopted the manner of a completely different character, apparently the defendant in the case: a pompous citizen whose mouth splashed spittle, a man given to haughty twitches of the shoulders and abrupt changes of posture from one rigid stance to another. By the end of this speech we were both laughing. I laughed until I coughed; my throat was feeling worn.

"I shall find myself whispering," I complained. "Or I shall hem and stammer fearfully, as Demosthenes did when young."

"I'll give you Demosthenes," said Aristotle, and began a parody which I remember quite well—a speech on preserving the ancient Athenian customs of laundering clothes. I remember it, but I shall suppress it in honor of both men. I think Aristotle resented Demosthenes most because that great but humorless philosopher believed that none but himself and those like him were patriots, and assumed that all who disagreed with him on any point were scoundrels in their hearts. Yes, I must suppress Aristotle's parody, though I cannot forbear remarking that the thing I found most amusing at the time, in my reversion to the mental level of a schoolboy, was not the penetrating wit but the broad humor of Aristotle's saying, from time to time, "Er—pardon me—while I put in a pebble." By the end of "Demosthenes' speech" he seemed to have a whole beach rolling under his tongue.

This performance lightened my spirits, and, indeed, I had learned from it in the most painless way, for Aristotle had incorporated into all three speeches some of my worst mannerisms.

On the next day, the day before the trial, I was permitted more rest, for the sake of my voice. That day Aristotle gave the speeches for the prosecution, acting as Polygnotos and as the accuser's witnesses; he invited me to consider what to say, or how to rearrange my own speech, if this point or that came up at a certain stage.

Both of us were worried about the possibility of a judgment being given against me for irrelevance, either in the middle of my first speech or at the beginning of the second. It is a law that accuser and accused must keep to the point in all four speeches. That law bears most heavily on the accuser in a trial of homicide, as is fair and just, preventing mere general abuse of the accused, but in my particular case it could be inconvenient, not to say fatal. My evidence was of course most deeply and entirely relevant—but I was pursuing a highly unusual course, and most of what I was going to say had not been produced in any prodikasia. If the herald blew his horn and cut off my advance, I was lost, and would have to fall back on repeating old tame matter. My defense was unique in that it depended on proving who was the real murderer; if I were not permitted to do so, then the accuser would have the advantage and Philemon might well be judged guilty. Then too justice would never be done, for the kin of Boutades would not again seek and try his murderer, and I, no kin of the victim, would of course never be able to bring what I knew to the light.

We discussed the unpleasant possibility that I might be prevented from making my case. I should have to be extremely crafty in my introduction of the (apparently) foreign material, weaving it in with my ostensible and straightforward defense of Philemon.

"I can see one way of preventing interruption," said Aristotle, "or of forestalling it, if you like. First, as the Areopagos is a court composed of just men—on the whole—the jury, although naturally sympathetic to Boutades and to Polygnotos' case, will wish you to be spared any unnecessary animadversions on Philemon's character. If Polygnotos calls the soldier as a witness, as you have reason to expect, the soldier's evidence might begin to sound like mere defamation; if true, extraneous. A delicate sense of justice might move the jury to cut off his evidence. Now, if it looks as if the soldier is going to be stopped, *you* must beg the court to allow him to continue."

"To *continue?*" I said in surprise. "I'd be glad to be rid of him."

"Yes, yes, but after swallowing the vinegar you come to the wine. What the soldier said isn't evidence. The man is a weak witness—if you can shake him, you will be able to make something in the accuser's case look dubious, and none of the identifications will seem quite so sure. Also, if you ask the court to allow the man to continue—and don't jump in aggressively, just ask humbly—then you make a good impression. You will seem to be a man who wants to come to the truth. Then you can legitimately hammer that bad evidence into the ground, and use it as a pretext for introducing other material. (We must hope that Polygnotos produces the soldier as a witness during the course of his first speech.) As you will have won favor by being so fair-minded, the court will be less willing to cut you off while you are pursuing your argument. If possible, don't let them see where your reasoning is tending until the end of your pleading. Keep weaving the rope—don't tie a knot until it's too late for protests."

It was going to be difficult. I would have to be clever enough to think of all these things while I was on my feet and speaking—I, an unpracticed speaker who would have found the simplest case about a bakery loaf something of an ordeal.

"The jury will certainly not be favorably disposed to the main meaning of my argument. I myself could not believe what the evidence said until you showed me beyond a shadow of doubt. They will be less willing. And they are disposed to convict Philemon and be done—I'm sure they are. After all, they are of Boutades' class and age."

"Yes, but, Stephanos, they are eager to see justice done against Boutades' murderer. Let any doubt about Philemon's guilt enter their minds, and they will be attentive. And do not forget that old graybeards are curious and inquisitive—just as much so as young men, although they require at least a show of reasonableness and thought. You can interest them. And a dignified, rational and natural manner is the best—for moving them slowly around to this new view. You have that manner now to perfection—no clumsiness, no false flights nor wooden expressions."

"How can it be natural now I've gone over and over the speeches and acted the manner?"

"Ah! That's one of the great points of rhetoric. Artful artlessness. Nothing sounds less natural in public than untutored efforts to be impressive. A law court and jury are no green grove and purling stream; it takes some intelligence to find what one's natural self is, there. Yourself now, uninstructed —your first impulses would take you to extremes both of pompous phrases and agitated mumbling. But you are really neither pompous nor inarticulate. No, the best of the natural is revealed by art."

On the morning of the trial I had to be awakened before sunrise, in order to be conveyed secretly back to my own home. My mother told me that she had done her part, and believed that no one knew where I had spent the last few days. She had also sent the money to Eutikleides, as directed. I dressed in the good clothes she had made ready—but not before she had bound some woolen strips impregnated with grease about my chest, to keep off the chill. She also gave me some pellets of honey, boiled down and hardened, "for your poor throat."

Aunt Eudoxia was pale and trembling—she laid her hand upon my arm.

"You'll do your best for my poor son, I know," she said. "Oh, Stephanos, save him! You must save him!" She pleaded with me as if I were a stranger who might or might not be disposed to grant a boon. That hurt me. The gods knew I was giving body, estate and soul to my effort.

I set out, followed by the sound of their prayers. I walked along as briskly as I could, collecting my witnesses at various points along the way. They were an ill-assorted crew indeed. One of them went ahead in a litter; the others trotted after me, in plain brown woolen cloaks and hoods. It was now the gloomy month of Gamelion, the coldest in the year. The sun was trying to shine, but gave little heat, and was perpetually interrupted by gray clouds.

We came to the Areopagos. There on the west of the hill was the open space for the trial, already filling with spectators. I saw Polygnotos advance with his train of witnesses. Eutikleides was one; thus he could not be on the jury. I was glad at least that I no longer had to look upon this accusing witness as a creditor, though he seemed scarcely pleased. I saw him cast me a baleful glance, yet with something of glee in it too, as a man looks at some noxious insect that he is vexed to find but pleased to crush. Polygnotos did not look at me.

Nothing seemed quite real. I felt as if I were going to watch a play. We seemed to spend a long time doing nothing. The crowd filled the place, and then all the jurors were waiting. The sacrificial ritual began. Soon all was ready for the oaths.

XXII

The Trial Begins

Polygnotos stepped forth first to the altar. He extended his hand over the offering—the cut pieces of a boar, a ram and a bull, slain in the particular manner demanded by the ritual of a case of homicide. Polygnotos looked grave and dignified, yet handsome and youthful withal. He gave utterance in a clear voice to the oath:

"I, Polygnotos, son of Eusebios, come here before this court and in the eyes of the gods and make accusation of Philemon, son of Lykias of Athens, for the murder of Boutades of Athens. I affirm that I am the nephew of the murdered man, and nearest adult kin.

"I swear by all the gods above, upon and below the earth, by Athena, Protectress of Athens, by fire, by the waters of Styx and by these holy things on the sacred altar that my accusation is true, and that Philemon of Athens is truly the deliberate slayer of Boutades. I come only to show to all men present and to this jury that this is so, and all that I have to speak will be on this cause only, with no matter not pertaining to this cause.

"If this accusation be not true, with all my statements pertaining to it, may a curse descend on my house, and destruction light upon my family and my wife and my wife's kin and my children, and utter destruction upon myself."

It is a terrible oath, indeed. Then the Horkotes motioned to me, and it was my turn to swear. I feared lest my hand should tremble as I extended it over the altar, and my nervousness be attributed to an intention to perjure myself. I began, "I, Stephanos . . ." and felt that my voice was pitched too high. My oath was the counterpart of Polygnotos'. I swore that I was Philemon's nearest kin and fittest to defend him, that he was innocent of the charge and that I came to prove it, inviting destruction on myself and all dear to me—and to Philemon and his house too—if my statements were false.

For a while I could see only the red meat on the altar, the bloody markings of a deed of blood. Then, raising my eyes, I saw the whole great multitude, all hushed. I became calm, for I knew that my cause was right, and that I could swear in all safety that Philemon was innocent. I sat down to hear Polygnotos' first speech.

The body of a murder trial has four parts. The first oration by the accuser is followed by the first oration of the defender; then the accuser speaks again, and then the accused (or he who stands for him, as in my case) has the last speech. This method gives every fair advantage to the man accused—truly, the law of Athens is most just. If the accused is guilty—or feels that the trial is going too heavily against him—he has the opportunity to withdraw from making a second speech at all, and can use the last chance to try to escape from Athens before he becomes subject to the law's penalty. In my case, I would have no personal need to withdraw, for if the law went against my case it would be Philemon and not myself who was subject to the penalty. But—if I spoke terribly badly? If everything went wrong, ought I to withdraw from the case before my last speech? Once I spoke even a sentence of it, that would count, and I could not then delay the trial's proceeding to a verdict.

Although I had gone over the case with Aristotle, I still wondered how much or how little to put into my first speech; whether it would be wise to mention this or that at the beginning or near the end. But I wrenched my mind from the problem of what I was going to say, and forced myself to listen to Polygnotos. Polygnotos, standing gracefully in the manner of a man of good family, gazed upon his audience in dignified grief. He looked strong, like a man made out of bronze, and his voice was clear and impressive (no need for honey-pills there). Almost every face in the crowd expressed admiration and sympathy as the audience leaned forward to hear the First Speech of Accusation in this famous trial for homicide.

Honored jurymen of Athens, most noble company, I, Polygnotos, come before you in my distress to tell you of a foul deed, wrought by Philemon in the treachery of his heart—Philemon, who took away my uncle's life deliberately, in the most vile manner. The manner of the killing aggravates even the heavy crime of murder. It is as secret-killing as poison, but more bloody; as bloody as the sword or dagger, but far more stealthy. Would that my tongue did not have to frame the horrible tale—of how Philemon came by night and shot my uncle with an arrow, shot him from without the window as my uncle sat peaceably in his study. Philemon, in the iniquity of his heart, so pierced the heart of Boutades that he let out his life-blood. It was I who found him lying on the floor with an arrow through his throat, dead or just dying."

Here followed an account of how Polygnotos had come into the room, awakened by a noise just at dawning; how he found the corpse and had seen someone through the window; how he had given chase in the garden and had seen the fugitive leaping over the wall.

"I here call the honored Telemon of Athens as a witness."

Telemon came up; the old hobblefoot was as splendid as might be and looked as smooth as a bowl of cream. Telemon swore the great oath that the accused Philemon was guilty. He then said much of what he had said before at the prodikasia, swearing he had seen and identified the villain.

"So it is," said Polygnotos. "I returned to the house and Eutikleides came in, in the company of some others. He will tell you what he saw. I call the honored Eutikleides of Athens as a witness."

Eutikleides swore also that the accusation was true and Philemon guilty. He gave a very full and moving description of his first view of the corpse of Boutades.

"There, sirs, he was, a piteous sight, his poor body just where it had been shot down—you could draw a straight line from the window to where he was standing before he fell. Hideous and ghastly to behold, gentlemen—the blood staining him, clotting his very hair."

He darted his eyes at me in no friendly fashion, as if he accused me, personally, of having struck down his fellow ex-arkhon.

"Nothing was said to me at that moment about the villain, because the nearest kin of that person was in the room at the time—very curiously. But, immediately after, Polygnotos told me that it was Philemon."

Eutikleides looked very impressive; the faces of the jurymen seemed to say, "Here is one of us. Here is one we can trust."

"So far, gentlemen," said Polygnotos, "we have heard only of what I saw, and what others have seen. No one denies that Boutades was murdered by an arrow—an arrow shot from a bow. Shot, as this object" (he held out the horn bow-tip) "will illustrate, by an arrow from a Kretan bow. This was found outside the window. But it will be objected, with some show of reason, that it was not a very good light, that I saw the killer only briefly, and Telemon too—and that our eyesight is not to be depended upon. I shall offer more proof that it was Philemon who was the slayer—the wretch who perpetrated this deed of blood.

"Pardon me, gentlemen, if I am unmanned and unmannerly. It was no common death we looked upon—and Boutades, remember, gentlemen, Boutades was to me even as a father. O wretched shade! See here your avenger!"

He stretched forth his arm—the crowd was affected. Polygnotos regained his composure and continued.

"We will adduce more evidence to show that it was Philemon, a man once exiled for manslaughter, and full of bitterness and wrath, who did this deed. The defense will assert that it could not have been he, for he was an exile. Foolish objection! Have not exiles returned ere now, illicitly? We will show that Philemon did indeed return—against the law—to Athens. Furthermore, we shall show you what manner of life he lived, what manner of man he was, so that it was inevitable he should return and do what he did."

The herald did not intercept Polygnotos; no one questioned the relevance of this promised discussion. I was more interested than anyone—on hooks to hear what he said. Would Polygnotos suddenly produce the fact of Philemon's marriage? Or give some distorted account of his connection with Boutades?

"I call Sosibios of Athens as a witness."

This was the soldier, who looked spruce and swaggering. He blinked at me a bit nervously, but gave his case much as he had given it at the prodikasia. When he came to the fight on the banks of the river, I saw the jurymen look dubiously at each other, and some began to glance at the herald.

I spoke in a low voice to the Horkotes. "Pray let him not be interrupted—this may be relevant—please let him continue." The message was transmitted to the Basileus, and the jurymen looked approving. They sat back to listen; of course, they wanted to hear about the battle, and only the most delicate sense of justice had made them feel that they perhaps ought to cut off the witness in a defamatory digression. I heard it all out, patiently. The rest of the soldier's tale was as he had given it before, but better worded.

"Thus," said Polygnotos, after pleasantly dismissing this entertaining witness, "we see that the accused, Philemon, did come back to Athens from the coast of Asia Minor. He had to leave the whole theater of war, for he had reason to fear any of Alexander's troops—he, a traitor. So he came. And, gentlemen, I will now produce a witness to show that he—Philemon—was in Athens on that fatal day."

Here was something new! There was a sensation in the audience, and people craned forward. I sat up attentively; the next witness had not been seen at any prodikasia.

This witness was one Kleophon of Peiraeus. Sworn, he made a statement that he had seen Philemon in one of the streets near the Peiraeus market place on the afternoon before the murder. This Kleophon was a fish-seller—a meek knobbly-looking little man wearing coarse but respectable clothing. He had probably been paid for his trouble, I thought, knowing the dislike men of Peiraeus had of getting involved in the affairs of great Athenians; the little man was obviously very frightened of the court. But I had no reason to think his statement untrue. He was very probably the most honest witness we had seen yet. He spoke at the risk of some trouble to himself; for, of course, if he had seen an exile, he should have reported him at once.

There was a great buzzing in the court after this witness had spoken. I could tell that the jury felt that Polygnotos was making his case. If Philemon had been in Athens, was not all plain?

"Thus, reverend sirs," continued Polygnotos, "we see that this violent man, this exiled Philemon, was in Athens at the time of the murder. He had already some experience of killing, remember. He had been to Krete, and doubtless knew well the capabilities of a Kretan bow. But why—why should he kill my poor uncle? I will tell you why, though the reason is strange enough almost to make one think the man was mad. I must tell you, gentlemen, that he, Philemon, was —although when exiled a man of nineteen years—much distressed by his lack of a father." [*Laughter.*]

Polygnotos permitted himself a tight smile. "I mean no rude jest, sirs—the matter is too grave. No, as we all know, Philemon was the true and legitimate son of Lykias. But his father had died, and this scapegrace was in poor circumstances. It became a fixed idea with him, a settled source of melancholy, that he ought to have the perquisites and expectations of a rich man's son. So my poor uncle became the object of his attention. Because Boutades once spoke kindly to him, he was possessed by the preposterous notion that Boutades ought to adopt him—against all reason. My uncle mentioned this to his wife and myself as a subject of mild mirth. But he said nothing about it outside the home, out of respect for poor Lykias' memory.

"Thus—we can see this wrathful young man whose life has been a sequence of self-created misfortunes. First he kills a man in a brawl, and is exiled. In exile he first wanders fecklessly over the seas; then, in the malignity of his heart, he joins the army of the Persians. Wounded in a great battle in which he was on the wrong side, and fearful of the triumphant army, he flies back home and re-enters Athens—enters it although it is a forbidden city to him. I think he had no settled plan of murder until he reached the shore—but who can tell? Once in Athens, alone and dispossessed, he decides in his desperate mind to take a revenge upon mankind for the consequences of his own errors—to take a false revenge upon my poor hapless uncle. Philemon would kill Boutades and take the property which he thought ought to be his, which would have been his had he been, as he wished, the son of a rich man. It was in this mad state of mind, surely, that he stole out in the night to take my uncle's life in the most vile fashion—yet with utmost safety to himself. Perhaps he felt satisfaction in seeing the man dead and bloody? My stirring prevented Philemon's committing the robbery he intended. Unfortunately I arrived too soon; a few minutes later I should have caught him in the act of robbery, within the house.

"It was a mad deed—but his madness is no excuse, for the murder was done deliberately, in full knowledge that he was causing the death of a man. Alas for my kind uncle, thus deprived of life! The madness of Philemon shows only that the gods themselves do curse him.

"And I curse and execrate him, Philemon, the murderer. And may I be myself accursed if I have uttered ought but truth in my accusation, by all the gods and by these holy things."

XXIII

The Areopagos in an Uproar

I felt as if the earth were crumbling under my feet. Polygnotos had mentioned nothing of motive at any of the prodikasiai. I could see that the jury was convinced. One of the major
points in my case would perhaps be seriously weakened. *I*
had meant to produce surprise in referring to Boutades' desire to adopt Philemon. But now it would be much easier for
the accuser to wave that aside, to say that it was all a figment
of Philemon's imagining, and to deny the documents as anything but forgeries. The only slight good of this new matter
was that it must now give me sufficient reason to take the
argument forward and raise matters which I had not mentioned at the prodikasiai.

I got up to speak. I saw my audience in a kind of blur. The
sky above us was gray and forbidding. I felt as if I was talking
to a world made of iron.

"Honored jurymen of Athens, I, Stephanos, come before
you to speak for my unhappy cousin Philemon, and to tell you
that he is innocent of this dreadful crime. I will try to take
the accuser's case, point by point.

"No one denies that Boutades was shot by an arrow, nor
that his body was seen by many exactly as the accuser and
two witnesses have described it—but the accuser can be mistaken about the killer, especially in a case where no one
claims to have arrived on the scene until after the crime was
committed. First, as to the killer's having been seen. It was
indeed a poor light—the light just before dawn breaks, in
which it is still difficult to tell black threads from white."

I went dutifully through the points I had made at the

prodikasia, and was especially emphatic about Telemon's short-sightedness. The jury listened dutifully, too, but without much interest.

I then passed to the case made by the soldier—here I was stronger. I questioned that witness, much as I had done before, although this time he was more wary. Still, he was a poor witness—cocksure and anxious to please his own side, so he could be thrown by an unexpected question. This time I managed to throw him off balance by some technical questions about arms and armor, of the Allies and of the Persians. He was caught appealing with his eyes to his own side for an answer when asked a simple question about Makedonian helmets. This folly cost him some credit with the jury; I was able to make my point that his "recognition" of Philemon was doubtful.

"In fact," I said, "this witness is not *entirely* wrong. Philemon was at that battle, certainly. He was fighting on the side of the Greeks and Makedonians at that great victory by Issos town. There he was indeed wounded—in honorable service. I have here the name of his captain, a Makedonian. Send to this man—" I passed the name about the jury, for all to see—"who is the captain in Alexander's army, and he will be able to tell you of Philemon's conduct in the battle. It is far to send—and I found out this fact only recently. But I beg of you to assist me in sending for this information before you brand Philemon a traitor in your minds.

"You will wonder how I know this—and why, knowing it, I did not act sooner. As you will have realized, I have communicated with Philemon since proceedings began. If this is a crime, I beg your mercy, but it is not, surely, a crime for a citizen to answer a letter sent by his nearest kinsman in great distress—nor to ask for a letter in return." (I was on dangerous ground here, and did not feel quite happy about the oath, although I was being careful not to utter a direct lie.)

"No, the law of Athens is just, and recognizes ties of blood. But it was only since the slander was uttered that I heard from the accused and could ask him about the war and hear from him the name of his captain. Philemon is, though an exile, still a patriot—he has been a warrior for the Greeks. He had no reason to slink away from Asia, nor, being one of the heroes in a glorious victory, had he cause to come to such a frame of mind as the prosecution suggests."

The jury were somewhat impressed by all this—not totally, but my confidence and the name of Alexander had their effect. I could see the first stirrings of any doubt about Philemon's guilt—at least, they were less willing to see him totally unfavorably as a traitor and hence as a mad revengeful man.

The fact that I had asked that the soldier be allowed to speak had told in my favor. I took this slight advantage and pressed on; the next part of my defense was not going to be so agreeable.

"Yet, sirs, I have an admission to make. But why be afraid? Who should be afraid to admit the truth before this court of Athenian justice? I ask no pity. I ask for justice, for equitable judgment. I know now what I did not know earlier—may the gods help me!—that Philemon was indeed in Athens. I knew it not when I confidently swore before the Basileus that the accused was not here and could not have been here. Now truly, in his voice to you, I plead guilty to trespassing against the laws regarding exile. And you may say, truly, 'For that he deserves death by the law.' O sirs, I beg you to consider that that case is not this one, and that though guilty in one thing he may be innocent in another. Find it in your hearts to see how this man felt—to see his condition. For after fighting for his country, he did return home, and was a trespasser in his own city.

"Why should he do this illegal thing? Ah, sirs, because he wanted to see his old mother, who is dying of an incurable disease. She knew of his coming, and no other member of the family knew it until very recently, when the wretched woman broke down and confessed to me. It is right that I now tell you of this. Punish me in my own body, if you will, for Philemon's offense—but do so after this trial is over. I am willing to be secured. But that case is not this one. Which among us has not done some wrong—not a crime, but a wrong—and yet is not horrified at the bare idea of committing some other wrong? All offenses are not one. We are hearing *this* case—and of this deed Philemon is innocent."

I wiped my forehead. The jury were looking very solemn. I could see the accuser and the witnesses looking as pleased as five carrion crows in a tree. Polygnotos looked proud, but sorry for me too; Eutikleides, however, was grimacing with satisfaction.

"Consider, sirs, that though Philemon may deserve death by your law—yet that law is not always carried out in its full rigor—he does not deserve that the horrible slander of the most foul crime should hang upon his name forever. Between the one act—return from exile—and the other—the most disgusting murder—there is a great gulf. Some of us may imagine committing the first; no man with a grain of honor and humanity left in him can imagine committing the second."

I could see that the jury, for the most part, agreed with me about the difference between the two crimes, but that most of them felt I had, in admitting Philemon's presence, given up the major point of the case. There was some sympathy for me (if grudging); none for Philemon. I had to dive deeper.

"But that is not all I have to say about his return. I shall shortly come to a tale which will interest you greatly, a complicated story about a family. Philemon came to see his old mother—true. But he also came to see a woman—his wife, Melissa—whom he had married secretly before his exile. He came to see her and his child.

"Now comes the strangest part of their case. This woman is of an Athenian family which had lived in Thebes. She, while in flight from the sack of Thebes in company with her father and servants, was seen and admired by Boutades. Boutades later found her after the marriage, after the birth of Philemon's child, and wanted to adopt the baby as his son."

There were cries from the audience: "This woman and child! Where are they?"

"In Makedonia," I replied mildly. "If you send Antipater's

envoy thither, you will find them in the chief city.

"This woman explained about her marriage, and it was then that Boutades decided he wished to adopt Philemon also—thus he would have a son and a grandson. Observe that the matter was somewhat as the prosecution suggests, but the other way around. Why, incidentally, did the accuser mention nothing of this adoption matter at any of the prodikasiai?"

Polygnotos looked reproachful, as if to say, "But I had only recently seen the connection." I was sure he would be able to handle *that,* anyway, in his next speech. Eutikleides played with the fringe of his robe and puffed out his lips.

"Lo!" I said dramatically, producing the tablets that Aristotle and I had found in their hiding place. "Here is the tentative agreement drawn up by the deceased citizen Boutades. This is the copy owned by the woman who is now in Makedonia. This unwitnessed document constitutes no claim as it stands: it is obviously a draft. Yet the tablets are written in Boutades' hand, and are signed with his seal. Notice that these tablets are *old*—they have not been made in the last few weeks; and let those who know Boutades' hand examine them closely."

I handed them to the Horkotes, who passed them first to the Basileus and then to the jury. There was a good deal of interest.

"I am sure that the accuser will cry 'Forgery!' Yet—who is the forger? Would a woman be able to write like that? Would she find the correct terms, even if she could write? Would my cousin—no scholar—be able to write like a man versed in law and business? How would Boutades' seal be imitated? Or his hand? If anyone, man or woman, were sufficiently daring and skilled to undertake a forgery, would he or she attempt to forge mere *drafts,* and not a document which would be advantageous in a court of law? These tablets could not be produced to claim adoptive kinship or right of inheritance. They are useless. They show us only that Boutades *did* think of adopting Philemon.

"You will ask, why was no copy of this draft agreement

found among Boutades' effects? A very proper question—one to which I shall return, for I myself have asked it.

"To begin to find an answer we must go deeper into the case. I realize that to most of you, who do not know Philemon, the picture painted of him by the accuser must seem plausible. But my cousin, a cheerful, good-natured man, is hardly this melancholy man of wrath. He had known the joy of victory in battle. He had a beautiful wife and a handsome child. He thought—with reason—that his valor in battle might lead to commutation of his sentence, and his wife's inheritance gave him some hopes of prosperity too. I ask you to imagine for the space of two minutes—just that—that it *might* be possible that Philemon did not do the deed. True, he had been to Krete, and everyone swears that Boutades was shot with a Kretan bow. Could no one else have had access to a Kretan bow? I call citizen Arkhimenos as a witness."

Citizen Arkhimenos was not a happy witness; it was he who had come in the litter, on the plea of not feeling very well. He did not look well, but he spoke clearly, frowning all the while, the two lines on his forehead graven deeply into his face so that one felt they must be marked on his skull.

Arkhimenos swore that Philemon was innocent and his statement true. Then he testified that he himself had possessed a Kretan bow, which had disappeared sometime in the summer. He described the place where it was kept, and the men who had been in the room and must have seen it.

"Remember," I interjected, "this is important. Not everyone knew Arkhimenos had the bow—not everyone knew that the bow was a Kretan bow. But some men did, and those men included Boutades himself and Polygnotos, and other men of good standing, and also some slaves and some sailors."

I turned to the witness again. "Why did you not report the loss of the bow?"

"I didn't know who had taken it," he replied in a low voice.

"Why did you not mention it, nevertheless? Did you think you knew who had taken it?"

"Yes. I thought it was Boutades himself."

"A little louder, please. You thought it was Boutades. But why?"

"For a kind of—of jest."

"A pleasantry between friends? You were friends?"

The man amazed me. He burst out, at me and the whole court: "I HATED Boutades! The man cheated me—he made my life a misery and a weariness. He exchanged with me a ship for a debt—a ship so ill-fitted that I would be ruined trying to make it good. He was dishonest in his heart. Nothing was beyond him! Nothing! He cared nothing for Athens, nor for the trierarkhy. Himself—his reputation and his money—that was all he cared for, but chiefly money. Sirs—" he turned to the jury—"look to yourselves and your ships, and examine closely all Boutades' accounts. Nay, I am sure there are those among you whom he cheated too—and some of you know it. But not one has been so much abused as I! Not one! I thought of killing myself—because of him! I am not the killer, but I love his death. If I had prayed a hundred years, I could have asked nothing better! The gods curse him in Hades, and Rhadamanthos condemn him!"

At the end of this astonishing outburst Arkhimenos was in tears—not a slight moisture in red-rimmed eyes, but tears cascading like those of a child, running over his face, pressing the furrows between nose and chin and dripping in rivulets down his khiton. He looked very old, very pitiable, very strange.

I think we all felt a touch—more than a touch—of madness, yet everyone believed what he said. There was a great stir among the jury; I am sure that Arkhimenos' words about men other than he having been cheated by the deceased citizen had struck home to a few of them, and all felt indignant at the account of Boutades' mean dishonesty. The reputation of trierarkhs in general is sensitive to such injury, and the pity which had been present for Boutades was suddenly lightened. Boutades was no longer the "good man" of the ballad. The crime of murdering him remained as grave as before, yet suddenly the atmosphere was easier for me to breathe in. Men were no longer implacably convinced by the prosecution; they became more willing to hear me.

"What Arkhimenos said appears true," I asserted. "Boutades was mean. But his avarice grew upon him during the last while. He became possessed with the notion of adopting a son—and grandson—and leaving a great inheritance. Possession became his whole object. But let us think of the bow. The murderer shot with a Kretan bow. Yes. But I will ask you again to do your painful duty and imagine the horrible sight. I call citizen Eutikleides, the witness for the accuser, to give again his account of the disposition of the body and the state of the room."

Eutikleides spoke again—with exaggerated patience. He gave a very smooth account, but when I asked him to describe what was on the various tables—there he hesitated, and was not able to give a complete description.

"But the body," I said. "You saw the body very clearly."

"Yes, certainly, lying just as I have said."

"And it was very bloody?"

"Yes."

"The hair too?"

"Yes. When they raised up that poor corpse, the hair at the back of the head was blood-clotted. I could see it."

"And his feet?"

"Yes. His slippers—the very soles—had blood on them. I don't see what's the good of all this," he added disdainfully. "The man was very dead, that's certain. I protest only that the defender is asking unnecessary questions in order to gain time."

I let him retire. No one else objected to my questioning.

"Look at the body—in your mind's eye, gentlemen. The accuser said that Boutades sat working at his table, facing the window. That is, he was working peacefully at the table at the end of the room, facing west. The murderer shooting from outside the west window could not have shot from very close to the window, for an arrow needs to be shot from some distance in order to gain its force. But—where was Boutades?

The body was facing in the right direction—the right one, I mean, for a man shot from the direction of the window. But the body was near the middle of the room. If Boutades had been shot while working at his desk—where the murderer could perhaps have seen him clearly from outdoors because the unsuspecting victim had a small light on the table—then he would have fallen at or on the desk. At the very least, his blood would have spattered the desk. Perhaps, you will say, he stood up, and thus received the blow standing, and fell back suddenly. But then, surely he would have fallen across or by his chair. The body was in the wrong place—in the middle of the room. If Boutades had seen his murderer through the window, and got up hastily and run toward the middle of the room—why, then he would have been shot in the neck, not the throat.

"Why was he in or near the middle of the room when the arrow struck his throat? And there are other curious facts as well. Everyone testifies that there was a great deal of blood. There was blood on the floor, on the man's khiton, blood on his slippers and in his hair. Now, the great vein in the neck is a vital place, and has a good deal of blood in it. But any soldier will tell you that a man shot with an arrow doesn't usually bleed very much, often, because the arrow itself plugs the wound. However, in this case, of course, blood would have gushed from the mouth as the body fell backward from the impact of the blow. But a very strong man moving swiftly forward might be able to move, say, one step, or two, before he fell, especially if the arrow, although lethal, was not shot from a *great* distance.

"Why were the soles of the murdered man's slippers covered with blood? I suggest it was because the murdered man was walking *forward*—forward toward the eastern door—when he was shot. And he took, shall we say, one step, or a step and a half, in his own blood before he sank to the ground. The desk was innocent of blood. Is this not strange? Either he was working at it—in which case the desk would have been the bloody field—or he was running away from it, in

256

which case his back was to the arrow. That is, *if* the murderer were outside. This is a problem, like a problem in geometry."

I paused to let this sink in, and allowed the jury time to work it out. They were curious. I had caught their attention with the problem.

"I suggest to you that it is a distinct possibility that the murderer was within doors—not outside. Though of course you will say the killer might have made his escape through the window—and that we will consider later. But if it is possible, nay even likely from the disposition of the corpse, that the murderer was within the house at the time, then it is very strange that no one saw him. Would not the murderer have had to escape quickly between the time he shot Boutades and the moment in which Polygnotos came in and saw his expiring uncle? He could hardly have left by the door into the hall. Could our murderer have been standing at the end of the room opposite to the window—with Boutades, shot directly through the throat, between him and the window? Yes. Could he—the murderer—have then escaped through the window? No. No, hardly, for he would have left tracks on that grisly floor, or traces of blood beyond the desk and on the windowsill.

"But I have further proof—proof, and not mere speculation—that the murderer was inside the house. There is, as you know, a famous vase, a beautiful commemorative vase, kept in Boutades' house. Some of you have seen it recently, some of you have seen it in days gone by. It stood on the side table against the painted wall, about six hand-lengths from the window wall, but to the far left of the window. In the days when Boutades lived and worked in that room, no passer-by could have seen the vase from the window. If the murderer had shot from outside, he could not have shot the vase from any angle at which a bow could be aimed, near the window or far from it. Nor could anyone reach the vase to touch or take it from outside the window. Yet—something happened to this vase at the time Boutades was killed. It was not a weapon. The body was nowhere near it, the murderer outdoors could not have been near it. Yet it is a witness. I ask for the famous Dionysia vase to be sent for, to be examined—then I will make my point clear."

I was afraid that the court might not consent, but after some puzzled confabulation between the Horkotes, the Basileus and the arkhons, a runner was sent to get it. Polygnotos objected strongly to this proceeding, which violated his property and his house, but was assured that the vase would only be looked at by the court, and that I would not touch it—and that it would immediately be returned. Telemon spoke to Polygnotos soothingly. Eutikleides was more angry, and kept making private objections to all the arkhons and jury, until the Basileus said, "I have spoken. Let it be." The other witnesses looked perplexed; I distinctly heard the man from Peiraeus say, "Phut! What's an old pot, after all?" which brave consolation won him no approval from the others.

"Sirs, you are patient. I assure you, this has very much to do with Philemon's case. I know you are asking yourselves, 'Whether the murderer were indoors or out, what matter, if Philemon was the murderer?' But he was not. I have admitted that he was in Athens as a returned exile; for aught I know, the worthy fish-seller from Peiraeus is perfectly right when he says he saw him the day before the murder. But Philemon was not in Athens when the murder itself took place. I call Philander of Athens as witness."

Philander of Athens was my old acquaintance Pheidippides, the cheerful rascal with the pouchy eyes who had offered me the chance to say bye-bye to the old moon. The work of a good barber and the gift of a secondhand khiton had made him less disreputable, but he was certainly, though brazen, not at home in the court, and I feared lest a certain shifty look about the eyes, when he glanced at the jury, would not tell in our favor.

He gave his oath in a good loud voice, but did not take too kindly to my delicate and necessary questioning about his occupation.

"Honest man. Potter's assistant," was all he would say at first.

"Yes, but you have had some experience of the sea, haven't you? I believe your father was a fisherman."

"Yes. Honest fisherman. Not that he was ever what you might call lucky in his catch."

"And you know how to manage a boat, don't you?"

"Yes, sometimes. Fact is, I pick up a few obols, when times are slack, rowing—or sailing. Old lady wants to get to Hydra. I'll take her. Always civil. Well-spoken Philander. Reasonable charges."

"And," I said coaxingly to this cousin of Kharon, "it is well known that you offer a ride in your boat to anyone—for reasonable hire. Anyone who knew Peiraeus at all might choose you and your boat, and offer hire for the journey?"

"Oh, yes. Well-known waterfront character. Anyone might. Mainly a potter's assistant, however," he added doggedly. "Known for an honest man—reasonable rates," he added again, emphatically. "Philander wouldn't spit in your eye. A few honest obols is all I ask, enough to buy the next meal and I'm laughing."

It was slow work, but I took my witness—so unlike the previous one—through his paces, and he finally divulged, very carefully, the information that he had taken Philemon in his boat on the night before the murder happened—taken him to one of the islands.

"Not as I knew it was that proscribed Philemon," he said desperately. "Didn't want to do wrong, you understand. I only knew it was he when he was out to sea—well out—and him such a big fellow, and handy with killing, like, so naturally I didn't say anything, being only a poor man. And then, *being* a poor man, I was frightened of telling the law— though usually I would—when I got back. For I was feared they'd say, 'My! You've let him slip away, and will have to take a penalty!' But I didn't in no wise wish to do what wasn't right, if agreeable to your lordships," he added to the jury. "And don't you be harping back to that now, if you please, for what's the use of crying after an egg long addled? And it's not as if it was important like this nasty murder here. 'I needn't worry about my aching tooth now,' as the man said when they led him to execution—not but what I hope that isn't a delicate subject here."

I got rid of my ingratiating witness, after having made the point firmly that Philemon was not in Athens at the time of the murder. I trembled for the judgment of the gods on this man, this Philander/Pheidippides, but the jury evidently felt that he was speaking the truth—as he was on the central point—and were amused, impressed and puzzled.

"Thus, sirs, it was not Philemon who was the murderer within the house that night. And the murderer was within the house, as I will prove finally when I both show you the vase and show that it was broken. Be patient with my paradox—a moment from now, when we view the vase, all will be clear. The vase was broken inopportunely, and at the time of the murder. It did not crash to the floor as a result of the press of people around the corpse of Boutades that morning. No—it was not there at the time; I ask all just men present, not connected with the case, who saw the room that morning to cast their minds back for any recollections of the Dionysia memorial. No—by that time the fragments of the shattered vase were all well hidden."

Voices from the crowd and jury cried out, "But the vase is still there! It never was broken!"

"Ah, sirs, it was. There were two shots that night. The first struck the pot, the second struck Boutades—who had already risen, turned around and walked forward when the second shot reached him. The murderer had probably intended that he should die by his desk, but the crash of the first shot as it shattered an object aroused the victim and gave him time to move. The murderer within the house intended that his victim should stand facing him to be killed, but not that he should be so far in the center of the room. He moved the body to face the right way. Doing so, he probably dislodged the arrow inadvertently, letting an abnormal quantity of blood escape. He could not move the corpse back close to the desk, as that was suspiciously far from the pool of blood. When the body was moved and turned around, the victim's hair became soaked and matted in blood, and the soles of his slippers were likewise stained.

"Only the nervous murderer was aware of the significance of the broken pot. The fragments were quickly gathered up and hidden in a large jar in the room—a long-necked fat-bellied wine amphora. The Dionysia vase which now graces Boutades' house is, I claim, but a skilled copy. The original vase was of fine Athenian ware, and, as everyone with a knowledge of pottery understands, Athenian clay is red. I prophesy that we shall find the vase taken from Boutades' house now is made of yellow clay. And here it is!"

The runner came up to the court and produced the vase before the Horkotes and the Basileus. There was a murmur of admiration. One wag shouted, "Take it to the Prytaneion, if you want to try a pot! That's the court for investigating malignant objects!" And there was nervous laughter. "Nay," I resumed, "we are not trying the pot. It was in no wise responsible for the man's death—it was a witness, as I say. Admire the vase as you wish, but hear me. The original jar was of red clay. The valuable fragments were hidden, after a copy was made. Hidden in a place where they were never expected to come to light until the end of all things.

"But, you are wondering, who is he, this murderer within doors? Who had time to dispose of fragments? Surely, the man who disposed of the fragments and had a cunning copy made was the man who knew that the destruction of the vase was connected with the murder, and who wished the murder to look quite different in circumstance. I repeat—no murderer from without could have hit the vase with an arrow, or touched it at all. Had anyone other than the murderer destroyed the vase, he would have mentioned it openly. Had an innocent man wished to have a copy made, a copy could have been made in Athens. Will you accept my reasoning?

"Will you accept that if this vase is a copy, and if the name of the man who had the copy *secretly* made can be discovered, then that man is the murderer? For he and no other would have had the knowledge, the will and the opportunity to do all this."

Some of the jury nodded; others remained silent, some still evidently trying to follow my train of thought.

"Here is the vase," I said. "It is not on trial, yet we will put it to the question as a witness. I ask that a small chip be taken from the base of it, to see if it be red clay or no. I ask the Horkotes to see to this."

There were protests—not least from Polygnotos. "It's a valuable vase," said the Horkotes, in distress.

"It may be—and may be not so valuable after all," I said. "Is a man's life, is his good name, of less worth than a vase? I do not ask that this vessel be destroyed or greatly harmed. Take but one chip from it and see the color."

Reluctantly, the Horkotes gave the vase to the Basileus where he sat among the arkhons. With visible distaste the Basileus very carefully touched the base of the vase with a knife.

"Look!" I cried. "What do you see? Red Athenian clay? Or yellow Korinthian clay?"

A gasp from the Basileus. "It is yellow!" He rose in his place and waved the vase aloft to the jury and to that great throng. "It is of yellow clay—it is a copy!" The word went from mouth to mouth, although not many could see closely enough. The Basileus handed the vase to the first rank of the jury.

"I call Onesimos of Korinthos as a witness."

Onesimos of Korinthos, a small quiet man, was a potter by trade. I had not met him until that morning.

"Do you see that vase?" I asked him, and the object was brought nearer. "Have you seen it before?"

"Yes. I made it. From fragments of an old one. It is a copy. A very good one," he added.

"When was it made?"

"In my shop in Korinthos, in the late autumn."

"And who was the man who commissioned you to make it?"

"His name, he said, was Periander of Megara. He seemed a rich man, though he traveled simply, accompanied by a red-haired slave."

"Have you seen him again?"

"Yes. Today."

"Can you point to him?"

And Onesimos pointed his finger. There were gasps—and uproar. I drew a leather bag from my waist and quickly opened it with trembling fingers.

"Yes!" I shouted above the noise. "And here is the original vase. These fragments were recovered by me from where the murderer had hidden them!" I held them aloft, displaying on the palm of my hand some of the fragments of brilliant painting on pieces of red clay. "They were hidden, I swear, in a most strange place—under the very tombstone of the victim!

"There is the murderer!" I had to yell now above the noise of the crowd. "His name is truly known to us. Who is the man who has a pressing need for money if he is to make a show before us soon? Who is the man who had most to lose if Boutades decided to adopt a son for the sake of delightful progeny? Who had most reason to wish Philemon and all dear to him to be ground into the dust? Who could murder from within the house, taking his time and choosing his assistant? Who could conveniently do the deed while naked, so no blood would be seen on him— with a slave to hold his clothes and a light, meanwhile? Who is strong enough to shoot, and to move a heavy corpse? Who had his leisure to gather fragments of a shattered bowl, and the time and opportunity to replace it? I declare Philemon is innocent, by all the gods, for the name of the real murderer is—Polygnotos!"

Caught up in my passion, I had run ahead of myself and packed all my evidence and everything else into my first speech. That is usually a mistake in legal tactics—I don't advise any other pleader to try it. I had lost my head, and had gone charging on, from the moment I first began to feel I had moved the jury. And no one had stopped me. Since the production of the pot, no one, not the Basileus himself, had thought to question the relevance of what I was saying. The jury were too curious, and too surprised.

Polygnotos was pale and shaken. He had turned astonishingly white when the runner was told to produce the vase. I think, however, that he had not remembered the countenance of the Korinthian potter, and hadn't realized who he was until the man gave evidence. Polygnotos was little used to noticing the lowly, unless they were handsome. Even then he had perhaps hoped to brazen it out—there were various lies he could have told (although his giving a false name to the potter was more damaging than if he had given his own). I think it was the resurrection of the fragments that shook him most. Now, in that excited crowd, there was a kind of hiss, and a visible shrinking away from him—his own witnesses began to move from his presence, as if there were contamination in it.

Then Polygnotos, for the first time in his life unpopular, completely lost his head. He may have had some confused idea of its being a trial for murder in which he was the accused, some feeling that he would be liable for sentence and execution if he made a second speech. He wavered on his feet for a few seconds—and then, with a wild cry, fled from the court and down the hill of the Areopagos.

"After him!" somebody cried—no person in authority, just someone—and the crowd began to move, shoving and tripping over each other. The Basileus sat there with the arkhons and the jury, trying to decide what to do. I sat down; somebody gave me a drink of thin wine.

I was in no condition to run after Polygnotos, nor did I wish to join in the mad hunt. I know only by hearsay what followed. Polygnotos ran down the hill into the city. He had a few minutes' start of everyone else, and he was a splendid runner. Somewhere in the city near the road to Peiraeus he found a horse. He took this and galloped down the Peiraeus road—that road I had myself so much cause to know—with the crowd following more slowly, about three stadia behind. Many of his pursuers dropped away.

It seems he arrived in Peiraeus and dashed down to the sea's edge, where he found two slaves working on a boat half in, half out of the water. He demanded of them—with threats and execrations, so they said—that they take him out to sea and down the coast. Frightened, they obeyed, although they made all reasonable protestations that the boat was not seaworthy, and that a storm was coming on. He appeared to hear nothing of these objections; he was, one of them said later, "like a god out of the sea—as if nothing could hurt him." So, against their will and judgment, the slaves set out, sure that they were about to lose their lives in the elements. The pursuers arrived at the beach to see Polygnotos in his craft just visible, moving away from them over the gray angry water. Then a storm of wind and rain moved across the water and a curtain of rain and cloud hid Polygnotos as if a god had taken him up. The watchers on the shore were soon drenched, and sought shelter.

So Polygnotos disappeared from view, and the wonder of his going lasted all that night—that night when I slept exhausted in my bed at home with my mother's and my Aunt Eudoxia's tearful expressions of gratitude ringing in my ears. Philemon had been formally declared innocent by the Basileus.

Next day there was more wonder. The two slave-boatmen had reappeared in the night, tossed up on a beach of Salamis like two logs—except that they were animate. According to them, the boat, which was leaking, had been submerged by the sea about two hours after they had taken Polygnotos aboard. The slaves had given themselves up for lost, but had managed to rip some wood from the boat and, assisted by floating planks, they had made it to shore. Of course, their one desire was to get to shore at the nearest point. But Polygnotos, they said, had set his face away from the Athenian coast, and had gone swimming on in quite a different direction. "It was no good talking or shouting, even," said one. "He was like a man made of marble—save that he swam well. He moved off like a dolphin."

So Polygnotos, with his face hard but serene, like a god—

how well I could imagine it—had set out for other shores in the midst of a storm. An Odysseus, but not swimming home. Nor did he meet a kind Phaiakian coast and a princess— though when we first heard the tale of the slaves, we all, I think, felt that somehow he would succeed, that he might be anywhere, that he would be living somewhere in this world.

He must have swum strongly, and for a long while, because he moved far away from the currents that would take him to Salamis or to Peiraeus, and managed to reach some point where the current swept him eastward. That was evident when he was found. For he was found—and in no godlike state. A week after he had disappeared, we heard that his corpse was discovered on the rocks around Aigina. It was blue and swollen and horribly mutilated—he (or his body) had been battered and flung about the rocks. But enough of his clothes remained to show that it was he, and his ring was still on his finger. Of his person, only his handsome curly hair was recognizable.

No Athenians wanted the corpse back. Some official persons who knew Polygnotos went reluctantly to identify it, but no one wished to pollute the grounds of the city by harboring the corpse of such a vile murderer, a man who was in effect a parricide, and displeasing to the gods. The gods had shown their displeasure in inflicting punishment themselves when the time was ripe—everyone agreed on that. The fact that the two slaves were saved from that odd wreck showed that the gods wanted to make it absolutely clear that their vengeance was intended strictly for Polygnotos. There was some trouble with the citizens of Aigina—they said indignantly that *they* did not wish to pollute their land either. Presents were given, and mollifying speeches made; it was pointed out that the gods, having sent Polygnotos there, evidently wished him to be there, and could have no feelings against the citizens of Aigina, as Polygnotos was not one of them. The body was reluctantly disposed of under a pile of stones on an unfrequented shore of the island. So the man who in life was so much sought after and courted, and invited to dine at the best houses, was denied proper burial and a proper grave. It could hardly have gone worse for him if he had been executed at the tympanon. Sometimes, but not often, and not until lately, I have found it in my heart to feel a kind of discolored pity for Polygnotos, whose ruthless hopes had promised him so much.

XXIV

After the Trial

The trial of Philemon had ended most irregularly, but the Basileus and the jury had pronounced him innocent, entering a formal judgment to that effect before an almost empty court. Much later an accusation was publicly made against Polygnotos for murder; there was no defender. The city underwent ritual cleansing; sacrifices were offered, and many of Polygnotos' personal possessions were cast out of the walls. In time, a second cousin of Polygnotos quietly took possession of the property; he was careful to offer expensive sacrifices on all the altars and to make handsome donations to the city funds and to the poor.

Those who had been witnesses at the trial of Philemon were dealt with leniently. Telemon, whimpering to anyone who would listen, said that Polygnotos told him he had seen Philemon that night, and he was sure he had seen *something*. He was merely despised. Eutikleides said that he was horrified to learn what a serpent he had taken to his bosom, and he underwent elaborate ritual cleansing for unwitting perjury in swearing Philemon's guilt; he was, however, careful to explain that otherwise he had said nothing which was not true, and made rather a point of the fact that it was some of his evidence that led to the exculpation of the innocent. Eutikleides also made large donations to the public weal.

No questions were asked of the irregular Pheidippides about his abetting a returned exile, and he was quite happy with his day in court—especially as he had been among the few who reached Peiraeus and saw the fugitive in his boat. Pheidippides must have been something of a runner, after all. I paid him some money for his trouble in appearing at the trial; I only hope that he cleared himself before the gods for his elaborate testimony to his own general innocence.

No questions were asked of me about the extent to which I had assisted a proscribed exile—and the full manner of my assistance never came to light. I was not altogether easy about some of my own utterances under oath, for, if I had not said falsely, I had certainly made fallacious suggestions about my communication with the accused man; I made some special prayers and sacrifices, and then communicated the matter to the Basileus, but not before I knew that Philemon had risen high in popular esteem.

The most important thing of all is that Philemon's sentence was not made any harder because of his offense in returning. The general opinion was that he was a much-wronged man, and a man whom the gods favored in spite of all. Before the end of the summer his sentence was commuted, and he was allowed to return with his wife and children—by then little Lykias had a younger brother. Aunt Eudoxia saw her grandchildren before she died; she lingered awhile, but departed almost exactly a year from the time that Philemon was first accused.

Even a few days after the trial it was evident that public opinion was in my favor, and I soon began to look about me with some hope. Eutikleides insisted on giving back to me the interest on the money which had been lent my father and which I had repaid with so much difficulty. I did not feel that my responsibility to our poor family allowed me to refuse. (I still did not *like* taking anything from Eutikleides, although I am sure that his charge of interest was outrageous.)

I lost my voice the day after the trial—and no wonder. Upon my recovery I was engaged in doing business and in entertaining the many who flocked to see me and offer congratulations (they had stayed well away from the door after the accusation). It was not until about a week after Polygnotos' body was found that I had a chance to have a proper conversation with Aristotle. I took him a small present, in humble testimony of my great gratitude, and we found ourselves discussing the whole affair again. Some things were still puzzling me.

"You told me," I reminded him, "the night we went to the Kerameikos, that Polygnotos was the murderer, and when I was at your house going over the speeches you told me the evidence that proved it was so. But—I want to know when you first thought Polygnotos was the murderer. And why didn't you tell me when you knew?"

"Oh, I knew it from the first," the philosopher said airily. Then he smiled. "Not quite from the first—no, I didn't *know* it. I thought it. I did think it might have been Philemon, you know. But what you told me of the disposition of the body made me think. And what motive did Philemon have? Had he some reason to be in the house? Had Polygnotos made or persuaded him to do the murder? All sorts of thoughts like that went through my mind, but they weren't satisfactory. I thought it must be either Philemon or Polygnotos. Then when Boutades' wife died . . . it was too convenient. And what you told me of the gossip of the slaves in the market place made me see what a strong motive Polygnotos had for getting rid of his uncle quickly."

"But—why didn't you tell me?" I said heatedly. "You sent me off on foolish expeditions—to Peiraeus disguised—when you knew all the time!"

"Knowing and proving are two different things. Strictly, I didn't *know*. I only *thought*. I could see no easy way of getting the sort of proof that would be required in such a difficult case. I hoped you might come upon something which I could interpret, or that evidence would come our way. Stephanos, I was frightened that you *might* suspect the truth. I blessed the gods that you did not. For you are no deceiver, my friend. You would have blurted out your thoughts at once —unsubstantiated, they would have sounded like frantic ravings, and you would have been in the greatest danger. As long as you were innocent and unsuspecting, still trying to work on the notion that Philemon wasn't in Athens at the time, you were harmless and desirable. You were useful to the accuser, for he wanted a proper murder trial, and Philemon convicted. He knew he could prove in the end that Philemon had been in Athens."

"You didn't tell me," I said reproachfully. "You let me go through all that without telling me—when it was my own cousin too."

"Where was the good?" he said mildly. "I preferred having you alive. If the murderer could also kill Boutades' wife with so little compunction, he was obviously not full of scruples. And I thought your case also might in the end have to rely on Aunt Eudoxia's Defense."

"So it did, to a large extent," I reminded him, and felt better. "But—some things don't fit in. When we were preparing the speech and the evidence, I asked you if Polygnotos had set fire to Melissa's house and attacked me, and you said, 'No. Leave that alone.' But now I want to know— wasn't it Polygnotos?"

"It was someone who hated you, Stephanos. Someone who hated you in a most peculiar way. Arkhimenos was horror-stricken when he heard the murder had been committed with a Kretan bow. He jumped to the conclusion that it was the bow he had lost (rightly, as it proved); he was terrified of the murder being brought to his door. For he had a very strong reason to kill the murdered man. I think in some peculiar way he felt guilty—he had wished for that man's death so often. Therefore he was delighted that it was Philemon who was accused, and wanted you and your family's name thoroughly blackened. He felt relief from shame, guilt and fear in hating you. Yes—you, Stephanos, became an object of compelling hatred in his mind. He followed you—and found what he supposed was your light o' love—and set fire to the house."

"He is ill now," I remembered. "He has never been the same since that outburst on the day of the trial. I was most astonished, I must admit, when you said he should be one of my witnesses. But yet you said it was Polygnotos who brought about the attack on me on the Hill of the Muses?"

"Yes, and I am convinced that is so, although now it can probably never be proved. The murderer became uneasy as the trial approached. You talk of your own sufferings during those months, Stephanos, facing prodikasiai and everything going against you. But—have you ever considered what the accuser went through? He had always to smile and be serene, while lying and planning and guarding himself. A most unnatural life. Even a condemned criminal is allowed to speak of what is uppermost in his mind. Yes, Polygnotos must have been unhappy—and frightened. He was frightened that his slave had revealed something. We have already discussed the probable scene of the night of the murder—the murderer naked so as not to be stained by the blood, the slave holding his clothes and a light. The Sinopean slave, so pale and terrified the morning of the murder, so happy, so well treated by his master afterward. I suppose Polygnotos always meant to murder the slave anyway, after the fragments were truly hidden in their final resting place—the fragments which the slave perhaps carried perpetually upon his person. Yet—Polygnotos, even he, might have hesitated to kill the one creature in whom he could confide—a creature devoted to him. I feel that you must have said something inadvertently —perhaps a remark directed to another person entirely— which made Polygnotos fearful that you might know or guess something which you were not to suspect. Something at any rate happened to make Polygnotos feel that he had to get rid of the slave right away."

I thought back, and remembered an unfortunate and foolish remark of mine which might indeed have been mistaken by the real murderer.

"So," Aristotle continued, "as we've already mentioned, Polygnotos killed the slave. This cannot have added to his peace of mind. And, suspecting you might know too much, he thought it better to get you out of the way, trial or no. Who knows what he felt? Perhaps he hated you chiefly at that time because in his eyes you had caused the death of his favorite. Probably, of all he killed or tried to kill, the slave was the only one for whom he cared."

"It would not have made him unhappy to kill me," I said. "He already loathed Philemon, whom he saw as the usurper, and did his best to crush him and his whole family. It is amazing that I wasn't done for—as I would have been if he had taken the same method with me as with the slave."

"Yes," Aristotle agreed, "but your case was too obvious— it might have been a murder too many. He decided to rely on hired help. We have already discussed how Polygnotos must have stalked the slave in the Parnes mountains and brought him down with a stone from a catapult. One can't help admiring his intelligence and mental flexibility. He had seen the danger of repeating himself. He committed three different murders with three different weapons. Always he felt it important to adapt to circumstances. He had a nice taste in weapons, too. Somewhere in that young man there was a sort of grim wit."

"You mean," I said hesitantly, "because he shot Boutades in his room—the place where Boutades looked after his money and had drafted adoption documents—"

"Yes, and pretended that the outsider Philemon had done it, from outside. He gave his uncle a legendary end —gruesome and memorable. He gave his aunt a feminine ending—he declined her in poison, perhaps secretly intimating that he thought her poisonous. He ended the life of the slave in coarse stone. He was capable of variation. He thought of hiring help to kill you—and that is appropriate as well as needful, for he regarded you with contempt, and he needn't sully his hands with you, as with one of the family.

"I would like, however, to know what we can't be sure of," Aristotle continued. "Where was the murder weapon, the bow—with its unwanted companion, the second arrow—at the time just after the murder? I have wondered if the bow and the arrow were worn by Polygnotos at the time when you saw him—say between the body and the khiton? You mentioned that he moved stiffly. If Polygnotos were not wearing it, it then would have been hidden somewhere in the room, perhaps in the tall amphora. Certainly there was no chance of finding the weapon. Bows and arrows can easily be burned."

"But the horn tip would have been broken off the bow before it was hidden," I reminded him. "He must have meant that to be found outside the window. It helped to connect the shooting with the imaginary shooter outdoors, and that shooter with Philemon."

"True. But the fragment of broken pot was dropped accidentally, probably at the same time." Aristotle chuckled. "That fragment—I told you pots were worth looking at. That sliver of potsherd must have come outdoors on Polygnotos' clothes, or his sandals. As he didn't know that it had been both lost and found, even his adaptable mind could not have prepared for its being used against him. I'm sure the broken vase was the most hearty vexation to him, nonetheless. It was the only thing in his plans that went wrong. Once I knew the fragment existed, and saw it, I surmised that a pot—an important Athenian pot—in Boutades' household had been broken at the time of the murder. When I realized that the Dionysia vase had not been present in the room just after the murder, I saw the way to the one bit of evidence that might stand firm for us. But by the time that I and other notables were invited to dinner, the Dionysia vase was on view in Boutades' house as before. What had happened in the meantime? Nothing very obvious—but Polygnotos had been to Korinthos. Do you remember my telling you that I once paid a visit uninvited and stopped to write a message?"

"Yes, I know," I said. "And when you paid a visit uninvited to Polygnotos, knowing he would be absent, you stopped to write a message in Boutades' old room, and that gave you the opportunity to examine the pot and scrape the edge of it. And I am *very* grateful to you for taking a journey to Korinthos to find out who made the copy. I wish you had told me —I could at least have paid—and I will—"

"Away with gratitude!" he said, twinkling. "It's the puzzle that counts. I was fascinated. Nothing could have kept me away. It is good to go to the source, to examine the facts. And I didn't want to feed you on hopes. Besides, you might have let something out—too dangerous for you," he added hastily.

"But," I said, "I still don't understand how you knew to look for the fragments under the tombstone. That night when you came to my house you told me that the vase had been copied, and that the original pieces would be where we found them—but how did you know they would be there?"

Aristotle looked slightly uncomfortable. "I was certain in my own mind that that was the logical place for them to be —although I hadn't had ocular proof. Perhaps mistakenly, I presented it to you as a fact."

"You didn't put the fragments there yourself, did you?"

"Dear me, Stephanos, what an exalted notion you have of both my strength and my iniquity. No indeed. I worked from deduction. By that time I had a good idea of the murderer's mind and how it functioned. I had seen that he displayed, in all this carnage, a strong sense of the appropriate. He was resourceful, and adaptable, yet in everything (including his behavior at the prodikasiai) he suited his actions to the occasion. He respected conventions. Now, one knew that the fragments of the pot would be needed until after the copy was made. And the slave could not be killed until after the fragments were disposed of and the new pot restored. Polygnotos could have thrown the fragments away in the Gulf of Korinthos, or otherwise disposed of them abroad. But a careful man would keep the fragments of the original until the new vase had been safely brought home. Polygnotos was careful as well as reckless. I thought he would do what anyone would do in a normal case: wait until the copy had well and truly arrived before disposing of the only pattern. So I took it that the fragments must have been disposed of between the return from Korinthos and the death of the slave

274

—but nearer the latter event. What had happened between? Only one noteworthy thing—the erection of Boutades' tombstone."

"Yes," I said. "I remember that day." And I recalled Boutades' white marble face proceeding along the street.

"Well," Aristotle went on, warming to his exposition, "as I said, the murderer had displayed a sense of the appropriate. He also had a strong sense of the family. In some ways he was remarkably like his uncle—retentive and acquisitive—people were of little value compared to things. I believe Boutades learned a new lesson, strangely, before his death, when he became infatuated with little Lykias—but that was because he needed someone satisfactory to pass his things to; he needed to feel as if he had had a child. Polygnotos never learned to value people—but he learned from his uncle's miserly example that at times it pays to spend. He had a respect for family possessions. And he said in my presence once that he liked to see things where they belonged—I think that was true, although Polygnotos had an ironic sense of his private meaning. When at the dinner party he quoted those lines from the *Iliad,* he was looking at the 'Dionysia vase'—the copy. Those words of Akhilleus come, as you remember, from the funeral of Patroklos—when the hero looks at the great pyre on which are sacrificed all sorts of possessions, and even the lives of men. The poet's words are associated with funeral rites and offerings. I think those lines had been running in Polygnotos' head quite recently. He too was like the hero sacrificing living beings—and he too was ensuring that things were done properly. He had already planned where the real vase should go, shortly. Heirlooms should not go out of a family. But when a rich man dies, valuables, even heirlooms, are often buried with him. On my way back from Korinthos, I remembered the quotation from the *Iliad,* saw its significance and was certain. The most appropriate place for the fragments of the beautiful Dionysia vase was the grave of Boutades. With that heavy and imposing monument on top of them, they would be safe forever—safely hidden and ironically restored to their proper owner."

"So you think he buried the fragments in the grave just before the tomb was put up?"

"I'm not sure. I think that would have involved unnecessary risk. Workmen could displace the earth. And the things were buried shallowly, you recall. No, I think Polygnotos and his trusty slave made a secret journey to the Kerameikos, much like our own—but to cover, not to discover. Two men could move the stone, as we know. And their expedition was not so hazardous as our own; Polygnotos would have had a satisfactory reason to offer any passer-by, for, after all, it was his own uncle's tombstone, bought with his own money. He could say that he had come to pay his respects, or that he had heard that the tomb had cracked or had fallen—or even that he had come to bury a forgotten offering."

"So Polygnotos went to all that expense and trouble. You are right—he was ready to spend when the occasion offered, wasn't he? Look at the funerals—and Boutades' tomb—and the copy of the pot. And I think he really was looking forward to sponsoring the Dionysia."

"Yes. We shall not have our Kheiron play, after all. I'm sure the story of Kheiron supplied our murderer with a private jest. Perhaps it was after deciding on that dramatic subject that Polygnotos decided how to murder Boutades. The arrow shot by Herakles, the strong hero who killed his instructor. Well, the actors are very sad, and rather poor."

"Money," I said. "Polygnotos had some, and wanted more. Wrath, Fear and Avarice—as you once said. Avarice seems more powerful than I had thought."

"But Polygnotos loved power better than anything else. The money was only a means to an end—or several ends. He made expensive investments. Hiring murderers, like being a khoregos, is suited only to the wealthy. And in both cases the performance may not be all that the sponsor desires. Arkhimenos, on the other hand, was in no financial position to hire attackers to murder you."

"Who was the man, then, who assaulted and maimed a slave-girl on the Megara road? Was it Polygnotos? Or was it Eutikleides?"

"Oh, Stephanos, haven't you guessed? That was Arkh-imenos. That is why Boutades had such power over him. Wrath and fear—and guilt too, which partakes of both—these took root in Arkhimenos' mind and gave him such great hatred of Boutades. Yes, if Arkhimenos had been coura-geous enough, he might have murdered Boutades. But—he is of the sort that vents hatred only upon weaker objects. He was always cruel with women. But you were not the weaker —he made a mistake when he made you an antagonist, did he not?"

I was mollified. "I suppose," I said, "that you did not bribe that witness, but threatened him somehow—that it was to Arkhimenos that you sent a message of your own, on the day before the trial?"

"I did not threaten, Stephanos. I merely reminded him that this was a fitting opportunity to avenge himself for the ill use Boutades had made of a certain incident. I am not sure, mind you, that Arkhimenos is not deserving of legal punish-ment for that past crime, but the gods are making him pay."

"So—Eutikleides is not guilty of anything," I said, rather disappointed.

"Well—Eutikleides may or may not have suspected that Polygnotos was the slayer. That is another of the things we shall never know. It is my opinion that Eutikleides guessed the truth almost at once—that he guessed and did not greatly care, but saw in Polygnotos' future rise to power a great opportunity for himself. He is not an old man, and was still ambitious. His family have made political errors and lost power, but here was a chance to retrieve the position. He could make himself indispensable to Polygnotos. Eutikleides certainly wished you and your family ground into the dust— to please Polygnotos, and to ensure that the trial would go smoothly. After all, you would be too poor even to hire a speech-writer." He smiled with self-approbation. Then he grew sober.

"That's the trouble with oligarkhs," he said gravely. "They have such bad habits. Polygnotos had the oligarkhic soul. So does Eutikleides. But Polygnotos was unusual—young, brilliant, daring. He trusted very much to his own luck. He trusted superstitiously that it would uphold him as long as he paid tribute to the conventions and satisfied that peculiar conservatism in himself which is manifest in the wild decorum of all his deeds. Yes, Polygnotos felt he was a fortunate man—one of those whom events obey."

"He seemed—so good," I said, remembering him. "He seemed admirable. You know, in a way, even I rather liked Polygnotos—or at least looked up to him."

"Yes," Aristotle sighed. "Polygnotos commanded the best rhetoric of all."